# The
# Bride's
# Sister

# BOOKS BY KATE HEWITT

# Kate Hewitt

## The
# Bride's
# Sister

**Bookouture**

Published by Bookouture in 2022

An imprint of Storyfire Ltd.
Carmelite House
50 Victoria Embankment
London EC4Y 0DZ

www.bookouture.com

ISBN: 978-1-80314-837-3
eBook ISBN: 978-1-80314-836-6

*Dedicated, as ever, to the lovely people of St Bees, who gave me and my family as kind a farewell as they did a welcome. Although we no longer live there, we still count it as a home. Also dedicated to my father, George Louis Berry, who did not live to see this book in print, but was always a tremendous encourager of my writing.*

# PROLOGUE

There is no letter, no address or greeting, nothing at all save for the single slip of paper that she slides out of the envelope, a sense of dread curdling like old milk in her stomach even though she has no idea, not yet, of what she holds.

Carefully she unfolds it, the paper cheap and scratchy, the stark lines of black ink written in a firm and unshaking hand. It takes her a moment to see what it is – an official document, or at least a copy of one, the columns darkly scored. *Sarah Mills, Aged twenty-two, River Cottage, Kendal.* She catches her breath as she reads the next lines: *Cause of Death: General Debility.*

"Love?"

Her husband's voice floats up the stairs of their little terraced house, kind and questioning, and her fingers clench on the paper as guilt washes over her in a scorching tide.

"Just a moment." She scans the lines again. *Date of Death: 24 May 1872.* Two months ago. Two months ago Sarah had breathed her last – how and why? And who had sent this to her? Realisation ices inside her. Someone has wanted her to know. This slip of paper is an accusation, as loud as a spoken threat, as frightening as a raised fist, a judgment handed down by some unknown witness.

*It's your fault Sarah died.*

She couldn't know that. She had no idea why Sarah had died, and yet... she has so much to atone for. So much to regret. When she'd seen Sarah last, she'd been healthy and whole, robust if resigned. She'd been twenty-one years old. When she'd seen Sarah last, she'd been rescued by her. Saved.

The sound of her husband's heavy, familiar tread on the narrow staircase has her slipping the copy of the death certificate into her apron pocket. She rises from her seat by the window and straightens her dress, taking a deep breath and tucking a few stray wisps of hair back into her bun. Her heart thuds.

"I'm coming," she calls, her voice trembling slightly, and she hurries from the bedroom, trying to push the terrible knowledge of that certificate from her mind. She's been good at that, too good, perhaps, at pretending the past hasn't happened. That she's a new person, a different person now, one with a husband and child she loves and adores. She won't let that certificate and its awful knowledge threaten what she holds dear.

The next morning, after her husband has gone off whistling to his carpentry workshop, the breakfast dishes have been scrubbed and put away and the dirty water poured out into the courtyard in back of the kitchen, she climbs up the narrow stairs to the little attic room at the top of the house. It is meant for a maid, if they had a maid, but her husband's work as a carpenter means she does all the housework, even the heavy scrubbing and washing, herself. And once she'd insisted she would have a maid when she married.

Grimacing faintly at her own childish folly, she thinks again of Sarah. Sarah had had to do all the washing and scrubbing, soaking shirts and old-fashioned collars until her hands were cracked and red from the harsh lye soap she made herself, and then having to starch the collars into hard points, spending hours with the heavy flat irons. Had the never-ending round of housework contributed to her death? *General Debility.*

The little room is cramped and airless, the cobwebbed eaves brushing her head, the one tiny window looking out onto rolling hills that lead to a slate-grey sea, churning and restless even on this summer's day, yet no less beautiful.

She remembers her arrival two years ago, how desperate and afraid she was, yet clinging to the one frail thread of hope that Sarah, in her generosity, had offered her. She'd clutched her single case, its side banging her knees, as Ruth had met her at the train and led her up the narrow, winding street, the smell of coal fires on the damp sea air. She'd glimpsed the sea, a twinkling promise behind the row of whitewashed cottages, and her heart had lifted. She'd always loved the sea. Back in Kendal there had only been the river, hemmed in on every side by the looming fells, so sometimes it felt as if the earth was enclosing her, a giant's teacup.

Now she crouches in the centre of the room, the slip of paper clutched in her hand, a dozen different memories tumbling through her mind, making her mouth tremble as she keeps the useless tears at bay. Sarah silently sweeping up broken crockery, her face set in determinedly placid lines. Sarah sitting slumped at the kitchen table, her head resting against her hand, her eyes fluttering closed, her other hand reaching out to Lucy, always to Lucy. Sarah pressing a rail ticket into her hand, her lips drawn tightly together, her eyes dark and troubled.

*Go. It's the only way.*

But had it been? *Had it been?*

It would be wiser to burn the death certificate, and with it her links to her old life in Kendal, those awful memories, the endless sense of reproach and the childish anger and hurt, but she knows she can't. It feels like a sacrilege, yet another betrayal of Sarah. But neither can she keep the thing, its stark lines a potent reminder of who she'd been, what she'd done. *Who had sent it? Who knew?*

With shaking fingers she pries up an old floorboard, a jagged splinter piercing deeply into her thumb, the pain feeling right and clean, somehow just, and then she slides the folded certificate into the dark, musty space underneath.

Dust rises in the air and motes dance in the sunlight streaking in from the window, making her cough. All around her the house is still and silent, waiting for the thing to be done. In the distance she sees the glint of the sea, a twinkling flash before the clouds cover the sun and all turns grey again.

She presses the floorboard back down and breathes a sigh of mingled regret and relief. It is finished.

"I'm sorry, Sarah," she whispers, pressing her hand against the floorboard, a farewell, the only memorial she can offer for a woman she's never had the decency or courage to thank. Silence stretches all around her, feeling accusing now rather than expectant, and with a quickly drawn breath she rises from the floor and then hurries from the room, closing the door firmly behind her.

# CHAPTER 1

## ELLEN

"Oy, love."

Ellen Tyson looked up from the third kettle she'd boiled that morning, slapping a smile on her face as one of the three builders who was redoing the little attic room lumbered into the kitchen.

"Yes?"

"Found this under the floorboards. Thought you might like to have a look."

"Under the floorboards...?" Ellen took the scrap of paper, brown and wrinkled with age, with a puzzled frown. "What is it?" she asked as she opened it. The builder just shrugged. "Sarah Mills... this is from 1872!" She looked up as if suspecting a practical joke, and the builder shrugged again. "Must have been under there a good while, then," he said. "That's milk with two sugars, yeah?"

"Right." The kettle switched off and Ellen scanned the paper again; it looked like some sort of death certificate. "River Cottage, Kendal," she murmured, flummoxed at how such a thing would end up under the floorboards of a cottage in Goswell.

As the builder tramped back upstairs she put the scrap of paper aside, her mind on the more pressing matter of brewing yet more cups of tea for the thirsty builders so she could get back to her own work waiting on her laptop on the kitchen table.

*This will be worth it*, she reminded herself as she loaded another tray with mugs of milky, sugary tea and headed up two floors of narrow stairs to the tiny attic room they were having redone as her home office. After decades of working at the kitchen table or on the sofa, always having to stuff her papers in a drawer or a file folder and tidy her laptop away, she couldn't wait for her own space.

"A room of one's own," she murmured with a small smile, even if it was a far cry from that now. The little attic room had been nothing more than a storage area for the twelve years they'd owned the house, filled with bins of baby clothing and Christmas decorations, a dressmaker's dummy Alyssa had picked up when she'd briefly been thinking of doing a course on fashion before she'd settled on a more sensible English degree.

Last week all of it had been trundled out to the new shed in the back of the garden, and Ellen had swept the room clean in preparation for the builders arriving. She didn't know why she'd bothered; within minutes they'd filled the place with dust and tarps as they'd plastered walls and pried up floorboards.

But in a couple of weeks she would have a brand-new room, with proper walls and varnished floorboards, heating and electricity, and a view, if you crouched and angled your head in a certain way, of the sea. Her home office. Her new beginning as a full-time freelancer after twelve years of snatching both time and space and always feeling hassled and harried.

Latching onto that hopeful thought, Ellen called up the stairs to the builders, just in case one of them was heading down with a ladder or something. They'd had a near-collision on the stairs yesterday; Ellen had only just managed to keep the tray aloft, although hot tea had slopped all over her fingers.

"Thanks, love," one of the men said as he hefted all three mugs in one hand and began passing them around. "We'll have another brew in an hour if you're putting the kettle on?" he added with a lift of his eyebrows, and Ellen smiled.

"Of course."

As she went back downstairs the phone was ringing, and with a sigh for her abandoned laptop – she'd managed all of two pages that morning – she reached for the phone, nearly tripping over their black Labrador, Pepper, who had been her nervous shadow since the builders had arrived, tail wagging in hopeful expectation of a walk to escape the hammering and clatter.

"Hello?"

"Ellen?"

"Alex?" Ellen reached down to give Pepper a reassuring pat as she registered the unusually sharp note in her husband's voice. He'd only left home a couple of hours ago, and he hardly ever called from work. As a research chemist at the nearby nuclear power plant, he worked in a high security clearance area that didn't allow for phonecalls or emails. The most she could hope for was a flirty text at lunchtime, although come to think of it, she hadn't had one of those in quite a while. "What's up?"

"Nothing," he said a touch too quickly, and the vague sense of unease that had been skirting the fringes of her mind since she'd picked up the phone now settled heavily into her gut.

"Why are you calling, then?" she asked, trying to sound reasonable rather than panicked, or at least starting to panic. She couldn't remember the last time Alex had called from work. Maybe when she'd been pregnant with Sophie and he'd been worried she'd go into labour.

Alex blew out a breath. "I just wanted to make sure you're going to be home tonight."

"Home tonight? Where else would I be?" With a ten-year-old daughter who needed help with homework, at least two bedtime stories, and an ever-lengthening tucking-in time, Ellen spent nearly every night at home. It was Alex who often worked late, despite his intention of having "flex" hours. But she wasn't going to nag him about that, not now anyway. She knew he tried his best both to provide for their family and be there for the children. "Is something going on?" she asked.

"No... not really. I just wanted to make sure we could talk tonight."

Ellen gave a slightly shaky laugh. "You're starting to scare me, Alex."

"It's fine," he assured her. "We just need to chat. I've got to go now. I shouldn't have been calling, anyway. You know how they are about security."

"Yes..." Before she could say a proper goodbye he'd hung up, leaving her with a dial tone and a thumping heart. Pepper nosed her thigh impatiently and Ellen gave her another half-hearted pat. *That had been weird.*

Admittedly, they'd been the proverbial passing ships these last few months, with Alex working long hours on a special project, and she... well, she'd been busy just with normal life. Keeping house and home going, not to mention body and soul. With Alyssa halfway through her first year at uni and Sophie starting to think about secondary schools, as well as her freelancing stepping up a notch and the volunteering she did with school, not to mention walking the dog at least twice a day... there hadn't been much time for romantic dinners, or even normal conversations.

Sighing, Ellen glanced at her laptop and decided she could manage a few more pages of her latest proofreading assignment. It was slow-going, a scholarly article for an economics journal, and the dense writing sometimes gave her a headache, but at least she could charge twenty-five pounds an hour, and she had almost that amount of time before the builders would want yet another cuppa.

She tried not to think about Alex's strange phone call for the rest of the day, but there must have been some sign of worry on her face, for her friend Jane Hatton, whose daughter Merrie was best friends with her Sophie, noticed it from twenty paces as they met on the high street for the school pick-up.

"What's wrong?"

Ellen gave a laugh and shook her head. "Why do you think something is wrong?"

"Because I know you," Jane returned as they went together up the steep little lane that led to the village's primary school. From the top of the lane you could see the village stretching down to sheep fields which led straight onto the sea, sky-blue on this May day. Ellen breathed in deeply, enjoying the view and the moment of sunshine, wanting to dispel the vague worries that she'd been trying to keep at bay all afternoon.

"Seriously, Ellen," Jane asked as they leaned against the stone wall and waited for the children to emerge from the school, tumbling down the stairs like puppies in pinafores. "Is something up?"

Ellen shrugged. "Nothing more than the usual. Builders everywhere, trying to get some work done, Pepper constantly under my feet..."

"Come to ours if you like," Jane offered. "You know we've acres of space. You could set up an office in one of the spare bedrooms—"

"I can't," Ellen cut her off, although the invitation was tempting. Jane and her family lived in the old vicarage, a massive Georgian edifice with eight bedrooms and even more fireplaces. They'd been doing it up slowly and were almost finished. Ellen had to suppress a serious pang of house-envy whenever she went over there. "The builders need their tea, after all."

"They could bring a flask—"

"I want to keep them happy. And Pepper would go ballistic without me home all day." Ellen smiled and straightened as the school doors opened and its first occupants were gleefully released. "Really, it's fine. I'm just having a bit of a moan over nothing." She wasn't about to tell anyone, not even Jane, about Alex's phone call. Not at least until she knew more herself.

"Mummy!" Sophie came running towards her, ginger plaits flying behind, and Ellen's heart squeezed with love. It was impossible to remain even the slightest bit gloomy with her golden girl around.

Sophie tackled her around the middle and Ellen let out a startled *oof* that morphed into a chuckle as her daughter tilted her head up to her and put on the cuteness with a huge, gap-toothed smile.

"Can Merrie come over today, please, please, pretty please, with sugar on top?"

Ellen thought of the plaster dust that had drifted down the stairs and coated every surface of every bedroom in fine white grit, as if someone had upended a bag of flour, or several, in every room. She'd decided not to bother dusting until they were done, but it was on its way to becoming a health hazard. She'd almost bitten into a dust-covered apple this afternoon before she'd noticed. "I don't know, Soph. The builders are still there..."

"Sorry, Sophie, but we can't," Jane interjected. "Merrie's got swimming lessons today."

Merrie made a face and Sophie visibly deflated, her mouth pulling down at the corners in a tragic frown.

"You have a future career on the stage," Ellen teased as she tugged gently on one of her daughter's plaits. "Another time, all right? When the house isn't in such a state. The pair of you live in each other's pockets as it is." Now that they were a bit older, Merrie and Sophie ran down the high street from one house to the other most weekends and many weekday afternoons. Neither Ellen nor Jane minded laying an extra plate for supper, and they'd both remarked how thankful they were their daughters were such good friends.

Ellen said goodbye to Jane and Merrie as they turned in the opposite direction, up to the narrow, terraced house on the high street that she and Alex had bought twelve years ago, right after they'd got married.

They'd been so happy then, irrepressible with hope, Alex having fallen in love with Goswell in this remote corner of Cumbria along with Ellen and her daughter, Alyssa, then only five years old.

Ellen remembered when they'd closed on the house, a falling-down wreck with "bags of potential" according to the overly optimistic estate agent. Alex had taken a photo of them all in front of the rusty gate, the sea sparkling in the distance. Ellen had stood there with her arm loped around Alyssa's shoulders as she'd grinned at her new husband and had thought, *I will always remember this moment. I will remember how perfectly happy and blessed I am.*

But why on earth was she thinking about that moment now, almost as if she wouldn't get another one? Muttering under her breath, Ellen wrestled with the gate's still-rusty latch. She was starting to feel positively maudlin. Alex might just want to talk about their half-term holiday, three weeks away and as yet unplanned and undiscussed. Maybe he had a surprise in store – a trip to Tenerife, or at least Devon. She pictured them both sprawled in deckchairs on a warm, white beach, Sophie building sandcastles. Maybe Alyssa would come for the weekend, work on her tan. Ellen liked the thought of them being all together again.

"Mummy, what's all that noise?" Sophie asked as she skipped into the kitchen. Upstairs it sounded like the builders had taken a pneumatic drill to the floor and Ellen watched dust shake loose from the kitchen rafters, drifting gently down onto the slate floor, with a sigh.

"Just the building work, Sophie," she said as she switched on the kettle. No doubt it was time for another round of tea.

"Ugh, there aren't any biscuits." Sophie peered into the empty tin before shooting her mother a look that managed to be both mournful and accusing. "Don't you go shopping on Wednesdays?"

"Usually," Ellen answered. "I didn't have time today." She reached for a browning banana from the neglected fruit bowl on the kitchen table and wiped the plaster dust off the peel. "You'll have to make do with this."

She handed Sophie the banana, glancing at the slip of aged paper she'd pushed aside that morning. That death certificate. Ellen reached for it, flicking it open and scanning the lines once more.

"What's that?" Sophie asked, standing on her tiptoes to peer over Ellen's shoulder.

"Watch the peel, Soph." Ellen removed a banana peel from her shoulder and lobbed it into the bin. "One of the builders found this under the floorboards upstairs."

"But what is it?" Sophie asked around a mouthful of mushy banana.

"A death certificate, I think." At Sophie's confused expression, Ellen clarified, "A report someone, a doctor most likely, wrote out when a person died."

Sophie's mouth turned down at the corners. "Someone died?"

"A long, long time ago," Ellen reassured her. "No one we know." She glanced at the paper again. "Sarah Mills. Aged twenty-two," she mused. "So young, even for back then."

"Back when?"

"1872, moppet." Ellen tugged on her daughter's plait. "I

wonder how it ended up under the floorboards. I guess we'll never know."

"You could show it to Merrie's mum," Sophie suggested. "She loves all that old history."

"So she does," Ellen agreed with a laugh. "Jane would eat this kind of thing up with a spoon." A few years ago her friend had found a shopping list from the 1930s under a slate shelf in the old vicarage, and had spent months researching the history of the house and discovering who had written the list. "I'm not quite as curious as she is, though."

The kettle switched off and Ellen dropped the death certificate back onto the worktop next to the microwave, where all the random paper they accumulated ended up – school notices, village magazines, till receipts that Ellen thought might need saving. Every couple of months she'd toss the whole lot into the bin, most of it unread and untouched.

"You should still show it to her," Sophie insisted.

"I will," Ellen promised. "Now, how about getting your reading book out?" The homework had been due two days ago.

Five hours later, Sophie was tucked up in bed after three chapters of her childhood favourite, *The Magic Faraway Tree*, and Ellen was back downstairs, a wary, surprised pleasure rippling through her at the sight of the kitchen cleaned, the big pine table scrubbed, and the pot that had held their supper's bolognaise sauce soaking in the sink. Even better, Alex had opened an unusual midweek bottle of wine and was pouring two glasses as Ellen came into the room.

"This is a treat," she said as she accepted a glass. No doubt this was in all preparation for their big talk, which had grown in import in Ellen's mind throughout the day, and certainly solidified now, with all this special treatment. She couldn't remember the last time Alex had cleaned the kitchen. He hadn't said anything beyond the basics since he'd arrived home an hour ago, just as they were finishing tea. Somehow she had a feeling he wasn't going to spring a self-catering cottage in Devon on her.

"What's the occasion?" she asked lightly, and Alex shrugged, not meeting her gaze as he took a sip from his own glass.

"Thought we could do with a bit of relaxing."

"Oh, yes?" Ellen moved into the conservatory that led off the kitchen, which had been one of their first improvement projects after they'd bought the house. She loved the octagonal-shaped room with its shabby sofas, rattan tables and a view on every side of their tangled garden that stretched downhill to the beck that emptied into the sea.

She sank onto one of the sofas, tucking her knees up under her as she gazed out at the garden now lit up by the last of the sun's fading rays.

The grass needed mowing and the flowerbeds were rampant with weeds. Once she'd enjoyed mucking about in the garden; after they'd bought the house she and Alyssa had discovered a huge tangle of overgrown raspberry canes in the back, and had spent that first, sweet summer picking all the juicy berries. It had motivated Ellen, albeit briefly, to plant some fruit and veg and attempt to have the kind of motherly, pioneering spirit that she quite liked the idea of but which had often eluded her in the busy chaos of raising children, keeping a cleanish house, and attempting to make ends meet.

The veg patch had become overgrown years ago, and last summer Alex had dug it up and grassed it over, which Ellen had had to admit looked better, even if she'd felt a bit nostalgic for the days of composting and sowing seeds, followed by the seeming magic of sprouting plants.

"So what did you want to talk about?" she asked. A few sips of wine had given her enough courage to ask the obvious question.

Alex didn't answer right away, which made the bands of

tension tighten around Ellen's head. What on earth did he have to tell her? "Alex?" she prompted. "Don't keep me in suspense here. I've had all day to imagine what could possibly be so important you had to ring me from work, and none of it has been good."

He sighed, the sound long and weary, and raked one hand through his sandy hair. The flyaway strands went in every direction, making him look like the proverbial mad scientist. Usually Ellen would have smiled at the sight, but now she felt too keyed up. "Well?" she asked, impatience edging her voice despite her desire to sound levelheaded and reasonable.

"Sandra rang today."

For a second Ellen didn't know whom he meant, which was ridiculous because there was only one Sandra in their lives. Sandra Tyson, Alex's ex-wife. Ellen had never met her, never even seen a photo of her. Alex hadn't brought any with him, and that had been fine by Ellen. More than once she'd been tempted to look up her profile on Facebook, but she'd resisted, deciding that ignorance, if not exactly bliss, was better. She preferred acting as if Sandra didn't exist at all.

Sandra had left Alex years – well, *a* year – before they'd even met. Alex never spoke of her except to say Sandra had decided she didn't want to be married any more, and cut Alex completely out of her life. He'd accepted a job up in Cumbria while Sandra had stayed in Manchester, and Ellen didn't think he'd spoken to her in years.

"Why on earth has Sandra rung you?" she asked.

"She wanted to talk about Annabelle."

*Annabelle.* Ellen stared down at her wine as a prickling, uncomfortable sense of guilt crept over her. Annabelle, Alex's daughter from his first marriage. She had to be seventeen now, a year younger than Alyssa. Ellen hadn't seen her in ten years, and as for Alex... maybe the summer before last?

In the early years of their marriage, Annabelle had visited

for one weekend a month and Ellen had done her best to make the little girl feel welcome. She knew all too well the pain of a father walking away from a daughter, as her ex-husband, Jack, had walked away from Alyssa, with barely a backward glance, after those first few years. Ellen didn't even know the last time Alyssa had seen or talked to her father.

She hadn't wanted that for Annabelle, and had done everything she could think of to make her stepdaughter feel like a welcome part of their little family. She'd made her favourite meal – some bizarre lentil casserole, since Sandra and Annabelle were both strict vegetarians – and bought princess sheets for Annabelle's bed. She'd even découpaged, rather inexpertly, a box for the toys Annabelle kept with them for those endless, awkward weekends.

Nothing Ellen had done had seemed good enough for Annabelle. The casserole remained uneaten by everyone, the princess sheets weren't the right kind of princess, and her ideas for fun outings condemned as babyish or boring. Ellen understood Annabelle's resistance to her father's second wife; of course she did. It was both expected and natural for any child to feel suspicion and resentment towards her father's new family. Still, it didn't make being the good-intentioned yet still-wicked stepmother any easier. With Annabelle she could never win.

Then, when Annabelle was seven, she'd come for an entire summer holiday. Sandra, a professor of Women's Studies at the University of Manchester, had been taking a sabbatical somewhere exotic, no children allowed, and she'd blithely traipsed off to who-knew-where while Alex went down to Manchester to pick up his reluctant daughter, all sullen eyes and sulky silences.

The holiday had been endless, rainy and cold as only a Cumbrian summer could be. Ellen had arranged trips for Annabelle and Alyssa to the farm park in Carlisle and the zoo near Keswick; despite the lure of such outings, Annabelle had remained unenthused as she made countless comparisons to Manchester, where everything was shiny and perfect and, if you were to believe Annabelle, paved in gold.

"It never even bloody rains in Manchester, does it?" Ellen had savagely asked Alex, and he'd stared at her, nonplussed, oblivious as only a right-brain scientist could be, to the emotional currents crackling through the house, charged and dangerous. Alyssa, after an initial foray into friendship, had chosen to ignore Annabelle, and the summer descended into a stand-off of tense silences and snippy exchanges between the two girls. Ellen, eight months pregnant and rather miserable herself, had felt like throwing it all in – or maybe just Annabelle, who had been so sneeringly unimpressed with everything, nothing good enough, Goswell considered the dullest place ever, the food and furniture and everything Ellen had to offer tatty and stupid and, Annabelle's favourite word at the time, *vile*. Ellen had started the summer with smiles and ended it by gritting her teeth to keep from screaming.

Alex had been working all the time on an important research project, often coming home after the girls were in bed. The holiday they'd planned in Devon had been cancelled because Ellen developed pre-eclampsia in the last month of pregnancy and had to stay in bed – yet another complication to an already difficult summer. It felt as if everything that could went wrong, and when Annabelle had finally gone back to Manchester, it felt as if the house itself breathed a sigh of relief, its very rafters relaxing.

That autumn Sandra had tartly informed Alex that from then on he could visit Annabelle in Manchester. Annabelle would not be coming to Goswell again. Ellen had heard Alex's terse replies and wondered what Annabelle had told her mother about Goswell, about Alyssa, about her. It burned to think that Alex's ex-wife assumed his daughter had been mistreated under Ellen's care, but she let it go. She was a few days off her due date and her blood pressure was already worryingly high. She couldn't add Sandra to her list of anxieties. In any case, she didn't particularly want Annabelle coming back to Goswell, either.

Now, however, all those memories made her cringe a little bit in shame. When Annabelle had first come to stay she'd been *six*. Had Ellen really expected a child that age to appreciate her attempts to make her welcome? Perhaps Ellen should have made *more* of an effort, thought of more ways to include Annabelle in their family. She could have overlooked the sneering slights; they'd been so *obvious*. Of course Annabelle had felt threatened. Why hadn't Ellen been able to look past the surly sullenness to the hurting child underneath?

But then Sophie had come along and somehow it had been easier to let Annabelle slip from her mind, to let Alex have his weekends away, and then to soothe her guilty conscience with generous gift cards for birthdays and Christmas, and the occasional awkward three seconds' chat on the phone when Annabelle rang Alex, a rare occurrence in itself.

At some point, the trips he took to see her became more and more infrequent; Annabelle had school trips and too much homework and holidays with Sandra, and weekends down south kept getting put off. Ellen couldn't actually remember the last time Alex had seen her.

"So," she asked, and took another sip of wine. "Why did Sandra want to talk about Annabelle?"

Alex hesitated for a moment, his gaze on the twilit garden, and Ellen tensed. She had no idea what to expect. "She's moving to New York."

"Annabelle...?" she exclaimed in surprise.

"No, Sandra." His breath came out in a hiss of impatience, making Ellen feel rebuked. "Sandra's moving to New York to take up some position with a university there, and she wants

Annabelle to stay in England to complete her A-Levels. She only has one more year after this."

Even then Ellen didn't quite get where Alex was going. Maybe she didn't *want* to get it, because surely it would be obvious to anyone with half a brain. But she just looked blankly at him and said, "So...?"

"So she wants Annabelle to live with me. Us. Until she finishes school."

"Live with us?" Ellen stared at him, trying not to let how appalled she was show on her face. "You mean... for a whole year?"

"Yes." Alex hunched a shoulder defensively. "She is my daughter, Ellen. As much as Sophie is."

Ellen blinked, hurt, though part of her recognised that she shouldn't be. What Alex had said was both true and fair. She just didn't like it. She had no idea what Annabelle was like now, but if the last visit was anything to go by...

She wrapped her arm around her knees as she stalled for time and tried to marshal her thoughts. "When did you last see Annabelle?" she asked, and Alex's expression closed up. Too late Ellen realised how her question could sound like a criticism. "I mean..." she tried to explain, but then only trailed off lamely.

"It's been a year," he said stiffly. "A little over. Last Easter, it was."

"Last Easter?" Why did she not remember this?

"I saw her during a business trip to Manchester. Anyway, the important thing is what happens now. She needs to stay in England to complete her A-Levels."

"But she's in the middle of them, isn't she? She must be doing her AS exams right now—"

"They're mocks, they don't count because of the new reforms, and she can come right after. Get stuck in as soon as possible and do the final year here."

"But what if Copeland Academy doesn't offer her subjects? Or uses different exam boards—"

"It's not ideal," Alex cut across her, his voice tight. "But then, Sandra's never been particularly thoughtful about things like that." He pressed his lips together, clearly not wanting to say any more, and it occurred to Ellen that in twelve years of marriage Alex had never criticised his first wife. He'd barely mentioned her at all. And while she'd thought she preferred that, right now she realised how much she didn't know, hadn't wanted to ask about. About Sandra, about Annabelle, about Alex's first marriage. She certainly didn't want to ask now.

"Well..." Ellen blew out a breath and tried to rally. Annabelle was seventeen, and from the sounds of it, her mother was practically abandoning her. She needed a place to stay, and that place was here. It had to be. "Of course she can stay here. What A-Levels is she doing? I can look into what Copeland Academy offers. And I suppose she can stay in Alyssa's bedroom, although it will be a tight squeeze when she's home from uni." Which was a massive understatement. Alyssa's bedroom could barely fit in her bureau and bed. Getting another set in there would take a miracle of engineering.

A look of relief passed over Alex's face and he visibly relaxed. "Thanks, Ellen, for understanding." He reached over and squeezed her knee. "I know it's not ideal, but..."

"It's fine," she returned, giving him a reassuring squeeze back and ignoring her own lingering unease about the whole situation. "Totally fine. Your daughter needs you, Alex. Of course we'll welcome her."

# CHAPTER 2

## SARAH

Goswell, 1868

Sarah Telford saw the smoke from the train first, cheerful white puffs against a slate-grey sky. Then the train came into a view, chugging past the grand Station Hotel like a gleaming, black, mechanical snake, a cheerful menace.

She and Lucy were the only passengers embarking from Goswell that morning, with the damp chill of last night's rain still hanging in the air. Her neighbour, Ruth Teddington, tugged on Sarah's best shawl, arranging it to cover more of her slight bosom.

"Keep you warm," she said gruffly, although Sarah suspected Ruth Teddington was thinking more of modesty than warmth. She'd already warned Sarah about chancers who took improprieties with wayward girls in empty train compartments.

"The rest of the world's not like here," she'd said, although as far as Sarah knew, Ruth Teddington had never left Goswell, save for the odd trip to Whitehaven, same as her. And if truth be told, Sarah would rather the rest of the world *was* different. Since her father's death, her life in Goswell had been marked neither by kindness nor good fortune; her mother's death a few weeks before had shown how little people's grudging charity could extend.

Sarah was dressed in her mourning best for this journey to Kendal, a dress of black wool that had faded to a dingy grey-brown, that she had cut down from one of her mother's old dresses, and her best pair of boots. She also wore her woollen petticoat as well as her mother's crinoline skirt that had been given to her by one of the ladies of the village who had pitied the curate's widow in her thrice-mended threadbare dresses. Sarah was grateful for the extra layer; it was cold for March and the third-class carriage would be icy. Besides, she and Lucy only had one small valise for the two of them and the crinoline wouldn't fit in it.

"You take care," Ruth said sternly, tugging on Sarah's shawl again. "And make sure to write and let me know how you've got on."

"Yes, Mrs Teddington."

Ruth's face softened as she glanced at Lucy. "I know you'll take care of her," she said gruffly, and Sarah did not reply. Only last week, after the last of the pennies and precious half-crowns in the old coffee tin kept on the high kitchen shelf had paid for her mother's funeral, Ruth had taken her aside and whispered that she'd have taken Sarah and Lucy as her mother had wanted, of course she would have, but she didn't have space or money for two mouths to feed, especially considering Lucy...

She'd trailed off, slightly shamefaced, and Sarah had yanked her arm away, drawing herself up. "You don't need to worry about us," she'd said rather coldly. "I can take care of my sister just fine."

"Ah, Sarah, don't be like that," Ruth had pleaded. "You know I want the best for you two lasses. I've known you since you were both babes in your mother's arms, God rest her."

"We'll be fine," Sarah said, not meeting her neighbour's eye, because the truth was she had no idea what awaited them in Kendal. In the twenty years since her mother, Victoria Hatley, had left her family to become the wife of a penniless curate, a former grammar school boy with no connections and therefore no prospects, she'd never returned to Kendal. Sarah had never heard from any of the Hatleys, and hadn't even known her mother had had a sister, Edith, until she'd been on her deathbed, clutching Sarah's arm and gasping out her last wishes.

"You must write to my sister, Sarah. Edith Hatley, in Kendal. We parted badly but she'll help you now. Lowther Street. She still lives there, I think..." Her mother had fallen back against the pillows, her face as bleached of colour as the faded pillow slip. "Edith always knew her Christian duty."

Sarah had not wanted to be anyone's duty, Christian or otherwise, but she recognised that she could not stay in Goswell. She was eighteen, with the sole care of her ten-year-old sister, and she had no money, no prospects, no hope. At least something waited for them in Kendal, even if Edith Hatley was more stranger than relation at this point.

The conductor strode forward, thumbs tucked into the pockets of his waistcoat, and Ruth gave Sarah a quick, hard kiss on the cheek.

"Godspeed," she whispered, her voice choked, and Sarah wondered if it was sadness or simply guilt that had her mother's closest friend blinking back tears as she and Lucy boarded the train.

Lucy slipped her hand into hers as they made their way down the third-class carriage, one large compartment with wooden bench seats, lit by a single, swinging oil lamp. The carriage was empty, and Sarah guided Lucy to a bench by one of the soot-grimed windows. Although it was draughty there, she wanted to see a bit of the world. In all her eighteen years she'd never been further than Whitehaven, four miles away.

With a great hiss of steam and a heaving, mechanical sigh,

the train started towards the coast. Lucy craned her head to watch Goswell's small platform disappear, and then the train was going around the curve, and the sea came up suddenly, churning grey froth that seemed to be only inches from the iron wheels.

Lucy gripped Sarah's hand tightly and she squeezed it with a reassuring smile. "Isn't it grand," she remarked, "being on a train?"

They'd been on a train before, going to Whitehaven, but never as far a journey as Kendal. There would be a change at Carnforth, and Ruth had packed them a dinner pail. Lucy's stomach rumbled audibly and Sarah wondered when she should let her have some of the thick ham sandwiches. At ten years old, slender as she was, Lucy always seemed to be hungry and growing.

Lucy squeezed Sarah's hand again and nodded towards the window. Through the sooty grime, Sarah could see the churning sea, and on the other side of the carriage, the rocky cliff side dropped away in a grey-green blur. Lucy had always loved the sea; whenever she'd had a spare moment, Sarah had taken her down to the wide sweep of beach so they could stare at the restless waves, and on sunny days, sometimes even take off their stockings and have a bit of a paddle. There would be no sea in Kendal.

Sarah closed her eyes, weary before her journey had even begun. She feared what awaited them at the end of the journey, despite Ruth's cheerful insistence that Kendal was known to be a lovely place, and Edith Hatley would surely welcome her sister's children as her own. Considering Ruth had never met nor even known about Edith Hatley, her assertions seemed like nothing but more sops to her own troubled conscience.

No, Kendal felt like an unknown, an end to life as Sarah had known it, growing up in Goswell, living with family who loved her, although in truth that life had ended long ago. For a few seconds, with her eyes still closed, she allowed herself the sentimental luxury of picturing her mother before she'd died six weeks before. The pale, thinning hair that had once been compared, rather ridiculously, Sarah thought, to silk; the faded blue eyes that could still sparkle with humour; the ever-ready smile, even as death loomed closer, a dark angel that Victoria Telford had, in the end, welcomed with weary, open arms.

Then, in an even more indulgent moment, Sarah pictured her father as she remembered him before his death when she'd been ten years old. Even now the shock of it could steal her breath; how could a person be happy and whole one moment, and wasted and lifeless the next? That's how it had seemed to Sarah back then; her father had come home one evening complaining of a headache and gone upstairs to bed. Four days later he'd been dead of a fever that had raged through him and wasted his body.

Now she pictured the soft black hair that had flopped across his forehead, his serious, dark eyes and surprising smile that had lit up his face the way the sun lit the surface of the sea when it was still. She could almost hear his laugh, that quiet, dry chuckle that always had her smiling in return, the way he'd lean closer to listen to what she said.

Tears pricked under her lids and she blinked them back impatiently. She shouldn't have thought of her father now. She didn't have the luxury of self-pity or even sorrow, not with Lucy to think about.

She glanced down at her sister, who was watching the sea churn and froth next to the train. The railway ran along the coast until Carnforth, when they would change trains to the Windermere line and travel inwards to Kendal.

Lucy's expression was placid, her eyes following the move-ment of the sea, and Sarah wondered what her sister was think-ing. Last night she'd crawled into Sarah's bed and wrapped her arms around her, rocking back and forth while Sarah had stroked her hair. Lucy might not have any words, but she could communicate her fears and feelings as well as anybody else. At least for now she was occupied with the novelty of being on a train. Who knew how long that would last, or if something unexpected would startle her sister, and make her act up. Sarah was ever on her guard against either change or surprise; Lucy didn't handle either well.

"What do you suppose Kendal will be like?" Sarah asked with as much cheer as she could muster. She was used to keeping up a monologue, and discerning Lucy's response from the duck of her head or the twitch of her mouth. "Reverend Hesham said it's bigger than Whitehaven." Reverend Hesham was the vicar of Goswell and her father's old employer, having paid his curate out of his own pocket and then conveniently forgotten to provide more than a pittance for his widow, although he'd advised them to apply to a charity in Carlisle that provided for clergy widows. Unfortunately, curates' wives were far down on their list of the deserving needy; vicars' wives who'd had generous livings tended to get a good deal more of the charitable purse.

For the last seven years the Telfords had made do with cast-offs and the vicar's parsing donations, as well as some sewing that came their way, although Victoria had never known what to do with a needle. Sarah had sewn shirts, but there was precious little business in a village the size of Goswell and too many skilled seamstresses eager to turn their hand to shirt-making to earn a few pennies.

Reverend Hesham had been as relieved as Ruth Teddington to see the back of the curate's orphaned daughters, one of them, Sarah had heard him whisper to a gossipy parishioner, not half a saddle-goose.

She glanced again at Lucy, satisfied to see her sister looked content for the moment. Lucy wasn't any trouble, despite what Ruth or Reverend Hesham seemed to think.

At least, she wasn't *much* trouble. Yes, she acted up, and people didn't like it when Lucy flailed about or banged her head in a rhythmic way that disturbed even Sarah, although she had become used to it. They didn't like how Lucy stared at people without saying anything, her eyes wide and unblinking, until Sarah gently whispered for her to look away. No one liked anyone noticeably different, and Lucy certainly was. But she wasn't stupid. She'd never said a word in her life, but Sarah believed her sister understood far more than most people assumed. Saddle-goose, indeed.

At Millom they were joined in the third-class carriage by half a dozen lads going down to Barrow to, Sarah quickly surmised, get drunk, judging by their lively chatter debating the merits of the beer at each of the town's two inns.

"Ah, but the neck oil at the Ship is much better," one man, dressed in a too-tight waistcoat of boiled wool and a greasy neck scarf exclaimed. He caught Sarah's eye and gave her an audacious wink. "Don't you think so, sweeting?"

Flushing, Sarah looked away. She drew Lucy more closely to her and they both stared out the window as the train continued to trundle down the coast. She hadn't realised on her short jaunts to Whitehaven just how noisy and dirty a train could be. The steady clacking rhythm created a ceaseless din in the carriage, and her best gloves were already covered with a thin rime of greasy soot. Lucy began to draw in the grime-covered window with one finger, and Sarah didn't have the heart to stop her. Perhaps there would be an opportunity to wash in Carnforth.

The young men got off in a noisy pack at Barrow, and a man and his daughter came into the carriage, their clothes worn and mended several times over, although they looked respectable enough. The girl couldn't be more than five or six, and she perched on her father's knee, occasionally resting her head against his shoulder. He rested one hand lightly on her back, a touch that to Sarah seemed both possessive and caring, and she felt a needle-prick of envy pierce her soul. Where were they going, a father and his daughter on this chilly March morning? She discovered soon enough, when she overheard them chatting, straining her ears over the relentless clacking of the train to catch the titbits of their conversation.

They were headed for Grange on Morecambe Bay, to have a cream tea at the newly built Grange Hotel and walk on the wide, sweeping beach. She pictured them there, hand in hand, watching the tide roll out and the gulls circle overhead. She imagined the father cautioning his daughter, telling her not to run too fast. She pictured his hand on her shoulder, loving and protecting her. That needle-prick of envy burrowed deeper, drew blood. Her father had once done such things with her. She could picture him on the beach at Goswell, squinting up at the sky as she and Lucy chased after the gulls, his laughter carried away on the wind.

The father caught Sarah staring and he gave her a disapproving frown. Too late she realised how she must look, staring like Lucy often did, desperate and hungry, wishing that she had a father to take her on daytrips, that she wasn't travelling to an unknown and uncertain future. Flushing, she turned back to her sister.

"I think we're almost there."

Lucy didn't turn from the window, absorbed as she was in her sooty drawing. Her hands were filthy.

They arrived in Carnforth a short while later, and ate their sandwiches while sitting in the Ladies' Waiting Room, although several well-turned-out ladies looked sniffily upon their sandwiches wrapped in wax paper. Sarah carefully cleaned it all up after they'd finished, folding the wax paper into a neat square and putting it back in the pail, her head held high.

"Let's get you cleaned up," she said to Lucy with a determined smile. "Your face is nearly as black as a skillet, to say nothing of your hands." Dipping her handkerchief in the basin of cold water available to ladies for washing, she scrubbed her sister's face and hands of coal smuts as best as she could. "There you are."

Gently, Lucy took the handkerchief from her and dabbed at Sarah's own face with a shy smile.

"I'm just as dirty, I'm sure," Sarah said with a little laugh. She held still while Lucy inexpertly scrubbed her face. "Thank you, Lucy."

She wrung out the handkerchief and carefully put it away. "You know to be a good girl for Aunt Edith," she said, not for the first time, keeping her tone gentle. Lucy gazed up at her solemn-eyed and nodded. Sarah nodded back, satisfied she understood. Lucy was never any trouble, not really, not unless something scared or unnerved her, and Sarah had long ago learned how to handle those episodes.

"We're as presentable as we're ever likely to be," she said cheerfully, and tugged gently on one of Lucy's fair plaits. She had the same wispy blonde hair as their mother, while Sarah was dark and sallow, like their father. More than one well-meaning neighbour back in Goswell had said how Lucy might have been able to find a husband, if she wasn't so addlepated. Sarah ignored them, and hoped Lucy didn't hear. Her sister would always have Sarah to take care of her. She didn't need a husband, not that either of them would ever be able to find one, with nothing to their names. All they needed was each other.

Dusk was falling when the train finally pulled into Kendal, the sky having darkened to deeper grey as the train turned inland, away from the familiar sea, the sweep of the fells barren and a bleak grey-green as they loomed up menacingly on either side, seeming to tower over the train. Lucy sagged against Sarah, half-dozing, and Sarah put a protective arm around her as she peered out the window at the scramble of stone buildings that now crowded the horizon. Kendal, a market town, the biggest one in all of Westmorland.

She glimpsed a big brick building with a sign reading "K Shoes" in bold letters; another factory was for "Kendal Brown Snuff, Samuel Gawith & Co." Everything seemed huge and dark and somehow threatening.

Then the train was finally slowing down and the conductor was calling out the stop. Sarah woke up Lucy, who scrubbed her eyes and blinked sleepily around her before they were hurrying from the carriage and out onto the empty platform.

No one was waiting for them. The telegram her aunt had sent had been brief, terse: *Send on train. Stop. Will meet at station.* Sarah had sent a telegram back, using precious pennies for her reply: *Arrive at Kendal on the afternoon train from Carnforth, March 26.*

It was the twenty-sixth of March, and here they were, the wind that shuttled down the platform icy and unforgiving, the other passengers hurrying away in the dark so they were completely alone.

"Come along," Sarah said briskly, determined to act as if she knew what she was doing. Lucy would worry otherwise. "Aunt Edith is most likely inside."

But Aunt Edith wasn't inside the station; no one was but the stationmaster sitting comfortably by the fire, a newspaper spread out before him, a pocket watch gleaming against his waistcoated paunch, and they lingered for only a moment in the room's inviting warmth before they came out on the other side, onto the street that stretched towards the River Kent and the town proper.

Just as Sarah was wondering whether to start walking towards the town, a figure emerged through the dusk, heels clipping smartly on the cobbles, one gloved hand holding her skirts away from the street muck.

"Sarah? Sarah and Lucy Telford?" Her voice rang out in the darkness and Lucy shrank back, fumbling for Sarah's hand.

"Yes, ma'am," Sarah called. "That's me. Us, I mean."

The woman, who Sarah thought must be her aunt, stood before her, tall, thin, and imposing, her hair brought back over her ears in a tight bun of greying blonde that peeked out beneath the low-brimmed bonnet she wore. Her dress was of black bombazine lined with crêpe, which heartened Sarah a little. Her aunt was in deep mourning for Victoria Telford, just as she was.

"Look at the state of you," Edith exclaimed. "Trains are so terribly dirty. I don't have a carriage, but there's nothing wrong with a brisk walk to improve the circulation as well as the humours. You'll have to carry your valise, but you're a strong-looking girl." With that she turned on her heel and began to sweep down the street. Sarah hefted her valise in one hand, took Lucy's in the other, and followed her aunt.

She couldn't see much of Kendal in the oncoming darkness; she heard the lap of the river as they crossed a stone-arched bridge that led into the town centre, and then the mournful peals of the clock on the town hall's tower as they passed the marketplace and finally arrived, Sarah's arms aching, at a narrow, terraced house on Lowther Street.

"Here we are," Edith said, and fished a key out of her reticule. She unlocked the door and Sarah stepped into the gloomy entrance hall behind her aunt, waiting while she turned up the gas lamps. They came on with a hiss, illuminating the little hall with a sickly yellow glow. They'd never had gas lighting in their little house back in Goswell, only lamps of colza oil that lent a greasy feel to the air.

And even though she could tell already that this house was grander than the set of rooms her mother had let as a widow, or the dear little house they'd lived in when her father was alive, Sarah felt a powerful wave of homesickness hit her for the faded little sitting room with the precious few pieces of coal for the grate, the Welsh dresser with its little ornaments – a pair of brass cats, a collection of shells they'd found at the beach – and most importantly, her mother in her rocking chair by the fire, a book in her lap, and her father bent over his desk, his fusty books lit only by a single tallow candle.

Here she saw heavy mahogany furniture, an umbrella stand and a marble-topped table, an elaborate wrought-iron plant stand with a bushy aspidistra and another stand for coats and shawls. The small space felt crowded and dark, the air heavy with the smell of coal fires and lavender polish.

"Well, then." Aunt Edith hung up her shawl and bonnet, every movement brisk and businesslike, giving Sarah the impression of a woman who was not accustomed to either giving or receiving affection. "Take off your things," she said, a touch of impatience in her voice. "And then we'll see about something to eat."

Slowly Sarah took off her shawl and bonnet, and then helped Lucy with hers. Their belongings looked faded and frayed next to Edith's things, and Sarah saw her aunt react, her thin lips pressing together as she assessed the sorry state of her nieces' possessions.

After they'd finished, Edith ushered them down the hallway, past the front and back rooms, to a narrow set of stairs that led down to the kitchen and scullery below.

"Sit yourselves down," Edith commanded, gesturing to the small table with two Windsor chairs. The room, although dark, with high windows overlooking the backyard, was spacious and comfortable, with a large wooden dresser filled with Willow-pattern china, an armchair, and a single-oven range that threw out a welcoming heat. A pot of something, soup or stew, simmered on its hot plate, and Sarah watched in fragile, dawning hope as Edith fetched bowls and spoons and began to dish it out.

"Get that in you," she said, placing bowls in front of both Sarah and Lucy, "and then you can have a wash."

"Thank you, miss," Sarah murmured, and Edith let out a sound between a sigh and a laugh.

"You might as well call me Aunt Edith," she said, "although I know as well as you that we've never clapped eyes on each other before today. The truth is, I didn't know the pair of you existed." Edith turned to give her a sad, wry smile, and for a moment, although she was taller and thinner and altogether sterner than her sister, Victoria, had been, Sarah could see the resemblance in the way her eyes crinkled, the cleft of her chin.

"We didn't know about you," Sarah said quietly, and Edith nodded towards Lucy.

"Does she speak?" The question was more matter-of-fact than unkind, and wordlessly, her mouth full of hot soup, Sarah shook her head.

Edith sighed. "Well, then," she said, and to Sarah it sounded like acceptance, and that fragile hope planted roots right down in her soul. Perhaps things would be all right here. Perhaps things might even, against all expectations, be good.

# CHAPTER 3

## ELLEN

A second bed was not going to fit in Alyssa's room. Alex had said as much and Ellen had known it already, but it took her husband attempting to manoeuvre it through the doorway to finally accept the obvious.

She stood in the hall, her hands on her hips, as Alex put the bed down with a groan. "I'll spare you the 'I-told-you-so'."

"You just said it," Ellen returned, blowing a wisp of hair out of her eyes. It was a beautiful, sunny afternoon, the kind of golden spring day that came rarely to Cumbria but made Goswell feel like the loveliest place on earth. Everything sparkled; the air was fresh and clean, and the view of the village nestled against the golden beach and sky-blue sea was worthy of a picture postcard. Ellen's heart had lifted that morning when she'd seen it, driving down from Whitehaven with a week's food shopping in the boot. Annabelle was due to arrive in three days.

"We could do bunk beds," she suggested, a bit dubiously, because even bunk beds would be difficult to fit in the narrow room with its low, sloping ceiling, and she couldn't see two teenaged girls wanting to share them. Alex shook his head.

"This room is tiny," he said. "Annabelle would barely have room to stand up."

Ellen kept herself from pointing out that the room had been tiny for Alyssa, and for Sophie before her. Sophie had only moved to the bigger room when Alyssa had gone to uni. And if her girls had managed perfectly well, couldn't Annabelle?

Somehow she didn't think that train of logic would go down very well, and so she stayed silent. Alex sighed heavily.

"I think Annabelle needs her own room."

"Oh, does she?" Ellen retorted before she could keep herself from it. The last week of preparing for Annabelle's arrival had left her a bit raw. The expense of new furniture, Alex on the phone every day to Sandra or Annabelle making arrangements... Even though Ellen had gone around Copeland Academy and talked to all the relevant teachers about Annabelle's A-Level subjects, Alex had done it again afterwards to satisfy his daughter. Apparently Ellen's efforts hadn't been good enough.

But she wasn't going to be bitter or resentful, she reminded herself for what felt like the twentieth time. If Alyssa were ever put in Annabelle's position, she'd want Jack's wife to be welcoming, loving, even, although she'd also probably want to claw the woman's eyes out for attempting to mother her own child. But Jack had never married again; he far preferred playing the field, just as he had during their marriage.

"How is she meant to have her own room?" Ellen asked, making sure her tone was reasonable, even a little curious. *Here is a problem we can solve together.* "We can't turf Alyssa out of hers when she comes home at the end of term."

"I didn't say that," Alex returned, irritation edging his voice, and Ellen wondered why everything between them recently had bordered on an argument. They always pulled back from a proper fight, but the pettiness could be heard in both of their voices, and tempers were definitely frayed. Even Sophie had noticed, silently glancing from Ellen to Alex when they'd been in a verbal tennis match over supper last night, talking about who should pick up the dry cleaning from Workington.

"Then what do you suggest?" Ellen asked, and Alex gave her a pointed look before heaving the bed back into the hallway, forcing her to move out of the way.

"There is a room going spare," he said, his head lowered as he continued to shove the bed further down the hallway. Where, Ellen wondered, was he trying to put it?

She retreated to the top of the stairs, one hand resting on the banister. "A room going spare? You mean my office?" Alex didn't reply, but then, he didn't need to. What other room was going spare in their little terraced house? The builders had only left yesterday, and the room upstairs smelled of new plaster and fresh paint. The bright white walls, the wide wooden floor-boards, sanded and varnished to a glossy shine... Ellen had stood up there last night, craning her head to glimpse the sea from the window, and had felt a desperately needed sense of peace settle on her soul. A room of her own. Finally.

Except, apparently not.

"It would only be for a year," Alex muttered.

A dozen different replies formed themselves on Ellen's tongue, none of them helpful. *It's only been twelve years that I've been waiting* was the hardest one to choke down. Ellen took a deep breath and counted to ten. *Think of Annabelle. Think of Alyssa, who could have very well been in the same position at some point. Except you'd never leave your daughter, to traipse across the world.* Ellen counted to twenty.

"Ellen?"

"Fine," she said, the single word clipped and decidedly ungracious. "Fine, she can have my room."

"If you're going to be like that..."

"How am I supposed to be?" Ellen exclaimed. "I'm giving up the room, aren't I?" She took another breath to hold back the tears that now threatened. "If you'd just asked me properly, Alex..."

"I did."

"Not like that." She turned away, swiping at her eyes, feeling like a big baby. It was a *room*. *For heaven's sake, Ellen, get over it.* "Never mind," she mumbled, and then drew a deep breath to steady herself. "Do you need help getting the bed up there?"

Later, when Sophie was in bed and Ellen was at the kitchen table with her laptop, wading through the last pages of the economics article she'd been working on all week, Alex came downstairs, bracing one shoulder against the doorway, his hands shoved in the pockets of his jeans.

"Did you say goodnight to Sophie?" Ellen asked.

"Yes, and read an extra chapter of that faraway tree book."

Ellen looked up from her laptop with a brief smile. "Softie," she teased, wanting to lighten the mood after the tension of that afternoon. She had, silently and a bit sullenly, helped Alex move all of Annabelle's new furniture up to the top floor. It had not eased the loss to see how well the furniture actually fitted.

They hadn't talked much in the hours since then, busy with domestic life – dinner, dishes, bedtime. Now the house was quiet except for Pepper's gentle snoring under the table, her muzzle resting on Ellen's foot.

"I'm sorry about before," Alex said abruptly.

Ellen raised her eyebrows. "Sorry...?"

"About the room." He nodded towards the stairs. "I should have been more... sensitive about asking for your office space. I know you've been waiting for it for a long time."

A smile twitched Ellen's lips; she knew this kind of emotive talk was difficult for her husband. He sounded like he was reading it from a manual. "It's all right. I understand the need, even if I don't always act like I do." She sighed, pushing away her laptop so she could rest her elbows on the table. "I'm sorry about this afternoon, too. This is hard for me, Alex. Maybe it shouldn't be, but..."

"It's hard for me, too."

"Is it?" Ellen stared at her husband, surprised by his admission. Alex was the classic scientist – unsentimental, coolly practical. He was definitely pulling out the emotional stops tonight, at least for him.

It had been that steady sense of certainty and purpose, his quiet strength, that had first attracted her to him when she'd met him at the pub, of all places. She'd been on a friend's hen night and Alex had been sitting at the bar, having a pint after work, new to Goswell, knowing no one. Ellen wouldn't have thought to talk to him; she'd met Jack in a similar way and had no interest in chatting up strangers again. Two years on from her divorce, she'd been tired, guarded, a single mum struggling to hold things together and make do on freelance work and what little maintenance Jack remembered to pay. She didn't have either the time or interest for romance and all of its complications.

But then Alex had glanced up with a wry smile, as if to acknowledge what a sad sack he was for drinking on his own, and Ellen, emboldened by two glasses of wine herself, had started talking to him. Alex had told her later that she was the first person outside of work to give him so much as the time of day, and he'd fallen in love with her right then.

Now, twelve years of marriage on, they were thankfully still trying to break through the awkward silences. Just.

"What's Annabelle like now?" Ellen asked, and Alex shrugged.

"I don't really know. I saw her a little over a year ago, for dinner at an Italian place. She had the mushroom ravioli."

Ellen's heart gave a painful little twist at this bleak statement, encompassing how little he knew of his daughter. "But you must have talked..."

"I asked her about her GCSEs. She was about to take her exams." He sighed, moving into the room, restless now. "It was all pretty hard going, to be honest. I'd ask a question and she'd give me a monosyllabic answer, barely even looking at me." He paused, his gaze moving to the window to rest on the darkening garden. They still hadn't mown the lawn. "It had been that way for a while."

"Then maybe this is an opportunity to deepen your relationship," Ellen suggested with determined optimism. "This could be a good thing for both of you, Alex. I know it might not be easy, but maybe it's what you both need."

Alex smiled wryly, his gaze moving to rest on her. "And what about what you need?"

"What I need is a husband who gets that this is challenging," Ellen said. "But it can still work. For all of us." As she said the words, she knew she believed them. She *felt* them. Her worries and jealousies of earlier that day seemed petty now. Annabelle deserved as much love and support as Sophie or Alyssa did, and Ellen wanted to give it to her. "This can work, Alex," she said firmly. "We can make this work."

Over the next three days, Ellen threw herself into making Annabelle's new bedroom the best it could be. She and Sophie painted the walls a pale lilac and she bought a fuzzy, purple rug for the floor. She also bought some throw pillows in different shades of purple and blue and a mirror with lights so Annabelle could do her make-up and hair upstairs rather than in the one small bathroom they all would have to share. By the time Annabelle was due to arrive, Ellen felt the room was as welcoming as she could make it, a private sanctuary for a teenaged girl.

She'd ended up cleaning the whole house from top to

bottom as well as stocking the fridge with sodas and treats she didn't normally buy. Was it bribery? Maybe. But she wanted Annabelle's introduction to their family to be successful, and if a can of cola helped, then so be it.

"So today's the big day," Jane said when Ellen met her at the school drop-off on Friday. "When does she arrive?"

"A little after five, on the train. Alex offered to pick her up in Manchester, but she said she could take the train all the way to Goswell." Which Ellen couldn't help but feel seemed like a slightly ominous harbinger of things to come, almost as if Annabelle was already refusing their welcome. Yet she wasn't entirely surprised; she doubted Annabelle was keen to come up to Cumbria and live with the father she barely knew and his second family. Who would be?

"It's going to be difficult at first," Jane said in sympathy. "Moving here is hard on anyone."

"As well you know." Jane had moved to Goswell from New York City two and a half years ago, and she'd struggled with the isolation, as well as the wind and rain, for months. "Well, we'll do our best," Ellen said, with as much optimism as she could muster. "And who knows, maybe Annabelle could do with a change." She had no idea what Annabelle's experience in Manchester had been. She'd gone to some swanky girls' school, apparently, so the local comprehensive was certainly going to be different. But maybe their hectic household could be a change, too, from living alone with her mother. A welcome change.

In reality, Ellen had no idea what Annabelle wanted or needed. She hadn't got much more from Alex about his daughter, and she'd stopped pressing because she could tell he was defensive about how little he knew, even though he tried not to be.

She'd ended up going through the old photo albums, looking for snaps from that one awful summer, something to jog her memory, and come to realise that she hadn't actually taken that many pictures. The few in the album were of Annabelle and Alyssa swathed in parkas looking woebegone and resigned, standing as far apart from each other as they possibly could, reminding Ellen of what an endurance test the whole summer had been.

But it would be different this time. She'd make sure it was. The weather was sure to be better, for one. The Met had forecasted a whole five days of straight sunshine. And she was older and wiser and hopefully a bit more patient. Plus, she wasn't pregnant, and Sophie was always good at making friends. Who couldn't warm to Sophie, with her clear blue eyes and infectious smile, her relentless good cheer and little acts of kindness, whether it was a home-made card or a clutch of wildflowers? Annabelle would love her. She would love them all. Eventually.

Ellen kept telling herself that as they all walked down to the train station to meet Annabelle a little after five that evening. The day had been as sunny as promised, the sea breeze a warm balm, and the view of the rolling sheep pasture with the sea glinting in the distance made Ellen release a sigh of pure contentment at living in such a beautiful place.

Sophie skipped ahead of them towards the level crossing and Ellen reached over to squeeze Alex's hand. "It's going to be OK."

He nodded tersely, and she could tell by the frown settling between his eyebrows, the tightness of the jaw, that he wasn't quite buying it. Judging by the nerves leaping around in her stomach like a bunch of grumpy snakes, she wasn't sure she was, either. Who knew what Annabelle was like now? Would she turn her nose up at their house, their lives, just as she had when she was seven? Except this time it would be even more scathing, because she was seventeen. She must have learned a little more finesse.

They came to the platform, the only people waiting for the five o'clock train, huddling together even though it wasn't cold. In the distance she could see the boxy shape of the old vicarage, the squat Norman tower of the church beside it.

"Do you suppose it's running late?" Ellen asked when five minutes had passed with no sign of the train. Alex shrugged. Sophie started jumping up and down the stairs that led to the footbridge, and Ellen didn't have the energy to caution her. She strained her ears to hear the coming of the train, but all she heard was the raucous cries of the rooks that circled over the church on the other side of the station, and some strains of music from the pub.

"Well, the train will come when it comes," Ellen declared finally, which she realised belatedly was the most inane statement ever. Sighing, she shifted from foot to foot and tried not to feel anxious.

Had she had *any* contact with Annabelle since she was seven? Besides the few tense phone calls there had been a dutiful thank-you letter to an especially large gift card they'd given her for her sixteenth birthday that could have been copied from an etiquette book or, more likely, off the internet. But a proper conversation? No. Not even close. It had been far too easy just to *forget* about Annabelle, and the lack felt far greater now, when she was about to come face-to-face with this teenaged girl seething with hormones and, no doubt, a fair amount of resentment. How was Ellen going to cope?

"The train's coming," Alex announced, his voice tight, and they all swivelled to see it coming around the curve from the south and the sea.

"She came from Lancaster?" Ellen confirmed, another inane comment. Alex nodded.

Her palms became clammy and her stomach started to cramp as the train slowed to a stop and then various passengers spilled out, mainly tired-looking commuters in sensible shoes, briefcases in hand, heads tucked low as they started trudging towards home. A crowd of twenty-something lads came next, noisy and boisterous in their football jerseys and faded jeans, heading straight for the pub. And then there was Annabelle.

Ellen drew a quick, surprised breath as she caught sight of the girl. Gone was the coltish seven-year-old with a cloud of brown hair and sullen eyes. Annabelle was beautiful, with long, caramel-coloured hair that flowed over her shoulders in a perfect, shiny sheet, her slender body encased in designer skinny jeans, and a tailored white button-down shirt she'd accessorised with a chunky gold necklace. Her knee-length leather boots were designer too, and the whole ensemble put Ellen's best jeans and colourful cotton top to shame. She felt instantly inferior, and annoyed with herself for being so. This wasn't a *contest*.

"Annabelle. Hey." Alex stepped forward, smiling, his arms awkwardly half-held out in a sort-of hug. Annabelle stepped down from the train, swishing her hair over one shoulder, her expertly made-up face completely closed. "Hey." She stepped out of the loose circle of her father's arms without having touched him.

"Hi, Annabelle." Ellen stepped forward as if presenting herself for inspection. She decided not to attempt a hug. "It's been a long time, but I'm Ellen…"

"I know who you are," Annabelle answered in a tone so dismissive that for a few seconds Ellen could only blink. O… K… Maybe introducing herself had been the wrong way to go. Of course Annabelle knew who she was. So what if they hadn't seen each other in ten years?

"Let me get your suitcase," Alex murmured, and reached for the single large case – also designer – that Annabelle had held. "Did you have more stuff than this?" Alex asked. The case was large, but not a coming-for-a-year size. Annabelle shook her head, her lips pressed together.

"Well, let's get back," Alex said. "Show you around." Sophie hung back by Ellen, uncertain but clearly wanting to be part of things.

"You haven't met Sophie yet," Ellen said, her voice a touch too loud. "She wasn't born when you were last here, but—"

"I remember," Annabelle interjected. "You were as big as a house."

"Annabelle..." Alex's admonition was half-hearted at best. Non-existent was more like it. He gave a wry, shrugging smile that made Ellen feel like he was actually agreeing with his daughter. *Yes, you're right, sweetheart, she was huge.*

It was hard not to be huge while pregnant when you barely topped five feet. Ellen took a steadying breath and tried to rally.

"You're right, I was. Absolutely huge. But you were worth it, Soph." She squeezed her daughter's shoulder, and with a hint of steel entering her voice, said to Annabelle, "Now's the time for you to be properly introduced."

For a second she held Annabelle's gaze, determined to ride this out, even though her heart sank at the stand-off that was happening just seconds into their meeting. She hadn't wanted it this way at all, but Annabelle *would* acknowledge her daughter. She deserved that much courtesy.

After a tense, teeth-gritting moment, Annabelle swung her indifferent gaze to Sophie, raking her from head to foot in one scathing second. "Fine. Hi," she said, and started walking down the platform.

Ellen glanced at Alex, whose expression was frozen and blank. She knew her husband well enough to know this didn't bode well. Was he angry at Annabelle, though, or himself? Or even her, for forcing an introduction?

Alex followed Annabelle and, holding Sophie's hand, Ellen fell in step behind him. They made a silent, awkward parade back up the high street to their house, no one saying anything to anyone. Ellen waved to a few neighbours, trying for a friendly smile although inside all her determined optimism was trickling away like air escaping a balloon, leaving her deflated and flat. How on earth was any of this going to work?

"Here we are," Alex announced in a too-hearty voice that Ellen knew was his way of trying. The gate squeaked as he opened it. Annabelle didn't say anything, just stepped across the slate path with exaggerated care, as if there was muck all over the ground that she had to avoid. All right, there *were* a few muddy puddles. This was Cumbria, after all. Those designer boots, Ellen thought with grim satisfaction, wouldn't last very long up here, no matter how sunny it was now.

"Let me show you your room," Alex said, a note of excitement and even pride entering his voice, and Ellen headed for the kitchen with Sophie. She would have liked to show Annabelle the room she'd given up and worked so hard on, pointing out the little girly touches, but she recognised that Alex needed a win with his daughter.

"Come on, Soph, let's dish up supper," she said. She'd made a vegetarian bolognaise, a meal she vaguely remembered Annabelle liking, or at least eating, ten years ago. Was she still vegetarian? She had no idea.

Sophie gamely helped her lay the table, and even went out to the garden to pick a few roses from an overgrown bush for the centrepiece.

Ten minutes later Ellen stood back and surveyed the scene with satisfaction. The table was laid with pretty, if mismatched, pottery plates in bright colours, and the roses in a glass jar in the centre were big and blowsy, releasing their heady scent into the kitchen which mixed pleasantly with the aroma of the sauce bubbling away on the stove. It was a homely, welcoming scene, or so she hoped. A creak on the stair had her looking up, and then Alex came into the kitchen, his expression as closed as ever.

"Annabelle...?" Ellen ventured and he shook his head.

"She's not hungry."

"She's not coming down?" Ellen heard the censure in her voice and so did Alex, for his mouth tightened.

"No," he said shortly, and then sat down at the head of the table. "Shall we eat?"

# CHAPTER 4

## SARAH

Kendal, 1868

It took Sarah a few days to gain the measure of her aunt, and adjust her behaviour accordingly. After plying them with soup that first evening, Edith showed Sarah and Lucy upstairs, to the smallest bedroom in the back of the house. Still, it was larger and more luxurious than their shared room back in Goswell, although Sarah could see it would be considered plain by many people's standards: a single bed, just big enough for both of them, a washstand with an enamel pitcher and bowl, a small chest of drawers and a cupboard built into the recess between the chimney and the window.

Edith moved to the window, opening it several inches so the cool, damp air rolled in. "Best to keep the room well ventilated," she said crisply. "Carbonic acid is poison."

Sarah nodded in agreement, although she'd never heard of carbonic acid, and the room would get very cold with the window forever open. The fireplace was swept clean and looked as if it hadn't seen a fire all winter, and the coal scuttle next to it did not hold so much as a speck of coal dust.

"I'll bring up some hot water tonight," Edith continued, "but it will be cold water from then on, mind. I can't be forever heating cans of water. I don't have much help here, just a woman to come in to do the heavy scrubbing. I've no need of a maid, but I imagine you both will be some help with the housework."

"Yes, miss. Thank you, miss." Hot water for washing was a luxury Sarah had long done without. As for housework... she was certainly used to that.

Edith glanced at her, the sharpness fading from her face and voice as she sighed. "You must learn to call me Aunt Edith. Though I know it is more than passing strange."

"Aunt Edith," Sarah repeated dutifully. It *was* strange. She did not know this woman, even if she thought she'd seen something familiar about her eyes and smile. Edith Hatley was a stranger, and one Sarah was still trying to understand. Would Aunt Edith lash out and strike, huff and sigh in disapproval, or be simply indifferent? Sarah could not yet tell. The hope she'd felt earlier, with a bellyful of hot soup, was a frail and fragile thing.

Edith brought up a full can of boiling water, as well as a cake of hard soap that Sarah had to rub vigorously between her hands to get any lather from. When Edith had returned downstairs, Sarah carefully washed Lucy's face and then her own, rinsing the square of muslin in the bowl of water until it was black with soot and grime.

After tidying her and Lucy's hair, she took the bowl of dirty water back down to the kitchen, careful not to spill so much as a drop. Edith was washing their supper dishes, and she glanced up sharply when Sarah came into the room.

"Pardon, miss – Aunt Edith. Should I pour this outside?"

"Yes, quite. The door is through there."

Sarah moved carefully through the scullery to the door that opened to the backyard. It was completely dark outside now, and she stepped carefully over the damp, slippery cobbles, breathing in the air that smelled of coal smoke and musty damp, rather than the fresh sea air she'd been used to at Goswell.

A pang of homesickness assailed her, sharp and fast, and she resolutely pushed it down. She did not have the luxury of remembering. She poured the dirty water in the corner of the courtyard and then turned to go back into the kitchen.

"Is there anything else I can do for you, Aunt Edith?" she asked as Edith poked among the embers of the range's fire.

"No, that will be all, Sarah. Get some sleep and we will discuss your duties tomorrow."

*Duties.* Sarah was used to hard work, goodness knows she'd had to be, but she still felt a ripple of unease at her aunt's brisk tone. What did her aunt expect of her – and Lucy? Now was not the time to ask, so she simply nodded, murmured her thanks for the soup and hot water, and then went upstairs to Lucy, who had already crawled into bed, shivering.

They lay there next to each other in the cold and dark, and then Lucy reached for Sarah's hand. Sarah pulled her sister in close, cuddling her like a baby.

"We've landed all right here, haven't we, Lucy?" she whispered. "Hot food and a nice room. We'll be all right." She stroked Lucy's hair until her sister fell asleep, and even though she was exhausted, she lay there gritty-eyed and anxious, for no matter what her words were to Lucy, she did not know if they had landed right at all. They were entirely dependent on their aunt's goodwill, and it wasn't a position Sarah liked to be in.

The next morning, Sarah was up before the bells of the town hall's clock pealed six. She crept downstairs for a can of cold water, and then washed and dressed as quickly as she could, for the room was terribly cold; it had rained in the night and the open window had made everything feel icy and damp.

Quietly she woke Lucy and helped her to wash and dress, plaiting her hair and reminding her to be good for Aunt Edith, before they both went downstairs to await their aunt's direction; Sarah standing by the range and Lucy crawling on her hands and knees, in search of a marmalade cat she'd seen peeking from under the table. Sarah had tried to make her rise, so as not to dirty her dress, but Lucy had resisted and Sarah knew that forcing her sister would only cause her to fight harder.

The first fingers of grey morning light slid across the kitchen's flagged floor, and the town hall's clock chimed seven before Edith came down, dressed today not in deepest mourning's black crêpe, but a more practical housedress in serviceable grey wool. She came up short when she saw Sarah and Lucy; Lucy had thankfully found the cat and was cuddling her in her lap. Sarah dipped a small curtsey.

"Good morning, Aunt Edith."

"Well." Edith bustled over to the range and stoked up the coals in the grate. "I'm glad to see such work-ready girls."

"Yes, miss," Sarah said, and this time Edith did not correct her.

Over a plain breakfast of stodgy but filling porridge and cups of weak tea, Edith told them their duties.

"This house may seem large for one person," she explained, "but it belonged to my parents and I've no wish to live anywhere else." She eyed them sternly, as if expecting them to disagree. Sarah wondered if that meant her mother had grown up there. She did not dare ask; her aunt had not been forthcoming with any family details, and her very expression, narrow-eyed and purse-lipped, positively forbade Sarah from saying so much as a word.

"As I said last night, I only have the one woman to help. She does the washing and the heavy scrubbing, but I manage the rest on my own. Your help will be of some use, I should think." Her beady gaze moved to Lucy. "Assuming she can work?"

"Lucy's no trouble," Sarah said firmly. After her father had died she'd kept her sister from having to do much in their little rooms back in Goswell, but she could see that here they would both have to earn their keep. Any hopes of feeling like family crumbled to ash. Still, she knew how to work, and Lucy could learn. It could still be all right.

"Goodness knows your mother wasn't much use around the house," Edith said with a touch of asperity. "Are you skilled with a needle?"

"Yes, Aunt Edith."

"Victoria couldn't manage to darn so much as a stocking. And my parents spoiled her, I'm afraid. We all did."

Sarah did not know how to reply, so she said nothing. She'd known, even as a child, that her mother was not accustomed to hard work. When her father had been alive, they had just about managed to live a life of very shabby gentility, with a maid living in and a clergy's scholarship place for Sarah at the girls' school on the high road. When he'd died, Sarah had been big enough to take over the responsibilities that should have fallen to her mother. Even at that age she'd understood that her mother would not be able to manage the household tasks of a maid – washing and scrubbing, cooking and darning – even before Lucy's difficult birth. She simply did not have it in her.

"Well, then." Edith nodded once. "I suppose we'll all rub along. It has long been my custom to work in the morning and visit the poor and needy in the afternoon." Her gaze raked over their drab dresses. "When you are suitably attired, you may accompany me. In the meantime, you will stay here and keep out of trouble."

How, Sarah wondered, were they to be suitably attired? She didn't have so much as two pennies to rub together. She and Lucy were entirely dependent on this stranger's charity, a fact which made her bow her head and murmur meekly, "Yes, Aunt Edith."

The days soon fell into a familiar and dreary pattern of housework. They started in the early morning, all together in the kitchen, eating a simple breakfast of porridge and a cup of tea, and then saying their prayers. Afterwards Sarah and Lucy washed and stacked the dishes while Aunt Edith went upstairs to read her prayer book or Bible. Then, depending on the day, there was a different job to do, for each room of the house was thoroughly cleaned on a separate day. Monday was the parlour, Tuesday the dining room, Wednesday the kitchen and Thursday Aunt Edith's bedroom. Friday the spare bedroom, Saturday Sarah and Lucy's bedroom, and of course no work at all on the Sabbath.

Sarah was used to housework, but she'd never spent so much time cleaning rooms that were barely used. Mop, sweep, dust, polish, drag the carpets and beat them outside; black-lead the grates for fireplaces that often stayed cold and empty, for Aunt Edith was stingy with coal.

She liked cleaning the parlour best, for it was by far the most interesting room, with its horsehair sofa and dark velvet curtains, its stiff-backed chair and nest of mahogany tables, a Chinese-painted fire screen and a mantelpiece bedecked with rosy-cheeked Dresden shepherdesses and milkmaids. On the wall there was a pair of heavy-handed oil paintings of bleak pastoral scenes under lowering grey skies, and several embroidered samplers with admonitory Bible verses among the needlework roses and violets.

Standing in that room, Sarah wondered if her mother had sat in that high-backed chair, feet stretched out to the fire, and read her Bible, or simply sat and daydreamed. It was hard to imagine her light, laughing mother, whose free spirit, some of the more spiteful ladies of Goswell had whispered, bordered on frivolous or even fey. "Not far off the daughter," Sarah had heard one housewife mutter, and she knew the woman hadn't meant her.

After each day's room was cleaned, they had a light luncheon and then spent the afternoon in decorous pursuits –

on that first day, Aunt Edith gave Sarah a pile of stockings to darn and set Lucy to stitching a sampler. Sarah sat close to Lucy, guiding her chubby child's fingers with the needle; when her sister pricked her thumb, tears welled in Lucy's eyes and she drummed her feet against the chair, on the verge of one of her episodes.

Thankfully Aunt Edith wasn't in the room, and Sarah was able to calm her quickly, finishing the sampler's stitches herself before she turned back to the stockings. Lucy rocked back and forth, her arms wrapped around herself, while Sarah darned as quickly as she could and Edith saw to their supper in the kitchen.

Supper was a quiet affair, and afterwards they all sat in the parlour while Aunt Edith read the Bible for what felt like a very long time. Then it was up to bed with a candle and the cold sheets. Sarah did not dare close the window, as much as she was tempted to.

After a week Sarah realised this dull pattern was not going to change, and she told herself to be grateful. Life was far more comfortable than it had been in Goswell; the house was spacious and fairly warm, despite the open bedroom window, and dusting and polishing was not such hard work. She did not have to make shirts to earn a few pennies, and she did not have to worry about money at all, unless it was her complete lack of it, but there was nothing she could do about that.

Best of all she did not have to do the laundry, which a cheerful, red-faced woman came in and did once a week. Sarah watched her heat endless water in the copper in the scullery and then scrub the clothes with the harsh lye soap before plunging the dolly and then working the heavy mangle. It was hard, backbreaking work, and it took the entire day. All Sarah had to do was step around the clothes and sheets draped about the kitchen, and she breathed a sigh of relief. Admittedly, there hadn't been much laundry in their rooms back in

Goswell; they hadn't had many clothes. But Sarah had been the one to do it, and she'd disliked it intensely. She still had chilblains on her fingers from plunging her hands in cold water so often.

Several afternoons a week, Edith went off to visit the poor, usually carrying a bundle of paper-wrapped bottles of beef tea or jam. She did not invite Sarah or Lucy to accompany her, presumably because they were in mourning and did not have the proper clothes, although Sarah wondered if they ever would.

At least when Aunt Edith was gone they could relax a little; Lucy would lay her head in Sarah's lap and Sarah would stroke her hair, singing songs or telling silly stories that sometimes brought a faint smile to Lucy's face.

Yet she could not keep from wondering, as she slipped from between the cold, slightly damp sheets and dressed for another day of dusting and darning, if the rest of her life would be spent in such meaningless drudgery. Would she and Lucy go on the way they were for another twenty or thirty years, until their aunt met her Maker? The thought was unendurable, yet Sarah could not see another way. Aunt Edith had clearly been living out this dull pattern for a long time and seemed perfectly satisfied with it.

The one highlight of the week was Sunday, when there was no housework to be done and they walked to the town's parish church, a large, gracious building with soaring ceilings and large stained-glass windows. Just being in there, letting the words and music wash over her, made Sarah relax – although not too much, for she was conscious of her aunt watching her out of the corner of her eye, making sure she didn't so much as slouch.

After church they returned home for Sunday lunch, and then an afternoon of sitting quietly, with nothing to do but read the Bible or look at Fox's *Book of Martyrs*. Aunt Edith was a stern keeper of the Sabbath; even Sarah's father had not taken such extreme measures, often going for a stroll on Sunday afternoon between services.

Lucy had trouble sitting still for so long; Aunt Edith did not tolerate any fidgeting. Sarah took to playing a little game with her, drawing a pattern with her fingers on her skirt that Lucy then copied with a sly grin for Sarah, knowing that their aunt shouldn't see. No matter what Reverend Hesham had said, Sarah knew her sister wasn't a saddle-goose.

On Monday the pattern started all over again, even though the house had barely been dirtied. Sarah wondered how her aunt could see the use of any of it, but she knew better than to utter a word. Aunt Edith hadn't been hard with them, stern as she was, but Sarah had no idea if that might change. There was a reason, she reckoned, that her mother had never mentioned her family or seen them in twenty years.

They had been in Kendal for a fortnight when, one sunny morning, Aunt Edith said she and Lucy could go to the Friday fish market and buy a piece of fish for their dinner. "A nice bit of char would do," she said, counting out pennies carefully. "And while you're at the market, you can stop by the haberdasher's on Stricklandgate and buy some more black thread. Two spools." She eyed Sarah's cut-down dress meaningfully. "One of your sleeves is torn."

Sarah murmured an apology but inside her heart was singing. A morning out in town with Lucy, without dusting or scrubbing or slopping heavy pails of dirty water in the yard! She felt freer than she had in a long time, and her step was light as she and Lucy walked to the top of Finkle Street where the fish market was held. She'd been out in town a few times before with Aunt Edith, but then she'd kept her eyes on the ground, conscious of her aunt's waiting censure. Now she looked around with bold curiosity, interested in the many shops, the carts of wares for sale in the market square, the noise and bustle of a place far larger than any she'd ever known.

Lucy slipped her hand in Sarah's as she gave her a shy smile. Sarah knew her sister was just as glad as she was to be free from the stuffy confines of the tall house on Lowther Street. Sarah glanced up past the market buildings and the impressive town hall with its coat of arms and inscription in Latin – *pannus mihi panis* – which Aunt Edith had told them meant "wool is my bread". The woollen mills were still important to the town, Edith had said, although the medieval days of making Kendal green cloth were long over.

Above the buildings the fells loomed, grey-green and faintly menacing, snow-capped even in April. Lucy tugged on Sarah's hand and Sarah glanced away from the jagged horizon to see her sister pointing to the Methodist church on the corner of Stricklandgate. Sarah's step slowed as she took in the sight of rows of children filing into the church. The girls wore starched white pinafores, their hair neatly plaited. They looked no older than Lucy.

"It's a school," she said, and Lucy nodded, her eyes bright. Sarah wasn't sure if Lucy understood what a school was; Lucy had never gone to school in Goswell, and Sarah had stopped when she was ten, when Lucy was barely out of leading strings. Sarah had tried to teach Lucy her letters, but it was hard to know how much her sister took in when she was as silent as a standing pool.

"Lots of children," she remarked to Lucy, and her sister looked at her with so much hope in her eyes Sarah had to look away. It wasn't fair to lock Lucy away as if she was something to be ashamed of, but that's what ended up happening, for her own sake. Who knew if children would sneer or stare, or worse, if she went to play among them?

"We'll see," she said, promising nothing, but Lucy smiled and nodded again, trusting, as ever, in Sarah. It made a lump rise in her throat and guilt flush her cheeks. She wanted more for Lucy than dusting rooms and sitting quietly; sometimes she felt as if they were both constantly erasing their existence from the house in Lowther Street, with dust rags and beeswax. Still, it was more than most children had. At least Lucy wasn't working at the mills on the outskirts of town, threading needles or collecting spindles from dawn to dusk.

The fish market was bustling with carts and peddlers, their sleeves rolled up over meaty arms, their faces red as they hawked and haggled over their wares. Sarah had never seen the like in Goswell, and inwardly she quaked at the thought of returning to Lowther Street with anything but the best piece of fish the whole market had to offer.

Lucy held her hand tightly as Sarah went from pushcart to pushcart, inspecting the freshly caught char and cod and haddock, wondering what would please her aunt. When inspecting Sarah and Lucy's work, Aunt Edith had been grudging but fair, so surely she would be the same about a piece of fish? Still, it felt like some sort of test; if Sarah failed in this, perhaps Aunt Edith wouldn't let her come out to market again, and she wanted to, very much indeed.

She finally settled on a fillet of char, and tucking the paper-wrapped parcel on her arm, she turned to head back to the market and the haberdasher's for the black thread.

For a moment, with the sun breaking from behind a thick bank of grey cloud and the town stretching all around her in a maze of cobbled streets and limestone, she wished she didn't have to return to her aunt and the dreary prospect of an afternoon of embroidery. Still, perhaps they could dally a bit on the way back, look in a few shop windows. It was the closest thing to a treat that Sarah could offer her sister.

At the haberdasher's she waited while the shopkeeper served a man in the black frock court and trousers of deepest mourning who was buying several yards of black crêpe. She knew many people who could afford it did up their whole house in black for mourning, taking the example of the Queen, who had lost her dear husband seven years before. She wished she could have done the same, but it was all she'd been able to manage, to cut down her mother's one black dress, made when her husband had died, to her size.

Finished with his transaction, the man turned, and his gaze snapped to Sarah's, surprising her. He was an average-looking fellow of middling height and weight, his hair wispy and brown, his cheeks pallid, although perhaps he simply looked pale because he was wearing such endless black. He had kind eyes, she noticed, before she lowered her gaze, disconcerted by his stare, which was as probing as Lucy's could be. It was only then that she realised he was looking at Lucy, his gaze far too open and searching for any respectable man – or woman.

"May I help you, miss?" the shopkeeper asked, and Sarah pulled Lucy towards the counter, avoiding the man and his strange stare.

"Two spools of black thread, please," she said, and breathed a silent sigh of relief as she heard the shop door close behind her.

# CHAPTER 5

## ELLEN

"So how is it, being stepmum?" Jane asked as she poured everyone glasses of wine. They were all seated by the fireplace in Goswell's pub, together for a rare girls' night out.

"Fine, fine," Ellen said, and then reached for her wine so she didn't have to look anybody in the eye. If it had just been her and Jane she wouldn't have minded admitting that just two days into Annabelle's stay she was feeling strung out, resentful, and incredibly tired. But with Jane's friend Marin along, as well as a couple of the other school-gate mums, she didn't feel like going on a big whinge.

"Stepmum?" Abigail Watson, a mum of a Year Five that Ellen only knew vaguely, raised her well-plucked eyebrows. "What's that about, then?"

"Alex's daughter from his first marriage is living with us for a year," Ellen answered. She was trying to sound relaxed and lighthearted, no problem here, none at all, but she could tell she sounded stiff. "While she finishes her A-Levels."

Abigail clucked sympathetically. "I didn't know Alex had been married before."

"Yes. Well. Second time lucky for both of us, eh?" She tried for a smile. Why was it all so difficult? She knew there would be a settling-in period with Annabelle. Of course there would be. The whole year would be a settling-in period, most likely, but at least it had an end point. Was it terrible that she was already looking forward to Annabelle getting her exam results and trundling off on the train back to Manchester and her mother?

In the two days since she'd arrived, Annabelle had made no effort whatsoever to fit into their family life. That first night Ellen had, after Sophie was in bed, brought a plate of bolognaise up to Annabelle's room, even though she didn't normally let the children have food upstairs. She'd knocked on the door, hesitant and a little timid, and there had been no reply.

"Annabelle...?"

Still nothing. Ellen had hesitated, torn between respecting the girl's privacy and tiptoeing away – which was by far the easier option – and making some kind of friendly overture. In the end she'd done something of both, opening the door a crack and peeking in. "Sorry, I thought you might like some tea..."

She'd trailed off as Annabelle looked up from her laptop, coldly furious. "Can't you respect my privacy?" she demanded in icy tones.

Ellen blinked, startled by the blatant hostility, even though she'd been telling herself all along to expect it. "I thought you'd want some supper," she said with as much dignity as she could.

"That?" Annabelle eyed the plate of soupy bolognaise incredulously. "It looks minging." She turned back to her laptop, effectively dismissing Ellen, who now felt like hurling the plate of lentils right into Annabelle's sneering face. Heaven help her, but this was going to be hard.

She took a deep breath, battling with various replies, and then decided silence was best. Easier, anyway, even though she hated the thought of Annabelle trampling all over her and knowing it. She closed the door, went downstairs, and scraped all of the lentil bolognaise into the bin. She wouldn't be making that again. None of them even liked vegetarian bolognaise, except for Annabelle. Except apparently Annabelle didn't like it any more.

She found Alex camped out in the conservatory, his laptop balanced on his knees, his expression brooding as he stared at the screen. Ellen perched on the arm of the sofa, trying to sound light-hearted.

"Seems like everyone is having some serious screen time tonight."

"Huh?" Alex flicked his gaze upwards before returning it to the screen.

"Annabelle," Ellen clarified, still trying to sound unconcerned. "She's on her laptop. I went upstairs to give her some supper but she didn't want it."

"Huh." Her husband was sounding delightfully monosyllabic.

"Have you spoken to her at all tonight, Alex?" Ellen asked. Alex kept his gaze glued to the screen, and Ellen resisted the urge to slam the lid down and force him to look at her. Why was she the only one trying here? "Alex..."

With a sigh as if this conversation was tedious, he looked up. "I'm giving her some space. This is difficult for her, Ellen."

"And difficult for us."

"Shh." He glanced meaningfully at the open door to the kitchen, and Ellen rolled her eyes.

"She's on the top floor with the door firmly closed, Alex. She's not going to overhear."

"Just in case."

"Fine." So Annabelle could call her food minging but she couldn't admit that any part of this was a tiny bit tricky. *Stop being childish*, Ellen told herself. *Stop feeling so slighted. This is no more than what you expected.*

It didn't make it any easier, though.

She and Alex hadn't spoken about Annabelle any more that

evening, and the next morning Ellen had put her own work aside to take Annabelle to Copeland Academy to register for school, meet her teachers, and buy the uniform. None of it had gone particularly well.

Annabelle flounced into the kitchen at ten to nine, right when Ellen was hustling Sophie out the door. Sophie had turned to her with wide eyes and a heartbreakingly friendly smile.

"Hey, Annabelle!"

Annabelle's reply had been an eloquent eye-roll that had Sophie frowning uncertainly and Ellen gritting her teeth. Again.

"Help yourself to cereal or juice," she said pleasantly. "I'm going to walk Sophie to school and then I'll come back to drive you to Copeland Academy."

"Whatever," Annabelle answered in a bored voice and Ellen decided not to reply. Silence was golden, after all. She had a feeling there was going to be a lot of silence. Either that or screaming.

"Why is Annabelle so cross?" Sophie asked as they walked down the high street towards the school. It was another glorious day, the sun bathing everything in gold, the sea breeze balmy and fresh. Who *couldn't* love it here, Ellen thought as she gazed out at the sea twinkling behind the rows of whitewashed cottages. Who couldn't think this was the most beautiful place on earth?

All right, perhaps she was a tiny bit biased, because she'd grown up here, in a little bungalow at the top of Vale Road, where the vicar now lived. She'd roamed these streets as a child, played in the sea and splashed in the beck, collected shells and crabs and, as a teen, lain out on the beach, breaking out in goosebumps, in desperate search of the ever-elusive tan. She'd eaten ice cream cones while sitting on the promenade, legs swinging, heart light. She'd walked up to the primary school just like Sophie now, arm in arm with her best friend, Lila, who had moved down to Barrow with her builder husband ten years ago.

A lot of people had moved on since her childhood days, her parents included. They'd sold up when Ellen had been eighteen and about to go to university. Her mother was from Dorset and she'd never liked the cold and wet, not to mention Goswell's remoteness. Ellen had been planning to go to uni in Bristol, so it made sense for them to move down south.

Then the summer before she was to start, Ellen had fallen pregnant, scrapped her uni plans and married Jack, and longed for a little parental support.

*Like Annabelle needs.* She had to keep everything in perspective. A seventeen-year-old girl needed her, whether she acknowledged it or not. Ellen wouldn't act the way her parents had, silently disappointed, struggling with disapproval. She'd *embrace* Annabelle, if only the girl would let her.

"Mummy?" Sophie prompted. "Why is she?"

"Annabelle?" Ellen sighed. "It's difficult for her, Soph. She misses her own house. Her own mum."

"Why can't she live with her own mum, then?"

Ellen sighed again. This was not a conversation she particularly wanted to have on the three-minute walk to school. Years ago she and Alex had sat Sophie down and explained the basics: how Alyssa wasn't Alex's daughter but he loved her just the same, and how he had a daughter from another marriage named Annabelle.

Sophie had looked confused, and Ellen couldn't blame her. The dynamics of second marriages were confusing for anyone, not just a ten-year-old, especially when there were children involved.

She hadn't asked too many questions, though, which relieved both Ellen and Alex, and then last week Ellen had told her Annabelle was coming to stay and Sophie had been curious and excited. Asking loads of questions Ellen hadn't been able to answer. And asking more now.

"Where is her mum?" Sophie asked, her tone turning insistent, demanding a proper answer.

"She's moved to New York City, in America," Ellen said, and Sophie brightened.

"Where Merrie used to live!"

"Yes, that's right." Before moving to Goswell, Jane had been a diehard New Yorker. "So why didn't Annabelle go with her mum? Didn't she want to?"

"Probably, but she has exams," Ellen said as she started to chivvy her daughter up the school lane. "It's complicated, Sophie, but the point is Annabelle is with us now, and we need to make her welcome."

Sophie frowned. "I don't think she likes me."

"Oh, Sophie." Ellen gathered her daughter in a quick hug, inhaling the clean, childish scent of strawberry shampoo and bubblegum toothpaste as she gave Sophie's slight shoulders a squeeze. "You can't say that. Annabelle doesn't even know you yet."

"I know, but..." Sophie shrugged, and Ellen's spirit sagged. When Sophie had been born, Alyssa had been in raptures over her baby sister, treating her like her personal living doll. Ellen's biggest worry had been Alyssa loving Sophie too much. Not much had changed in the ten years since then; admittedly Alyssa had had the usual distractions of boys, exams, and impending uni, but she'd always had a soft spot for Sophie. The last time Ellen had spoken to her on the phone, Alyssa had suggested Sophie come down to York and stay with her for a weekend. Laughing, Ellen had suggested Alyssa wait a year or two. Why did Annabelle have to be so different? So hostile?

"Just give Annabelle some time," she told Sophie, managing to get in one last squeeze before her daughter scampered off to join the other Year Fives heading towards the Junior entrance.

Squaring her shoulders, Ellen turned back to home – and Annabelle. When she arrived in the kitchen, she discovered a spill of sugary cereal across the worktop, the milk and orange juice left out, and the fridge door open. Annabelle was nowhere in sight.

Taking a deep breath, Ellen tidied everything up and then headed upstairs in search of her stepdaughter. She found Annabelle in her bedroom, still in her pyjamas, lounging on her unmade bed, a bowl of cereal balanced on her stomach as she watched some lurid video on her laptop.

"Annabelle." The single word came out too reproving, and so Ellen tried again. "I thought we were going to visit Copeland Academy?" She raised her eyebrows, managed a smile. "See your new school, get your uniform?"

Annabelle didn't look up from the laptop. "Maybe later."

*Maybe later?* Was this girl for real? "Actually," Ellen said, still managing – just – to keep that jovial, easy tone, "I have to work later, so it would be better to go as soon as possible."

"Better for you," Annabelle answered, contempt audible in her voice, and Ellen's hands curled into fists before she deliberately straightened them out, made herself relax.

"Yes, better for me," she agreed. "And better for you. Your teachers are expecting you. I said we'd come right after nine—"

"Fi-i-ine," Annabelle drawled, managing to elongate the word to several sneering syllables. "After this episode." And she angled herself away from Ellen, towards the laptop, spilling cereal in the process. A dismissal, then.

OK. Fine. Ellen went back downstairs and made herself a coffee. It wasn't until she was pouring the milk that she realised her hands were shaking. She was literally shaking with rage. *Deep breath, Ellen*, she told herself. *Deep breath. You can handle this. She's seventeen.* Even if she was acting like she was six.

Forty-five minutes and two coffees later, Annabelle came downstairs dressed like a punk rocker in designer-distressed jeans – shredded so Ellen could see most of her skinny thighs – and a midriff-baring top. Ellen glanced at that strip of perfectly toned, tanned flesh and tried not to feel envious.

"You might want to wear something a bit more... professional," she suggested, and Annabelle subjected her to a dead-eyed stare. "OK, then," Ellen said, grabbing her car keys with so much force that they cut into her hand. "You can go in that for all I care."

Annabelle snorted, and in that sound Ellen felt as if her stepdaughter had scored a victory. *She wants me to lose my cool*, she realised, wondering how she could have been so slow on the uptake. Of course she did, so she could complain to Alex about what an awful stepmother Ellen was.

Well, she'd kill her with kindness, Ellen vowed. Even if she died trying.

Things didn't improve when they arrived at Copeland Academy. Annabelle acted bored and uninterested, embarrassing herself along with Ellen with her monosyllabic answers and sulky hair flicks. Ellen had to bite her tongue to keep from apologising to the kindly woman at reception who helped with the uniform. And she gritted her teeth when she wrote out a cheque for ninety pounds for a school blazer, tie, and games kit and Annabelle didn't so much as bat an eyelid.

"Do you want to meet your teachers?" she asked, and Annabelle shrugged. "We'll leave it for another day, then," Ellen decided. Maybe Annabelle would realise she was only hurting herself with this terrible attitude. Back in the car Annabelle slouched in the front seat, skinny arms folded tightly across her chest as she blew a strand of hair away from her eyes.

"You know, Annabelle," Ellen began carefully, unable to keep from offering some advice even though she had a strong gut feeling that her stepdaughter wouldn't appreciate a word of it. "You're only hurting yourself with this attitude."

Annabelle merely snorted and stared out the window, her

arms still ominously folded. Belatedly Ellen realised how sanctimonious she'd most likely sounded. "All I mean is, you want to
make a good impression," she tried again. "With your new
school and your teachers. This is your last year of school and if
you want to go to university—"

Another snort. That made three this morning, Ellen
thought, her hands clenched on the steering wheel as she
turned onto the beach road that led back to Goswell. The sun
was streaming over the sheep pasture, and the sea was a haze of
blue on their left. Annabelle wasn't looking at any of it.

"All I'm saying," Ellen persevered, determined to finish this
one-sided conversation, "is that you might regret burning your
bridges right at the beginning. You're going to be here for a
year—"

"You think I'm *staying*?" Annabelle's voice dripped scorn,
her face angled towards the window so Ellen could only see the
round sweep of her cheek, making her look younger.
Vulnerable.

"What do you mean?" she asked, after a pause.

"I'm not staying here," Annabelle clarified flatly, her face
still turned towards the window. "You must be mad to think I
would."

"But..." Ellen hesitated, at a loss as to how to navigate this
unexpected development. "Where would you go? I mean... you
want to finish your A-Levels, don't you?"

All the response she got was a bony-shouldered shrug.
They'd crested the hill that led down into Goswell, the village
nestled in its valley, a few wisps of cloud lazily scudding across
the sky above, when Annabelle spoke again.

"I'm going back to Manchester. I'm sorting it with a friend.
I'll live with her and go to my old school."

Ellen couldn't deny the relief that coursed through her at
this prospect. It made much more sense, and yet—

"Your mother didn't mention anything about this—"

"Only because she has this rubbish notion that I need to spend more time with my dad," Annabelle interjected, turning to Ellen with an over-the-top eye roll. "As if. I don't even know him."

Ellen was driving down the main street now, her eyes on the road as she pulled behind a battered Land Rover to let a Royal Mail van go by. "He wants to know you, Annabelle," she said quietly.

"Whatever." Annabelle had perfected the bored drawl. "I'll be out of here in a couple of days. And you can't say you won't be glad," she added viciously as Ellen pulled into the space in front of their house.

"I—" Ellen began, but Annabelle was already flinging open the car door and slouching towards the house, leaving her alone and floundering for words. *No*, she silently finished. *I can't say that at all.*

She didn't tell Alex about the conversation, which felt like the coward's way out, but if Annabelle really did have plans to return to Manchester, then she could jolly well tell her father herself. Ellen wasn't about to butt in and cause more acrimony.

In any case, she had other things to worry about because at half past eight that evening, just when she'd been hoping to get an hour's work in, Sophie came downstairs, trailing her teddy bear and tearful.

"Sweetheart..." Ellen pushed her laptop away and propped her elbows on the kitchen table. "What's wrong?"

"I forgot the bake sale is tomorrow," Sophie said, a sob catching in her throat. "And I told Miss Davies that you'd make meringues..."

"You did?" Vaguely Ellen recalled a conversation several weeks ago about bake sales and meringues.

"Sixty-four," Sophie clarified. "Can you do it, Mummy? The chocolate ones with whipped cream and strawberries?"

She'd brought mini Pavlovas to a bake sale a few years ago

and it had become her thing, something she was not entirely happy about. Why couldn't brownies-from-a-box be her thing? "I suppose," she said after a moment. Making sixty-four meringues would take hours, and then there was the faff of whipping the cream and chopping strawberries... if she even had any strawberries. Did she really want to run out to the supermarket at this time of night?

"Oh, thank you, Mummy," Sophie cried with obvious theatrics, but Ellen's heart softened all the same as her daughter threw her arms around her and pressed her cheek against hers.

After the day she'd had with Annabelle, she craved a little childish affection.

She didn't finish the meringues until after eleven, putting everything in plastic containers in the fridge before heading upstairs. Alex was already in bed, lights out, snoring softly, and Ellen tried not to mind. He'd spent the entire evening on his laptop in the conservatory, and Annabelle had not made an appearance for most of the day, except to come downstairs at four o'clock to make toast, leaving crumbs and butter and dirty dishes in her wake. She had refused supper yet again, and Alex had merely shrugged.

"She'll come down when she's ready."

Ellen told herself not to mind. She could see the point of giving Annabelle some space, although it felt a bit like giving someone enough rope to hang themselves. Eating nothing but toast and watching YouTube all day couldn't be good for anyone, especially a homesick, hormonal seventeen-year-old. But she knew better than to push, or perhaps she simply didn't have the energy to make the effort. Annabelle wasn't her daughter, after all. These were Alex's decisions to make.

The next morning Ellen was consumed with getting the meringues to school, and then she was cheerfully conscripted to help at the bake sale until noon, wrapping biscuits and fairy cakes in plastic and taking twenty pence pieces from children's grubby hands.

When she returned to the house, Annabelle was still closeted upstairs, the only sign she was still alive the mess in the kitchen that Ellen once again tidied before making herself a much-needed coffee and settling down to work.

The rest of the day passed much the same as the last, and now she was out in the pub with her friends, trying to relax over a glass of wine and not mind when Abigail Watson murmured, "It must be so difficult, having all that emotional baggage."

*Yes, Abigail, it bloody well is*, Ellen answered in her head. Abigail had married her husband, Geoff, when she was twenty-two. No ex-spouses lurking in the cupboard, no inconvenient stepchildren to deal with and worry about. Must be nice.

The conversation thankfully moved on, and a little while later Jane squeezed in next to Ellen on the settee. "You OK?" she asked quietly, and Ellen felt too weary to prevaricate.

"Annabelle is just about doing my head in at the moment but it's nothing surprising, really," she said as she took a large sip of wine. "It will pass."

"When does she start school?"

"Monday. And she's going to spend every moment until then in her bedroom, on her computer, scoffing cereal and crisps."

Jane smiled. "Sounds like a normal teenager, then."

"Perhaps." Alyssa hadn't been like that, had she? In the sixth form, her daughter had been driven, studying all the time, sometimes too stressed to eat, so Ellen had made her warming soups and plates of buttery toast, cajoling her to try something. She'd been worried about Alyssa in her last years of school, but she would gladly trade Annabelle's attitude for those concerns now.

"Why don't you all come over for supper one evening?" Jane suggested. "Natalie's in the same year as Annabelle. So is

Marin's sister Rebecca, as a matter of fact. The three of them might hit it off."

Inwardly, Ellen shuddered at the thought of unleashing Annabelle on her friend, but maybe her stepdaughter would be friendlier to strangers. And it would be nice not to feel so alone in this. *Because Alex isn't much help.*

Pushing the uncharitable thought away, Ellen smiled at Jane. "That would be lovely," she said. "How about next week?"

# CHAPTER 6

## SARAH

Kendal, 1868

A month after Sarah had arrived at Lowther Street she came downstairs one evening to use the privy before bed to find her Aunt Edith in the kitchen, a chair drawn up to the warmth of the range, tears streaking her face and a frame clutched in her hand.

Sarah stood in the doorway, frozen with shock at the sight of her aunt in such a state. She'd never seen so much as a gleam of sentiment in her aunt's eyes, much less actual tears. Her aunt had approached everything with the same brisk efficiency she'd exhibited on their first meeting. Sarah had become used to it, found she appreciated her aunt's plain speaking – mostly.

Now Edith looked up with a sniff, and then she let out a choked sob as she caught sight of Sarah standing in the doorway in her nightdress.

Sarah wobbled where she stood, unsure whether to flee back upstairs and try to pretend that this had never happened, or stay where she was and accept her aunt's undoubted anger at being caught in such a moment of weakness.

In the past month Sarah had become accustomed to the monotonous round of housework, the endless drudgery relieved only by the occasional trips to the market and church every Sunday. She'd considered asking her aunt about the Methodist school for Lucy, but in truth she wasn't sure her sister could manage school, and she didn't have the courage to hear her aunt's undoubtedly incredulous response.

"You must be all agape, to see me like this," Edith choked out as she wiped at her eyes.

It was enough of an encouragement for Sarah to venture cautiously into the room. "Aunt Edith... is there anything I can do to help?"

Edith shook her head, still wiping her eyes, and then she glanced down at the frame she held. It was double-sided, hinged in the middle, and coming closer Sarah saw it held two silhouettes cut from black paper, both of young girls, with round cheeks and snub noses, their hair falling down their backs in thick waves and curls.

"Victoria and me," Edith answered the question Sarah had not had the courage to voice. "When we were children. My mother cut them, from our shadows on the wall." Her voice broke again, and she averted her head.

"Were you..." Sarah licked her lips, her heart thudding as she worked up the courage to voice her next question. She had not dared yet to ask Aunt Edith about her mother. She had not dared to ask Aunt Edith anything. "Were you close?"

"Close?" Edith drew in a long, shuddering breath and then, seeming to compose herself, straightened in her chair. "Yes. Once, we were close." Edith stared at the silhouettes again. "When we were younger you could hardly tell us apart. There is – was – only a little over a year between us."

Shocked, Sarah said nothing. She'd assumed Edith was far older than her mother had been, judging by the lines on her face and the grey in her hair.

"I suppose you thought I was much older?" Edith surmised shrewdly, and sniffed again. "Nursing my parents stole my beauty, what little of it I had. But there's no use in vanity." Which could have been embroidered on one of the parlour's samplers.

"Mother was beautiful," Sarah offered. "Until the sickness."

"Yes, Victoria was lovely," Edith agreed. Her expression had become distant and unfocused. "She had no end of admirers before she ran off with that curate." She shook her head. "No sense at all, either." Sarah held her tongue although everything in her boiled up to defend her father. "We looked alike as children," Edith continued. "Mother used to dress us alike in the sweetest dresses, all white lace." She swiped tiredly at one tear-stained cheek. "But then I grew up tall and lanky, all awkward angles and elbows, while Victoria was so dainty, like a china doll, only prettier." She sighed, the sound one of sadness, and looked again at the silhouettes.

"Yes," Sarah agreed quietly. Her mother had been doll-like in her pale, blonde loveliness, but also in her bright, childlike view on life. What did money or food or coal matter, as long as they had each other? Her father had kept them fed and clothed and treated them like ladies, but Victoria hadn't cared about any of it. Sarah remembered her mother clasping her hands and spinning her around their shabby rented room, merrily saying they could dance to keep warm, and Sarah had yanked her hands away, furious, stating coldly that she'd rather have coal.

"What was it, in the end?" Edith asked. She turned to stare at Sarah, red-eyed and hollow-cheeked. "What killed her?"

Sarah hesitated. "She was never quite right after Lucy's birth," she said after a moment. "It was... difficult." It was indelicate to talk of such matters, but she knew no other way to say it. Edith pursed her lips, nodding.

"Is that why Lucy isn't right in the head, then?"

"She isn't—" Sarah began heatedly, but stopped, sensing this was not the time to talk about Lucy. "The birth took a long time," Sarah explained. She could still hear the echo of her mother's screams as she'd laboured, her father pacing downstairs and Sarah crouching in her room, her hands over her ears, terror crowding in her heart. "Mother took a long while to recover, and Lucy..." Lucy had been an alarmingly placid child, hardly ever crying, late to sit or crawl, and Victoria Telford had blithely accepted her good fortune in having an easy baby, until it became all too clear that Lucy wasn't like other children. But she wasn't *stupid*, not the way so many people assumed. Sarah was willing to acknowledge that her sister might be a bit slow about certain things, and that she became agitated in new or trying situations, and she'd long accepted it was her duty to shield Lucy from the harsher realities of the world and the many people who could be carelessly cruel. But Lucy, Sarah believed, had far more personality, more possibility, than anyone gave her credit for.

Of course, there wasn't much possibility for either of them in the house on Lowther Street.

"So Victoria was an invalid?" Edith surmised, a quaver in her voice. "Bedridden?"

"Only at the end." But since Lucy's birth Victoria had tired easily, and then her father had died, and there had been no going back to anything the way it had once been. They'd moved out of their little house near the church, into a set of rooms with damp and draught, having to hoard pennies and depend on charity.

"I knew it would kill her," Edith said in a low voice. Her head was bowed, her gaze on the glowing embers in the range's grate. "How could she even think it?" She let out a ragged laugh. "She told me she loved him, as if love can keep you warm or put food on the table. Victoria was as addlepated as your sister, in her own way." She shook her head, her mouth curling in contempt, and Sarah drew back, stung for both Lucy and her father's sakes.

"Mother did love him," she protested. "And he loved her. Father would have given the world to Mother if he could have. The whole world." Her voice shook and sudden, surprising tears trembled on her lids. She couldn't bear to hear her father maligned. He *had* tried. It hadn't been his fault that they'd had to eke out a gentleman's existence on a pittance, or that the vicar was stingy with both money and praise, or that Daniel Telford hadn't had the social connections to obtain a living of his own.

"But he couldn't," Edith finished flatly. "And never would. I warrant he didn't earn more than fifty or sixty pounds a year. Your mother was used to more, Sarah."

Sarah glanced around the spacious kitchen, silently acknowledging the luxury of the place. All of it, from the heavy furniture in the parlour to the modern range in the kitchen, was more than they'd had even when her father had been alive.

Aunt Edith might be stingy with coal, but she filled up Sarah and Lucy's plates and didn't seem to hold to the common belief that children should subsist on little more than bread and dripping and boiled puddings. All of it made her realise how little she knew of her mother's background.

"What did my grandfather do?" Sarah asked, still cautious in case her aunt grew cross with her curiosity.

"He started as a clerk with Gawith Hoggarth & Co." Sarah stared at her blankly and Edith clarified, a touch of impatience in her voice, "The tobacco manufacturer's. You must have seen their snuff works at the end of the street."

"Oh, yes..." She hadn't known what the big stone building at the end of the street was actually for.

"He became a senior clerk and then an accountant." Edith glanced around the kitchen with a weary, resigned air, her shoulders rounded and slumped, the framed silhouettes slipping from her hand. "Your mother's actions shamed him. He was never the same."

"There's no shame in marrying a man of the cloth," Sarah protested.

Edith's gaze narrowed. "There is if she was already betrothed to someone else."

"What..." Her breath came out in a rush. "What do you mean?"

"What do you think I mean? Victoria was engaged to a junior clerk at the tobacco company, a perfectly respectable man who earned a hundred and fifty pounds year. It was all arranged, the banns about to be read, and then she met Daniel Telford at a church picnic and that was that. She ran away with him just a week later, shocking everyone. None of us could hold our heads up for shame for years."

Sarah felt a prickly flush spread through her body. She didn't want to believe her mother had been so reckless, or that her father had countenanced it, and yet... her father had been desperately in love with his wife. And her mother hadn't had much sense, just like her Aunt Edith had said. That much Sarah had always known. But to break off an engagement... to run away... It was deeply shocking.

"You never knew," Aunt Edith said flatly. "But now you know why we didn't speak these twenty long years. She shamed all of us." Aunt Edith's voice trembled. "I was going to marry a young man, a lawyer. Samuel Vickers. He'd come to court me, of an evening. I was waiting for him to make an offer. We all were."

Sarah caught her breath, shocked further by this admission. A doomed love! She would not have thought it of practical Aunt Edith. "What happened?" she asked in a whisper.

"Your mother ran away and Mr Vickers didn't appreciate the scandal. I begged him to wait until things quieted down, but then my mother became ill, and my father after. I nursed them both until their deaths, and Samuel Vickers didn't wait. He married Rose Allerton and they live up on Finkle Street now, with their four boys." She rose from her chair, brisk once more, and Sarah saw something in her face that suggested she regretted this entire conversation. "What are you doing up at this hour?"

"I had to use the privy..."

"Well, then see to it, girl. Don't dawdle." Edith turned away with a swish of her skirts, and Sarah hurried outside. Although it was April and the trees were beginning to bud, the night air was cold and damp from the river. She picked her way across the puddle-filled yard to the privy in the back, half-wishing she'd used the chamber pot instead of venturing out alone in the night, but as she was the one who had to empty and clean the chamber pots, she knew she'd rather face the cold and dark.

She quickly finished her business and hurried back into the house, but the kitchen was dark save for the embers settling in the range's grate, and all was quiet. Aunt Edith must have gone to bed, and Sarah wondered if they would ever talk like this again. She looked for the framed silhouettes, but her aunt had taken them with her. Sarah wished she could have examined them more closely, as she had nothing to remind her of her mother save for a lank curl of hair Ruth Teddington had snipped off at her deathbed. Sarah didn't particularly like the faded strands but she'd accepted the keepsake in the spirit it had been given.

Now Sarah tiptoed up the stairs and then snuggled in bed next to Lucy, wishing she dared to close the window Aunt Edith insisted must be kept open, her mind still full of all her aunt had – and hadn't – said. Had her mother really run off in such a shocking way? Why had her father, a man of the cloth, allowed such a thing? And did Aunt Edith resent her and Lucy because of what had happened so long ago?

More worrying than the unanswered questions of the past

was the bleak picture her aunt had painted of Sarah's own future. Would she be like Edith, nursing a relative to death, losing her looks and any chance of love while she withered away darning stockings and polishing silver no one ever used? Shivering, Sarah drew closer to Lucy and closed her eyes.

She didn't want to end up like Aunt Edith, brisk and brusque and yet without any real hope or happiness. She didn't want to, but in truth she wasn't sure how she could avoid it.

# CHAPTER 7

## ELLEN

Ellen knew she shouldn't put all her hopes on the forthcoming supper with the Hattons, but after an interminable week with Annabelle, she couldn't help it. Annabelle had spent the weekend closeted in her bedroom, while Ellen got on with catching up on housework and taking Sophie to ballet and the beach, and Alex worked.

Sunday evening, the night before Annabelle was to start at Copeland Academy, Ellen broke and confronted Alex, who seemed to have spent more time than usual hiding behind his laptop.

"Don't you think you should talk to her?" she asked, as she spritzed the kitchen countertops in her before-bed ritual of attempting to keep the house tidy.

"I told you before, I'm giving her a little space to settle in."

"Yes, but it's been five days, Alex, and she's meant to be part of this family." Ellen blew out a breath as she scrubbed at a hardened stain. Was that ketchup or blood? "She shouldn't be spending every spare moment in her bedroom and only coming downstairs to help herself to food. This isn't a hotel."

Alex lifted his gaze from his laptop. "Things will be different when she starts school."

"How? If anything, they'll be even more tense and fraught. The year before uni is an important one." Ellen shook her head, new implications of Annabelle's year with them assailing her. "What about her UCAS applications? And her personal statement? Or going to university open days..." Alyssa's last year had been a whirlwind of stress and drama, making the applications, spending hours on her personal statement, visiting a university on what felt like every other weekend. And now she was going to have to do it again with Annabelle, who would probably sulk and eye-roll her way through everything? Or would Alex do it, and leave Ellen to soldier on alone at home? Neither option particularly appealed.

"That's not for ages," Alex dismissed. "It's been five days, Ellen. Give her a chance to get used to us."

"And when do you think that will happen? You think one day she'll magically decide she's settled and pop downstairs for dinner, help with the washing-up?" Alex didn't answer and Ellen realised that was exactly what he thought. Or hoped for, anyway. "*Alex*. Why won't you talk to her? She might like to hear from you. Be reassured that you're glad she's here."

He sighed, raking a hand through his hair as he gazed out at the garden, now cloaked in purple twilight. "I don't know what to say to her."

Ellen came to perch on the end of the sofa. "Maybe start with something simple, like, 'How are you doing?'"

"I'm not sure she'd even answer that. We haven't talked properly in ages, Ellen." Alex gave her an unsettlingly bleak look before he glanced away. "I think the last real conversation I had with her was about plastic pony toys, which gives you an idea of how long it's been."

"You still need to try," Ellen said, although she was disconcerted by Alex's honesty. She should have realised how badly

Alex and Annabelle's relationship had fallen apart, especially considering she'd known how little they saw each other, but it still felt like an unwelcome shock. She really had just pushed Annabelle out of her mind, content with the happy family she'd created for herself. "We both need to try," she said with as much conviction as she could. "Annabelle deserves more from us, and frankly I don't think I can cope with the way things are now for an entire year." She tried for a smile, a joke, or at least a semi-joke. "We'll all end up having nervous breakdowns."

"Fine." Alex pushed away his laptop but didn't move. "What should I say?" He sounded uncertain, like a little boy asking for help with a homework assignment.

"Like I said, start simple. Ask how she is or if she needs anything." Ellen thought about Annabelle's assertion that she wouldn't be here long and wondered if she should tell Alex about her plans to move back to Manchester. Or would it just make him feel more inadequate? Annabelle hadn't mentioned it again – not that Ellen had actually talked to her all weekend – but she was meant to start Copeland Academy in the morning. "Ask her if she's ready for school tomorrow," Ellen suggested. "Or if she's looking forward to it." Although the answer to that would undoubtedly be a vehement no. "Something."

"OK, OK." With a sheepish smile, Alex rose from the sofa. "I get it. I'll go up there. I'm sorry, it's just... I'm not very good at this."

"I know, but you can still try." The flip side of the strong, silent type, Ellen had long ago discovered, was that he some-times possessed the emotional intelligence of a hermit crab. But he tried. At least, he'd tried with Alyssa. Ellen remembered watching Alex and Alyssa play dolls together, Alex sitting cross-legged, endearingly serious, while Alyssa fed him his doll's lines which he parroted back in an earnest monotone. Ellen's heart had swelled with love for this man who so wanted to get it right. So much more than Jack had, with the endless arguments and the way he'd breezed in and out of their lives, promising ponies and trips to theme parks before disappearing again. Why was Alex having so much trouble with his own daughter?

Alex headed upstairs and Ellen abandoned the kitchen counters to sink onto the sofa, tired and wrung out at the end of the day. She wasn't even sure why Annabelle exhausted her so much. She'd barely seen the girl all weekend, and yet... Annabelle's presence felt like a malevolent force in the house, almost a threat. Or was she being melodramatic? Maybe Annabelle was just acting the way most teenagers did. It just felt worse, because she wasn't Ellen's.

Precisely three minutes later Alex slunk back downstairs and hid behind his laptop once more. "Well, that went well," he muttered. "Not."

"What happened?"

"I asked her if she was looking forward to school and she gave me the death stare of stupidity."

Ellen choked back a laugh. "The death stare—?"

"You know the one. It makes you feel like you just asked the most idiotic question in the history of the universe."

A smile tugged at her mouth. "Yes, I think I know that one." All too well. But it felt so much better to be sharing it with Alex than struggling on her own, feeling inadequate and uncertain. "Then what happened?"

"I asked if she needed anything and she said no. So then I said I hoped it went well tomorrow and I got the classic eye roll. End of conversation."

"Still, you tried," Ellen encouraged. "She's registered that, whether you realise it or not."

Alex nodded morosely. "Yeah, maybe." He seemed on the verge of saying something else, something important, and Ellen tensed, both hopeful and afraid, at what he might admit. Then the moment passed, Alex immersed himself in his work, and Ellen decided to head up to bed.

Monday morning, in what felt like a miracle, Annabelle appeared at 7:45 to take the bus to Egremont. She wore the straight black skirt, white blouse, striped tie, and black blazer that was Copeland Academy's sixth form uniform, but she managed, as Ellen had no doubt many teenaged girls did, to make it look borderline pornographic.

"You might want to tug your skirt down a little," she suggested as mildly as she could. Annabelle had rolled the waistband up so the skirt ended mid-thigh. Paired with sheer black tights and three-inch spike heels, her tie loosened and the top two buttons of her blouse undone, she looked more like a stripper than a student.

As she'd expected, her suggestion was met with disdainful silence and the cooked breakfast she'd made, ignored.

"Don't you want to eat..." Ellen began, but Annabelle was already swinging her designer leather bag over her shoulder and catwalk-strutting out of the house. "Have a good day," Ellen called, and the door slammed.

That afternoon Jane came over for coffee and a chance for Ellen to moan, although she didn't know if complaining about Annabelle was a good idea or not. It felt good to get it all off her chest, but then she felt guilty for complaining about her step-daughter, talking about her rudeness and awful attitude.

"What really is the problem?" Jane asked in a no-nonsense way that Ellen usually appreciated but now found she cringed under. "Annabelle's acting like a typical teenager. Mopey, ungrateful, hormonal... you've been there before, haven't you?"

"Alyssa was never this bad," Ellen muttered.

"Perhaps not, but she wasn't a saint, either. I remember you telling me the war stories about how she sneaked out of the house one weekend to go to the pub with some mates when you'd forbidden her. And she had a fake ID for a while, to go to the clubs in Whitehaven... you found it in the wash, remember?"

"I'd forgotten about that." When Alyssa had turned sixteen she'd started dating a bad boy type and gone through a wild phase that had been thankfully brief. Amazing how quickly some memories fogged over.

"So? Why is Annabelle getting up your nose so much? It's almost as if you're taking it personally."

"It's kind of hard not to, when she's so insulting," Ellen answered, and then leaned back in her chair with a groan. "I know I shouldn't. I know this shouldn't faze me, but..." She paused, unsure if she could explain all that she felt. Uncertain whether she actually wanted to. Because it wasn't just Annabelle's attitude that bothered her, she realised with a prickle of discomfort, but Annabelle herself. The very fact that Annabelle existed, that Alex had had another wife, another life, and so had she. All the mess their first marriages had created, that they were still now cleaning up. "It's just so fraught and complicated," she told Jane. "All the dynamics. I want Alex and Annabelle to get along, but I can't be the person to make that happen. Annabelle resents me and I understand why, but I don't know how to get over it. How to *fix* things, for all of us."

"Oh, Ellen." Jane squeezed her hand and Ellen blinked back the sting of unexpected tears. "The world is a broken place. There's nothing you can do about that but make do and mend as best as you can."

"I know that," Ellen answered through a too-tight throat. But what if her best wasn't good enough?

Annabelle's first day of school passed without comment; she returned home at 4:30 in the same slutty get-up that she'd left in, the skirt still hiked high, the blouse buttons undone. Ellen didn't comment on any of it, just asked how the day went.

"How do you think?" Annabelle snapped before stomping upstairs, leaving Ellen to wonder what she was supposed to infer from that. Nothing good, obviously.

Two more days passed in similar succession; Alex made

another well-meaning effort, going upstairs to ask Annabelle about her day, and giving Ellen a shrugging what-can-I-do apology when he returned to the kitchen five minutes later. Sophie tried, too, making Annabelle a card congratulating her on finishing her first day of school.

"Why don't you give it to her up in her room?" Ellen suggested, and Sophie shook her head.

"I don't think Annabelle wants me to go up there," she whispered. "Can I leave it down here?"

So they left it on the kitchen counter, and Ellen couldn't keep from pointing it out to Annabelle when she appeared the next morning for school.

"Sophie made you a card," she said brightly. "Congratulations on surviving your first day of school." She pointed to the colourful card leaning against the salt and pepper shakers, and Annabelle's gaze flicked over it before she reached for her bag. "Annabelle!" Ellen heard how sharp and accusing her voice sounded and inwardly she winced. "Aren't you going to read it?"

For once Annabelle looked her full in the face, and the contempt and anger she saw in her stepdaughter's hazel gaze chilled her. "No," she stated flatly, and then she walked out of the house.

Now, seven days after Annabelle's arrival, they were all heading down to the Hattons' for supper. Ellen held a lemon drizzle cake – another one of her specialties – and Alex carried a bottle of wine. Sophie skipped ahead of them, ridiculously excited to see her best friend for a midweek meal.

Annabelle hadn't wanted to go, until Ellen had blown up at Alex, telling him it would be rude for Annabelle to refuse, considering that Jane had made the invitation for her sake.

"Either she's part of this family or she's not," Ellen had fumed. "She needs to make some effort, Alex. She can't just run roughshod over all of us."

Ellen wasn't sure what Alex had said to her, but Annabelle had sulkily agreed, and to Ellen's surprise she'd appeared in the kitchen without prompting when it was time to go, and even more amazingly, she was wearing a nice and normal pair of skinny jeans paired with a pink cashmere jumper, the kind of outfit she'd worn on her arrival, expensive and classy. It left Ellen wondering if Annabelle had multiple personas and was just deciding which one to inhabit. Maybe she saved the slutty clothes and attitude just for them.

The tension was palpable as they walked down the high street and then across the sheep pasture to the old vicarage.

It was a beautiful evening, and Ellen made a comment about the weather that no one replied to. It hadn't always been like this, she thought with a mixture of self-pity and irritation. It felt as if Annabelle was bringing out the worst in all of them, so they all either snipped at each other or lapsed into morose silences.

Jane's husband, Andrew, opened the door as soon as they knocked, and the next few minutes were spent in a flurry of hellos and introductions.

"You must be Annabelle," Andrew said, stretching out a hand for Annabelle to shake. To Ellen's amazement, Annabelle shook Andrew's hand and murmured her thanks for having invited her. So she did possess basic good manners, after all.

The surprises continued all evening. Natalie introduced herself to Annabelle, who smiled and chatted politely back, asking Natalie what A-Levels she was doing. It turned out they were in the same history class and a lengthy discussion ensued about the course topics that had Ellen's jaw nearly hitting the floor.

Jane gave her a slightly smug, pleased look, as if to say, *See? This is all it took. Annabelle's a nice, normal girl, really.*

And maybe she was, but... it was like seeing a vicious dog turn suddenly, scarily docile as Ellen watched Annabelle chat to everyone, smiling and laughing, admitting she wasn't looking forward to the rain and wind she'd heard about, and how she couldn't wait to go hiking.

*Hiking,* Ellen repeated silently to herself. *Aren't you laying it on a bit thick?* Or was she being an utter cow for being so suspicious, so cynical?

"Seems like it's going well," Jane whispered to her when Ellen helped clear the table. She dumped a load of plates in the sink, managing a smile.

"Yes, amazingly well. I can't believe it." Literally. Why had Annabelle done a complete about-face? And why couldn't Ellen trust it? It would be nice for something to finally be simple. Easy, even. It would be amazing.

"Maybe she just needed a friend," Jane said quietly, and Ellen felt unreasonably stung. *I was trying to be her friend,* she almost said. *I've been trying bloody hard, but no one seems to notice.*

This wasn't about her. She needed to stop whingeing about it and simply be pleased that Annabelle was finally turning a corner. Maybe they all were. This was their new beginning, brought on by her dear friend, Jane.

"Yes," she told Jane as she brought out the lemon drizzle cake for dessert. "Maybe that's what she needed."

She'd almost convinced herself this was the case, that Annabelle had changed her tune, come out of her sulk, whatever, as they walked home in the twilit darkness, Sophie humming softly to herself, Annabelle walking behind, hands jammed into the pockets of her jeans.

"That was lovely, wasn't it?" Ellen said, and Alex loped an arm around her shoulders.

"It was. We should get out more." He shot her a quick, apologetic smile. "Sorry I've been so busy with work."

"It's all right," Ellen answered. Gazing at the hills and meadows now cloaked in violet, the sound of the incoming tide a gentle shooshing in the distance, she felt she could be magnanimous. Things were going to be better now, for all of them. She glanced back at Annabelle and smiled, inviting her to share in the good mood, in the beauty around them, waiting for her to smile back, willing it, even, but when Annabelle caught her eye she only gave her a cold, stony look, worse even than the death stare of stupidity.

Ellen faltered, the smile slipping from her face as she stumbled in her step. Alex caught her elbow.

"Watch it there," he teased. "Andrew was plying you with the wine, I know."

"Right," Ellen murmured, and turned back to him. Surely she'd been imagining that awful look of Annabelle's. For a second it had almost seemed as if... as if Annabelle *hated* her. Hated her, specifically, rather than having had to move or Cumbria or go to Copeland Academy or whatever. No, for that fraught moment it had felt as if there was only one thing, one person, Annabelle utterly despised. Her.

# CHAPTER 8

## SARAH

Kendal, 1868

Sarah didn't know what to expect from Aunt Edith after that strange conversation they'd had in the kitchen, amid the darkness and the tears, but in the weeks following she thought she detected a faint thawing in her aunt's brisk, unsentimental demeanour.

The housework continued apace, but at least the days were a bit warmer, the trees in bud and the distant fells enlivened with colour. Aunt Edith seemed a little softer, allowing Sarah and Lucy to go to market more often and even fetching a can of spillikins from a cupboard for Sarah to play with Lucy one rainy afternoon. These small changes made Sarah's life a little more pleasant, although she still wondered what the future could bring. Aunt Edith couldn't be much more than forty, and in front of her all Sarah could see was years of cleaning empty rooms and waiting for Sunday.

A few weeks after the conversation, Sarah worked up the courage to ask Aunt Edith if Lucy could attend school. Her aunt had stared at her, nonplussed.

"School? What on earth can you mean? The child doesn't speak, Sarah."

"I know, but she is only ten, and she likes being with other children."

Edith looked mystified. "How on earth do you know that? She doesn't say a word. She's a simpleton."

Sarah gritted her teeth, even though simpleton was a far kinder word than many others had used. "There are other ways of communicating," she said stiffly. "I can manage the house-work on my own, and the Methodist chapel has a school for children. I saw it."

"Yes, but..." Edith shook her head. "There can't be much point to it, surely."

"A little schooling could hardly go amiss," Sarah said, trying to keep her voice reasonable and pleasant. Her aunt would not want her to insist or argue, but oh, she wanted this for Lucy. Her sister surely deserved a little happiness, a bit of hope. "Please, Aunt Edith. It... it doesn't cost money, does it?"

"It's a charity school," Edith said, after a moment. "But in any case..." She sighed. "I suppose I have been remiss with both of you. You need new dresses, for a start."

The sudden turn in the conversation had Sarah gaping. "New dresses..." She had not had a new dress since she'd been a child; everything had been given to her second hand or cut down from her mother's. "Do you mean it?"

"I can hardly have a relation of mine in rags, can I?" Edith answered with asperity. "We have some standing in this community, you know, despite the scandal your mother caused. You and Lucy look like paupers' children, although I suppose that is what you were."

Sarah remained silent, not wanting to jeopardise the allure of new dresses with a pointless argument about her father.

"And school..." she reminded her aunt hesitantly. Edith frowned.

"I suppose she could go to Sunday school," she relented. "And see how she gets on."

It was better than nothing, and Sarah was honest enough to admit that she was a bit relieved her sister would not be attending school all week long. She could not imagine enduring the long, dull days with only her aunt for company, and she didn't want Lucy to be teased or bullied.

The next week Edith took them to a dressmaker's in a yard off the market square. It was a small, cramped place, filled with bolts of cloth and plenty of buttons and fripperies, and Lucy seemed to find it wondrous, gazing around in rapture.

They examined the colourful bolts while Edith selected both the fabric and cut for two dresses each; Sarah's would be black, while Lucy's were white muslin.

"It's not proper for a child to be in mourning," Edith said briskly.

The styles she chose were plain, without any ornament or bustle, and her mother's crinoline skirt would stay packed away for the time being.

"A crinoline!" Edith had exclaimed when Sarah had shown it to her. "What silly vanity. Victoria did always think too much of her looks."

Still, a new dress was a new dress, and the fabric felt fine even if it was dull black. Sarah was satisfied.

The dressmaker, Mrs Seaton, seemed happy for the custom, and as they left the shop Edith gave a little grimace.

"But for God's grace and Father's planning, I would be in a similar state," she told Sarah as they stepped out onto the street. "Many a gentlewoman has been reduced to plying her needle to make ends meet. Thank Providence my father left enough for me to be provided for."

Sarah murmured some suitable reply. She understood the seamstress's precarious position all too well, having sewn shirts for the few gentlemen who required them in Goswell. She was grateful that despite the large darning pile and endless samplers her aunt always managed to provide for her, she did not have to take in sewing for money. Yet, anyway. She still did not know how far her aunt's charity would extend, or for how long.

A man all in black caught Sarah's eye, and she stiffened. It was the same man she'd seen in the haberdasher's, who had looked at Lucy with such an unsettling earnestness.

"Aunt Edith." Sarah reached for her aunt's arm, staying her brisk stride. "Who is that man?"

Startled at being so handled, Aunt Edith stiffened. "I do not appreciate—" she began, and Sarah responded quickly, "It's only that I've seen him before, and he was looking at Lucy."

Edith's gaze narrowed as she glimpsed the man. He'd stopped on the other side of the street, his hat in his hand, one boot on the kerb, as he gazed at them.

"Mr Mills," Edith said after a tiny pause, her voice cool. "He lost his wife a few months before you came, as I recall. She was friends with your mother when they were girls. That must be why he's looking at Lucy. She's very like her, you know... Victoria."

"Yes." Sarah still didn't like the way Mr Mills looked at them. It was unsettling to be so stared at by a stranger.

"He was friends with your father as well," Aunt Edith continued, her tone reluctant. "Introduced them, if I'm not mistaken." Her cool gaze clashed with that of Mr Mills before she looked away. "We have nothing to thank him for, I warrant." She started walking down the street, away from Mr Mills, and Sarah had no choice but to follow. Still she craned her neck to glimpse the man once more. Friends with her father and her mother...! She wondered what he could tell her, if she ever worked up the courage for an introduction.

A few weeks later the thing was managed, when an older woman in green bombazine sailed up to Sarah at church. "I wonder that you have not met Mr Mills before," she said, smiling at Sarah. "He works at Gawith Hoggarth & Co. and knew your grandfather as well as your mother." Her eyes brightened with speculation as she added under her breath, "And your father, I shouldn't wonder."

"I knew them all," Mr Mills agreed as he stepped forward. He was clean-shaven, his teeth a bit crooked and his cheeks rather pale, but his eyes did seem kind, although his stare could be a bit intense. "I was good friends with your father, Miss Telford. We went to the grammar school together."

"My father wasn't from Kendal, though," Sarah said. Her voice sounded thin and scratchy. She could barely believe they were talking about her father, that she'd actually met someone who had known him as a boy.

"No, he wasn't. He was from Preston, as I recall, but he moved up here to live with his aunt when his parents died." He smiled, and that was kind too. "He went on to theological college in Durham, and then took his place at Goswell, as you know. He was visiting here on his way to his curacy when he met your mother."

"I never knew. They never said anything." Her voice was low and she found she was not bold enough to meet his gaze.

"No." Mr Mills paused, and when he spoke again his voice was as low as Sarah's. "I know it set tongues to wagging, but I always considered your father an honourable man. He must have loved your mother very much."

"He did," Sarah answered, her voice throbbing with sincerity. "I know he did."

"Aren't you as pretty as your mother," Mr Mills said to Lucy, and her sister moved closer to her, slipping her hand into hers.

"Lucy doesn't speak," Sarah explained when Mr Mills' smile faltered. "But she's clever," she added, a bit defiantly.

"I'm sure she is," he replied, and then stepped aside for a young woman with curling blonde hair and a face like a milk pudding to step forwards. She was dressed in pink satin, with three tiers of deeper pink flounces on the hem. "This is my daughter, Clara," he said, and Sarah heard the unmistakable note of pride in his voice. "She's my light as well as my joy, since her mother died six months ago."

"Pleased to meet you," Sarah murmured, and Clara held out one limp hand.

Spoiled, Sarah surmised, as she shook the girl's hand. She couldn't have been more than fourteen or fifteen but she was dressed like a lady, and a far too fashionable one at that.

Just then, Sarah saw her aunt scowling from the other side of the church and her insides jumped in alarm. "My aunt is calling me," she said hurriedly. "I'm pleased to make your acquaintance, Mr Mills, Miss Mills." With a hasty nod that bordered on rudeness she hurried away, pulling Lucy along behind her.

"Why were you talking to Mr Mills?" Aunt Edith demanded as she bustled from the church.

"A lady introduced us—"

"Prudence Barton, no doubt, always looking for a good bit of gossip, even on the Sabbath." Aunt Edith shook her head, disgusted. "We've nothing to say to that man, Sarah."

"He seemed kind," Sarah dared to venture quietly.

"He encouraged your parents' match! That alone should deem him unsuitable. And he spoils that girl of his, turning her into quite the drapery miss. I wonder at the dowry he thinks he'll settle on her. He's only a junior clerk. His wife was a frivolous miss as well, and quite sickly. He spent all his money on medicine powders and brown bottles of false hope." With a huffy sweep of her skirts as she stepped out into the street, Aunt Edith glanced back to give Sarah and Lucy a quelling look. "I don't want you talking to him again."

"No, Aunt Edith—" The words were torn from her throat as the next few moments seemed to slow down and speed up at once – Sarah heard the clatter of hooves on the cobblestones, the snap of a whip and a groom's urgent shouting, and then the awful screech of iron wheels sliding across the cobbles. She stared in shocked horror as her aunt's body flew up in the air and then landed with a sickening thud in the middle of the street, and was still.

# CHAPTER 9

## ELLEN

A week after the meal with the Hattons, Ellen came upstairs to call Annabelle for supper, pausing at the closed door, one hand raised to knock, when she heard the sulky voice within.

"I feel like I've fallen off the edge of the earth here. I mean, *honestly*. There's no Starbucks, like, in the entire county." Ellen almost smiled at that, because Jane had had a similar complaint when she'd first moved to Goswell. "It's so boring, and I'm probably going to fail my exams because the school is that bad." Completely unfair, Ellen thought, bristling. Copeland Academy got very good results.

She knew she shouldn't eavesdrop on Annabelle's conversation, and yet she felt rooted to the floor. After two weeks of sulky silence and outright hostility, she was finally getting some insight into her stepdaughter's mind. And Ellen was afraid if she tiptoed away now the stair would creak and Annabelle would know she'd been listening.

"I don't see why I can't just stay in Manchester," Annabelle huffed. "I'll be eighteen in October. I could rent a flat..." Her voice trailed away and Ellen strained to hear the reply coming, no doubt, from Annabelle's ever-open laptop. It must be Sandra she was talking to, she realised with a ripple of unease. Sandra, the other woman Ellen had never let herself think about. Was she sympathising with her daughter for having to slum it in Cumbria?

Apparently not, for Annabelle growled something unintelligible before snapping, "I don't *want* to get to know him. And I don't want to live in the middle of *nowhere*." Another growling sound and then Annabelle slammed her laptop shut. Ellen jumped back from the door, half-expecting Annabelle to wrench it open and start yelling at her. But then she heard the most surprising sound: a sob.

At least she thought it was a sob. Small, mewling, and utterly heartbreaking. Ellen almost opened the door to go in to comfort Annabelle, but then she realised how well that would go down.

The sound subsided almost as quickly as it had begun, and after a few large sniffs, Annabelle put on some music, something loud and obnoxious that had been thumping through the floorboards for the last two weeks. Last night Ellen had heard Sophie singing some awful pop lyrics under her breath and had stopped in her tracks. She'd asked Sophie where she'd learned that song, and her daughter had gazed back at her, wide-eyed, and shrugged. "Annabelle," she'd said simply. Ellen wondered if it was too much to ask for her stepdaughter to wear headphones.

Now she counted to twenty just to be on the safe side and then, taking a deep breath, knocked on the door. No reply, so she knocked harder. Finally, with a long, world-weary sigh, Annabelle bid her come in.

"Dinner's ready," Ellen said in that over-bright tone with a hint of steel that she seemed to instinctively reserve just for Annabelle. "I thought you might come down and join us tonight." Even though she never had before.

Cue the death stare. "I'm not hungry."

"Even so, Annabelle, it would be nice if you joined us."

Ellen felt as if she were tiptoeing, or perhaps stomping, through a minefield. It was only a matter of time before her words blew up in her face. "We're meant to be a family, aren't we?"

Why had she made that a question? Annabelle stared at her in scornful disbelief. "Are you serious? We're not a *family*. I don't even know you."

"You could get to know me," Ellen continued steadily. Her heart was thumping, her hands slick. This felt harder than asking somebody out on a date, which she hadn't done since she was a teenager herself. "I could get to know you. But we can't, if you're determined to avoid or ignore us."

"So it's all my fault, is it?"

"I didn't mean that—"

"Get real. You don't even want me here."

*Why would I*, Ellen was tempted to snap, *when you act like this?* "I know this move hasn't been easy for you," she said. "I can appreciate that."

"*OK* then," Annabelle snapped. "Sorted."

"What do you want from me, Annabelle?" Ellen asked. Her voice had risen, and she didn't miss Annabelle's smirk. "What do you want me to do? To say?"

"Absolutely nothing," Annabelle returned, triumph audible in her voice. Ellen stared at her, fuming, feeling set up.

"Fine," she said, knowing she was falling right into Annabelle's obvious trap and yet unable to keep herself from it. "Because that's what you're going to get."

She managed not to stomp down the stairs but she had to take a trembling breath, feeling near tears, before going into the kitchen. Sophie and Alex were already at the table; Sophie was dipping her fingers in her milk and sucking them and Alex was checking his phone.

"Sophie, don't be disgusting," Ellen snapped, and her daughter looked up, all injured innocence.

"Mummy..."

"You know not to put your fingers in your milk." For good measure Ellen pushed Sophie's hands away from her glass. "If you're going to do that you won't get any milk with your supper."

Ellen saw the first telltale sheen of tears in her daughter's eyes and she bit her lip. She was taking her frustrations out on Sophie, which was the last thing she wanted, and yet... Something had to give. Alex hadn't even asked where Annabelle was.

"This can't go on," she told him flatly later that night, when they were getting ready for bed.

Alex looked up from loosening his tie, eyebrows raised. "What can't go on?"

"Can you really not know what I'm talking about?" Ellen demanded. Alex blinked, clearly taken aback by her sudden fury.

"What's got into you tonight?"

"What's got into me?" Ellen shut the bedroom door with a firm click. "Your daughter, that's what." As soon as she said the words she realised they weren't the ones she wanted. They were too hostile, drawing lines, picking sides. *Your daughter*. Why had she said that? The answer, Ellen knew, was because she'd meant it.

Alex's frosty silence had her cringing even as she held her ground. "I'm serious, Alex. We need to talk."

"And you certainly seem in the mood for a reasonable discussion," he returned, yanking his tie from his collar and flinging it in the general direction of his cupboard.

"You never seem in the mood for any discussion at all. It's been two weeks and you're still perfectly happy for Annabelle to hibernate in her room, helping herself to toast and cereal, and treating me like her servant—"

"Isn't that what every teenager does?"

"It's different." She was tired of the teenager argument. "This is different, because Annabelle is not *my* teenager."

The irritation she'd seen sparking in his eyes vanished, replaced by an awful, cold flatness. "So that's how it works?"

"It's not working at all," Ellen cried. "Can't you see that? Annabelle isn't *settling*. She's trying her best to get out of here and she's been incredibly hostile towards me—"

"What are you talking about?"

"I overheard her talking to her mother about renting a flat in Manchester. And before that she was trying to fix things with a friend, but I'm guessing that didn't work out."

"You're eavesdropping on her conversations?"

Ellen stared at him in disbelief. "After everything I've said, *that's* how you respond?"

"How am I supposed to respond?" he replied, his tone turning heated. "If anyone is sounding hostile, Ellen, it's you. You can't cut Annabelle some slack because she's not your biological daughter? Seriously?" He turned away to unbutton his shirt and Ellen sank onto the edge of the bed, reeling from his curt words. Were they actually having an argument? Another benefit of the strong, silent type was you didn't fight, not like she had with Jack, when it seemed like every single night they were at it with raised voices, tears and accusations, followed by his exasperation and indifference.

"I'm not trying to be hostile," she whispered. She felt as if she'd been flayed, and so very, very tired.

"Well, maybe you need to listen to yourself."

"And maybe you need to listen to yourself," Ellen retorted, rousing herself a little. "I'm sorry, but you're sounding rather sanctimonious, Alex. At least I'm trying."

"Trying to do what? Make Annabelle feel unwelcome?"

Tears pricked Ellen's eyes and she blinked them away furiously. "You know that's unfair. I gave up my office. I decorated the room myself. I took her to school, I've stocked up on snacks, I've tried to be patient—"

"And all the while racking up an impressive list of what

you've done." He shook his head. "Maybe she sees that, Ellen. Maybe she realises that your heart isn't really in it."

"So it's my fault I can't love a teenaged girl I barely know who is making my life a misery?" Ellen cried. "I'm sorry I'm not a saint, but—"

"You could love her for my sake," Alex burst out. He yanked on his pyjama bottoms, his whole body taut with tension. "Isn't that the point?"

Ellen stared at him, feeling more wretched than she could ever remember. "Alex..."

"At least I thought that was the point," he continued, pulling back the duvet and getting into bed. "I've never considered Alyssa only *your* daughter."

*You just did*, Ellen almost said, but she felt too heartsick to snipe. She and Alex had never argued like this before, but far worse than the fact of a fight was the reality of what they'd both said. *Your daughter*. So much for the cosy little family Ellen had thought she'd been nurturing, cobbled together but working and strong.

Silently she undressed and slid into bed; Alex had turned onto his side, his back like a brick wall facing her. She lay on her back, staring up at the ceiling, feeling as if sleep was a million miles away... and so was her husband. No words could bridge this arctic silence, and after about ten minutes she heard Alex's breathing even out and she knew he'd fallen asleep.

The tension was still there the next morning as they got ready for the day, moving around each other like polite strangers. Alex left the house before either Sophie or Annabelle had got up, and without speaking to Ellen. Great start to the day, then.

Downstairs Ellen made coffee while Sophie ate her Weet-abix, a book about ponies propped against the back of the box. Annabelle clattered down the stairs in her too-high heels at ten to eight, and Ellen forced herself to stare her in the face, feeling the full force of her contempt.

"Annabelle. I'm sorry for the sharp words we... I... said yesterday. I'd like to start again, if we can." Sophie looked up from her book, wide-eyed. Annabelle hitched her bag higher up on her shoulder and said nothing. Ellen's smile flickered like a dodgy light bulb. "Please."

"You know," she said after a moment, and her voice sounded high and thin, without its usual sneer, "you should have invested in some soundproofing."

Ellen felt herself go cold. "What do you mean?"

"My room is right above yours," Annabelle said, and now there was the sneer. "I heard every word you said last night."

Two hours later Ellen was in Jane's kitchen, her head in her hands as Jane plied her with strong coffee and an almond croissant.

"I'm the worst stepmother alive," she said with a groan. "The worst mother. Even Sophie got it from me last night. And Alex..." Ellen stopped, her throat going tight. She didn't want to admit how awful the argument between her and Alex had been. How *frightening*, because in that moment she'd felt as if the solid ground beneath her feet had shifted, the bedrock of her marriage crisscrossed with cracks she hadn't even seen until last night when they'd both spoken those awful words. *Your daughter*. And Annabelle had heard them.

"Well, I don't know what happened last night," Jane said as she sat across from Ellen and popped a flaked almond from her own croissant into her mouth, "but I do know you're neither of those things, Ellen. You're a lovely mum and by default a lovely stepmum."

"By default?" Ellen echoed hollowly. "How does that work?"

"You're a good person. You can't be the wicked stepmother to Annabelle's Cinderella, no matter how hard she tries to put you into that role. And I suspect that *is* what she's doing, no matter how sweet she acted when she came round here."

Ellen lifted her head. "So you think it was an act, when we came for dinner?"

Jane shrugged. "I don't know. But something seems to be going on, so why don't you tell me what it is?"

"I'm not sure I can." Ellen took a sip of coffee and gazed out the long sash window, weak sunlight streaming through from between grey shreds of cloud. The sunny weather had finally broken, just in time for half-term. "It just feels as if everything has gone wrong from the moment Annabelle came back into our lives. Just like last time, really."

"Last time?"

"Have I not told you? I suppose I put it out of my mind." Ellen pretended to shudder, although in reality she didn't know how much was pretence. "Annabelle stayed with us the summer before Sophie was born. It was awful. And that was the last time I saw her. Alex visited her in Manchester after that. Dismal failure on all fronts, really." Glumly she picked at her croissant, her appetite non-existent. How had she managed to mess everything up so spectacularly? Because after talking with Alex last night, she felt as if this was all her fault. Or at least, everyone else thought it was.

"From where I'm sitting it all looks pretty normal," Jane said. "Pretty dire to you, I know, but nothing out of the ordinary. Nothing you can't make up for." She raised her eyebrows. "Unless something huge happened last night? Like you tossed Annabelle out on her ear?"

"No, of course not." Ellen tried for a laugh but didn't quite manage it. "I just asked Alex to make more of an effort. He's been almost avoiding Annabelle since she arrived. I understand that it's awkward, and he probably feels guilty for their lack of relationship, but it's been putting the burden on me." She felt guilty for admitting that much to Jane. Alex would hate it if he knew what she'd said.

"And what did he say?" Jane asked.

"He put it right back on me. Said I wasn't being genuine with Annabelle, or something like that, and the truth is…" Her throat went tight again and she took a sip of coffee to ease it. "The truth is he's right. I don't feel genuine. I don't like her, which makes me an awful person because I know I should feel sorry for her. She's young and miserable and homesick, and her mother has basically shunted her onto us like some unwanted parcel. But all I want is for her to go away." She said the last on a gasp, horrified by her honesty. "That makes me incredibly self-ish, I know."

"It makes you normal, Ellen," Jane said, reaching over to squeeze her hand. "Stop holding yourself up to this impossible gold standard. Annabelle hasn't given much reason for you to like her, has she?"

"Not yet…"

"Why don't you do something together?"

Ellen blinked, utterly nonplussed by the suggestion. "What are you suggesting?"

"A girly day at the spa? A trip to the cinema, or shopping in Carlisle?"

"I think Annabelle would turn her nose up at the shopping delights of Carlisle," Ellen replied dryly. "And I think she'd see it all as bribery, anyway. She isn't impressed by any effort I make, and I'm not just having a whinge when I say that."

"I know, but…" Jane frowned. "What about a project together? Painting her room, or—"

"I've already done that, before she came."

"Découpage—"

"Seriously, Jane?" Ellen rolled her eyes, feeling strangely like her stepdaughter.

"All right, all right." Jane held up a hand, laughing. "I'm reaching, I know. But can't you think of something?"

Ellen was about to shake her head when a sudden image drifted through her mind of a folded scrap of paper, brown and wrinkled with age. She'd completely forgotten about the death certificate that had been found under the floorboards. Would Annabelle be interested in it? She was doing history A-Level, after all.

"Well?" Jane asking, leaning forward, intrigued by Ellen's silence.

"I don't know," Ellen said slowly. She knew if she told Jane about what she'd found, she'd get excited. Too excited, because she'd found that old shopping list in her house a couple of years ago and it seemed to have given meaning to her whole life. Ellen had no illusions about the death certificate. If anything it would do the opposite; it was a *death* certificate, after all.

And yet she realised she was a little curious about the thing. And maybe Annabelle would be too.

*Who are you kidding,* her inner cynic mocked, but for once Ellen silenced it. With her awful argument with Alex still ringing in her ears, she was willing to try just about anything.

# CHAPTER 10

## SARAH

Kendal, 1868

Sarah sat next to her aunt's bedside as the shadows lengthened and the town hall clock chimed the hour. Ten o'clock at night. Her aunt hadn't stirred all day.

It had been nine days since she'd been hit by the carriage on Kirkland, nine endless, awful days. Sarah thought those first few suspended moments would stay emblazoned in her brain forever. Her aunt's pale, startled face, the sickening thud as her skull met the cobblestones, and then the terrible silence afterwards that seemed to echo through the whole town, through Sarah herself, a whistling wind that went right through her.

Then, after those few suspended seconds, everything had happened in a horrid rush; the driver of the carriage had stumbled forward, calling for a doctor; people spilling from church had hurried over, and someone had taken Sarah by the arm. She'd looked wildly around for Lucy, and seen her sister's face, as pale and shocked as Aunt Edith's, her mouth opened in a soundless scream.

*"Lucy,"* she'd choked out, and her sister had hurled herself

at her, wrapping her arms around her middle, her whole body shaking.

Somehow they'd got back home; Sarah wasn't sure how. Someone from church, the lady in green bombazine who had introduced her to Mr Mills, Sarah realised later, shepherded them into the stuffy little parlour and plied Sarah with precious sherry kept in a dusty bottle on the top shelf of the larder.

Two men, one of them the shaken driver, brought Aunt Edith into the house and upstairs to bed.

"Don't look, love," the woman – Prudence Barton, her name was, Sarah remembered – said, but Sarah wrenched away and hurried upstairs, coming to a shocked halt in the doorway of Edith's bedroom.

She'd only been in there to dust and polish, moving around the double bed and heavy furniture with careful precision. But now the bed's cover of embroidered Broderie Anglaise was pulled back and Edith lay there still in her Sunday best, her face ashen, blood on her temple, her eyes closed, her body still.

"Is she..." Sarah's breath hitched and for a few seconds the room spun. "Is she dead?"

One of the men hunched forward to take her pulse. He exchanged a quick look with the other man, a look that lasted mere seconds but seemed to speak volumes. "She's breathing, lass," he said, and then muttered under his breath, "Just."

The room reeled again and Sarah clutched at the doorway. "Has someone sent for the doctor?"

The other man, the one who wasn't the driver, gave her a look so full of pity Sarah winced. "Aye, someone has. But it might not do much good."

"Aunt Edith." Sarah took a few steps closer to the figure lying so still and pale on the bed. Her aunt's face was nearly the colour of the coverlet, and her chest barely rose and fell. "Aunt Edith, can you hear me?" There was no reply.

The doctor came and went, a corpulent man in a dusty

black frock coat who shook his head and clucked his tongue. Sarah disliked him intensely.

"It's impossible to say," he intoned, speaking as if in front of a large audience. "Quite impossible with these types of head injuries. She might wake in the morning, or she might expire in the night. She might remain like this for days or months or even years. And if she does wake, she might be like a child or even a vegetable. Completely insensible, perhaps."

"Thank you," Sarah answered stiffly, "but is there nothing we can do?"

"Nothing at all but keep her in relative comfort," the man answered. "I'll come back in the morning."

"For his bill, I shouldn't wonder," Prudence muttered, and Sarah blanched. *Bills.* She had no idea how much money her aunt kept in the house, or if she could get more from the bank. And if her aunt actually *died...* what would become of them? Sarah couldn't even think of it.

The days passed and her aunt didn't speak or even open her eyes. Sometimes Sarah had to make sure she was breathing. She stayed by her bed as much as she could, but Lucy was anxious and fretful, and meanwhile it seemed everyone in Kendal was coming for his bill.

The doctor alone had cost four shillings, which seemed excessive considering how little he'd done. Within days of her aunt's accident, messenger boys were coming to the door with bills from the butcher, the baker, the grocer, and the tea dealer's. Sarah had long exhausted the few coins her aunt had kept in the house, and with mounting desperation she applied to the Kendal Bank where she knew her aunt had business.

The clerk who listened to her, however, was shaking his head before she'd finished. "I'm very sorry, Miss Telford, but I cannot release your aunt's funds to you without her consent." Pity flickered in his eyes but he remained firm. "You will have to apply elsewhere for financial help or, if the Lord wills your aunt to pass from this world, when her will is read. I assume she had a will?"

"I... I don't know."

Her mind whirling, Lucy's hand clutched in hers, Sarah headed back to the house on Lowther Street where Prudence Barton had been sitting with her aunt.

"No change," she said as she rose from the chair by Edith's bed. "God rest her."

Sarah murmured something suitable in reply, but inside she was wondering what would happen if God *didn't* rest her aunt. She couldn't get any money, and the bills were mounting as the news of her aunt's accident travelled around the town. Shopkeepers were anxious to be paid, and rightly so, but Sarah didn't have any money and no clear way to get any.

"I suppose I could take in some sewing," she murmured to herself as she made supper for her and Lucy. Her aunt's debility had made her realise how much Edith had done for her and Lucy – making their meals, seeing to their clothes. She was ashamed for how easily she'd accepted such charity – and wanted for more. She would gladly take the dull drudgery of life on Lowther Street to the unknown that loomed so terrifyingly in front of them. What on earth were they going to do?

In the end she did not have to wait very long to find out. A fortnight after her aunt's accident, Edith opened her eyes. Sarah was sitting next to her, having half-fallen into a doze, while Lucy played with a rag doll Sarah had fashioned from scraps long ago. Weak, watery sunlight filtered through the drapes, touching the grey in Edith's hair.

She tried to speak, her mouth working silently while her eyes stared blankly ahead, and Sarah lurched forward to grasp her hand.

"Aunt Edith... Aunt Edith, it's me, Sarah. Can you hear? Are you well—" Sarah choked on a sob, clinging to her aunt's hand, willing her to be well even as she knew she would not be.

She recognised the agonised look in her aunt's eyes, the desperate way her claw-like hand clutched Sarah's before relaxing so terribly, so finally.

Her aunt made an awful sound, something between a groan and a sob, her eyes bulging and spit dribbling from the corner of her mouth as she struggled to say something Sarah couldn't understand.

"Aunt Edith," Sarah said again, helplessly, tears in her voice and eyes. "Tell me..."

But her aunt's eyes closed again and her head fell back against the pillows. A shuddering breath went through her, and then all was still.

"Aunt Edith," Sarah whispered, but she already knew it was too late. In just seconds the tiny breath of life that had kept faint colour in her aunt's cheeks and her chest rising and falling so slightly had been extinguished. Already Edith's cheeks had become hollowed, her skin taking on a waxy, yellow tinge. In seconds her aunt no longer looked alive; she was like a wax effigy, so still and silent and somehow empty. Lucy looked up from her doll, wide-eyed, and Sarah let go of her aunt's hand.

She'd seen death before, too many times. She knew exactly how it looked. How it felt, the hollowness inside, the incredulous despair that felt too big an emotion to absorb, so instead she simply felt flat.

"Lucy," she said, keeping her voice soft and steady, "go outside the room." Lucy shook her head, the movement frantic, her mouth opening and closing soundlessly much like Edith's just had. "Lucy." Sarah took a deep breath. "Go to the pump and fill a can with water. I'll heat it on the stove, for washing." It was something for her sister to do, and she would need to wash her aunt's body before the undertaker came.

*And then what?*

Sarah forced back the useless panic that threatened. She needed to be calm. Numb, as she had before, when her father had died and her mother had sobbed and Sarah had been the one to tell the undertaker, to wash his body, to dress him in his Sunday suit, forcing stiff limbs into trousers and a shirt, fingers fumbling on the buttons. She'd been ten years old.

Lucy was still standing by the window, her panicked gaze on her aunt's horribly still body. Gently Sarah took her by her shoulders and looked her in the face.

"It's going to be all right. For both of us, it's going to be all right." Lucy's mouth opened and closed and she shook her head again, so hard Sarah worried that she'd hurt herself. Sarah drew her in for a quick, tight hug. "It's going to be all right, I promise," she said. "I'll always take care of you, Lucy. You must believe me." Even if she didn't know whether to believe herself.

The next few days passed by in a terrible, stilted blur. Prudence Barton helped Sarah wash and dress her aunt's body, and then the undertaker came and took it away. The house felt strangely empty without it – her aunt had been as silent as Lucy in those terrible days before death, but Sarah found she still missed her presence.

She went back to the bank, and then to the solicitor who had handled the Hatley family affairs. And then she learned that the house on Lowther Street was rented at forty-five pounds a year, and that in her will, unchanged for over a decade, her aunt had left everything she owned to the parish church.

"You mean... there's nothing?" Sarah whispered to the kindly man who wore a lorgnette and sat behind a big desk.

"Do you have other relations?" he asked, and distantly Sarah acknowledged that was not the response she wanted to hear.

"No... my father was an orphan and my mother's family is all dead." Could she go back to Goswell and throw herself on Ruth Teddington's charity? She didn't even have enough money for the train fare. "What am I going to do?" she asked, and for the first time true panic entered her voice. She had not envisioned a scenario as bleak as this. No money at all! She'd expecting something from Aunt Edith, even if it wasn't the whole of her estate. Something to keep them clothed and fed, a roof, no matter how humble, over their heads.

Could she ask the vicar if he would give her some of her aunt's inheritance? Did she dare? He seemed a stern and distant figure in the pulpit, and considering how little Reverend Hesham had wanted to help them, back in Goswell... Sarah could still remember the sorrowful shake of the vicar's head, his lips pursed in disapproval. No, she couldn't throw herself on the mercy of indifferent clergy again.

Yet she must, Sarah realised, because she had no alternative. The solicitor, Mr Browning, had suggested she find employment. "Whitwells is hiring mill girls," he said. "You could earn up to eight shillings a week, and your sister could work on the floor, cleaning under the machines for another three. That would see you set up in a boarding house."

Sarah drew back in dismay. Lucy work in a mill, scrambling about on dirty floors! She couldn't. In any case, her sister wouldn't be able to; she'd get distracted or upset and they'd both be fired inside a week. And what would eleven shillings a week get them? A life even more destitute than that in Goswell, living in a rented room, pinching pennies for bread and coal.

"Thank you for your help," she said with stiff dignity, and that afternoon she called on the vicar. It was his curate who answered the door, a book in his hand and a ready smile on his young face. He only looked a few years older than she was, tall and as lanky as a clothes prop, dressed in a dusty black clerical frock coat, his white cravat inexpertly knotted, his sandy-brown hair in tufty disarray.

"Hello!" He glanced at the book in his hand and then snapped it shut with a wry smile. "I'm afraid I'm on door duty this afternoon. The poor housemaid has the grippe."

Sarah clenched her hands together tightly as she bobbed a quick curtsey. "I'm here to see the Reverend Cooper, if you please, sir."

The curate frowned, sensing her distress, and then he stepped aside so she could come in. Sarah did so, breathing in the rich scents of beeswax and books. "Of course, Miss—?"

"Telford, sir."

"Telford. I'll tell him you're here." He paused in the doorway, his smile both whimsical and understanding. "Whatever it is that is troubling you, Miss Telford, I hope that we can be of help."

Sarah fixed him with a rather grim smile. "As do I, sir."

John Cooper was a dignified-looking man in clerical black, with wispy white hair and a full set of whiskers. He stood as Sarah came into his study, a large, important room with a huge desk and shelves full of important-looking tomes.

"Miss Telford. I am so sorry, of course, to hear about your aunt's untimely demise." His smile was kind and it heartened Sarah. "You are here to discuss the funeral, I presume?"

She blinked, realising she had not even begun arrangements for her aunt's funeral. She'd only been taken away two days ago, but already it felt like a lifetime, a different life, one where she'd worried merely about drudgery. She felt a sharp, urgent contempt for the girl she'd been, dissatisfied with a life that she now saw had had no end of comfort.

"No, sir. That is, I do wish to discuss the funeral arrangements, but I have a more pressing matter on my mind at this moment."

"Indeed." He sat down and gestured to a pair of Windsor armchairs in front of his desk. "Please take a seat, Miss Telford, and tell me what is so pressing."

Sarah sat down, taking a deep breath to buoy her courage. "It concerns my aunt's will," she stated. "I met with her solicitor today, and he informed me that in her will she has left all her worldly goods to this church."

An expression flickered across the Reverend's face and was gone, too quickly for Sarah to guess what it was. He did not seem surprised. "She spoke to me of those arrangements some years ago," he said after a brief pause. "When I first took charge of this living."

"Indeed." Another breath; she felt light-headed. "Then you know she was not aware of my existence at that time, or that of my sister's."

"I do not believe she was."

His careful response alarmed her; there were no reassurances. He sounded like a man hedging his bets and guarding his income. "We have been left with nothing, Reverend Cooper. Nothing at all." Sarah's voice trembled and she clenched her hands together, fingers knotted, her gloves damp. "My own father was a curate, a poor one, it's true, with no hope of obtaining a living, and upon his death my mother was left quite destitute. I have no relations or resources whatsoever except for my young sister, who depends on me utterly, and so I must throw myself on your Christian charity." It was as bold and desperate a speech as she could make, and yet the Reverend's expression did not change.

"What are you asking of me, Miss Telford?" he finally said, his voice gentle and yet possessing a hint of iron that alarmed her.

"I believe if my aunt had had time to change her will, she would have left us provided for. She certainly intended to provide for us while she was alive." The Reverend was looking at her with watchful eyes and so Sarah continued, emboldened beyond all measure now, her voice far too strident. "I'm asking for you to provide for us as my aunt would have, and release enough from her inheritance to see us situated in modest circumstances. Otherwise you will condemn us to the mill or the workhouse or worse."

Ire flickered in his eyes and then was damped down, and with a plunging sensation in her stomach Sarah knew she had gone too far.

"My Christian responsibility is to your aunt and her wishes," he said after a moment, his words clipped and precise, like those of a schoolmaster or a judge. "And as you had been living in her household for several months I believe her wishes remained in accordance with what they were when she first made her will. She certainly had adequate time to change it if she'd wished to do so."

It took a moment for his words to sink in. Sarah stared at him, the flinty eyes, the pursed lips. The only sound in the room was the relentless tick of the mantel clock. "So you are refusing to help?" she finally whispered.

Reverend Cooper puffed out his chest, one hand tucked into his waistcoat. "My dear, you are a very young woman and entirely impressionable," he said, his tone turning genial now, as well as earnest. "It would be quite remiss of me, and indeed impossible, to release such a substantial sum of money to a young female such as yourself. You would not be able to manage it, and would most likely either succumb to all manner of frivolity or worse, become the victim of whatever unsavoury character chanced to take unscrupulous advantage. I could not allow you to be subject to such a thing."

He smiled, seeming genuinely regretful, and Sarah knew he believed what he said. He thought this was for the best – for her and certainly for his church. What would her aunt's money fund? A new roof or repairs to the crumbling steeple? The church had leaked the last time it had rained; there had been buckets in the aisles, the steady *plink plink* competing with the Reverend's stentorian tones.

Resentment burned deep inside her, a hot, punishing

flame. She should have realised this would happen. She should have expected this, because it was what had happened before, when Reverend Hesham had looked just as regretful. The world didn't look favourably upon young women without families or protectors. Just as in Goswell, she would be expected to live a life of moral rectitude and dignity without any money at all.

"Very well." She drew herself up and managed a stiff nod. She would not appease his conscience with a smile. "What would you suggest I do then, Mr Cooper? As I am without any resources, either financial or otherwise? May I ask for your advice, as my spiritual counsellor?"

For a moment Reverend Cooper looked discomfited. He shifted in his chair, drumming his fingers on the top of his desk. "You can, of course, apply to the various societies that have been so generously founded for women and children in your situation," he said. "Or indeed, Miss Telford, you could find appropriate employment as a governess, or...?" He trailed off, not quite able to bring himself to list the alternatives. Maid, Sarah wondered sourly. Laundress? Mill girl? She could do none of them with Lucy in tow.

"I have my sister to think of," she said.

"Indeed. And while your devotion to your sister is laudable, of course..." He hesitated, and Sarah tensed, her hands bunching into fists. "Perhaps you should consider her greater need, as well as your own?"

"What are you suggesting, sir?" Sarah asked, her voice shaking. She could tell from the apologetic downturn of his mouth what it was. She just wanted to make him say it.

"It is unfortunate, of course, but your sister is an imbecile," he stated baldly. "If you do not have the resources to take care of her, she belongs in the workhouse where others can see to her needs and free you to work."

Sarah rose from her chair, her whole body trembling with

fury. "Good day to you, sir," she managed to gasp out. She strode from the room without looking back.

The curate was waiting in the hall, and he jumped to attention, casting his book aside, looking even more rumpled than before, as Sarah went to the door.

"Miss Telford—"

"The church has not helped me, sir," Sarah told him, her voice low and furious. "Not one whit, nor has it ever. What do you say to that?" Without waiting for a reply, she wrenched open the door and stormed from the house.

# CHAPTER 11

## ELLEN

The Friday of half-term Ellen drove across the A66 from Goswell to York to pick up Alyssa, enjoying the hazy blue skies and barren fells dotted with stone farmhouses and sheep. Her eldest daughter had decided to come home for the weekend, a prospect that filled Ellen with equal measures of joy and relief. She needed someone on her side.

It had been a week since the argument with Alex, and the following tense morning with Annabelle. Nothing had been resolved. Coward that she was, or perhaps simply too tired, Ellen had tiptoed around both of them rather than force yet another confrontation.

As for the idea that she pal around with Annabelle, researching that death certificate... the idea seemed absurd now. What was she supposed to do, merrily suggest that Annabelle might like looking through microfiche reels in the local archives, to find out who Sarah Mills was and why her death certificate had ended up under the floorboards of her bedroom? Annabelle would look at her as if she was crazy.

Ellen's spirits lifted as she drove to the University of York's campus in the south-east of the city. She was meeting Alyssa outside her hall of residence, and Ellen hoped her daughter would let her take her out to tea in the city. She could use a break.

Alyssa was more than amenable to the idea, and within half an hour Ellen had found parking and Alyssa had led her to a tearoom on the Shambles with tiny round tables and Victorian teapots with mismatched cups.

"What a sweet place," Ellen commented as she perused the laminated menu. "Two full cream teas coming up, with loads of jam."

"Sounds good to me," Alyssa answered cheerfully.

Ellen lowered the menu to gaze fondly at her oldest daughter. She looked good, more sophisticated than she had as a round-cheeked sixth former; she'd been blessed with Jack's silky, dark hair and lean build, and now she'd glammed herself up with make-up and charity shop chic. Ellen felt frumpy in comparison, but she didn't mind. "How are you, love?" she asked. "Not working too hard?"

Alyssa had worked herself to near-exhaustion achieving the three A grades she'd needed to study English at York, and Ellen knew her daughter was still driven. "No, not too hard," Alyssa answered lightly. "Just enough, I hope."

"And you've made some good friends?" Alyssa had gone skiing with her room-mates from university at Easter, and had spent the entire Christmas holidays catching up with local friends. Ellen felt as if she'd barely seen her daughter since she'd started uni, and she had an urge to cling now, to strengthen the bond between them and reassure herself that she was still a good mum.

"Yes, some good friends." Alyssa's glance slid away and Ellen felt that first fingertip of unease trail along the nape of her neck. What was her daughter not telling her? She had a sixth sense for these things, and she didn't think it was just paranoia now, even though she had reason enough to be a little jumpy after her experience with Annabelle.

"And boys?" she asked, her voice as light as her daughter's. "Anything happening there?" Considering her own experience at around Alyssa's age, she hoped not.

"Not really." Their cream teas came then, and the conversation stopped so they could both slather clotted cream and strawberry jam on their scones and take delicious, gooey bites.

Ellen tried to keep up the chat after they'd polished off the scones, but Alyssa's answers seemed evasive and she could feel her heart starting to sink. This had not gone as she'd hoped, she thought despondently as Alyssa disappeared to the loo and she paid for their teas.

"How about a wander round the city?" she asked as they put their coats on. "Try some make-up samples, or..."

"Actually, I'd rather just get home," Alyssa interjected. "If you don't mind." She made a little apologetic face. "Sorry."

"No, it's fine. Sophie will be dying to see you."

"And how's Annabelle settling in?" Alyssa asked as they walked back to the car. She didn't sound particularly interested.

"Oh, you know. It's a tough move for her." Ellen didn't feel she could say anything else. Alyssa was not the person to confide in about her troubles with Annabelle.

"Mmm." Alyssa got into the car as Ellen tossed her bag in the back. "She always seemed kind of sad, to me."

"Sad?" Startled, Ellen turned to look at her daughter. "What do you mean?"

"Well, I didn't see it at the time," Alyssa answered with a laugh. "I just thought she was stuck up, with her nose in the air, always going on about how everything was better in Manchester."

*Not much change then.* Ellen pursed her lips to keep from saying it.

"But did you notice how her mother never even called?"

Alyssa continued. "I don't think she rang once that whole summer." She glanced at Ellen who was focusing on navigating York's narrow streets. "Do you remember if her mother called?"

"She must have," Ellen said after a moment, but she heard the note of uncertainty in her voice. Had Sandra called? Surely... "She was staying somewhere remote," she recalled. "In Asia, I think. There wouldn't have been much reception..."

"But there would have been a phone." Alyssa shrugged. "Anyway, I was thinking about it later and it seemed a bit weird."

"She's talking to her mother now," Ellen said, recalling the Skype conversation she'd overheard. "A little bit, anyway."

They both lapsed into silence as Ellen navigated the traffic out of York, thoughts of Annabelle and Sandra whirling through her mind in an unwelcome maelstrom. Why didn't she know anything about Sandra, really? Why had she never even asked Alex about his marriage or how and why it had ended? She hadn't asked *anything*, hadn't wanted to know, and Alex, being Alex, had been content to let things remain unspoken.

Now Ellen felt the weight of all those unspoken conversations, all the knowledge she hadn't been prepared to deal with. And what about Alyssa? She glanced at her daughter, who was staring out the window at the fields flashing by, her lips pursed slightly in thought. Something was on her mind. Something she didn't want to tell her mother.

Suppressing a sigh, Ellen refocused on the road. She'd try harder with Annabelle, she promised herself. And with Alex. Somehow she'd make a way forward through this swamp of sullen silences, one heavy, soul-sucking tread at a time.

When they got back to Goswell, the house was quiet, Sophie already in bed, having been picked up from Merrie's by Alex after work.

"Hello?" Ellen called into the silence, slightly annoyed at

the lack of welcome even though it was nearly ten at night. "Anybody at home?"

"Hey." Alex padded out of the conservatory, his hair sticking up as usual and a tired smile on his face. "Hey, Alyssa. How are you?"

"Hey, Alex." Alyssa smiled and waved, and Ellen watched them covertly. Why didn't they hug? Had they never hugged? And why did Alyssa calling Alex by his name bother her a little now? Not bother exactly, but... she noticed it. Alyssa had never wanted to call him Dad, even though Ellen had cautiously suggested it once or twice, when she'd been younger. She'd told herself it didn't matter, that they had a good relationship, but now for some reason everything was rubbing her raw, making her wonder and doubt.

"How's university?" Alex asked and Alyssa made some positive reply while Ellen sifted through the post on the kitchen table, trying to pretend she wasn't listening to their conversation. Except there was no conversation. After her reply, Alyssa headed upstairs and Alex wandered back into the conservatory. Ellen wondered if she was being hyper-paranoid by questioning their relationship now. What if Alex and Alyssa had never really got along? Had she had blinders on about everything?

"Hey." She stood in the doorway of the conservatory, dusk starting to settle on the garden. "How was work?"

"Fine."

"This big research project you're on..." She realised she didn't even know what it was. Alex was usually researching the properties of radioactive isotopes or something like that. Ellen had stopped trying to understand it a long time ago. "How is it going?"

"Fine."

"Look." Ellen took a breath, trying her best to navigate the treacherous waters of marital discord. "The other week. I'm sorry for the way I sounded." Alex made a waving motion with his hand that Ellen couldn't interpret. "I'm just feeling a bit stressed about everything," she continued.

"Understandable," Alex said, but his tone was as impossible to gauge as the hand gesture.

Ellen tried for a different tack. "How's Annabelle been?"

"I haven't seen her."

"Really?" The disbelief crept into her voice of its own accord. Alex's mouth tightened.

"I was busy fetching Sophie and then seeing her to bed," he said shortly. "Annabelle came down for something to eat while we were reading stories."

"OK." She was going to try harder, remember? "So what shall we do for half-term?" Ellen injected as bright a note as possible into her voice and it sounded false, jarring. "We haven't made any plans…"

"I need to work," Alex said with a shrug and then, relenting a little, added grudgingly, "I could most likely take a day or two off."

"All right." It was far too late to book anything anyway, Ellen knew, and their finances were stretched tight due to the room renovation. Still, she felt disappointed, and dreaded the thought of a week at home with both Annabelle and Sophie. What on earth would they do all day? "Well, perhaps we can at least take Alyssa out to dinner. I could ring the pub for tomorrow night…"

"Just Alyssa?" The sharpness to Alex's voice took her by surprise.

"I meant everyone, but because she's home…" Why did absolutely *everything* have to become a minefield? "I'll make a reservation," Ellen muttered, and retreated to the kitchen, switching on the kettle. She needed a cup of tea even though it was past her usual bedtime. Sleep felt very far away. From the conservatory she could hear Alex tapping on his laptop keyboard and upstairs the sound of Alyssa moving around.

A few months ago she would have enjoyed this moment of peace, revelled in it, even, feeling content and maybe even a little smug that all was right with her world. She would have looked around her kitchen, cluttered but comfortable, and rested on her laurels of another day done, her work as mother and wife and freelance proofreader all ticking along, everything going as well as always. And if she had probed her sense of entitled contentment a bit more deeply, she would have told herself that she deserved this. That after one difficult marriage of endless arguments and acrimony, the bitter heartbreak of being left, the hurt of having tried and failed, she deserved a peaceful, loving marriage, a happy household. But, Ellen wondered bleakly, did anyone actually deserve anything?

"Mum?"

Ellen looked up to see Alyssa standing in the doorway. She was wearing her pyjamas and biting her lip and Ellen felt dual waves of concern and dread.

"What's going on, love?" Because something obviously was. At least Alyssa was going to tell her about it now. Hopefully.

"It's just..." Alyssa took a step into the kitchen, lowering her voice. "Dad's been in touch."

"*Dad?*" Ellen blinked, stunned into a second of silence. *Dad?* Jack hadn't been in touch with Alyssa in years. Had he? Or did she really not know anything about anyone any more? Perhaps she never had. "Why? I mean, I'm glad he's making contact, but... it's been a while, hasn't it?"

"Yes. A couple of years, at least."

Something in the way Alyssa answered made Ellen think she knew exactly when she'd last seen her father. She just didn't want to tell Ellen. And Ellen didn't understand why.

The kettle switched off and Ellen moved like an automaton, her mind spinning like wheels stuck in mud, to get the mugs and teabags. "Tea?" she asked Alyssa.

"Yes, please."

She spent a few minutes pouring boiling water and dunking teabags, fetching milk and spoons. It kept her from having to think about what to say, how to act. Nothing felt natural or right any longer, and that both scared and saddened her. "So what did he want?" Ellen finally asked when they were both sitting at the kitchen table, mugs of tea cupped between their hands.

"To see me." Alyssa took a too-hot sip of tea, wincing slightly, before she looked up at Ellen in obvious apprehension. "Is... is that OK?"

"OK? Well... why wouldn't it be OK?" Except it didn't feel OK.

"Because..." Another sip of tea, another wince. Ellen tried to keep her expression relaxed, interested, the typical *I'm a parent and I'm here to talk* look she'd perfected over the years. Or thought she had. "Because it always seemed like you didn't want me to see him."

"What..." The word escaped Ellen in an exclamation of surprise; she felt like she'd been kicked in the stomach. "Why would you think that?" she managed. Her tone sounded strangled, and she had no idea what her expression looked like any more. So much for relaxed.

"I don't know." Alyssa hunched a shoulder, her silky dark hair sliding in front of her face. Ellen could hear the klaxon alert of a teenager shutting down. Immediate damage control was necessary.

"I only meant," she tried, "that I've always wanted to support you seeing your father. Of course I have. I've been..." She swallowed down the end of that sentence, *disappointed when he hasn't stepped up. When he's failed us both again and again.* Not helpful right now.

Alyssa didn't answer, and Ellen felt the beginnings of a headache band her temples. She could tell she hadn't said the right thing, but it was so hard to know what the right thing was. And just talking about Jack made her tense; maybe it had been easier when he'd been completely out of the picture. In the past, whenever he'd called or come round, it had brought on unreasonable expectations on every side, wild hope followed by inevitable disappointment. She wanted to protect Alyssa from that. She wanted to protect herself from the emotional whiplash.

"So are you going to see him?" she asked, and Alyssa glanced up.

"Maybe."

"Oh. Well. Good." Ellen took a sip of tea and then tried to smile. It felt like an elastic band stretching across her face. *Snap.* "When?"

"I don't know. Maybe next weekend."

"Is he still in Birmingham, then?"

"He moved to Sheffield years ago, Mum." Alyssa's voice held a slightly reproving note, as if Ellen should have known this.

"Oh," she said. "Right."

Alyssa slid off her chair and went to dump her mug in the sink. "Thanks for the tea," she said, and then she was disappearing upstairs, leaving Ellen feeling once again that things hadn't gone as she'd hoped.

How did she feel about Alyssa seeing Jack? The question pinged around her mind like a pinball in a machine. She didn't know how she felt, not at this stage. She'd always tried to be supportive of Jack's visits, especially when Alyssa had been younger, and yet...

There had been so much hurt, so much bitterness, involved in her divorce. So many tears and hurled insults and accusations, so many arguments and visits that never happened, Alyssa waiting by the window, her nose pressed to the glass... did her daughter not remember *that*?

She'd always tried to take a breezy stance with friends and school mums alike, trotting out the tired phrases. *It was for the best. We're both happier now. We were driving each other mad. Alyssa's much more settled, really.* None of it hinted at the anger she still felt simmering beneath her air of determined optimism, the resentment, the hurt, the *fear*. She'd never even admitted those feelings to herself, because what was the point? Her marriage hadn't worked. She'd met Alex. *He* was her happy ending. He was her children's happy ending.

Except no one seemed very happy now.

"Ellen?" Alex appeared in the doorway of the conservatory, his laptop under one arm. "You ready for bed?"

Was his question a peace offering, a way to bridge the tense silence of the last few days? Ellen couldn't tell, but she decided to treat it as such.

"Yes, more than ready," she said, and followed him upstairs.

They got ready for bed in silence, but at least it didn't feel frosty. Once under the duvet Ellen scooted over to Alex's side and rested her head on his shoulder; she felt his surprise as a tremor through his body. Then he adjusted his arm to wrap it around her, drawing her in full and comforting contact with the hard wall of his chest. Biking eight miles to work twice a day made Alex enviably fit.

"You OK?" he asked softly, and sudden tears stung her eyes.

She didn't feel OK. She didn't feel remotely OK. But she was glad Alex had asked. "Yeah," she whispered, and closed her eyes. Her last thought before sleep was that she hadn't gone up to see how Annabelle was, or so much as say hello.

*Tomorrow*, she told herself as sleep thankfully claimed her. *Tomorrow I'll ask Alyssa about her dad, and tell Annabelle about that death certificate, and feel like I'm on top of everything again. Tomorrow.*

# CHAPTER 12

## SARAH

Kendal, 1868

The wolf was at the door. That was how it felt, in those awful days after her aunt's death, when the landlord told her she had until the end of June, just ten days, before she had to vacate the premises.

It felt as if the wolf was wearing a clerical collar when Reverend Cooper took her aunt's funeral and went on about Edith Hatley's generosity to the church. His generosity towards Sarah and Lucy was in allowing Aunt Edith's funeral to be paid out of the money that was soon to flow into the church's coffers rather than Sarah's empty pockets.

Sarah found she could not begrudge Reverend Cooper as much as she wanted to, for it soon became clear that he was not alone in his thinking. Prudence Barton came by to help her sort her aunt's belongings, and lowering her voice so Lucy wouldn't hear, she said, "You haven't much choice, have you, dear? And really, it would be the best thing. Lucy can be taken care of properly if she goes into college," she went on, using the euphemism for the workhouse that many preferred.

"I wonder," Sarah answered with asperity, "if anyone is taken care of properly in *college.*"

Prudence dropped the smile of sympathy as she gave Sarah a frank look. "She's a millstone around your neck, make no mistake. How can you find yourself a decent position, or make a marriage come to that, with her to care for? It's the only way."

And it was, Sarah knew, the way that most people believed was right for someone like Lucy. One person at church had helpfully pointed out that there was a room for imbeciles at the workhouse, complete with padded walls and a locked door.

"So they won't be a danger to anyone," the woman had explained kindly.

"Lucy isn't a danger," Sarah had replied stiffly, and then turned on her heel and left the woman standing alone, as rude as that was.

In truth Lucy had been difficult to handle since Aunt Edith's death, even for Sarah, who was used to her sister's moods and tantrums. She'd cover her ears with her hands and rock back and forth when anyone spoke to her, and when Prudence Barton had tried to give her a motherly hug, Lucy had wrenched herself away and kicked at Prudence quite savagely before Sarah had managed to subdue her, her arms wrapped around Lucy's slender body as she whispered soothing nonsense in her ear.

"Mark my words, that child belongs in a workhouse," Prudence had snapped, her face flushed with affront. She drew herself up, as impressive as a sailing ship in green bombazine. "She's a danger to every God-fearing Christian."

"She's only upset," Sarah said in a low voice, her arms still around Lucy, who had buried her head in Sarah's shoulder. "She's taken Aunt Edith's death badly. And she doesn't like to be touched." At least, not by near-strangers such as Prudence Barton.

"You won't have any choice, you know," Prudence said

grimly. "Not if you're to secure a position. Better to get the girl accustomed to life in college now."

Sarah did not reply, just kept comforting Lucy, one hand rubbing her sister's narrow back. She could feel the tremors wracking Lucy's thin frame. She did not trust herself to say something civil, and Prudence Barton did not come back to Lowther Street again.

At night Lucy was achingly compliant; when Sarah slid into the bed they shared, Lucy would snuggle into her like a little child, resting her cheek against Sarah's bosom, her arms tight about her waist, clinging to her as if afraid Sarah would slip away if she didn't.

And who could blame her? Everyone they'd ever loved or even liked had disappeared from their lives. Father, Mother, even their neighbour Ruth Teddington, who'd had a kind word for Lucy on occasion, was gone. And now Edith; there was no one left. No one but her.

Once, when Sarah had held Lucy at night and tried to keep her own swirling anxieties at bay, staring gritty-eyed at the ceiling and wishing with futile desperation that things, *anything*, had been different, Lucy had reached up and gently touched her fingers to Sarah's face, wiping away the tears Sarah hadn't even realised had slipped down her cold cheeks. Sarah had held Lucy's hand in hers and squeezed.

"You're a good girl, Lucy," she whispered. "You're a good sister to me." She would not consign her sister to the hopelessness of the workhouse. She could not.

Yet she had no idea what she could do to keep them both housed and fed. She scoured the back pages of *The Westmorland Gazette*, looking for suitable positions, and found nothing. A job as a housemaid or a governess? She didn't have a reference, and according to every interfering busybody Sarah encountered, no Christian household would accept Lucy along with her. It simply wasn't done. She was too strange, too too different, too unsettling. Never mind that Lucy wiped away her tears or had a smile like a sunbeam, sweeping away the looming grey clouds of worry and discontent. The injustice of it festered inside Sarah like a canker, eating away at any hope or happiness she might have clung to.

She considered pawning some of aunt's possessions, and even took the silver out from its cabinet in the dining room, inspecting the now-tarnished apostle spoons she'd polished many times, only to put them back regretfully. It belonged to the church now, and she could not bring herself to stoop so low, desperate as she was, to steal her aunt's things. Besides, she wouldn't even know where to go to sell them.

Two days after the funeral, the curate came to her door. He was dressed as usual in his fusty black, looking like a dark scarecrow with his long, lanky limbs, rumpled clothes, and squashed hat.

Sarah stood in the doorway, her arms folded, her expression deliberately cool. She had not been back to the church since the funeral, and she did not intend to return. She'd had enough of sanctimony and Sundays, and let the good people of Kendal think of that what they would.

"Reverend Cooper wanted you to have this," the curate said, sheepishly proffering an envelope.

"Oh, yes?" Sarah took it between the tips of her fingers, suspicious of anything the Reverend wanted for her. Was it an eviction notice? A warning not to take so much as a teaspoon from what now belonged to him? Perhaps he wished to come and make an inventory.

"And he also bid me to tell you that of course you should take whatever of your aunt's possessions you wish to keep," the curate continued awkwardly. "For sentimental reasons."

As opposed to economical? Somehow Sarah didn't think Reverend Cooper's charity extended to the silver. She nodded stiffly, not inviting him to come into the house. She'd had quite enough of social niceties.

"Well, then." He turned his hat over in his hands, his face red, his expression apologetic. "I wish you well, Miss Telford. Please do know if we can be of assistance, any assistance at all..."

"I did let you know," Sarah cut across him, her voice hard, "and Reverend Cooper declined to help me. So I'm afraid I have no use for either of you, sir, or your church."

"Reverend Cooper wishes to help," he insisted. "But you must consider his position, Miss Telford. He cannot go against your aunt's wishes. It would not even be legal."

"So he just has to line his own pockets instead?" Sarah replied with a cynical laugh. "How convenient for him. Good day to you, sir." And with that she shut the door in his face.

She was breathing hard, furious and yet near tears, and she was of half a mind to tear the Reverend's wretched envelope in two. But curiosity as well as common sense won out, and she opened it. Inside was a bank draft for twenty-five pounds.

Sarah let out a long, low breath, relief and resentment mingling inside her. Twenty-five pounds was enough to keep her and Lucy fed and clothed for a few months, but Sarah suspected it was only a fraction of the money her aunt had possessed. She'd found a ledger of household accounts and seen that her aunt had been living on a hundred and fifty pounds a year, and her grandfather had left three and a half thousand pounds in the Kendal Bank when he'd died fourteen years ago. How much of that was left Sarah had no idea, but it was all going to the parish church now.

Still, twenty-five pounds would keep her and Lucy off the street, for a little while at least, and for that she was grateful.

Then, a week before she and Lucy were to leave the house and go who knew where, another visitor came to the door. Sarah opened it, blinking in surprise to see Mr Mills of all people standing there, his hat in his hands, his eyes as kind as she'd remembered.

"Good day, sir," she said, and he smiled.

"I hope my visit is not inconvenient?"

"It is not, but I am here alone with my sister," Sarah said. Lucy was pressed to her side, one hand fisted in Sarah's skirts, her eyes wide and wary. "I don't know if it is proper..."

"I believe it to be proper when you consider what I intend to say," Mr Mills returned.

Sarah shook her head slowly. "But I do not know what you intend to say."

"Would you be so kind as to give me a few moments of your time? I believe that what I am about to suggest will be beneficial to us both."

Intrigued but more than a little suspicious, Sarah reluctantly stepped aside. She led Mr Mills into the parlour, deciding against offering him tea, and stood in front of the fireplace, hands folded at her waist like the staidest of matrons, Lucy still pressed against her while Mr Mills perched on the horsehair sofa, his hat resting on his knees. His collar, she saw, was wrinkled, and there was a coffee stain on his cravat, surely signs of a man without a wife.

The last time she'd seen him had been right before her aunt's accident, when he'd told her about her parents. More than once Sarah had considered that if she had not been so bold as to speak to Mr Mills, if she hadn't wanted to ask him about her father, her aunt would not have died. She had been in high dudgeon as they'd left the church, annoyed with Sarah for consorting with the man, and so she hadn't looked where she was going. It was, Sarah had reflected bleakly, all her fault.

"It has come to my attention, Miss Telford, that you are in difficult circumstances."

"Indeed." Sarah clutched her hands together tightly and Lucy leaned into her even more, her cheek pressed against

Sarah's side. She supposed half of Kendal knew about her "diffi-cult circumstances".

"I am in difficult circumstances as well," Mr Mills contin-ued, "although of a different sort." He gave her a sad sort of smile. His brown eyes crinkled at the corners in a way Sarah decided she liked. "My dear wife departed this earth six months ago, leaving my poor Clara quite motherless. I am aware I indulge the girl, out of love for her, and because she has no mother. But I realise she needs a woman's influence – as do I, I am sure!" He let out an awkward laugh and Sarah managed a stiff-lipped smile. She had no idea what he was trying to say. "The truth is, Miss Telford, that I need a wife. And I think, perhaps, you might need a husband."

It took Sarah a few shocked seconds to realise this was actu-ally a proposal of marriage. She could not countenance it. "Am I correct, sir," she began haltingly, "in believing that you are suggesting..." She found she did not have the courage to continue, in case she'd completely mistaken his meaning.

"I am suggesting we marry," Mr Mills said quietly. "For the sake of our loved ones, if nothing else." His gaze flicked to Lucy, half-hidden among Sarah's skirts. "We want them cared for, do we not?"

Sarah stared at him, taking his meaning, realising that he was offering both an escape and a prison. *Marriage.* She had not ever dared to dream of such a thing – and yet she barely knew this man. *He has kind eyes*, she reminded herself, but it did not seem nearly enough to base a marriage on. What if he treated her badly? What if he treated Lucy badly?

"I... I do not know what to say," she finally stammered, and Mr Mills smiled.

"I have taken you by surprise, I see."

"Yes..."

"Would you think on it? I am not as well situated as your aunt's family, I admit, as I am only a clerk at Gawith Hoggarth

& Co., but my house is comfortable enough and you would never be in want, nor would your sister." He smiled at Lucy but her sister just cowered even closer to Sarah, practically disappearing behind her skirts.

"And what of your daughter?" Sarah asked, thinking of the sour-faced girl wearing too many frills. "Clara? How old is she?"

"She is fourteen, nearly fifteen. A young miss in need of a steadying hand. She will marry eventually, I hope, and I would like a woman to teach her the gentle ways of domestic life."

*Gentle ways indeed*, Sarah thought sourly. There was nothing gentle about the domestic life, in her opinion. It was hard and harsh and unrelenting. "I must think on this," she said, when she realised Mr Mills was expecting a response. "In truth I barely know you, sir. I do not even know your Christian name."

"It is James," he answered. "And yours is Sarah?"

"Yes."

"And this is Lucy." He turned his kind gaze once more to Lucy. "How are you, poppet?"

"She doesn't speak," Sarah reminded him, a bit tartly.

"I know, you told me before." James turned his smile on Sarah. "But she still understands, doesn't she?"

Tears pricked Sarah's eyes. He was the first person since her aunt's death to treat Lucy with such common courtesy. "Yes," she whispered. "She understands nearly everything, as far as I can tell."

"Clever girl." His smile directed at Lucy made Sarah ache with a hope that she was afraid to give into. To have Lucy cared for, understood and maybe even loved...

"Why, sir?" Sarah burst out. "Why would you propose marriage to me? You barely know me. And I am not..." She stopped, not wanting to dissuade him, yet still suspicious. She was not pretty or well-connected; she was an orphan, a pauper, with nothing whatsoever to recommend herself.

"I was fond of both of your parents," James said quietly. "And especially your father. He was a dear friend of mine from school, and I always wished him well."

"So this is charity?" Sarah couldn't keep the disappointment from her voice, even as she inwardly berated herself. What else could it be? He did not know her. She was plain, poor. Of course it was charity.

"No, it is common sense," he replied. "This is a practical arrangement for both of us, Miss Telford, but I would hope that, in time, we could perhaps come to care for one another. I would like that." His smile, touched with sad whimsy, tore at her heart, and she looked away. Lucy pressed closer.

"I cannot give you an answer today."

"And I would not expect one." He rose from the sofa, settling his hat on his head. "I will leave you to think on it for a while."

"I am to leave this house in a week's time," Sarah blurted. "I fear I do not have the luxury of too much time."

"But you must be sure," James answered. "And in any case, it would take three weeks for the banns to be read. Do you not have anywhere to go?" Wordlessly she shook her head.

"Leave it to me," James told her, and Sarah felt only relief that finally there was someone she could perhaps trust, someone who might actually take care of her. This was a burden she did not, perhaps, have to shoulder alone.

Later that day James sent her notice by afternoon post that he had arranged for the rent to be paid for another fortnight. She and Lucy could stay on Lowther Street until the middle of July.

*And then?* Sarah wondered. Then, perhaps, she would marry James Mills.

She considered the prospect as she lay in bed that night, Lucy snuggled next to her, the moonlight spilling through the curtains. She'd kept the window open to the night air, although some stubborn part of her had wanted to close it simply because she could, but then she thought of Aunt Edith's stern face softened in sadness, the pair of silhouettes in her hand, and Sarah felt a welter of grief and anger that her aunt had been taken from this life so soon, and left her and Lucy in such straits.

And what of James Mills? Sarah pictured his gentle, whimsical smile and kind eyes and could not quite imagine being his wife. Kissing his face. Bearing his children one day, perhaps.

Why had he proposed to her? Surely another woman, one with connections and reputation, would be willing to accept him. Was it simply because of his association with her father? She did not know how old James Mills was, but she guessed him to be a similar age as her father would have been now, several years over forty and many more than her own eighteen. What would he be like as a husband? What would it be like, to be a wife?

She'd never imagined it, never even dreamed of such a possibility. She would be mistress of her own kitchen and home, a thought that brought a tremulous smile to her lips. She wondered what James Mills's house was like. Perhaps smaller and cozier than Lowther Street, which wouldn't be a bad thing.

He'd said she wouldn't want for anything, and that prospect alone made her inclined to say yes. It had been a long time since she had not had to worry.

And yet... she did not know him at all. She did not know if he could be trusted or relied on, if he would treat her with consideration and, yes, she dared to think of it, with love. And could she love him? Part of her thought she could love just about anyone who treated her and Lucy kindly. It wouldn't really take much at all. Another part shrank back in fear at loving anyone, because those she'd loved had been taken away so terribly, and she had no desire to suffer such a loss again.

But when it came to marriage, she wasn't sure she even had a choice, love or not. What was the alternative, but to scrape a living in a miserable set of draughty rooms, sewing shirts and living on bread and dripping, with hunger and debt, even the dreaded workhouse, always at the door? She wanted more for Lucy. She dared to want more for herself.

Two days after James came to visit her, Sarah wrote him a letter and sent it to the address he'd left, River Cottage, in the morning post.

*Dear Mr Mills,*

*I have considered your offer, and I am pleased to accept. Please advise on how we should proceed.*

*Yours sincerely,*

*Sarah Telford.*

She let out a shuddering breath, unsure whether she felt relieved or terrified by her decision. Both, most likely. The letter sent, she cleaned the house on Lowther Street from top to bottom; Reverend Cooper would have no criticism to make of her.

Taking the Reverend at his word, she put aside a few things of her aunt's to keep: the pair of silhouettes she'd found in her aunt's drawer, and two of her aunt's wool dresses with fine linen collars and cuffs as well as a lace shawl.

Then, filled with trepidation and fragile hope, she waited to hear from her husband-to-be.

# CHAPTER 13

## ELLEN

The first Saturday of half-term Ellen did her best to be Super Mum. She made American pancakes for breakfast, a favourite of Sophie and Alyssa's, and gave Annabelle a dazzling smile when she slouched downstairs in her pyjamas to have some.

"Annabelle, you remember Alyssa? The two of you shared a huge tyre swing at that farm park ages ago, do you remember?" It was the one positive memory Ellen had been able to recall from that awful summer. For about five minutes the two girls had got along, lying on their stomachs on the huge swing, all gap-toothed grins and dangling legs.

"Yeah, I remember," Annabelle said, shaking her caramel-coloured hair away from her face and giving Alyssa a darkly speculative look.

Ellen busied herself with dishing out the hot, fluffy pancakes and didn't say a word when Annabelle absolutely drenched hers with the costly maple syrup. It was all good. Nothing was going to annoy her today, nothing at all. She'd make sure of it.

"So it's not too bad out," she said in the super-bright tone that bordered on manic and seemed to be her default these days. "I thought we could take a picnic down to the beach. The tide will be out right around lunchtime."

"Oh, yes," Sophie squealed. "Can Merrie come?"

"Not today, love. This is going to be just for family." She smiled meaningfully at Annabelle, who rolled her eyes. No worries. She could handle it. "Then some ice cream at the beach café, and later dinner at the pub. Sound good?"

"Actually, I was going to go into Whitehaven with some mates," Alyssa said with a guilty smile. "Becca's home from Hull, so..."

"Ah. Well." Ellen poured herself more coffee, determined to take this in stride. "Can you make dinner at the pub, at least?"

"Yeah, sure."

That was something, at least. Ellen steeled herself to look at Annabelle. "What about you? Sunbathing and ice creams sound appealing?" She winced as she said it – what, was Annabelle six?

"OK, sure," she said without any real enthusiasm, but Ellen's jaw nearly dropped.

"Great," she said after a second too long of silence. "That's great."

Annabelle gave her a cynical look and dug into her pancakes. Ellen sipped her coffee, her mind starting to spin. Was this the beginning of a new era, a new hope? Happy Families take two... or maybe three.

It took Ellen a little while to dig out all her day-at-the-beach supplies; they hadn't gone since last August. Still, in a spirit of optimism or perhaps just foolishness, she dug out the lilo, the beach towels, the buckets and spades and even the sun cream. Alex watched her slather herself in the stuff, a bemused look on his face.

"You do realise it's only fourteen degrees out at the moment?"

"The sun's meant to come out properly later," Ellen answered. "Anyway, it's warmer at the beach."

"Maybe," he answered, but at least he'd agreed to come, putting away his precious laptop for the day so he could be with his girls – both of them.

The spring breeze *was* rather brisk as they all headed down the beach road, laden down with bags stuffed with towels, drinks, and optimistic tubes of sun cream. Alex carried the sagging lilo, in the shape of a deflated dolphin, on top of his head. More than one person gave them a bemused aren't-you-hopeful look, for the closer they got to the beach the more Ellen realised how chilly it actually was.

Still it was beautiful, a lovely stretch of flat, damp sand scattered with tide pools and smooth humped rocks glistening like the backs of seals.

They set up camp on a drier bit of sand near the rocks, and Ellen busied herself setting out all the prerequisites of a day at the beach: a plastic-backed blanket that wouldn't get wet, for sitting on even the driest-feeling sand left you with a wet bottom after a while; a cooler of drinks and sandwiches; nets for catching crabs, and buckets and spades to dig and build. She couldn't quite see Annabelle constructing a sandcastle, but who knew? Everyone became a bit of a child at the beach.

"I think I'll keep my fleece on," Alex said as the breeze buffeted them. Ellen suppressed a shiver.

"And you call yourself a Cumbrian," she teased.

"I didn't think I could lay claim to that title for another twenty years," Alex answered with a smile. He stretched out on the blanket and leaned back on his elbows. "What do you think, Annabelle? Does anything beat a Cumbrian beach?"

Annabelle, dressed even more optimistically than Ellen was in short shorts and a tee-shirt, the hot pink straps of her bikini visible underneath the thin fabric, was shivering visibly.

"I prefer the Caribbean," she said, her lips pursed, and Ellen gave her a commiserating smile.

"Come to that, so would I," she said. "But Cumbria is the next best thing. Here you go, love." She handed Sophie a bucket and spade and her daughter went scampering off. Ellen sat back with Alex while Annabelle stood there, managing to look both mutinous and uncertain, clearly unsure how to handle this situation.

Alex glanced at her and then tugged off his fleece. "Here you go, Annabelle. I have to admit, it is freezing out here."

Annabelle took the fleece with a muttered thanks and pulled it on. "Do you want to sit down?" Ellen asked, gesturing to the empty stretch of blanket on the other side of Alex.

"It's too cold to just sit," Annabelle muttered, and with her shoulders hunched, her hands lost in the sleeves of her father's fleece, she started walking down the beach.

Ellen watched her go, letting out the breath she'd been half-holding in a long, low rush. "Well, that went sort of OK," she murmured.

"We'll get there," Alex said with so much conviction Ellen couldn't keep from raising a sceptical eyebrow. But she did resist making some kind of snippy rejoinder; she was working hard today, trying to keep them all on course. Happy family, right here, right now.

"Thanks for this," Alex said after a moment.

Ellen looked at him in surprise. "Thanks for what?"

"Bringing us to the beach. Organising it all." He gave her a sheepish, sideways smile. "For putting up with me."

Ellen hesitated, torn between wanting to accept his apology and smooth everything over as quickly as possible and knowing there was more to say. More to know. But maybe not today. She just wanted to enjoy a day at the beach, chilly as it was. "Well, you have to put up with me too," she said as lightly as she could. "I'd say we're even."

Alex smiled, and Ellen didn't think she was imagining the relief in his eyes. Her strong, silent, emotionally limping husband wanted simply to smooth things over as well.

"I was thinking about doing something with Annabelle," Ellen said. "Just the two of us."

"Oh? What were you thinking of?"

"I don't know. Maybe a girly day at a spa or a shopping trip in Carlisle…" Both options, Ellen suspected, would pale in comparison to the equivalent in Manchester. "Or actually I was thinking about involving her in a little research project."

Alex raised his eyebrows. "Research?"

"The builders found a death certificate beneath the floorboards upstairs," Ellen explained. "From 1872. Sarah Mills, aged twenty-two, in Kendal."

"Jane's rubbing off on you, is she?" Alex surmised with a little smile. "You think there's some story behind it all?"

"There's bound to be, isn't there?" For the first time Ellen felt a proper flicker of curiosity about the unknown Sarah Mills. "Why would a death certificate from Kendal end up under our attic floor?"

"Well, the room was for a maid back then, wasn't it?" Alex said practically. "So this Sarah Mills was probably a relative of the maid. She received the death certificate and it slipped beneath the floorboards."

Served her right for having a scientist for a husband. He thought of the most obvious and uninteresting answer. "What if it was put there on purpose?" she asked. "To hide it?"

"Why would anyone hide a death certificate?"

"Exactly."

"It's a public document," Alex persisted. "It would have had to be registered, and you must have found a copy. Hiding it would serve no purpose."

Ellen stretched her legs out in front of her, toes wiggling in search of the sun. "Perhaps you need to think outside of the box, Alex."

"Research it by all means," Alex said with a laugh. "Jane will want you to. I'm sure the historical society will know something about the house, at least. You could find out who was living there in... what was it? 1872?"

"Yes." Ellen squinted at the sea; the sun had come out from behind the clouds and it actually felt fairly warm. Ish. "I could do that, couldn't I? Perhaps Annabelle would be interested." Alex didn't answer and she laughed, shaking her head. "What am I like? She's seventeen. She probably couldn't care less."

"Still, you could try," Alex said quietly. "That's the main thing, isn't it? That's what you told me, anyway."

"Yes." Ellen took a deep breath, keeping back the words that sprang so easily to her lips. *I have been trying already. I've been trying bloody hard, thanks very much.* No, she wouldn't say that, because she agreed with Alex, really. She needed to try in a different way with Annabelle. Somehow.

"Maybe I'll go and talk to her," Alex said. He nodded towards Annabelle's tiny figure now a quarter-mile away, down by the sea. "See how she's getting on."

"That sounds like a great idea."

Ellen watched him go, her heart feeling as if it were climbing up her throat as he jogged towards Annabelle and then fell in step beside her. Obviously she couldn't hear what they were saying. She couldn't even tell if they were talking. Alex was talking, she decided, judging by the way he'd angled his head towards Annabelle and was gesturing with his hands. But was she saying anything back? Or was she giving him yet another version of the death stare of stupidity?

Watching them even from this distance felt like an intrusion, and so Ellen scrambled up from the blanket and went to help Sophie with her sandcastle.

They spent a companionable time building what Sophie called an "epic" sandcastle, complete with pebble-reinforced moat and slightly wonky towers decorated with shells, rocks, and a few slimy strands of seaweed.

After about twenty minutes Annabelle came over with Alex, her arms wrapped around herself, her hair whipping about her face. The almost-balmy breeze had kicked up into a proper wind.

"Want to join us?" Ellen asked. "We're making a seriously huge castle here." Inwardly she waited for Annabelle's derisive snort, the incredulous eyebrow lift. *Build a sandcastle? Seriously? Um, no thanks.*

"Sure," she said, and sat down on the opposite side of the castle from Ellen. Alex gave Ellen a quick, encouraging smile, and she smiled back. Happy families. They were actually doing this.

They worked together, the breeze buffeting them, Sophie scampering around, the castle's chief architect delighted to have so many willing helpers.

Ellen and Annabelle ended up reinforcing the moat together, pressing pebbles into damp sand. Ellen noticed Annabelle was making a patterned mosaic with the different coloured pebbles.

"Hey, nice," she said, and Annabelle gave her a quick, uncertain smile that lifted Ellen's heart. For a moment, with the sulky mask dropped, Annabelle looked normal. Young. And it made Ellen say quietly, so Alex and Sophie on the other side of the sandcastle couldn't hear, "I'm sorry about – you know. You overhearing." Annabelle's expression froze and then she looked down at the moat, her slender fingers pressing the pebbles deeply into the sand, her hair hiding her face. "I was stressed and frustrated," Ellen continued, her throat starting to feel squeezed so it was hard to get the words out. "But I should have been..." She searched for what she was trying to say, what she felt Annabelle needed to hear. "More sensitive. More patient."

"Forget it," Annabelle mumbled, her hair still hiding her face, and Ellen considered whether to press the point and continue the conversation, painful as it was. She decided not to. They'd had enough progress for one day.

After they'd finished the sandcastle and the tide started its relentless roll in, they had a picnic lunch, eating slightly soggy sandwiches gritty with sand, and fruit and crisps that had become a bit squashed in the bottom of the bag.

"Perfect beach picnic food," Ellen teased as Sophie refused a bruised-looking banana. "How can you resist?"

Annabelle, she noticed, had gone quiet, but it didn't look like a sulk so much as a thoughtful inward gaze. Maybe Annabelle was repenting of all her attitude. *Hallelujah.*

After their picnic they took turns daring each other to dip toes and even knees in the sea; the water was icy and turning choppy as the wind continued to pick up. Finally they went for ice creams at the café, eating them on the walk back home, everyone windblown and a little sunburned despite the cool weather.

"I guess we didn't need the lilo," Alex said as he tossed it back in the garden shed and Ellen began to unpack the basket of now-soggy towels, unfortunately mixed with the detritus of their picnic lunch.

"Live in hope, eh? I've booked the pub for half six."

"I'll just grab a shower, then."

Ellen nodded absent-mindedly as she picked a discarded banana peel from a wet towel and lobbed it towards the bin, coming up short when she saw Annabelle standing there.

"Oh! You scared me."

"Sorry," Annabelle muttered.

"No, no, it's fine. I just didn't realise anyone was here."

Laughing a little, unnerved by Annabelle's hesitant expression, for once absent of any malice or contempt, Ellen tried for a smile. "What's up?"

"Dad said you had something to show me."

"What...?" For some reason the *Dad* surprised her. She realised she hadn't actually heard Annabelle call Alex Dad in a long time. "Oh. Did he tell you about the death certificate?"

"Death certificate?" Annabelle drew back, surprised and more than a little nonplussed. "He just said you found something in my room."

"Yes, a death certificate from 1872. It was hidden under the floorboards, and the builders found it when they redid the room. Wait." Ellen scrabbled among the stack of random papers, noticing the late permission slip for a school trip, in search of the aged paper. "Here it is." She handed it to Annabelle, who unfolded it dubiously.

"Sarah Mills, Aged twenty-two, River Cottage... what *is* this?" She looked at Ellen as if suspecting a trick.

"A death certificate. From a long time ago."

"But why would I be interested in this? Why would Dad tell me I needed to talk to you?"

Typical Alex, Ellen thought in bemusement. Trying to help but having no clue. "Well, I thought you might be interested in it," she said, trying not to sound as awkward as she felt. "Because of your history A-Level and because it was in your room. I mean, it's a little interesting, don't you think? Why would someone hide a death certificate underneath the floor?"

Annabelle glanced up, a spark of curiosity entering her eyes. "You think it was hidden on purpose?"

"It seems likely." She'd just forget Alex's practical suggestion about it falling between the floorboards by accident. How dull could you be?

"She was only twenty-two..." Annabelle stared down at the certificate again. "What does 'General Debility' mean?"

"General Debility?" Ellen moved to peer over Annabelle's shoulder. "Where's that written?"

"Here, under cause of death. Do you know what it means?"

Smiling, a new hope buoying her flagging spirits, Ellen shook her head. "No, but we can find out."

# CHAPTER 14

## SARAH

Kendal, 1868

Sarah married James Mills on a Tuesday morning in mid-July. It was a small, quiet affair, considering they were both still in mourning. No one looked askance at a man taking a wife as soon as he could, but a woman in mourning was a different matter entirely. Sarah suspected more than one tongue wagged about the young miss who'd lost her mother and her aunt and then turned around and married the first man who offered for her, in black crêpe, no less. She told herself she didn't care about wagging tongues. She was going to be happy as Mrs James Mills. She'd make sure of it.

Reverend Cooper married them, with only Lucy, Clara, Prudence Barton, and a thin young man from the tobacco company in attendance. His name was Edwin and he had a serious air and a sudden, girlish laugh that Sarah didn't like. She wondered if he was her husband's closest friend, but when she asked, James just shrugged and said, "We get along, I suppose." And yet he'd invited him to his wedding. It was one of many things she was coming to realise she did not understand about her husband.

They'd spoken and seen very little of each over the last three weeks, while the banns were read. Sarah would have been glad of a little company, a little reassurance that the man she was marrying was indeed a good one and someone she could trust. Instead, James remained busy with work, his daughter, Clara, in the care of an elderly neighbour who had not deigned to come to the wedding.

Sarah did not understand why he would not seek her out, reassure himself that he was marrying a woman he liked, but perhaps he simply did not care enough. Perhaps he did not care at all. By the time she and Lucy arrived at the church, Sarah was wondering if she'd made a terrible mistake.

The sight of James in a clean frock coat and cravat, his hair smoothed back with pomade, made her heart lift a little. His smile was warm, his eyes crinkling at the corners as they had before. Surely he wasn't a bad man.

They said their vows in murmurs, the church yawning emptily around them. James slipped a thin gold band on Sarah's finger; she saw initials engraved on the inside, along with a date, although she did not have time to examine them, but it heartened her that James had gone to such effort.

There was no wedding breakfast after the service; considering their recent bereavements, Sarah supposed it was inappropriate, although there had been no discussion. She did not really mind; she'd rather get onto the business of living. Still, she was a bit taken aback when James expected them all to simply walk back to River Cottage; he had not even hired a carriage.

It was a warm, muggy day, the sky low and grey with heavy clouds, the air so damp Sarah's dress stuck to her back and under her arms. She held Lucy's hand as she walked next to James, Clara, in a dress of violently purple silk, walking on his other side.

Sarah glanced covertly at Clara, who had barely spoken a word the whole morning. The dress's vivid shade didn't suit her fair colouring and was far too mature for a girl her age, but Sarah supposed Clara liked it, since the new dyes were all the fashion. It had three tiers of flounced ruffles and no end of furbelows and fripperies. Sarah had never seen the like on a woman, much less a girl of fourteen. It looked, she thought, quite ridiculous.

James had told her he lived by the river, and Sarah had, in a vague and pleasant way, imagined a dear little home with a garden overlooking the Kent. She'd pictured Lucy playing in the garden, the sun shining benevolently down, the world smiling. Happiness at last.

The reality, she discovered, was disappointingly different. River Cottage was not a cottage at all but a small terraced house of bleak grey stone with a single window on the first floor and a narrow garden at the back, hemmed in by its neighbours on either side, that led down to the river. The roof was missing slates and the wall in the front had half-fallen down; James did not seem to notice.

He unlocked the front door, standing aside so Sarah and Lucy could go first; Sarah ducked her head to avoid hitting the low stone lintel and stepped into her new home.

The front door opened directly into a small sitting room that was stuffed with furniture; Sarah glimpsed a sofa, two armchairs, an upright piano and a glass cabinet that held all manner of expensive-looking ornaments. There was barely room to move, and she stepped carefully around a plant stand – there was no plant – so James and Clara could come in behind her.

"It's not much," James said, a touch of pride in his voice, "but I do think it is comfortable. I'll show you the rest of the house."

The rest of the house comprised a small dining room with

table and chairs and a cupboard for china, and a kitchen that was so small and dark and dank Sarah drew back instinctively. James did not show her the upstairs.

"I hope you'll be happy here," James said as she surveyed the kitchen with its old-fashioned, open range, the stone slab floor and the spots of mildew that speckled the flaking white-washed walls. A single gas jet illuminated the dank space.

She swallowed hard. "I'm sure I will." Lucy was clutching her hand so tightly it hurt, and she could feel her sister's fear like a palpable thing, a creature with a hard-beating heart and fluttering wings. Or perhaps it was her own fear she felt, perching in place of her heart; this was all so *strange*, and so much less than she'd hoped for or even expected.

The sensible part of her insisted that River Cottage was not as bad as the rooms she'd lived in with her mother back in Goswell; they had been smaller and colder, and they'd had to cook on an open fire. She could make do with this; she'd known worse, certainly, so why feel so appalled?

Yet back in Goswell she had not lived with strangers, and the comforts of family had been precious. Even in the darkest of days, when there were no shirts to take in and the pennies were few, she'd felt safe. Here she felt as if she were stumbling in the dark, married to a stranger.

"I hope the ring fits," James continued in a quiet, shy sort of voice. Clara had gone upstairs, so besides Lucy they were alone. "It belonged to my wife."

Sarah stared at him, even more appalled. She wore a dead woman's ring? The initials and date on the inside of the band must have been from his first marriage. She fought the urge to yank the thing off her finger, managing to nod instead.

"Thank you," she whispered. "It's lovely."

"Perhaps now you will make some dinner?" James suggested hopefully. "It's past noon, and I will need to return to work this afternoon."

Sarah stared at the kitchen, her stomach feeling as if it were lined with lead. "Yes, of course. Is... is there no maid?"

James frowned. "I've had a woman come in to do the heavy work since Amanda... and a neighbour has provided us with most of our meals. We have no room for a maid and now that we are wed..." He spread his hands, shrugging, and Sarah understood completely.

Now that they were wed, he had no need of a maid, or perhaps even a woman to come in for the heavy work. The gentle ways indeed.

"Very well," she said, her voice stiffer than she would have liked. "I shall have dinner ready within the hour."

James smiled, pleased, and disappeared upstairs while Sarah set to work. Still holding Lucy's hand, she discovered all that the kitchen lacked; there was no separate scullery, so the food preparation as well as the laundry would have to be done in the kitchen itself, with the range throwing out a dangerous heat. The larder was nothing more than a cupboard, and the only running water was a tap in the coal store, a crawl space beneath the house accessed by a tiny door. When she opened the back door, she drew a deep breath of dismay; the garden she'd imagined Lucy playing in was flooded with dark, murky water from the river. In the winter it would most likely come right into the kitchen.

Sarah closed the door and then stoked up the fire in the range. She looked for what food there was in the larder; she found nothing more than some leftover mutton that looked as if it might soon go off, a heel of bread and a few shrivelled-looking potatoes and onions. And from this she was to make a meal?

She took another deep breath, willing back the tears that had stupidly sprung to her eyes. This was the life she had chosen; this was the only choice she'd had. She would have to make the best of it.

"You can scrub the potatoes, Lucy," she said, for she thought her sister would do better to keep busy. She fetched a pail of water from the tap in the coal store, hitting her head on the low ceiling, and then set some in the basin on the plain deal table and poured the rest into an iron pot she placed on the grate over the fire. She thought longingly of the modern closed range back in Lowther Street, and then pushed the thought away. This was her home now.

While the water boiled, she chopped the vegetables and mutton and then added them to the pot; a bit of salt was the only flavouring she could find. Then she sat in one of the rickety chairs and waited while the stew simmered; it would be a poor dinner indeed.

Lucy sidled next to her and even though she was heavy, Sarah pulled her onto her lap, sensing that they both needed the comfort. Lucy laid her head against Sarah's shoulder as she stroked her hair.

"This room needs a bit of work, eh, Lucy?" she said, trying to inject a note of cheer into her voice that she did not yet remotely feel. "Nothing that a bit of cleaning won't cure, I expect." She could set to work tomorrow, scrubbing the walls free of mildew and black-leading the range; it looked as if it had not been cleaned in an age. And she could go shopping; Sarah brightened at the thought of buying some fresh, good food for them all to eat. She would be mistress here, even if it was smaller and poorer than she'd expected. That was something.

Still, as she rose to set the table, she wondered why James lived in such poor circumstances. A clerk usually earned a hundred pounds or more a year; in his mid-forties, with plenty of experience, James might be earning twice that. He could surely afford a house nearly as fine as the one in Lowther Street, and a maid, and a new range, for that matter. He was certainly able to afford far too many fancy frocks for his daughter. She did not understand why his living circumstances were as poor as they were, but she knew it was not her place to ask.

She set the table in the dining room with the china she found in the cupboard; it was of decent quality, with plenty of pieces, from a gravy boat to a soup tureen with an elaborate lid. Another mystery, it seemed. She thought of the piano in the sitting room, and the many ornaments in the glass-fronted cabinet; James Mills had plenty of *things*. Why did he live in such a state, then? Was it simply the lack of a wife, or a stinginess she had not guessed at?

With Lucy a dogged shadow by her side, Sarah went in search of her husband. She found him in the sitting room, reading the newspaper. He looked up with a smile. "Is dinner ready, then?"

"Yes, but I'm afraid it's not very much. I shall have to buy some things for supper."

"I'm afraid we haven't kept much food in the house. A neighbour supplied most of our meals for a small sum, and it worked very well for us."

"Very kind of her," Sarah murmured and James rose from the sofa to stride into the dining room. Sarah went upstairs to call Clara; she knocked on the door of the second bedroom, poking her head round when there was no reply. Clara was sitting in a chair by the window, flipping through a book of dress patterns. Sarah registered the sulky expression on her face and tried for a smile.

"Hello, Clara," she said as kindly as she could. "It's time for dinner."

Clara flung the pattern book aside and flounced past Sarah in all of her finery; Sarah stepped out of the way, her gaze moving around the room with its single bed, chest of drawers, washstand, and chair. A cupboard built into the wall by the fireplace was half-open and Sarah could see the froth of satin and silk that told her Clara had many more dresses just like the one she was wearing. But what alarmed her was not Clara's many dresses, but the fact that this was the only other bedroom in the house. Where was Lucy going to sleep?

Slowly Sarah walked downstairs. Yesterday James had hired a wagon to collect her and Lucy's few possessions; she'd seen her valise in the front bedroom but she wondered where Lucy's things would be kept. Would she share with Clara? Sarah knew instinctively that arrangement would not suit; even worse, she suspected James would not suggest it.

She dished out the watery stew and sliced the bread, noticing Clara's pouty look at such poor fare.

"I shall have to go to the grocer's today," she said after they'd said grace. Lucy was sitting next to her, looking pale and almost as sullen as Clara. It did not feel like a good start. "Yes, yes," James said. "We have credit with most of the shops on Highgate."

Sarah murmured something acceptable, and then realised she could wait no longer. She needed to know her sister's situation. "Mr Mills—" she began, only to have James interrupt her.

"Oh, we do not stand on formality here. You may call me James, Sarah, in the company of family." He gave her an indulgent smile, and Sarah nodded stiffly.

"James." It was the first time she'd called him by his Christian name, and it felt odd. "Where is Lucy to sleep?"

Something flickered across his face; Sarah could not tell what it was but it did not seem like a harbinger of good news. "River Cottage is small," he said with a flick of his fingers, as if dismissing her question entirely. "I thought she could sleep in the kitchen."

Sarah stared at him, dread seeping into her stomach like the dank river water rising in the garden. In the kitchen…! Only the lowliest of servants would sleep in the kitchen, where it was so dark and *uncomfortable*, with beetles scuttling across the stove and mice nibbling their way into the larder. And James expected her sister to sleep there alone, in the cold and the dark?

Lucy had gone still, her eyes wide and unblinking as she looked from James to Sarah, sensing the tension but not seeming to understand it.

"Surely something more suitable can be found," Sarah said quietly. Her hands were trembling and she hid them in her lap. "She is only ten years old, and she is used to sleeping with me."

James let out a little laugh. "She can hardly sleep with you now, my dear. I'm sure we can make the kitchen quite comfortable." He glanced at Lucy with the same kind of indulgence he'd shown Sarah. "Don't worry, poppet. We'll see you settled."

Sarah stayed silent, knowing there was no point in arguing. The dread in her stomach rose, a wave that threatened to drag her under. It hurt to breathe.

As soon as the midday meal was over, James left for work, promising to return by seven o'clock and clearly expecting a hot supper. Sarah rose from the table to say farewell, and then turned back to Clara who was sitting there sulkily, her arms crossed over her chest in an unbecoming manner.

"Well, Clara," Sarah said, unable to summon a note of cheerfulness and settling for brisk instead. "Shall we see to the dishes?"

Clara's fair eyebrows rose and her mouth curled in an unpleasant smile. "*I* shan't be seeing to anything."

Sarah gazed at her for a moment, taking the girl's measure. She was spoiled past all reason – that much Sarah had worked out already. She was not a particularly pretty girl, despite her fair hair and big blue eyes. Her jaw was heavy, her cheeks too round, and her hair, fair as it was, was lank and dull. In later years she would likely run to fat if she was not careful.

"Your father wanted me to teach you how to manage a household," Sarah said evenly. "For when you are married."

"Managing a household will not require me to wash dishes,"

Clara returned, meeting Sarah's gaze with childish defiance. "I intend to have a maid when I'm married."

"Chance would be a fine thing," Sarah retorted before she could think better of it. Clara's eyes narrowed and Sarah felt any advantage she might have had slip away from her. She needed to get along with Clara; life would be difficult indeed if she did not. But she could not, she realised, force Clara to help her in this moment. "Come along, Lucy," she said, and with her head held high she began to gather the dishes. Lucy rose to help her, and they worked together to bring all the dishes into the kitchen while Clara simply watched.

Sarah considered the matter as she filled a pail with water and heated it on the range; the antiquated nature of the kitchen's arrangements made even a simple washing of dishes a cumbersome chore. Her skirt – her wedding dress – was already stained with coal smuts. She brushed a strand of hair away from her cheek and focused on the problem at hand.

Clara did not intend to lift a finger to help in the house, she surmised, and Sarah suspected James would not welcome any complaints about his daughter – something Clara undoubtedly already knew.

What was she to do? Befriend the motherless child – for despite her fancy frocks, Clara Mills was most certainly a child. And Sarah knew what it was to be without a mother. Perhaps if Clara softened towards her, she would have a chance of winning the girl's affection – and gaining her help in the house. Sarah could see no other way, but inwardly she trembled at the thought of wooing Clara, unpleasant as she could be, with patience.

After the dishes were done, Lucy having dried them and helped put them away, Sarah fetched her bonnet and shawl and then went upstairs to where Clara was lying on her bed, her boots on the coverlet, flipping through an old copy of *Lady's Magazine*. She did not look up when Sarah opened the door.

"Lucy and I are going out," Sarah announced. "I intend to do some shopping on Highgate. You may join us, if you wish."

Clara lifted her head and stared at her for a moment; Sarah waited, chin lifted, expression deliberately neutral.

"Very well," Clara said on a sigh, and tossed her magazine aside.

They spent a surprisingly pleasant hour walking up and down Highgate; Clara looked in the windows of various drapers and tailors while Sarah set to the more mundane task of buying food for both supper and breakfast. It felt odd to introduce herself as Mrs James Mills, and more than once she felt a prickle of alarm at the rather sympathetic looks the various shopkeepers gave her.

"So he's married again?" the butcher's wife said as she handed her some veal collops wrapped in paper. "I can't say I'm surprised. Poor Amanda, with her six bairns laid out like wee dolls. I wouldn't wish that on anyone."

Not wanting to gossip, Sarah struggled with a reply. "Six...?" she finally repeated stiffly. The look the woman gave her was tinged with pity.

"Aye, six babes she had, all born too early, and all dead before a day or two was out. One wee lass made it to a month or so, but it took it out of the poor woman, and as for Mr Mills..." The woman's mouth tightened ominously.

Sarah decided she did not want to hear the butcher's wife's opinion on her husband. "Thank you for the veal," she said hurriedly. "It looks delicious." She swept out of the shop before she could hear any more, her mind and stomach both churning.

*As for Mr Mills...* what on earth did that mean? She would, Sarah suspected, discover the answer before long.

That evening James returned as promised at seven o'clock, and Sarah had, with no thanks to Clara, supper waiting: veal collops with potatoes and currant jelly, and an apple pudding for dessert.

"Now, isn't this a treat!" James exclaimed, rubbing his hands together. "A proper hot meal, and a pudding as well! We are spoiled, aren't we, Clara?"

Clara did not reply and Sarah suppressed a sour smile. She knew of one person in the room who was most certainly spoiled.

They ate in silence, since James did not seem inclined to talk; he ploughed mechanically through his meal and then retired to the parlour with Clara until bedtime, while Sarah and Lucy did the washing-up. It clearly did not occur to James to ask his daughter to help with the chores, and Sarah did not have the courage to insist or even ask. As she cleared the dishes from the table she could hear them playing spillikins and resentment simmered in her belly, a fermented stew that made her work even more laborious.

By the time she'd put the last plate away, emptied the dirty water in the flooded garden outside, and then swept the kitchen floor, she felt exhausted in every inch of her body. And the night was still to come.

She was not so ignorant as to be unaware of what happened between a husband and a wife, and she dreaded the moment James would summon her upstairs. For all his kindnesses towards her, he was still a stranger – and one she did not quite understand. How could he be so complimentary about supper, and yet see no harm in Lucy sleeping in the kitchen? How could he smile at Sarah and pay for her rent and then expect her to work like a skivvy while he spoiled his daughter?

"Sarah." James stood in the doorway of the kitchen, one hand outstretched, his smile as kind as ever. "It is time for us to retire."

Sarah's hands trembled and she hid them in her skirt. "Yes, of course." She took a deep breath and glanced at Lucy, who had been methodically wiping the tabletop and then trailing her fingers through the rivulets of water, leaving it streakier than ever. "Let me see my sister settled first."

"Of course." James' smile was easy as he turned to Lucy. "It shall be quite comfortable for you, poppet, never fear."

Sarah did not think it was comfortable at all, and she was amazed that her husband had the gall to suggest it was. Yet she knew there was nothing she could do about it now. Tomorrow she could give the whole room a good clean, but until then...

Yet, really, it didn't matter how clean the room was. Lucy had slept with Sarah since she was little more than a baby. She would be terrified on her own.

"James," Sarah tried. "Couldn't... couldn't Lucy sleep upstairs? On the floor of Clara's room, at least? I worry for her down here, all by herself, when it's so dark and damp..."

James' smile stayed in place as he shook his head. "I am afraid not, my dear. Your devotion to your sister is admirable, but I could not presume on Clara in such a way."

*Of course not*, Sarah thought bitterly. He did not presume on Clara at all. For the next few minutes she busied herself in making the driest corner of the kitchen as comfortable for Lucy as she could, piling the blankets high and plumping the pillows. It still looked like a sad little nest of covers, but there was nothing else she could do.

"Well, then, Lucy." She turned to her sister with a smile and Lucy gave her a puzzled frown in response, her gaze searching her face, looking for answers, for reassurance. Here was something Lucy did not understand. Sarah knew her sister could not fathom her ever leaving her in such a way, and she had no memory of a father, so she wouldn't even understand why Sarah had to sleep with this man who had entered their lives so abruptly and then taken complete control.

"I must go upstairs with Mr Mills," she explained. "James. And you will sleep here."

Lucy stared at her wide-eyed for a long moment, her body as taut as a wire, and then she frantically shook her head.

"It must be this way, Lucy," Sarah said softly. "Be a good

girl for me, please. I'll be here first thing in the morning, I promise, to wake you up and make breakfast. We shall have a lovely
time together, then."

Lucy shook her head harder and then scrabbled at Sarah's
sleeve, her mouth working as if she were trying to form words.

A pressure built in Sarah's chest, a sob so strong she felt as if
her whole body would shake with it. She swallowed it down.
"You'll be all right," she said, drawing her sister into a quick,
fierce hug. Lucy clung, refusing to let go as Sarah tried to with-
draw. "Lucy..." Sarah knew James was waiting, and he might be
cross if she kept him for too long. She did not want to anger her
husband on their wedding night. "Please," she whispered.
"We're safe here, aren't we? We can be happy. You must be
good for me, please. Just at night, Please, Lucy." But Lucy
wouldn't let go and Sarah had to pry her sister off her, tears
spilling down her cheeks as she took a forceful step away.
"Goodnight, Lucy," she said as firmly as she could, her voice
breaking.

Lucy stared at her for one long, terrible moment, and then
she hurled herself onto the floor, banging her head against the
stone.

"Lucy... please!" Sarah reached for her shoulder but Lucy
shrugged away, distraught.

"Sarah," James called from upstairs, a touch of impatience
to his voice.

"I'll be back," Sarah promised her sister, her voice choked,
and with no choice but to obey her husband's summons, she
turned and left Lucy in the kitchen, closing and locking the
door behind her, everything in her resisting such a heartless
measure.

Upstairs she stood with a hand on the knob of the bedroom
door, wiping the tears from her cheeks. Taking a deep breath,
she opened the door and went inside.

Hours later, with her body aching in unfamiliar places and

the whole business of being a wife pulsing through her like a bad dream, she crept downstairs to check on Lucy.

From the flickering light of the candle she held, Sarah could see that her sister had not moved from her spot on the hard floor where she'd thrown herself, and she did not respond when Sarah crept closer.

"Lucy... *Lucy!*" Sarah shook her sister's shoulder and, wearily, Lucy lifted her head. Sarah stifled a cry at the sight of her sister's face, a huge, purple bruise marring her forehead and her lip bitten through and crusted with dried blood. She must have been hitting her head against the floor for hours, trapped in her own frightened misery. "Oh, Lucy," Sarah whispered. "What are we to do?" With tears starting in her eyes she gathered her sister up in her arms and brought her to the nest of blankets, where she stayed till morning, cradling her and grieving for all they'd both lost, and all they'd hoped to have.

# CHAPTER 15

## ELLEN

The Monday of half-term, Ellen rang up the chair of Goswell's historical society, a man she knew only by sight, and explained about the death certificate.

"How fascinating," he said, a note of laughter in his voice. "It seems like people are finding all sorts of interesting things in their houses. First Jane, and then Marin, and now you."

"Oh yes, Marin found something in her garden, didn't she?" Ellen said. She felt silly for a moment, as if she was just chasing a trend. "Well, this is probably nothing. My husband, Alex, has the dullest reason why it would have ended up there, and I'm sure he's right. But I thought it would be fun to look into it."

"Of course. I can do some digging, see who lived in your house before you. 1872, you say?"

"Yes, that's right."

"I'll have a look through our files and records and get back to you in a day or two."

Ellen thanked him and rang off, turning to see Annabelle coming into the kitchen. Since Saturday she felt as if they'd silently agreed on a truce; Annabelle hadn't been particularly chatty or friendly, but she'd ceased – mostly – with her theatrical sulks and sneers. They'd all had a good time out at the pub on Saturday night, or at least Ellen thought they had; Alex had asked Alyssa about her course and Annabelle had become a bit animated when she learned Alyssa was doing English, since that was one of her subjects. Alyssa had made things easier, too, by being friendly and relaxed, joking with Annabelle about the various teachers and horrors of Copeland Academy.

"Is the girls' bathroom by the gym still a cesspit? The toilets always overflowed. It was like something out of Harry Potter, Moaning Myrtle included."

"Yeah, no one goes in there," Annabelle had answered, looking more animated than Ellen had ever seen her. "It's revolting."

"Completely," Alyssa had agreed. Content to let them criticise the school, Ellen had sat back with her glass of wine and breathed a sigh of relief.

This morning Alyssa had taken the train back to York – without any more discussion about visiting her father – and Alex had gone back to work. Ellen was left with two very different daughters to manage, and she hoped she could find something to interest them both.

"So." She turned to Annabelle, who was coming downstairs. "I was just speaking to the man who runs the local historical society. He's going to try to find out who lived here back in 1872. Perhaps it will tell us something about the death certificate, and why it was under your floor."

"Mmm," Annabelle said without any enthusiasm, and reached for the cereal.

Ellen watched her, battling a familiar frustration. Now that the weekend was over and the fun people had left, would Annabelle be back to her old tricks? Judging by the way she was slouching around the kitchen, trailing cereal all over the floor and seeming not to notice, Ellen suspected that might be the case.

"So I thought we could visit my grandfather today," Ellen said, and Annabelle turned to look at her, clearly appalled by this suggestion. "He's in a nursing home near Whitehaven and he loves having visitors. He's eighty-seven but fit as a fiddle, for the most part, anyway. His memory is starting to go a little bit."

"Why would I want to visit him?" Annabelle asked in a *well-duh* tone that Ellen did her best to ignore, telling herself in actuality there was no compelling reason for a teenaged girl to want to visit her stepmother's grandfather.

"Because he's lovely," she said firmly. "And funny, and he might know something about this house and who lived here."

"He wasn't alive in 1872," Annabelle pointed out in the same *well-duh* tone. "And anyway, who cares who lived in this house?"

Yes, Unpleasant Annabelle was back in full force. "I care," Ellen replied, as nicely as she could. "And you might care, if you look into it properly. You could do a history project on it—"

"We're studying the French Revolution."

"An EPQ, then," Ellen insisted, remembering the Extended Project Qualification from Alyssa's sixth form. "They're as good as an AS exam. You could do one on the history of the house or women's roles in Victorian England – why do you think Sarah Mills died so young, anyway? Twenty-two years old. That's not much older than you, Annabelle, and the only reason was 'General Debility', whatever that means. Who knows what kind of life she had?"

Annabelle stared at her, and Ellen could see she'd snagged her interest just a little, even if she didn't want to admit it. Deciding it was better not to press the point, Ellen stayed silent, bustling around the kitchen and avoiding Annabelle's gaze.

"Fine," Annabelle relented, and Ellen only just kept herself from doing a little victory dance. "But we're not staying long, are we?"

Half an hour later, Ellen, Sophie, and Annabelle were

walking into the nursing home on the edge of Whitehaven, a pleasant, one-storey building that overlooked the town, the harbour glinting in the distance. Tulips filled the borders, and a small garden with a few chairs and benches stretched to the side of the building with a view of the sea.

Annabelle took it all in and gave a theatrical shudder. "I'd hate to live in a place like this. I'd rather you shot me first."

*I just might*, Ellen answered silently as she held the door open for both girls. The smell of antiseptic and old age wafted towards them, and Ellen admitted Annabelle might have a point. She couldn't imagine living here, either.

"Great-Granddad likes it here, though, doesn't he?" Sophie said as she skipped ahead of them. "He always seems so happy."

"Granddad is the most cheerful person I know," Ellen answered as they signed in at the reception desk and then headed towards her grandfather's room. "And he hasn't had an easy life, mind." Annabelle didn't respond and Ellen felt compelled to explain, "He was born in the 1930s to a single mum at a time when that kind of thing was very much frowned upon. He grew up with it hanging over his head, and during the War – the Second World War – he and his mum, Flora, were taken in by the vicar and his wife. The Jameses." It was actually Jane who had discovered all of that, when she'd been researching that old shopping list. Ellen hadn't even known, because her granddad had never liked to talk about the past. Learning about it had made her appreciate his sunny attitude all the more.

"Hello, Granddad." Ellen stepped into the room, raising her voice a little, for in addition to some bouts of memory loss, James was going a little deaf. His smile, however, was as wide and welcoming as ever.

"Why, hello! And whoever can this pretty young lady be?" he said to Sophie, who grinned up at him.

"Granddad, you know who I am."

"I certainly do. But I'm afraid I don't know this lovely young lady." He smiled at Annabelle, who was hanging back by the doorway, looking uncertain. "Who might you be?"

Ellen could tell her grandfather already sensed the troubled dynamics between Annabelle and her simply by his determined smile.

"Granddad, this is..." For a second she paused, struggling with how to introduce Annabelle. *Alex's daughter* made it sound as if she was trying to distance herself from Annabelle, but *my stepdaughter* didn't sound right either. She barely knew Annabelle. Trying to call her her daughter would surely only annoy. "Annabelle," she finished when the silence had gone on a couple of seconds too long, and Annabelle gave her an angry little smirk, as if she'd expected Ellen to mess up at that point but was still annoyed by it. Mentally, Ellen heaved a great big sigh. Sometimes she really felt like she couldn't get anything right.

"Annabelle," James repeated genially. "Pleased to meet you. I'm James."

Ellen realised she couldn't be sure if she'd ever even mentioned Annabelle to her grandfather before. She'd been visiting him once a week for years, but had she ever even said that Alex had a daughter? And what about when Annabelle had come to stay ten years ago? Ellen racked her memory to think what she might have said, but her grandmother, Doreen, had been alive then and she had a feeling she and James had been travelling in their caravan that summer. Twelve years of marriage and she'd never thought to mention that her husband had a daughter. That she was going to stay with them for a summer.

The realisation gave Ellen a cringing sense of guilt mixed with annoyance that she couldn't untangle. It was all just so *complicated*. For James, however, it was amazingly simple. Annabelle was a pretty young woman who had come to visit him, and he was happy to engage her in conversation, asking about her school subjects, her friends (Ellen hadn't even known she'd made any, but apparently Annabelle was hanging out with a girl named Trix). Annabelle gave reluctant, monosyllabic answers but James wasn't deterred.

It was only when Ellen attempted to insert herself into the conversation that it all derailed. Of course. "Annabelle is staying with us for a year," Ellen explained when an awkward silence had descended onto the room. "While she finishes her A-Levels." This received a venomous look from Annabelle.

"That's right, I'm *staying*," she practically hissed, and Ellen blinked, utterly nonplussed. What had she said now?

James deftly turned the conversation to Sophie, who was happy to tell him all about her latest Brownie exploits, until a half hour had passed and Ellen realised she hadn't mentioned anything about the death certificate and who might have once lived in their house.

Quickly, as she could see her grandfather was fading, Ellen explained what they'd found. "So do you remember who lived in our house, Granddad? When you were a boy?"

James screwed up his face in concentration as he considered the question. "Let's see... you and Alex are in that terraced cottage across from the Walkers', is that right?"

"Yes, that's right." The Walkers were an elderly couple who had been living in their bungalow since Ellen could remember. Florence Walker had used to slip her boiled sweets when she'd walked past on her way to school.

"The Dillons lived in it back when I was a lad," James said. "They rented it from the people up at Moreton Hall."

"Moreton Hall? But didn't that used to be a hotel?" It was empty now, a huge, Gothic wreck of a place with a commanding view of the sea. Ellen always thought it was a shame it was empty; it must once have been incredibly lovely.

"Yes, it was a hotel after the War, when they had to sell up.

Nobody could afford those grand places any more. But back in the thirties and before that a couple lived there – Lord and Lady something, why can't I remember it now? They used to give presents to all the schoolchildren at Christmas." He shook his head ruefully. "It's not easy getting old, I'll tell you."

"I can sympathise," Ellen replied with a smile. "I'm always forgetting things. Can't keep my own head screwed on most days."

"She is," Sophie chimed in helpfully. "She forgot about the meringues for the bake sale the other week. *And* she forgot I had a ballet performance once. I needed a sparkly tutu and a tiara, and we didn't have *either*—"

"I think Granddad gets the point, Soph," Ellen interjected hurriedly. She caught Annabelle's eye and saw her step-daughter was smiling a little. Ellen smiled back and Annabelle looked away. "Well, the Dillons in the 1930s. I'll see if that registers anything with the historical society. It would have been sixty years before Sarah Mills' time, but you never know."

"1872 is a little before my time," James teased. "I'm not that old, you know!"

"I know, Granddad." Ellen rose to kiss his cheek. She could tell her grandfather was getting tired by the way his eyelids had started to droop. "We'll come next week, all right?"

"All of you, I hope," James answered as he patted Ellen's hand. He aimed a smile at Annabelle. "I want to hear how you did on that history essay, young lady."

Annabelle looked startled, and she stammered out some-thing before they turned to go. Ellen always felt a pang of sorrow for leaving her grandfather there; with her parents down in Dorset, he didn't get many visitors. No matter how many bingo evenings or craft sessions the home put on, it was still a lonely life.

Annabelle and Sophie must have felt something similar, for they were both quiet as they headed out to the car.

"Do you have grandparents on your mother's side, Annabelle?" Ellen asked as they got into the car. She knew Alex's parents had both died before she'd met him.

Annabelle shook her head. "Mum was raised in foster care. She doesn't have any family."

"Foster care?" For some reason this disconcerted her – perhaps because she didn't like feeling any sympathy for Sandra Tyson. "How sad."

Annabelle shrugged, her face turned towards the window. "Mum said it made her strong. Strong enough not to put up with any of Dad's crap." She bit her lip, as if she regretted saying it, but then she slid Ellen a sly look to gauge her response.

With effort Ellen kept her expression neutral. *Alex's crap.* What did *that* mean? Again she felt that twisting unease that she knew so little about Alex's marriage. All he'd ever said was that Sandra had decided she was finished with it. Ellen had been happy to leave it at that, more than happy to blame the far away stranger Sandra, the over-the-top feminist who *sounded* unreasonable, for everything. But what if there was more to the story? Could she cope with some kind of terrible revelation?

"Well," she finally said, struggling to keep her voice light as she pulled out onto the road that led to Goswell, "I wouldn't wish foster care on anyone. It's got to be incredibly difficult to grow up without a family."

Annabelle disappeared upstairs as soon as they got home, and feeling a need to do something fun for half-term, Ellen got out the mixing bowls and scales and made fairy cakes with Sophie before turning her attention to tea. Alex came home just as she was sliding a lasagne into the oven, smiling as he sniffed the air.

"Lasagne?"

"You guessed it." Ellen closed the oven door. "You're home early."

"Well, it is half-term. How was Annabelle today?"

Even though the question was entirely warranted, Ellen could not quite suppress a little sting of hurt that he was asking about Annabelle rather than Sophie. *Get over yourself, Ellen*, she thought crossly. "Pretty good, actually."

Alex arched an eyebrow. "Actually?"

"Yes, actually," Ellen returned. "It hasn't been easy going, as you very well know."

Alex was silent, and Ellen tensed, feeling as if they were on the verge of starting a full-blown fight *again*, and part of her almost wanted it. Stupidly, because they were finally all getting along, more or less. Why rock the boat now? Alex's "crap" still rang through her mind, wanting answers.

"I know that," Alex said quietly, and Ellen deflated a little.

"We went to see my granddad. It was nice."

"Good."

"What did you talk about at the beach, anyway? Because she seems to have turned a page since then, thankfully."

Alex shrugged. "I just said I was glad she was here, and I hoped we could spend time together."

Which he should have said in the beginning, but never mind. Ellen blew out a breath. "Well, good. It seems to have worked. For the moment." She thought about asking Alex about Sandra, about his crap, but now was definitely not the time, and in truth she wasn't sure she had the strength for that conversation.

Tea passed uneventfully enough, with Sophie excited about her fairy cakes, and Annabelle deigning to eat one and pronounce that they were "all right".

"Hey, Annabelle," Alex said casually as Ellen was clearing up. "I thought we could go to the cinema in Workington to see a film tonight."

Everyone stilled, all shocked by this suggestion, unexceptional as it might have been in a normal situation. Annabelle looked warily at her father for a few seconds before saying, "I'm not sure there's anything decent on."

"There must be something," Alex said. "And I'll even watch a chick flick if necessary."

A small smile tugged at Annabelle's mouth and she nodded. "OK."

"Great." He slid out his phone. "I'll check the show times."

"Sounds like a nice evening," Ellen said. Not that he'd said a word to her about going out, or leaving her and Sophie alone. Not that it mattered, not in the grand scheme of things. It was much more important for Alex to bond with his daughter. She got that. She really did.

"There's a film on in half an hour," Alex said, and handed the phone to Annabelle so she could look.

"Oh, I've heard of that," she said. "It's supposed to be all right."

"We'd better get a move on, then," Alex said, and rose from the table. Annabelle did too, and Ellen watched them, trying to mask her incredulity that this was all happening without so much as a glance in her direction, that after having just arrived home, Alex was leaving again.

"We'll be back around ten," Alex called over his shoulder, and Ellen's eyes narrowed as Annabelle tossed her a catlike smile before disappearing down the hall, after her father.

"Well, Soph. Looks like we're on our own tonight." Taking a deep breath, Ellen took a load of dirty dishes and dumped them in the sink.

# CHAPTER 16

## SARAH

Kendal, 1868

After that first terrible night Sarah began to leave her marriage bed as soon as James was asleep, and creep downstairs to sleep with Lucy in the kitchen. It was the only way she knew how to keep Lucy from retreating even further into the solitary darkness of her mind; the livid bruises on her face that first morning after had shocked both James and Clara.

"I didn't realise she'd hurt herself," James said in a low voice while Lucy stared straight ahead, her porridge untouched, as if some vital part of her had withdrawn from the world. It had taken hours for her sister to stop shaking as Sarah had held her in the night, whispering reassurances and promises she desperately wanted to be able to keep.

"She's not used to being alone," she told James, her voice stiff. No matter what intimacies had passed between them the night before, she did not know this man. She was no longer sure if she even liked him.

"I'm sorry," James said, and she thought she saw true contrition in his eyes. "If I'd known how agitated she would become..."

"Then can she sleep upstairs, James?" Sarah asked, her voice edged with desperation. "Please? Even if it's just in the hall? She needs to be nearer to people, to me..."

For a wonderful few seconds, Sarah thought he was going to relent. His face softened, and his gaze flicked to Lucy, an unhappy frown settling between his eyebrows. Then Clara snorted, a most inelegant sound.

"In the hall? Really, I don't know what our household has come to," she murmured, and took a sip of tea. From the corner of her eye Sarah saw Clara's blue eyes light up with spite, and she had to keep herself from reacting. Her hand itched to give the girl a good slap, a slap she certainly deserved.

James's mouth pursed and he shook his head. "She needs to know her place, Sarah. If we give way in this, she will take all sorts of liberties."

Liberties? What kind of liberties could Lucy take? He made her sister sound like a beast that needed to be tamed, or a wild dog to be kept under control with well-placed kicks.

"The sofa, then..." she began, only to have James shake his head.

"No, Sarah. She is quite comfortable where she is."

Sarah bit her lips to keep from saying something sharp that she knew would do her cause no good. After less than a day of marriage she was beginning to see her husband's flaws; kind though he could be, like nearly every other man she'd encountered, he did not like to be opposed.

She had, at least, washed the kitchen, scrubbing the walls and floor, sweeping the corners free of dust and spiders, and laying traps for the beetles and other vermin that were a constant threat in the damp, draughty house, so close to the river. It made the room a bit more habitable for Lucy, but it still tore at Sarah's heart to leave her alone there every night. Lucy's wild desperation of the first night had been replaced by an even more alarming stoic bleakness. It was all too easy to become accustomed to suffering.

Sleeping on the hard floor and creeping to and from bed every night left Sarah aching with exhaustion, stumbling through the long days of housework and laundry. James's decision not to employ a maid left Sarah with more work than she'd ever had before. Once again she realised how much Aunt Edith had worked, for in addition to the dusting and polishing Sarah had done at Lowther Street, she now had to make all the meals, do all the laundry, and keep up with darning, shirt-making, and all the other tasks a household required. And despite James's desire for his daughter to learn the gentle ways of domestic life, Clara was no help at all.

After that first day, Sarah had not bothered to ask Clara to help her. It irritated her, how the girl would drift about the house in her ridiculously frothy dresses, but she felt a surprising stab of pity for her as well. She was nearly fifteen years old, plain-faced and fancily dressed, and with absolutely nowhere to go. James's social circle seemed non-existent; besides a few well-meaning neighbours, it did not seem Clara or James had any friends, and Sarah felt the lack.

"When your mother was alive," Sarah asked Clara one afternoon as she dusted the sitting room while Clara simply lazed indolently on the sofa, "did you go out together? To visit with friends?"

Clara shook her head. "Mother was too poorly."

"Our mother was poorly too," Sarah said, glad to have a point of sympathy with the girl, even if Clara would not acknowledge it. "But you must have friends from school?"

Clara shrugged. "I went to Miss Elizabeth Wade's Ladies' Boarding School for a little while. Most of the girls weren't from Kendal, and I stopped when I was thirteen."

"What about the girls who were from Kendal?"

Another shrug, the movement restless and discontented. "It's not as if I could invite anyone here, is it?" Her gaze moved around the small, crowded room before settling on Lucy, who was sitting quietly on the piano bench, her doll on her lap. Since coming to River Cottage, Lucy had fewer episodes, which would have been a relief if Sarah hadn't felt she was losing her sister in increments.

"Especially with *her* always sitting in the corner," Clara continued, her voice rising to a high quaver. "Staring with her bulgy eyes. She'd scare anyone off. She'll have to be shut in the kitchen if a suitor ever comes to call!"

Sarah jerked back as if Clara had slapped her. She felt assaulted, shocked by the viciousness of Clara's words. She moved to Lucy, putting one arm around her protectively. "Lucy is no harm to anyone," she said in a low voice. "Not like you, with your hateful words. I don't suppose you will get so much as a single suitor with a tongue like yours." As soon as she'd said the words, Sarah regretted them. She watched Clara's eyes widen and thought she saw a gleam of triumph light them before she leaned forward and yanked hard on Lucy's plait.

Sarah let out a shocked gasp as Lucy clapped one hand to the side of her head, her eyes wide with surprise and pain.

"You wicked girl," Sarah burst out before she could help herself. "What has Lucy ever done to you?"

Clara glared at her for a long moment, a small, vindictive smile curving her mouth, and then without bothering to reply, she flounced out of the room, slamming the door behind her.

"Lucy... oh, Lucy." Sarah sank onto the piano bench next to Lucy and drew her into her arms. Lucy sniffed and shivered, burrowing her head into Sarah's shoulder. Sarah closed her eyes.

Why had Clara been so horrible? Sarah knew the girl must resent her presence, but to take it out on *Lucy*...

But that, of course, was the best way to hurt Sarah, and

Clara had known it. Clara must truly hate her, to act in such a way. Sarah closed her eyes, overcome with regret and sorrow. In the month since she'd married James she had felt adrift, uncertain, trying to salvage the situation for both her and her sister and find some fragile happiness.

There had been good moments, although admittedly few. James had taken them out to tea one Saturday, and she and Lucy had enjoyed scones with jam and clotted cream, as well as dainty little chocolate cakes. He'd bought Sarah a new shawl, a lovely lace thing that must have cost him dearly, and Lucy a little wooden dog on wheels that she'd played with for hours.

He laughed easily and often, and seemed pleased with her efforts at cookery, always complimenting her on her meals, even when the potatoes were lumpy or the meat overcooked, which unfortunately happened more than Sarah would have liked.

And yet despite all these kindnesses, James could be remarkably unaware of the struggles Sarah endured. He did not seem to see anything amiss with their domestic arrangements, the lack of a maid or a modern range, even though Sarah suspected he could afford both. He was, despite having seen Lucy's bruises, perfectly content for her to stay in the kitchen. He had no friends that she knew of; no one called at the house and the shopkeepers viewed her with more pity than she liked. Several times she'd been tempted to ask what they knew that she didn't, but she was too proud to admit her ignorance.

Now, with Clara having turned against Lucy as well as herself, Sarah wondered if it would have been better, far better, for her and Lucy to rub along together in a set of rented rooms, taking in sewing and eking out Reverend Cooper's twenty-five pounds than live like this.

And what if Clara made trouble with James, and told her father what Sarah had said to her? Sarah did not want to risk her husband's ire. She found him difficult to deal with already, never knowing when his easy smile would slide into a frown, when his relaxed manner would change into stiff disapproval.

She discovered the truth later that night, as she was bringing the veal collops to the table, and Clara rushed to the front door the moment James entered.

"Papa, Papa," she cried, the plaintive wail of a child, and Sarah tensed. She glanced at Lucy, who stared back at her unblinkingly. From the parlour Sarah heard lowered voices, Clara's disconsolate tones and James's replies. She could not make out any words, and she realised she had no idea how he would respond to Clara's complaints. She had been married to the man for nearly a month, and she did not understand him at all.

Her heart began to thud as she heard James's heavy tread towards the kitchen. Dear heaven, what if he hit her? She knew some husbands did, although her own father had been gentle and adoring to her mother. She had not incurred James's anger yet, merely a few frowns, but he indulged Clara so... Her hands shook as she reached for a dish of boiled potatoes. Lucy, sensing her agitation, sidled closer to her, sticking her thumb in her mouth.

James did not come to the kitchen, though. In truth it was a women's room, and one he rarely visited. Managing to steady her hands, Sarah brought the potatoes to the table.

James did not smile at her as she came in the dining room, but neither did he frown or glower. The meal passed in silence, as it often did, and Sarah felt her nerves stretch tighter and tighter, in expectation of what was to come. The trouble was, she had no idea what.

After supper James retired to the parlour, and Clara played the piano while Sarah and Lucy did the dishes as usual. As she wiped the plates clean in the kitchen, one sputtering gas jet their only light, Sarah flitted between gratitude to be on her own and resentment that James continued to treat her like a skivvy.

She let out a heavy sigh, only to have Lucy still her with one hand on her arm.

"What is it, Lucy?" Sarah asked, and silently, always silently, Lucy put her arms around Sarah and held her in a wordless embrace of comfort.

That evening, after she'd said goodnight to Lucy and headed upstairs, a candle in her hand, James confronted her. Sarah had just closed the door to their bedroom, steeling herself for what was ahead, when he spoke, his voice unusually clipped.

"Clara mentioned you had harsh words with her this afternoon."

Sarah tensed, one hand on the door, the other holding the candle. "Yes," she said at last. "We did."

James didn't speak for a moment and Sarah moved from the door, determined to keep busy rather than give in to the fear fluttering in her breast. She had changed into her nightdress, plaited her hair, and was about to slip between the covers when James, already in his nightshirt and observing all of her movements, finally spoke.

"I know Clara is spoiled," he said quietly. Sarah stilled, the candle sending flickering shadows over the bed covers. "I indulge her because she is all I have. All I had," he corrected swiftly, with a small smile for Sarah. She stared at him blankly for a few seconds before she grasped his meaning; he had *her* now. Sarah said nothing and James went on, "We lost many children, Amanda and I. That is, my first wife. Six, altogether." His mouth turned down, his face drawn into such sad lines that Sarah felt a surprising urge to comfort him. This was not what she'd expected at all. She almost put a hand on his sleeve, something to convey her compassion, but she did not quite have the courage.

"I'm sorry..." she began hesitantly.

"It wasn't easy," James continued, his gaze distant now. "And Amanda... it cost her her health. Her life. But as a result, Clara is very precious to me." His gaze refocused on her, and Sarah trembled inwardly at the coolness she saw there. Here, then, was the rebuke she'd been waiting for.

"You must be patient with her, Sarah. You must bear with her girlish ways. I cannot allow anything else." An implacable note had entered his voice and Sarah nodded jerkily.

James seemed to believe the matter was finished, and yet Sarah knew she could not leave it at that. Not after the way Clara had treated Lucy so cruelly. "James..." she began, her voice sounding thin and papery. "It's only... I worry for Lucy."

James's eyebrows snapped together. "What on earth can you mean?"

"Clara..." She faltered under James's stern gaze. "She was unkind to Lucy."

His gaze did not yield. "It is your duty to keep both Clara and Lucy occupied," he said. Sarah blinked. "They are under your care, and you must see to their needs. Now." He leaned over her to blow out the candle. "I trust I've made myself clear."

Sarah nodded as darkness descended on the room and the lumpy hair mattress shifted beneath James's settling weight. She slipped down beneath the covers and squeezed her eyes shut, grateful that their argument – if it could indeed be considered such – kept James from reaching for her. Instead he rolled over onto his side and Sarah lay there, miserable, her heart so heavy she wondered how she could even breathe.

She drew a shuddering breath, willing the tears back. At least she and Lucy were safe. They had shelter, food, clothing. And James could be kind. As for Clara...

A shudder escaped her, halfway to an unruly sob, a sound she hadn't made in a decade. She amazed herself, making it now. Being that weak. That sad.

"Sarah."

James's voice in the darkness had her stiffening in alarm. Had he heard? Would he be angry?

"Sarah," he said again, gently, and then he reached for her. Sarah remained tense, silent and unresisting to his fumbling caresses. But then she realised he was not attempting to assert his husbandly rights – no, he was actually hugging her. Comforting her. His hands found her cheeks and he wiped away her tears with his thumbs.

"I do not wish to make you sad," he whispered.

"I'm sorry," Sarah whispered back, because she did not know what else to say. She could beg for him to relent and let Lucy sleep upstairs, but she feared raising that yet again would only make him angry. And as for Clara... he'd made his position clear there.

No, she realised as James drew her into a deeper embrace, here was the paradox of her husband. He did not wish to make her sad but he would anyway... and there was nothing, it seemed, that she could do about it.

# CHAPTER 17

## ELLEN

After Alex and Annabelle had left for the cinema and Sophie was in bed, Ellen got out her laptop, poured a large glass of wine, and retreated to the conservatory to spend some time on the internet. She felt anxious and yet resolute as she opened up Facebook and typed Sandra Tyson into the search box. This was new, unfamiliar territory, not actually forbidden but dangerous. And she wasn't even sure why she was doing it, why she wanted to know.

Had it been Annabelle's "Alex's crap" comment, or the revelation that Alex's ex-wife had grown up in foster care, or simply the complete absence of any knowledge of this woman that was now sending her diving off the precipice of ignorance into the huge, seething sea of internet searches?

There were hundreds of Sandra Tysons. A scientist in Glasgow, a housewife in Georgia. A drunken selfie of a university student in Nottingham. A human rights activist in India. Ellen scrolled through them all, gazing at all the different Sandra Tysons of the world and not seeing someone who had the University of Manchester under their name.

Of course, Alex's Sandra – how she hated to think like that – might not have a Facebook account. She might not link her name to her profession. And her name might not be Sandra Tyson at all. Women's Studies lecturer that she was, perhaps she'd reverted to her maiden name. And Ellen had no idea what that was.

She laid her hands on the keyboard, unsure how to proceed since Facebook hadn't panned out. She could see if Annabelle had a page and was friends with her mother, but it felt a little too much like cyber stalking. And what did she really want to accomplish here? If she wanted to know something about Sandra or her marriage to Alex, she needed to ask her husband.

With a sigh Ellen closed the laptop and pushed it away. She tucked her knees up to her chest and sipped her wine as she gazed out at the twilit garden. Maybe she needed a project. She could plant a vegetable patch again, since the weather had been so fantastic, although it was a little late to sow from seed. Or she could focus on her freelancing which was already going apace, update her website, send letters out to universities and publishing houses advertising her services. So far she'd just depended on word of mouth, but maybe she should think about stepping it up another notch, especially since Sophie would be going to secondary school in another year.

Another year. Then Sophie would start at Copeland and Annabelle would be going to university and things would be back to normal. Except the trouble was, Ellen didn't even know what normal was any more. She had a sinking feeling they couldn't go back. Annabelle's entrance into their lives had created too many questions, shone a glaring light on too many uncertainties. She needed answers, even if she'd rather let things lie.

Draining her glass of wine, Ellen reached for her laptop again. This time she typed Kendal Historical Society into the search engine, and with a few clicks she'd reached the email address of the society's secretary. Before she could think too much about it, she fired off a quick email.

*Hello,*

*I am a resident of Goswell and I have found a death certificate from 1872 in Kendal under my attic floorboards. I was curious about the woman named on it and I wondered if you could help.*

   *Her name was Sarah Mills and she lived at River Cottage, Kendal. She died of General Debility in 1872. If you could point me in the right direction of how to research more about her life, I'd be very grateful.*

*Many thanks,*

*Ellen Tyson*

There. Ellen shut the laptop again. That was something, at least. Maybe she'd find something about this Sarah Mills, something she could share with Annabelle. Although what she could find that would be interesting or encouraging, she didn't know. Sarah Mills's short life seemed like a tragedy that had had its full enactment over a hundred years ago. If the Kendal Historical Society came up with anything, it would probably just be a footnote to what Ellen suspected was exactly what it seemed: a young woman living in a difficult time who died of illness or perhaps just hard work. Still, she supposed with a sigh, it would be good to know. Jane had found something encouraging in Alice James's quiet life; perhaps Ellen could source her own inspiration from the unknown Sarah Mills.

Ellen was in bed by the time Alex and Annabelle returned, propped against her pillows and attempting to read the latest literary tome for her book club. She'd been stuck on the same page for a quarter of an hour, unable to find the frame of mind to appreciate the poetic prose.

Alex came in quietly, tiptoeing, and Ellen lowered her book. "How was the film?"

"Oh, you're awake."

"It's only ten."

"I know." He shrugged out of his jacket and Ellen watched it fall to the floor with pursed lips.

"Well?"

"It was fine. Good, actually, for a chick flick. Annabelle seemed to like it."

"Good."

And then silence, a silence that felt strained, at least to Ellen, as Alex began to get ready for bed. He smelled of popcorn.

What was she waiting for? What would ease this tension coiling inside her, this restless, latent anger that she didn't really understand? A *thanks for understanding*, maybe, or an admission that he should have checked beforehand about haring off to the cinema the moment tea was finished.

Or maybe she just needed to relax. Chill, as Alyssa or even Sophie would say. Annabelle, too. *Chillax, Ellen. It's no big deal.*

"Do you think you could spend some time with Sophie this week?" she asked. "Maybe go for a bike ride up to Nethertown?"

Alex sighed, his shoulders slumping, and Ellen wondered why this had been the wrong thing to say.

"Yes, Ellen," he said and she tensed at his dutiful tone. "I'll spend time with Sophie."

The next morning Ellen found an email in her inbox from the Kendal Historical Society.

"That was quick," she murmured as she took a sip of coffee,

a leap of excitement in her belly. She realised she really did want to find out something about Sarah Mills.

*Dear Ellen,*

*Thank you so much for your enquiry. A death certificate – how fascinating! Any idea how it came to be in your attic in Goswell? I can do some digging on our end, but I can tell you now that River Cottage was torn down nearly a hundred years ago. As for Sarah Mills, it is obviously a common name and I'll have a look through the archives to see if I can find anything, but you might have more luck looking through the parish registers, if you fancy coming up to Kendal for the day.*

*Best regards,*

*Ian Fletcher*

"Hmm." She wasn't actually any closer to finding something out about Sarah Mills, but perhaps she could be. "Hey, Soph." Her daughter looked up from her bowl of cereal, eyebrows raised in expectation. "How do you feel about visiting Kendal today?"

An hour later they were in the car heading south. Ellen had decided to go the scenic route rather than head up to Penrith and down to Kendal on the M6.

"Have you ever been to Windermere?" she asked Annabelle, who gave a shrugging non-answer as she tapped a text out on her phone. Annabelle hadn't wanted to come to Kendal, but Ellen had cheerfully insisted, promising lunch out and a trip to the shopping area as well as a browse through the parish register – assuming the vicar was around and she could get access to it.

It was another gorgeous day if a bit chilly, the pale blue sky dotted with fleecy clouds, the sea sparkling and ruffled with white. Sophie bounced up and down in the back seat while Annabelle propped her trainer-shod feet on the dashboard.

"So why are we going to Kendal, Mum?"

"To find out about the woman named in the death certificate. Remember I showed it to you?"

"Ye-es..." Sophie sounded uncertain, and Annabelle picked up on it, lifting her head from her phone to roll her eyes at Sophie.

"Yeah, exactly. *Why* are we looking into this?"

"I thought you were interested," Ellen replied as mildly as she could.

"Not that interested. I mean, Kendal is what? An hour away?"

"More like an hour and a half," Ellen returned, and Annabelle let out a theatrical I-am-so-bored sigh. *Off to a good start, then.* "Why not go to Kendal?" Ellen challenged, trying to keep her voice mild. "What's the alternative? Sit in your room and watch YouTube?"

"Sounds loads better," Annabelle muttered.

"I wanted to see Merrie today," Sophie chimed in, her voice nearly matching Annabelle's for truculence.

"Well," Ellen said, and now she didn't sound so mild, "we're going to Kendal."

They didn't talk for the rest of the journey, and Ellen tried not to mind. Perhaps if she kept her expectations low, she'd feel less disappointed. Less hurt.

She parked in the public car park next to the church, and Sophie and Annabelle fell in behind her, dragging their feet, as she walked across the green and into the church.

It was bigger than she'd expected, although the website she'd briefly looked at that morning had informed her the church was large, with five aisles rather than the usual three, and a light, airy interior.

As she stepped inside, Ellen was struck by both the size and quiet. Goswell's church was considered large, but Kendal's dwarfed it. A few tourists were wandering around the aisles and side chapels, and a steward by the entrance gave them a welcoming smile.

What was she *doing* here?

Ellen took a few more steps in, breathing in the scents of polish and dust that seemed reminiscent of every church she'd ever been in. Not that she'd been in many – she'd gone to church in Goswell as a child and had been married there. Somehow in the normal busyness of everyday life she'd stopped going. Sophie hadn't even been baptised.

Now for a few seconds she wanted only to drink in the peace, to sink into one of the pews and let the tranquility wash over her, soak into her pores. Maybe then this unease, this unhappiness, would finally leave her, and she'd find her way back to how she used to be... cheerful, ever-optimistic, perfectly content Ellen Tyson. That was who she really was. She wanted to get back to that place again.

"Mum?" Sophie tugged on her sleeve, and Ellen looked down to see her daughter doing a proper sulk. "What are we doing here?" Behind her Annabelle stood, arms folded, one hip thrust out as she ostentatiously blew a strand of hair away from her eyes.

"We're going to try to find out about Sarah Mills, Soph." Ellen mustered a smile. "Why don't we take a look around?" Slipping her hand into Sophie's reluctant one, she started walking around the church. Annabelle, with a loud sigh, followed them.

It was, at least, an interesting church, with chapels for the Parr family and the Border Regiment, and plenty of fascinating memorials and stained glass to peruse. Ellen could have spent an hour simply wandering around and enjoying the peaceful space, but she acknowledged it wasn't exactly a thrill a minute for a teen and tween on a sunny morning in half-term.

And what were they doing there, really? Did she actually expect to stumble upon some clue to Sarah Mills's life among the hymnals and memorial plaques? Maybe Sarah hadn't attended this church. Maybe she'd been a Quaker or a Methodist or even a non-churchgoer, although in Victorian England Ellen supposed the last was somewhat unlikely. Although in reality she didn't know much about Victorian life. Unlike Annabelle, she hadn't done an A-Level in history.

"Mum." Sophie tugged on Ellen's sleeve again as she stood in front of the tomb of William Parr, the first baron Parr of Kendal. "Annabelle and me want to go now."

"Annabelle and I," Ellen corrected on a sigh. "Let me at least ask the steward about the parish registers." Although it seemed like searching for the proverbial needle in an ecclesiastical haystack.

The girls trailed her back to the front of the church, waiting with obvious impatience while Ellen stammered out an explanation of what she was looking for and why.

"Oh, we get loads in here asking about their ancestry," the woman said with a smile, to which Ellen replied, stammering even more, "Oh, I'm... I'm not actually related—"

"You can ask about the parish registers in the office," the steward explained. "They should be able to direct you."

With more sighs and even groans from the girls, Ellen went to the church office only to discover that all the old parish registers were kept next door, in Abbot Hall.

Determined now, she walked across the green to the hall, and there discovered that she needed to fill out a research access form to look at the parish registers from 1872 or any earlier.

Duly Ellen filled it out, although now she really wondered why was she was bothering. Jane hadn't had this sort of faff, she thought crossly as she handed the form in. She'd just nipped over to the church and the lovely vicar, Simon Truesdell, had found the information for her in a trice.

"Now can we please go shopping?" Annabelle asked in the martyred tone of someone who was about to be pushed past all endurance.

Ellen glanced at the entrance to the Museum of Lakeland Life & Industry, part of Abbot Hall, and then decided she'd pushed the girls enough.

"Very well," she said, and they headed to the market square and its shopping delights.

After a lunch at a pizza place, they browsed through the shops in the quaintly named Elephant Yard and Stricklandgate. Even with the neon and plastic of the modern shopfronts, Ellen could see hints of the old Kendal in the bow-fronted shops and narrow, cobblestoned yards. Her mind kept going back to Sarah Mills, wondering what kind of woman she'd been. Only twenty-two years old... had she been married or had a child? It would be common at that age, surely, in Victorian times. Who had mourned her besides the resident of her attic room back in Goswell?

A feeling of intangible melancholy settled over her at the thought of Sarah's short and unexceptional life, one she couldn't shake despite Sophie's smiling insistence that she try on a sparkly tiara, which Ellen gamely did, and Annabelle's improved mood after Ellen bought her a lipstick in shocking red.

Actually, she noted as they walked down Stricklandgate back towards the car, Annabelle and Sophie seemed to be getting along, despite the seven-year age gap. They'd bonded a little bit over make-up and jewellery, and while Ellen wasn't thrilled with the temporary tattoos Annabelle had suggested for Sophie, she was grateful for the reprieve from the tension and discontent.

Back at home, Annabelle and Sophie both disappeared upstairs and Ellen had to face the kitchen, the breakfast dishes still stacked by the sink, and tea to be made. All in all, it hadn't been a bad day. Despite Annabelle and Sophie's reluctance to be dragged through the aisles of the parish church, they'd both cheered up enough to have made the trip worthwhile. And Ellen had managed a few exchanges with Annabelle that hadn't been loaded or fraught. Nothing earth-shattering, just random comments about classes and fashion and pop music – not that Ellen knew any pop music, but while they'd been at the pizza place a song had come on that Annabelle and even Sophie had known, and they'd shared a complicit eye roll at Ellen's ignorance. But that was OK. She could be the butt of her jokes. It was better than everyone being at odds, surely.

Deciding the breakfast dishes could wait another hour, Ellen took her laptop out to the garden and, dusting off a canvas chair that hadn't been sat on for about ten months, she pulled her computer onto her laptop and typed *Sarah Mills Kendal 1872* into the search engine. Maybe she wouldn't have to wait for her research access permission. There were six hundred and sixteen thousand results, and after skimming the first few pages, Ellen didn't think any of them were relevant. She typed in *Sarah Mills Kendal History* instead, and got two million results that were even less relevant – history professors named Sarah, genealogy websites about families who had the name Mills. None of them could be her Sarah.

*Her Sarah.* Ellen let out a snort of disbelief. When had she started identifying with this unknown woman, and why?

Frowning, she rested her hands on the keyboard and tried to think of another way to get closer to the Sarah Mills of the death

certificate. She tried a bunch of different searches for Sarah
Mills, for River Cottage, for death certificates from 1872. Nothing. Why did she suppose one solitary person from nearly a
hundred and fifty years ago would have registered on the
internet?

"Mu-um?" Sophie called. "When's tea?"

"Soon," Ellen answered, although she hadn't even looked in
the fridge, and the breakfast dishes still waited. "Soon."

She drummed her fingers on the keyboard and a bunch of
random letters appeared in the search engine box, which she
duly deleted. Then she typed *Kendal Mills parish register
1870s* and waited.

The first result, a list of Kendal genealogy resources, seemed
promising. Mills had come up as a surname, along with the year
1871. Feeling a little irrepressible leap of excitement, Ellen
clicked on the link and then scrolled down the various lists and
documents in search of the elusive mention of Mills.

"Come on, Sarah," she murmured. "Where are you?"

But it wasn't Sarah Mills who was listed, Ellen realised
when she found the mention and clicked on the link. It was a
Lucy Mills, aged thirteen, from a register of inmates of the
Kendal workhouse. Ellen read the word "imbecile" next to her
name and frowned. *Imbecile?* Chilled, she opened another
browser window and typed *Imbecile Victorian definition.* She
came up with an encyclopedia entry: *Imbecile was a medical
term for people with moderate to serious intellectual disability.*

Which had Lucy Mills been? And had she been any relation to Sarah Mills, who had died just two years later?

"Mu-um," Sophie called, impatience edging her voice. Her
ten-year-old daughter was definitely working the tween vibe.

Ellen stared at the workhouse register for another moment,
amazed at how unsettled she felt. How sad. She didn't even
know if Lucy Mills was related to her Sarah. And yet... *imbecile.* Medical term it might have been, it still sounded callous

and cold-hearted. And to put someone with a mental disability in a *workhouse*...

"Mum!" One sharp note, a demand.

"Coming, Soph. Keep your hair on." With a sigh, Ellen closed her laptop and went to find something in the fridge to make for tea.

# CHAPTER 18

## SARAH

Kendal, 1869

A year passed, the days long and hard, the months slow, the weather grey. Nothing seemed to change, not Lucy's silence, not Clara's sly digs or sheer laziness, not James's smiling ease or lack of understanding.

Sarah swept and scrubbed and cooked and accepted James's surprising gifts – a dress that must have cost several pounds at least and was every bit as fancy as one of Clara's frocks – and a china doll for Lucy that was just as fancily dressed, and most likely just as expensive. In August they took a trip to Grange and spent three nights in an elegant hotel, strolling on the wide beach and eating meals in restaurants. Sarah had never known such luxury, and it both amazed and appalled her that people actually lived like this and were accustomed to it. And then they returned to Kendal and she swept and scrubbed and cooked.

The one real disappointment in all the months of house-work and drudgery was that she did not fall pregnant. She could tell James was disappointed by this lack in her, although of course they never discussed it. But every month or so he'd look at her with an expectant hopefulness that Sarah could not answer, and she washed her monthly rags along with all the other laundry, wondering if she would experience the same female troubles her mother had. In any case, she could not imagine caring for a baby along with all the work she did already, and there was no room for one in their cramped house, unless James insisted Clara share. Perhaps their baby would sleep in the kitchen with Lucy. In her darker moments, Sarah could countenance James suggesting such a thing.

That September, fourteen months after she'd first married, Sarah stood in church after the service and watched from the corner of her eye as Clara flirted with the curate on the front steps. She'd learned his name a while back – Andrew Fairley – and he always tried to have a kind word for her, even though Sarah treated him with the stiffest, coldest courtesy that she dared to. She did not speak to Reverend Cooper at all. In the almost year-and-a-half since her aunt's death the church had been reroofed.

A year had not added to Clara's beauty. Her jaw was still heavy, her hair still lank, and her overwrought clothes did her no favours. Yet as the year had dragged on, Sarah had come to the conclusion that only one thing could improve her and Lucy's situation: Clara's marriage.

With Clara out of the house, so many of the ills that had dogged her would finally abate. Clara would cease her sly torment of Lucy, and Lucy would, Sarah hoped, be able to sleep in Clara's bedroom. At night Sarah lay in bed and considered the life of veritable ease she could enjoy without Clara's malevolent presence. It was enough to make her smile in the darkness, envisioning that promising day.

Of course, the difficulty lay in finding someone to marry her – and someone Clara was willing to marry. Sarah supposed Clara could be made to look presentable enough, if she would only wear less ridiculous clothing and style her hair in a more becoming manner. She'd taken to curling her hair with tongs most mornings and the result was crimped, singed-looking curls that lay flat against her head.

And as for Clara's other charms... Sarah did not think she was unfairly biased in believing they were few. Clara did not possess any skill in the domestic arts, despite James's initial hope, and Sarah had stopped trying to get the girl to help in any way nearly from the beginning.

Beyond her lack of ability, she did not always present a pleasing manner. Her face often settled into a sulk, and what she seemed to consider flirting to Sarah seemed like an unpleasant simpering. Sarah could not see how a man might contrive to fall in love with her, or even believe she might make a suitable wife.

Yet it remained Sarah's only hope of improving the lot in life she'd first considered in her aunt's cold parlour, when James had smiled at her and she'd thought he had kind eyes. And, she considered as she stood in church, if Clara was flirting with the curate, perhaps that was the place to start. She suggested the idea to James that afternoon, over Sunday lunch.

"The curate seems a nice man," she said as James began to slice the joint of mutton. "Perhaps we could invite him to supper."

James looked up from the meat, his eyebrows drawn together in a frown that Sarah decided was more surprise than disapproval. She'd learned to read her husband more accurately over the last year; indeed she'd learned a great deal about her husband. She'd discovered through the butcher's gossipy wife that James had turned to "a flutter" when his wife's health had declined; when Sarah had looked blank, she'd leaned closer and explained about the horse races at Cartmel that James went to on occasion, sometimes coming back with full pockets and sometimes with ones that were all too empty.

Sarah had noted the gleam of speculative glee in the woman's eye, and knew she had enjoyed shocking her. Sarah had murmured her thanks for the meat and left the shop. From then on she bought her meat from a shop on Stricklandgate that sent a boy round with a barrow twice a week.

James's gambling, sporadic as it seemed, certainly explained both the unexpected gifts and the poor state of the house. He was not a man to be trusted with money.

In addition to the gambling, Sarah had come to realise her husband was not a particularly ambitious or practical man. He had not risen in Gawith Hoggarth & Co. in his twenty years of service there, and did not seem bothered by his lack of promotion. He wanted things to be easy, and when they were not he became annoyed. He could be kind, but it was a careless kindness, costing him nothing. He did not consider buying a new range or moving to a better house because the lack did not bother him and the cost did. He liked giving presents, but he had no interest in improving his lot – or Sarah's.

It had been a long, hard year of accepting James's faults and learning to live with his weaknesses. Perhaps the most unsettling aspect of her discoveries was realising her father had been good friends with James. Had Daniel Telford shared James's spendthrift ways? Had he been as charming and feckless as her husband seemed to be?

A year ago Sarah would have denied such an accusation with her every breath. Now she wondered. What kind of man, after all, ran away with a respectable young woman upon one week's acquaintance, and then kept her in genteel poverty with no hope of improvement?

In marrying James, Sarah felt as if her own past was being rewritten, and that disturbed her most of all.

"The curate?" James said now, his voice guarded. "I'm not sure I really know the fellow."

"Mr Fairley. He seems a decent sort." Sarah glanced meaningfully at Clara. "Unmarried."

James stared at her blankly for a few seconds before realisation dawned. "Ah," he said, and nodded mechanically. "Ah."

It was arranged for that Friday evening. James made the invitation, which precluded Sarah from having to talk to the curate. It had occurred to her that there was likely to be a certain amount of awkwardness in having a man to supper whom she'd barely spoken to in the last year and been very rude to before, but she pushed that thought aside. All that mattered was seeing Clara married off.

And for that, she needed to see to Clara. She confronted her the next day, taking a deep breath and summoning all of her courage and conviction to deal with the matter at hand.

Clara was at the kitchen door, batting her eyes at the butcher's boy. Slamming the door in the boy's sheepish face, Sarah turned to her stepdaughter.

"You can't make eyes at a boy like that, Clara!" she said, in more temper than she'd wanted to be. Clara's face drew into familiar sulky lines. "He's completely inappropriate for you. If you wish to marry, then set your sights a little higher than that gormless lad!"

Clara looked set to fly into a temper of her own, but then she merely kicked the door instead. "It's so dull here," she said. "We never go out, I never see anyone at all..."

And whose fault was that? If James had chosen to live in a better neighbourhood, and spend money on a proper house and entertainments and education for his daughter... Sarah took a deep, steadying breath. There was no point in pursuing that line of conversation.

"All the more reason to think of marriage."

"And whom shall I marry?" Clara demanded.

Sarah gazed at her sullen, reddened face and wondered

anew who would have her. "The curate, Mr Fairley, is coming to supper on Friday evening."

"The curate..." Clara began derisively, only to stop and consider the matter. Sarah held her tongue, knowing anything she said was likely to be met with disdain. "He's handsome enough, I suppose," Clara said. Sarah stayed silent. As if that was all that mattered! "But he's poor," she continued. "He doesn't even have his own house. He lodges with Reverend Cooper."

"As a married man, he would have to find a house," Sarah returned. "And he might be a mere curate now, but one day he's likely to have his own living. A rectory somewhere..." She let that idea trail off beguilingly and suppressed the flicker of guilt she felt for feeding Clara such half-truths. Yes, he might possess his own living one day, and a grand rectory as well, but it was just as likely that he would not. Many curates remained so their whole lives, never climbing the ecclesiastical ladder to having their own parish. But surely Clara's lot would be improved even as the wife of a poor curate than if she stayed here and mouldered?

For a few seconds Sarah let herself picture the small house back in Goswell with its carefully furnished rooms; her father's desk and her mother's rocking chair, the maid, Elsie, who had lived on the top floor. It seemed the height of luxury now, and yet even as a child Sarah had felt the pinch of poverty, had accepted that she was on the fringes of a world where many others revelled in a surfeit.

Yes, Clara would do better as Andrew Fairley's wife.

"And what if he doesn't take a liking to me?" Clara asked, and for a moment her sullen mask dropped, to reveal the frightened face of a young and vulnerable girl. To her own surprise, Sarah's heart twisted with pity. "I know I'm plain."

"You have lovely eyes," Sarah said, "and your hair is quite a fashionable blonde. We can have you looking your best for

Friday evening, and the rest is up to your charm and the hand of Providence." Not that she set much store by those fickle fingers. No, Sarah knew she would have to intervene herself, as discreetly as she could.

That afternoon she went through Clara's many dresses, dismissing them all, much to Clara's irritation.

"You're only jealous," she said as she flopped on her bed, her arms crossed over her bosom. "You haven't got half as many nice dresses."

"And nor should I want them," Sarah returned. "I'm only just out of mourning, you know. But in any case, you must remember Mr Fairley is a man of the cloth. He would like to see you in something a bit more modest, I'm sure, rather than wrapped up like a parcel in fripperies and furbelows."

They settled on a gown of pale blue muslin, made simple after Sarah carefully unstitched several fussy bows and two rows of flounces. Clara thought it quite the dullest thing ever, but she seemed, to Sarah's relief, to accept her wisdom in these matters.

Sarah spared no effort and little expense in providing a decent meal for Mr Fairley. James was in one of his more exuberant moods, no doubt due to a recent Saturday jaunt to Cartmel, and so Sarah was able to serve a five-course meal: hare soup, oyster patties, saddles of mutton with mashed potatoes, and Cabinet pudding with custard.

Her cooking had improved in the last year, and she surveyed all the dishes waiting in the kitchen with satisfaction as James paced the parlour, unusually anxious, and Clara fluttered about upstairs.

"Shall we see if Clara has singed her hair?" Sarah asked Lucy, who managed a small smile in return.

In the last year Lucy had continued to sleep in the kitchen, and Sarah had crept down to join her as often as she could. For one week last winter, when Lucy had caught a chest cold, James had allowed her to sleep on the floor of their bedroom. It had, despite her sister's worrying illness, been a wonderful week; the constant anxiety that pressed on Sarah's breastbone had, for a few short days, mercifully eased.

Lucy had adjusted to this new life, a fact that James had smugly referred to more than once, claiming her sleeping arrangements hadn't harmed her. Sarah disagreed, although she never said as much, knowing James would not appreciate her dissent. Her sister might have adjusted to this new life of Clara's casual cruelty and the kitchen as a bedroom, but Sarah felt Lucy had lost a vital part of herself. At times Lucy seemed to have withdrawn completely, so Sarah had to shake her by the shoulders and peer directly into her face to get any reaction at all.

Now, however, with the kitchen full of good smells and the prospect of Clara's marriage – admittedly a distant and unlikely prospect, but one nonetheless – Lucy picked up on Sarah's buoyant mood and smiled shyly. With a complicit smile back, Sarah gave her the custard spoon to lick while she went to check on Clara.

She found her stepdaughter in one of her sulks, stomping about her room, the smell of singed hair lingering in the air.

"Oh, dear." Sarah eyed the pale blue muslin askance. "What happened?"

"It was so *dull*," Clara complained, and picked at one of the bows she'd very inexpertly tried to sew back on.

"And now it looks like something a child patched together," Sarah answered with a sigh. "I'll unstitch the bows for you – and then we must see to your hair."

A quarter of an hour later, Clara came sedately down the stairs, dressed in the unadorned blue muslin, her hair styled in modest loops over her ears. Sarah dabbed a bit of custard from Lucy's chin as they all waited for Mr Fairley to arrive.

In retrospect, Sarah supposed she'd pinned far too many

hopes on a single evening. It was strange to see Mr Fairley outside of church; she'd deliberately avoided him since he'd given her the envelope from Reverend Cooper and she'd shut the door in his face, out of both guilt and dislike. She might attend church every Sunday, but the hymns and sermons didn't move her as they once did, and the whole experience left her flat and cold, an exercise in hypocrisy for everyone involved.

Now he smiled at her as she took his hat and James offered him a glass of sherry.

"How are you, Mrs Mills?" Mr Fairley asked as he accepted a glass from James. Clara hung back with Lucy, hiding her hands in her skirts and biting her lips. "I never seem to have an occasion to speak to you after services."

*Nor should you,* Sarah wanted to reply but she nodded stiffly instead and answered, "I am well, Mr Fairley, thank you." She motioned to Clara to come forward. "Of course you know Clara. I saw you chatting with her after church last week."

Mr Fairley looked slightly taken aback by this remark, but he turned to Clara with a game enough smile. "Yes, of course. You are well, Miss Mills, I hope?" His tone was pleasant but perfunctory and Sarah's heart sank a little. This was not a promising start to her marital aspirations for Clara.

It only got worse as the evening progressed. Despite Sarah having arranged the seats so Mr Fairley was sitting next to Clara, he spent most of the time talking to James or attempting to engage Sarah in conversation. She kept her replies polite but terse, and rose often to see to the next course. He did not talk to Clara beyond the barest of remarks; considering Clara sat next to him like a blancmange in blue, Sarah could not entirely blame him.

Still, she tried her best, inviting Clara to demonstrate her mediocre skills at the pianoforte while Sarah and Lucy cleared the table. She was just wiping the last of the plates, Lucy at her side, when he appeared in the kitchen.

"Mr Fairley..." Sarah took an instinctive step backwards, shocked to see him there. A guest should never come into the kitchen, even in a home as small as theirs. She was embarrassed by the room's shabbiness, and angry that Mr Fairley had presumed to enter it. "Is something the matter...?"

"No, I only wanted to thank you for the lovely meal."

"You're welcome, of course."

He took a step inside the room, his sweeping gaze taking in all of its lack of comforts. "I also wanted to ask... are you well, Mrs Mills?"

She stared at him, unsettled by his seeking gaze, the perceptive light in his brown eyes. Her hands were wet from the dishes, the apron covering her dress spattered with grease and soap. "I told you I was well."

He gave a soft, wry laugh. "But what I really meant to say is... are you happy?"

Sarah stared at him, as silent as Lucy. *Happy?* She couldn't even remember what that felt like. He gazed at her steadily, a small, sad smile touching his lips. His hair had tufted up in several directions despite what looked like a liberal application of pomade.

"Your question is impertinent, Mr Fairley."

"Is it?" A faint blush touched his cheeks at her rebuke. "I did not mean it to be. I only ask because I have often thought of you, Mrs Mills, since you first came to the rectory over a year ago now."

"Have you?" Sarah knew he should not be here, saying these things. If James saw, or even Clara... and yet she found she could not quite make him leave. Not yet. "Why?"

"Because..." Mr Fairley looked down briefly before glancing up again to meet her gaze resolutely. "Because I fear we – the church – did not treat you rightly in your time of need. And I fear that as a result you have resented us." His gaze was unwavering, direct and yet kind, and Sarah felt skewered by it.

"It is in the past," she finally managed. "It has to be." She felt bizarrely near tears. Words were cheap, and the curate's sentiment cost him nothing now, and yet... She knew he meant it. And that meant something to her.

"But you are happy?" he asked in a low voice, and the question felt intimate, exposing.

Sarah shook her head. "My happiness is not your concern."

"Of course," he murmured. "I understand." He paused, still not making to leave, and Sarah looked away, unable to bear a moment more of this strange and unsettling conversation. Lucy had been drawing patterns in the soapy water but now she glanced up at Mr Fairley, her gaze as enquiring as his.

"Please," Sarah finally said, although she did not even know what she was asking.

"You would say..." he began, his voice low, "if something was amiss...?"

"No, I would not." Sarah forced herself to meet his compassionate gaze. "None of this is your concern, Mr Fairley, and you take appalling liberties in addressing me in this way. Thank you for coming to supper." It was a dismissal, as curt as any exchange they'd had in church, and the curate nodded his acceptance and said farewell.

Alone in the kitchen with Lucy, Sarah released a shuddering breath and sagged against the table. She felt utterly drained by the conversation.

A noise had her lifting her head, and with sinking spirits Sarah saw Clara glaring at her from the doorway.

"And you thought he was interested in *me*," she spat, and turned and flounced from the room.

# CHAPTER 19

## ELLEN

*Imbecile.* The word kept haunting Ellen, popping into her mind at inopportune moments. *Imbecile.* A word that had gone out of fashion, having become an insult that was no longer politically correct. No one called anyone an imbecile these days, did they? And yet Lucy Mills, all of thirteen years old, had been labelled one and stuck in a workhouse.

In the week after half-term, with Annabelle and Sophie back at school and a lull in her freelancing projects, Ellen spent several hours on the internet, surfing various research sites and learning more about the Victorian attitude towards mental illness and disability. It didn't make for pleasant reading.

She read of people being locked away in asylums, strapped to chairs or given shock treatments, treated as if their disability was a moral failing rather than a physical condition. She wondered if Lucy Mills had experienced any of the atrocities she read about, and she inwardly shuddered.

Yet, why did she care? She didn't know anything about Lucy Mills. She didn't know if she was related to Sarah of River Cottage, and for that matter she didn't know anything about Sarah Mills, either. It was all a wild, emotional goose chase, but at least it distracted her from the stresses and worries of her own life.

Not that she should be so stressed. Annabelle had ceased overt hostilities, for the most part, but the ensuing calm felt eerie and untrustworthy. She'd started bonding with Sophie, which left Ellen smiling uncertainly at the full makeover Annabelle enacted on her ten-year-old daughter with her heavy, high-end make-up. She didn't particularly enjoy seeing Sophie going for the heroin chic look at her age, with dark eyeshadow and heavy eyeliner, but she was glad Annabelle was making the effort. Sort of.

Sophie had taken to spending evenings up in Annabelle's room, and Ellen listened to the high, girlish laughter and the techno thud of pop music, and tried to feel positive about it all. "Isn't it good they're getting along?" Alex asked one evening in mid-June, after Ellen had voiced some doubt as to the amount of time Sophie was spending with Annabelle. "Isn't this what you wanted?"

He sounded so exasperated that Ellen felt unable to continue with her point. Any comment about Annabelle had become a criticism or complaint in Alex's mind, and it made conversation tricky indeed.

He and Annabelle seemed to be getting along, at least. They'd taken to having a father-daughter night once a week, dinner at a restaurant or catching a film, and while Ellen knew this was a good thing, she couldn't help but feel as if she and Sophie were being just a little bit cut out. Sophie had never had a weekly father-daughter night. Ellen had not yet worked up the courage to point this out to Alex; she knew he would only be annoyed.

When Alyssa rang, informing Ellen that she would be going to Lanzarote with her father for the first week of the summer holidays, Ellen was left wondering if she was getting it right with any of her children.

"Lanzarote?" she repeated. "I mean, wow. And you haven't seen him in..."

"I saw him last weekend," Alyssa said quietly. Stung, Ellen struggled with a response. "Oh. Well. Good. I mean, how was it?"

"Good," Alyssa answered. "I know he hasn't been the greatest dad through the years, but he's trying now. He wants to try." She sounded defensive, even though Ellen had been trying hard not to sound sceptical or even surprised.

And yet she was. How could she not be, when Jack had been the classic deadbeat dad for so many years? Missing child support payments, promising a trip to a theme park not once but twice, only to flake out at the last moment both times. Did Alyssa not remember standing with her nose pressed to the window, decked out in her fairy princess finery, her suitcase packed, waiting for Jack to pick her up for her weekend trip to France? She'd been six, and had talked of nothing else for weeks. Ellen had been apprehensive, but Alex had encouraged her to give Jack the chance to spend time with Alyssa.

And then the call had come, just as Ellen had known it would. She'd stood in the kitchen, the phone pressed to her ear, her gaze on Alyssa, as Jack had babbled incomprehensibly about emergency calls and a problem at the construction site where he was working.

"What about the plane tickets?" Ellen had asked. "The tickets to the theme park? Won't it all go to waste?"

The ensuing silence had told her all she needed to know. He'd never even bought the tickets.

But that was twelve years ago, and Alyssa was an adult now. She could handle her own heartbreak, even if Ellen still wanted to protect her from it.

"So what are you doing in Lanzarote?" she asked brightly. "Besides working on your tan?"

"We're renting a villa," Alyssa said after a tiny pause. "With his fiancée."

Fiancée. Oh. Ellen hadn't known about that. "Great," she said after a moment. Her voice sounded strangled. "Great."

"Do you mind, Mum?"

"Why would I mind?"

"I don't know. It's just... you've always been so touchy about Dad. About me spending time with Dad. I don't want you to be... jealous."

"I'm not jealous," Ellen exclaimed. "I just don't want you to get hurt."

"I won't," Alyssa insisted, and she sounded defensive again.

After Alyssa had hung up, Ellen made herself a coffee and took it out to the garden, trying to untangle her jumbled thoughts and feelings as she sat among the overgrown rose bushes and wisteria. She wasn't jealous... was she? She wanted Alyssa to have a good relationship with her father, but if she was honest, she'd given up on that notion years ago. And yes, maybe with a little bit of relief, because it was exhausting trying to build a relationship between two people, one of whom she found it extremely difficult to talk to. But jealous?

*You're jealous of Annabelle and Alex.*

That treacherous little voice whispering inside her head made Ellen wince. Yes, all right, she was jealous. Jealous of the relationship they were forming which she had no part of, and more worryingly, that Sophie had no part of. Sophie, who had never had movie nights or trips to restaurants, who hadn't had her relationship with her father damaged enough to need that kind of intensive repair.

*Stop being so petty, Ellen.*

Taking a sip of coffee, Ellen reached for her laptop and decided to immerse itself in genealogy sites and research into Victorian times. She really did need the distraction.

She spent an hour surfing various Victorian sites, reading

absently about the food they ate and the clothes they wore without getting any more information about Sarah or Lucy Mills. Impatient with herself, she pushed the laptop away and called to Pepper for a walk. She needed to clear her head.

She walked to the beach, enjoying the brisk breeze and the sunny sky, the sea stretching out to the horizon in a blue-grey sweep. She threw a grungy old tennis ball for Pepper, who ran after it with exuberant joy, only to be distracted by the seagulls and leave it for Ellen to retrieve.

She was so tired of feeling discontented. Worried. Stressed. She wished she could just shake it all off, focus on the positive. And there was so much to be thankful for, so many good things. She had two healthy daughters, a good marriage, a job she enjoyed, a home she loved. She had friends she could count on who cared for her, parents who lived far away but liked to Skype...

Honestly, she felt like a spoilt baby, whinging about how her life wasn't perfect. *And yet...*

Ellen let out a weary sigh as Pepper bounded off once again, leaving the tennis ball floating on the incoming tide. She went to retrieve it, whistled for Pepper, and kept walking down the beach.

A spur of the moment decision had her turning off the path that cut through the sheep pasture on the way home and into the curving drive of the church and vicarage beyond. She ought to go to church more, she thought guiltily as she walked past the Norman tower. She'd gone to Sunday school as a kid and yet somehow she'd just forgotten about that part of her life. When had she last prayed, or considered there might be some greater hand at work than her own? She couldn't even remember.

"Ellen!" Jane answered the door, coat on and car keys in hand.

"You're going out?" Ellen surmised. "Sorry, I should have rung."

"I was just contemplating the weekly shop," Jane answered, "but I'd much rather have a cup of tea. Come through and I'll put the kettle on."

Ellen left Pepper to dry out in the porch before following Jane to the back of the house and the large square kitchen with its cheerful Aga and the high sash windows letting in lemony sunlight. It was such a comforting, welcoming picture that Ellen felt a lump form in her throat.

"What is it?" Jane asked after she'd plonked the big brass kettle onto one of the Aga's hotplates. "You look like you're about to burst into tears."

"I just might," Ellen admitted on a shaky laugh as she sank into a chair at the kitchen table. "I don't even know what's wrong, not really."

"Is it Annabelle?" Jane asked as she ripped open a packet of chocolate digestives and handed Ellen two. "Go on. You need the sugar hit."

"Maybe." Ellen nibbled a digestive and tried to gather her thoughts. "It's not Annabelle," she said at last. "At least, it's not just Annabelle. She's settled down a bit and she's actually making friends with Sophie. And Alex has started having weekly date nights with her, for want of a better term. I'd say it's all going really rather well."

"But?" Jane prompted. "Because you certainly don't look like it's all going well."

"But everything feels like a mess, inside my head," Ellen admitted slowly. "A tangled-up disaster... of mistakes and failures and oh, everything." And then she was crying, a single tear that slipped down her cheek. Ellen dashed it away impatiently, managing a laugh as she shook her head. "Honestly, look at me. I'm ridiculous."

"No, you're not," Jane answered firmly. "You're just having a hard time." The kettle started to whistle and Jane whisked it off the hot plate, giving Ellen a few moments to compose herself. Honestly, she was embarrassed by how stupidly maudlin she was being. What was *wrong* with her?

"So, mistakes and failures," Jane said as she poured two cups of tea and pushed one across the table to Ellen. "Which would those be?"

"Having Annabelle come here has made me realise how little I know about Alex's marriage," Ellen blurted. "I never even asked him about Sandra, or why his marriage broke down. I just wanted to pretend it had never happened."

Jane took a sip of tea. "Surely you must know something," she said. "The basics, at least."

"We had one conversation about it. Alex said Sandra had decided she didn't want to be married any more, and then she left. I think I asked why she'd changed her mind and he shrugged and said he didn't know. She'd just... gone off marriage." It sounded so lame now that Ellen couldn't help but cringe. How could she have been such an ostrich about something so important? But she hadn't wanted to think about Alex's first marriage, or her own, or the complications and hurts that still existed from both of them. She'd just wanted to be happy.

"And now you feel like there's more to it?" Jane asked.

"There has to be, doesn't there? I mean... something. And Annabelle's said a few things..." Ellen sighed. "It's not just that, though. It's everything. It's Alyssa reconnecting with her father—"

"She is?" Jane's eyebrows shot up as she took a sip of tea. "But that's a good thing, surely?"

"I don't know. She's been reluctant to tell me about it because she thinks I'll be jealous."

"Jealous—"

"I don't think I am," Ellen said, a lilt of uncertainty entering her voice. "I never thought I was but now I feel like I'm questioning everything about myself. Why am I so annoyed that Alex is going out with Annabelle once a week? I should be happy. I *know* that, but if I'm honest, I'm not. And I don't really like Annabelle and Sophie hanging out together... I can't believe Annabelle is a good influence, and I don't entirely trust her. And I feel like there's all this baggage from both of our marriages, from these lives we had before. I used to pretend it wasn't there but now it feels like it's weighing me down. Crippling me." She sighed heavily, wishing she felt better for blurting all of that out but knowing she didn't. "Sorry. I'm whinging, I know."

"You're not whinging," Jane said quietly. She took a sip of tea, her brow furrowed in thought. "But I think you need to talk to Alex about all of this, Ellen. Ask him about his first marriage. It's a conversation I think you should have had a long time ago, but you can still have it now. Information can only help."

"Speaking of information, I found out something semi-related to Sarah Mills," Ellen answered. A while back she'd told a bit about Sarah to Jane, and what she'd discovered. Jane, being Jane, had been wildly enthusiastic and had offered to do some digging herself, but Ellen had declined. Sarah Mills felt like her project. Now, however, she was desperate to change the conversation after she'd volunteered way too much personal information, even to a close friend like Jane. "I found a record of a Lucy Mills in Kendal. She was admitted to the workhouse when she was thirteen, listed as an imbecile." Jane made a face and Ellen nodded. "Sounds awful, doesn't it? And especially when you read about the workhouse conditions... it was practically like prison, or worse."

"So is this Lucy related to Sarah?"

"I have no idea. Mills is a common enough name, so probably not."

"Hmm." Interest sharpened Jane's expression. "I wonder how you could find out."

"I sent an email to the head of Kendal's historical society. Beyond that, I'm not sure what I can do."

"And what about who lived in your house? Any more on that?"

Ellen shrugged. "Seems like a dead end. Alfred from the Goswell Historical Society sent me an email a few weeks ago and apparently there was a mention in some register that Samuel and Clara Frampton lived in the house around that time, but I have no idea who they could be, or if they're related to Sarah Mills." Ellen rose from the table and took her empty cup to the sink. "Not sure any of it really matters. It's been a bit of distraction, but Annabelle isn't really interested and I think any potential leads I might have had have petered out. Anyway." Ellen turned around with a bright smile. "I'd better get on. Thanks for letting me vent."

"Anytime, you know that." Jane's smile was genuine but troubled. "Are you sure..."

"I'm fine, Jane, honestly," Ellen interjected hurriedly. "Don't worry about me." She went to fetch Pepper, pulling on her welly boots and half-wishing she hadn't stopped. Talking about everything had definitely not made her feel better.

And yet, she reflected as she headed up the high street to home, perhaps Jane was right. Perhaps she needed to ask Alex about his marriage, deal with both of their mistakes of the past. Maybe that would help her accept her present – and shape her future. She didn't relish the conversation, though.

The home phone was ringing as Ellen let herself in, groaning inwardly as Pepper bounded through the downstairs, leaving muddy paw prints all across the hall and kitchen.

"Hello?" she answered breathlessly on about the sixth ring.

"Hello, Ellen, it's Margaret down at the school."

"Margaret. Hello. Is everything all right?" Fear clutched at Ellen's chest with a cold hand. Margaret was the primary school's receptionist, a cosy, grandmotherly type whose perfunctory calls about forgotten PE kit or needing lunch money turned into comfortable chats. She sounded grave now, though, and even more so when she continued.

"Sophie hasn't fallen ill or anything like that. But... Miss West is asking for you to come down before school ends and have a chat."

"Miss West?" That cold hand plunged right inside Ellen. Miss West was the head teacher, a stern and formidable woman who intimidated Ellen more than a little. She'd never been called into the woman's office to "chat". The prospect filled her with alarm. "Do you know what's going on, Margaret?"

"I couldn't say," Margaret answered, and Ellen heard a note of sympathy in the older woman's voice that scared her all the more. "But you should come in this afternoon. Would half past two be all right?"

Ellen glanced at the clock; it was only a little past noon. "Yes, of course," she said, and then Margaret rung off, leaving Ellen still holding the phone, Pepper butting her legs, and her heart beginning to hammer in fear.

*Calm down*, she told herself. *It might be nothing. It probably is nothing.* Just because it hadn't happened before didn't mean it was serious.

Did it?

She'd just replaced the receiver when the phone rang again, making her jump.

"May I speak to Ellen Tyson?" a man's voice barked cheerfully down the line.

"Speaking..."

"Hello there, it's Ian Fletcher from the Kendal Historical Society. I thought I'd ring rather than email on the off-chance you might be home. I found a few interesting bits and pieces about the woman on your death certificate. Sarah Mills?"

"Oh, yes?" Her anxiety about Sophie lessened for a few blessed seconds. "Thanks for ringing. What did you find?"

"I found the register of her marriage to James Mills at the

parish church in 1868. She was Sarah Telford before that. And I also found her grave, in the church's cemetery."

Ellen's breath caught. "You did?" Why hadn't she thought to look for Sarah Mills's grave? "Did it... did it tell you anything?"

"I can tell you what the inscription was, although it took me awhile to decipher it, it was that faded." He cleared his throat. "'Sarah Mills, Wife to James, Beloved Sister to Lucy.' Does that help at all, do you think?"

"*Lucy...*" Inexplicable tears pricked Ellen's eyes. *Beloved Sister.* But then, how and why had Lucy ended up in the workhouse at only thirteen years old, while Sarah was still alive?

"Does that mean something to you?" Ian asked, curiosity audible in his voice.

"Yes... I found a mention of Lucy Mills in the Kendal workhouse." She had to clear her throat before she continued. "She must be the same one, don't you think?"

"In the workhouse?" Ian sounded surprised. "It would be strange for one sibling to be in the workhouse and another not. Not impossible, I suppose..."

"She was listed as an imbecile."

"Ah. I see," he said, his voice full of regretful understanding. "I suppose it was fairly common for people with mental disabilities from families with few resources to end up in the workhouse. Sad."

"Yes, very sad." Ellen thanked him again before ringing off, her mind caught between the present and the past; her daughter, who might be struggling somehow, and Lucy, almost the same age as Sophie, her life ended most likely more than a hundred years ago, and yet who must have also struggled, terribly. *Beloved Sister.* How, Ellen wondered, could that be?

# CHAPTER 20

## SARAH

Kendal, 1870

The dinner with Andrew Fairley had been, Sarah recognised in the weeks and months after the event, a complete disaster. Not only had he not shown any interest in Clara, but his conversation with Sarah in the kitchen had intensified Clara's hostility towards both her and Lucy; what had once only been skirmishes of rudeness, with sly digs and hidden taunts, became a declared war.

Life had become near-unbearable, with Clara's endless sulks and pouts, the pinches and slaps she doled out to Lucy, not bothering to hide them from Sarah, a gleam of defiant malice in her eyes. Lucy had taken to hiding to avoid the older girl, often spending hours under the kitchen table, her face smeared with coal smuts and tears.

Sarah tried to talk to James about it, but her attempts to enlighten him about Clara's behaviour were met with chilly silence and reminders that it was she who was to manage the household.

Sarah had long stopped trying to manage Clara. Now

nearly a woman grown, Clara often went out without telling Sarah where, and spent the rest of her time lounging around or tormenting Lucy.

"What is to become of you?" Sarah, at the end of all patience, exclaimed once, her hands on her hips, as Clara lay on the sofa and ate chocolates James had, in one of his fits of indulgence, brought home the night before.

Clara stared at her with indolent indifference. "Why do you care?"

"Because I'd like to see you well placed," Sarah answered evenly.

"You mean you'd like to see me out of this house."

"That too," Sarah answered before she could stop herself. "Why wouldn't I? You don't lift a finger to help me and you make Lucy's life an utter misery. Why shouldn't I want to see you gone?" She turned on her heel, angry with herself for losing control, but not before she'd seen hurt cause Clara's face to crumple, making her seem like a child still, and almost, but not quite, making Sarah pity her.

Sarah had considered inviting other suitable men to supper, and she'd asked James if Clara could attend a sewing circle as a way to make suitable acquaintances, but while James had agreed to both prospects, Clara had refused.

"My stitches are terrible," she said flatly, to which Sarah remained tactfully silent. "And there is no point inviting anyone to supper. He'll only make eyes at you."

"Mr Fairley was not interested in me, Clara," Sarah said quietly. "He was only concerned because of my... situation before I married."

But Clara wasn't interested, flouncing away, her eyes gleaming with anger even as her lips trembled. She really was a child, and despite Clara's sulks and slaps, pouts and pinches, Sarah began to feel at least a little sorry for the girl. Her father had done her no favours, spoiling and indulging her, yet with casual indifference, buying her dresses and baubles but ensuring neither her marriage nor her future.

Clara, Sarah acknowledged tiredly, did not try to help herself, either. It seemed a hopeless situation that would endure forever for all of them.

And then, just after Christmas, everything seemed to turn on its axis, for Sarah discovered she was pregnant. She'd given up on falling pregnant after the first year, had stopped looking for the signs she remembered seeing in her mother.

Then one morning she threw up her porridge, and after it happened again for the next two days, she realised it might not be the grippe that she'd feared, but something far better. Something actually quite wonderful.

She held the knowledge tightly to herself, not wanting anyone to guess, not until she was sure herself, completely certain. *A baby.* Part of her quaked in fear at the prospect; how would she manage a child on top of everything else? And what if Clara tormented her son or daughter the way she did Lucy? Would James countenance it? Would he love their child as much as he favoured Clara?

The questions circled around in her mind as the nausea continued and her breasts became tender, her belly swelling just a little, so the buttons strained on her dress and she had to let out the seams. *A baby.*

In March, when the wind was still chilly and the fells were capped with snow, Sarah decided she could wait no longer. She cleared their supper dishes away as she always did, while James retired to the sitting room and Clara went upstairs, no doubt to read illicit novels and eat the last of the chocolates her father had bought.

With Lucy by her side, Sarah headed to the sitting room, pausing in the doorway. James was sitting in one of the wingchairs by the fireplace, his boots stretched out to the fender, a newspaper held in front of him.

Sarah stepped into the room. "James."

He looked up from his paper, his eyebrows drawn together in the beginning of a frown. "Yes?"

"There is something I need to tell you." Nerves fluttered in her stomach, making her feel nearly as sick as she had that morning, losing her porridge in the privy. She thought James would be pleased, but what if he wasn't? But no, he'd said before that he wanted children. Surely this would be happy news, and yet...

Even after a year and a half of marriage, Sarah felt she could not predict her husband's responses. She enjoyed his moments of kindness, was thankful for what he provided, but was wary all the same. She knew she couldn't trust him.

"Sarah?" His eyebrows rose, his mouth puckered, and he rustled his paper. "What is it?"

"A happy occasion, I hope." Her voice sounded thin and quavery. James continued to stare and this time Sarah spoke firmly. "I'm..." Words failed her for a moment; every phrase seemed indelicate. "I am in a blessed state," she finally said, fumbling for words. James looked at her blankly. "That is, I am expecting a child."

His face cleared as his jaw dropped. "You *are*..." Sarah nodded, gulping, and Lucy sidled up next to her and slid her cold hand into hers. Did her sister understand what she'd just said? What it meant? Sarah had no idea.

"Oh, Sarah!" James rose from the chair, his hands outstretched. To Sarah's surprise he caught her up in an embrace, kissing her on the lips. His expressions of physical affection had always been relegated to the bedroom, to those evenings when he would roll over to face her, one hand lying heavily on her shoulder as he fumbled with the laces of her nightgown.

He drew back, smiling widely. "I'm so pleased. After all this time I was beginning to wonder... but no mind. You are expecting! What a happy, happy day this is." He kissed her again, and then drew her down to the sofa. "But you must rest! You are delicate."

She had not been delicate this morning, when she'd dragged the copper out and done all the washing in the frigid air. And as conscientious as her husband was now about her allegedly frail health, Sarah knew he would still expect his shirts and collars washed and ironed, the meals put on the table. But she wouldn't think about that in this moment.

James sat next to her on the sofa and held her hand, every inch the doting husband and father-to-be. It was enough to make Sarah smile; she almost felt like laughing. She'd never seen him look so pleased, not even when he'd come home from Cartmel with a wallet full of notes and extravagant presents for all of them.

"Do you know when...?" he asked hesitantly, almost timidly. His cheeks were slightly flushed.

Sarah laid one hand against her middle in an instinctive, protective gesture. "I think perhaps in the early autumn. The end of September or thereabouts." It was only a guess, but James looked even more pleased.

"You must take care," he said, quite seriously, and Sarah simply stared. "You must not overtax yourself."

"I will try not to," she murmured, and then, because she'd never seen him in such a good mood, she added, "Perhaps if you could be so good as to find some help for the washing? Just while I'm..." She laid her hand against her middle once more.

James stared at her, his forehead furrowed, and Sarah schooled her face into one of placid contemplation.

"I suppose," he said at last. "I wouldn't want you lifting heavy things." He nodded once, his mind now clearly made up. "Yes, we must have a woman come in for the washing and scrubbing. If you arrange it, Sarah..."

"Of course." She could scarcely credit that it had been so

easy. A year and a half of backbreaking work, ended in an instant, and on a whim. It was so like James she didn't know whether to laugh or cry or simply shake her head at his fickleness.

The very next week Sarah hired a woman to come to wash and scrub, a cheerful, red-faced farmer's wife with an accent as thick as treacle and a booming laugh. Sarah sat at the kitchen table and watched her drag the copper out to the muddy yard and could have wept with relief.

The following week James came home, exuberant and secretive, telling Sarah he had a surprise for them all on Saturday.

"You do?" Sarah answered warily, trying to look pleased even though she was never certain about James's surprises. She did not want an extravagant gown or useless bauble, a waste of money both.

But what James showed her was far better than either of those. They left the house on Saturday afternoon, walking towards the market square. Clara was animated, expecting presents, and even Lucy seemed caught by the excitement in the air. She smiled shyly at James and he tugged gently on one of her plaits.

"Just you wait, poppet."

Sarah walked sedately next to James, Lucy's hand in hers, feeling as if they were on parade, just as they'd been that Tuesday morning a lifetime ago, when they'd walked from the church to River Cottage, newly married, holding onto hope. Now she didn't know what to feel.

They passed the market square and the town hall with its clock tower and Latin inscription – *pannus mihi panis* – and then James turned down a narrow street off Stricklandgate lined with modest but well-presented villas, recently built. Sarah's heart started beating hard.

He stopped in front of number four, Belmont, and with

great flourish produced a key from his pocket. Sarah pressed one hand to her chest, hardly daring to hope.

"Welcome to your new home, Mrs Mills," James said grandly, and walked up to the front door, shiny with fresh black paint, and unlocked it.

Sarah stepped inside the entrance hall, breathing in the scents of both dust and paint, old and new. "Do you really mean it..." she asked faintly.

"We can hardly live in River Cottage when the baby arrives," James said. "We'll need another bedroom at least. Come and see."

Sarah followed him through the empty rooms: a front parlour and a back one, both with gabled windows, along with a dining room, and a kitchen below stairs with a separate scullery and larder, a closed range and a cold water tap. Upstairs there were three good-sized bedrooms, along with, wonder of wonders, a bathroom with another cold water tap, a deep tub made of tin, and a gas geyser to heat the water. On the top floor was a small bedroom, presumably meant for a maid.

"I thought Lucy could sleep up there," James said with a kindly smile. "It's time you had a proper bed, isn't it, poppet?"

Lucy blinked shyly, caught, like Sarah, between wariness and hope. It felt too good, too unbelievably wonderful, to be true, and she knew she couldn't bear to be disappointed.

"What do you think to it, Clara?" James asked as he turned to his older daughter. Clara had been quiet since they'd entered the house, following Sarah and James about the empty rooms, saying little. Sarah had no idea what her stepdaughter thought about the proposed move, but surely it could only mean good things for all of them. They would be in a respectable neighbourhood, with so much more space and so many comforts. Moving here would elevate Clara's prospects along with her own.

"It's nice enough," she said, and Sarah watched James's face fall a little at his daughter's indifferent assessment.

"It's the loveliest house I've ever seen," she said quickly, earning a glower from Clara. "Truly, James, it's like a palace." It wasn't quite as big as Aunt Edith's house on Lowther Street, but it was light and airy, with many more modern conveniences. "When shall we move?"

"Soon," James said, jangling the key in his pocket. "This summer, perhaps."

A finger of unease trailed coldly up Sarah's spine. She'd thought James had already arranged it all, but it sounded as if he hadn't. "Can you afford it?" she asked, and he frowned.

"There's no need to talk about money," he said shortly. "I am quite in control of my finances, thank you."

"Of course," Sarah murmured. "I'm sorry." It had been stupid of her to ask, and now James's mood had soured and it made her think they really couldn't afford it. Perhaps this house was another gamble, a different dream.

James treated them to luncheon at the King's Arms, and Sarah tried to recapture the optimism of the morning. She wanted to believe in the future James had offered, as tempting as the apple in Eden, but the fear of disappointment was a metallic taste in her mouth. She didn't think she could bear to have another hope snatched away, and not one so important, so dear.

And yet, why shouldn't they move to number four, Belmont? It wasn't as grand a house as all that, and a respectable clerk should well be able to afford it, as long as he did not indulge in too many trips to Cartmel. And even without any household help, Sarah would enjoy the modern conveniences such a house provided – a separate scullery, a closed range, running water and a bathroom...

As the weeks passed, Sarah dared to hope. To believe. James signed the lease on the house, and her belly continued to swell.

She began to sew a layette: long clothes, napkins, day and night caps. Everything looked so tiny and delicate, she almost didn't want to touch them. When she'd finished each item, she folded it neatly and put it in a chest in her bedroom.

In May, Sarah felt the first flutters in her belly, and she clasped Lucy's hand to her stomach, laughing in amazement. Lucy grinned.

It felt as if the whole world shimmered. When Sarah stepped out onto the narrow street she'd called home for nearly two years, she breathed in the air, smoky from a hundred coal fires, as if it were fresh. The fells that had loomed so menacingly upon her arrival now looked majestic; the river flowing sluggishly by the end of the garden, flooding the yard, sparkled.

In June, Sarah began to prepare for the move, wrapping the ornaments that had once belonged to Amanda Mills in paper, packing their linens in chests. Each act felt like a deposit to secure their future. This would happen. They would start again, in a new and wonderful place.

Never mind that Clara still sulked and pouted; Sarah didn't understand why her stepdaughter wasn't more pleased about the move, but she refused to let the girl blight her fragile happiness. At last Sarah was looking forward to the future for both her and Lucy and no one, not even Clara, was going to spoil it.

# CHAPTER 21

## ELLEN

"I'm sorry to say Sophie has misbehaved."

Miss West's angular face looked particularly stern as Ellen perched on the edge of a hard plastic chair in the head teacher's cramped office, her handbag clutched on her lap.

"Misbehaved...?" she repeated uncertainly. Amazing how sitting in a room like this, with a woman like Miss West, could make her feel like a scolded Year Six.

Miss West sat back in her chair, steepling her fingers under her chin in a posture Ellen suspected she reserved just for moments like this one. "Has Sophie been having trouble at home, Mrs Tyson?"

A blotchy flush swept over Ellen. She could feel it prickling all over her face, a dead giveaway. She swallowed and managed through stiff lips, "We've been having some adjustments. My husband's daughter from his first marriage came to live with us in May and it's been a bit challenging." That was as honest as she was prepared to be, and in any case, it hadn't been *that* challenging. She was the one with the problem, not Sophie. Sophie was getting along with Annabelle. Wasn't she?

"I see," Miss West said. Her tone sounded ominous. Ellen felt a flicker of annoyance beneath the trepidation. Miss West didn't have to act like quite such a harbinger of primary school doom.

"So what exactly was this misbehaviour, if I may ask?"

Miss West's mouth tightened. "She was bullying another student. And I have to inform you, Mrs Tyson, that we take bullying very seriously at Goswell Primary."

"Of course you do," Ellen murmured. Her mind spun uselessly, like wheels in mud, unable to gain any traction with this idea. Bullying? *Sophie?* Ellen would have said it was ridiculous. Impossible. *Before Annabelle, it was.* "Could you give me the details, please?" she asked, her voice a lot less tetchy than it had been thirty seconds ago.

Miss West hesitated, her fingers still steepled, her mouth pursed primly. She had a small wart by her eyebrow. *Witch.* It was unfair, Ellen knew, but she couldn't keep herself from it. Calling Sophie a bully! She couldn't be. She just couldn't be.

"Why don't we ask Sophie to explain it to us," she said, and Ellen shrank from that idea. But no, maybe it was better. Maybe Sophie would explain everything. Of course she would.

"Yes," she said, trying to match Miss West's no-nonsense tone. "Let's do that."

Five tense minutes later, a pale-faced Sophie came into the room, making it seem smaller than ever. Ellen had never seen her daughter look so subdued.

She hung back in the doorway, hunching her shoulders and lowering her head so her golden ringlets fell in front of her face.

"Sophie." Miss West's voice had that ominous, overly even note of teachers confronting a pupil in trouble. "Why don't you take a seat?"

Ellen budged over so Sophie had more room; she tried to give her daughter a reassuring smile but Sophie wasn't looking at her. She sat in the chair next to Ellen's, her head lowered, her hands clasped in her lap. Her nails were raggedy, bitten to the quick. No one said anything for several audible ticks of the clock.

"Sophie," Miss West finally said, all sonorous authority, "why don't you tell us what's been going on these last few weeks?"

*Weeks?* And this was the first she'd heard of it? Ellen bit her lip to keep from saying something unhelpful.

Sophie hunched her shoulder in what Ellen supposed was a shrug. "I don't know." She sounded sulky, so unlike the cheerful, friendly, lovable girl Ellen knew, but underneath the attitude she sensed a genuine fear and unhappiness, and her breath bottled in her throat at the realisation that she might have missed something big going on in her daughter's life.

"Soph?" she asked gently, not caring if Miss West resented her interference. "Can you tell me what happened, please?"

No reply. Ellen took a careful, even breath, torn between anger, exasperation, and the strong desire to simply bundle her daughter out of this cramped, stale-smelling office so they could deal with this at home.

"Maybe we should ask Chloe what happened," Miss West said, and it sounded a little bit like a threat.

Chloe? Chloe Dawson? Ellen didn't know the girl very well, or the family for that matter. They'd moved to Goswell last year from somewhere down south, Southampton or Exeter or somewhere like that. A bit la-di-da, Ellen had thought privately, and she knew a few of the Cumbrian born-and-bred mums had eyed the mother askance, in her designer jeans and high-heeled leather boots, trailing scarves and an alligator-skin handbag (imitation, Ellen supposed) as she picked Chloe up from school.

But Sophie bullying *Chloe*? It seemed an even more unlikely scenario. Sophie would steer clear of someone like

Chloe, surely. Ellen had seen Chloe in the playground, doing her best to be her mum's mini-me, affecting airs and wearing designer something, even with her school uniform. She'd got her hair professionally highlighted and she was only ten years old. Girls like that didn't get bullied. If anything, they were the ones who were doing the bullying.

"Did Chloe do something to you, Sophie?" Ellen asked.

"That isn't really the point, Mrs Tyson," Miss West interjected in frosty disapproval.

"Isn't it?" Ellen challenged. It was all falling into place. Chloe must have been teasing Sophie, and Sophie finally broke and gave as good as she got for once. But why hadn't Ellen known any of this? Why hadn't Sophie told her?

"No, it is not. I'm afraid we have a clear case of bullying in this incidence, but perhaps Sophie should tell us about it."

"Sophie." Ellen turned to her daughter, near to trembling with indignation on her behalf. "Tell Miss West what happened."

Sophie pressed her lips together and crossed her arms. "Nothing."

A tense few seconds of silence ensued, seeming to stretch on and on. "Sophie..." Ellen stared at her daughter, at a loss. The folded arms, the jutting chin, the downcast gaze... this was not her daughter. All right, yes, Sophie had been a little bolshy these past few weeks. Part of growing up, Ellen had assumed, and had tried to take it in stride. But this...

"Tell Miss West what happened," she said in a quiet voice that brooked no disagreements, the voice she used rarely, saving it for a DEFCON 1 situation. And here it was.

Sophie glanced at her out of the corner of her eye before resuming her intent study of the floor. "I was just joking," she muttered.

"Chloe didn't think you were joking, Sophie," Miss West said severely.

"Chloe's a twit."

"*Sophie...*" Ellen could feel herself flushing in mortification. "Don't."

"Well, she is." Sophie glanced up, blue eyes glittering with anger. "She swans into school every day bragging about her designer clothes and bags and her boyfriend at Copeland and everybody is tired of it." She stared at Miss West defiantly. "I just told her what everybody else was thinking."

Miss West's expression was resolute. "Chloe says you pushed her."

Sophie said nothing. Ellen's heart felt like it was being squeezed through her throat. *Pushed?* "Sophie..." she began, and then stopped, because she honestly didn't know what to say.

"I think," Miss West said, her tone clipped and decisive, "we'll leave you to think about this for a day or two, Sophie. And perhaps after you've had a think you'll realise the seriousness of your actions. We consider bullying a very grave matter." Miss West eyed her silently for several beats before she rose from the desk, turning to Ellen. "Sophie will be welcome back at school on Friday."

"Friday..." Ellen repeated blankly, before the penny dropped with a thud. "You mean, she's *suspended?*"

"For two days, yes. I think that is reasonable considering the infraction."

"But..." Ellen swallowed dryly. "This is the first time..."

"Actually, Mrs Tyson, it isn't."

"What?" Ellen swung round to look at Sophie, who was back to staring at the floor. "What do you mean? Why did no one inform me that this happened before?"

"Sophie's teacher, Miss Forrester, sent a note home in her bag."

"She did?" Ellen felt herself start to flush again. She wasn't all that consistent about checking Sophie's bag for notes from school, figuring her daughter would tell her the important stuff. "I would have appreciated a phone call."

"Miss Forrester left two messages on your home machine."

"What..." All right, so she hardly ever checked the home machine. It wasn't even a machine, just a number you had to dial that informed you if you had messages. Who remembered to do that, especially when most calls these days came through to her mobile? "I see," she said, chastened, feeling as scolded as Sophie. It was her fault that it had got this far. She should have been on top of it, realised something was going on. But Sophie had been spending so much time with Annabelle, and Ellen had convinced herself that was a good thing. Or had she just been lazy?

"Thank you," she murmured, and rose from her seat. Sophie followed, and they went in silence to collect her things from outside the Year Five classroom. Fortunately the other pupils were busy in a maths lesson and no one noticed them slip out of the school and walk down the steep little lane. Neither of them spoke a word all the way home, Sophie scuffing her school shoes along the pavement, Ellen in a complete daze.

She let them in the house, Pepper bounding about them joyfully, pushing her nose against Ellen's thigh. She'd forgotten to walk her this morning, and she wouldn't have a chance now. Sophie started for the stairs.

"Sophie." Ellen stared at her daughter, torn between concern, anger, and fear. What was the right response here? The proper tone to take? She'd never once imagined Sophie could be capable of bullying, or Alyssa, for that matter. Her children were far more likely to be bullied than bully, and yet...

Here they were.

"Please come into the kitchen. We need to talk about this."

With a loud, drawn-out sigh of martyrdom, Sophie flounced into the kitchen and then flung herself into a chair. Ellen went to the kettle automatically, filling it up and banging it on the hob because she needed a moment to think, as well as a cup of tea.

"Do you want to tell me about it?" she finally asked.

"No."

"This isn't like you, Sophie." Ellen sat down across from her daughter. "This isn't like you at all." She searched Sophie's face, looking for clues, but all she saw was an unfamiliar pout, her gaze lowered, her eyes hidden. "Was Chloe mean to you? Is that why you... lashed out?"

"Chloe's a pain."

Not exactly the answer she was looking for. The kettle began to whistle and with a sigh Ellen rose to make the tea. She poured a glass of milk and fetched a couple of slightly stale biscuits from the cupboard and put them in front of Sophie, who looked at them askance and didn't touch them.

"Why is Chloe a pain?" Ellen asked. No reply. "Sophie? I can't help you if you don't talk to me." Ellen could hardly credit she was saying such a thing. This was *Sophie*, who tended to talk her ear off, who hid nothing, her expression as clear as a pool. "What has she done?" she pressed even as she knew it was futile. Sophie wasn't saying anything.

With a sigh Ellen rose from the table, her tea untouched. "I suppose we'll talk again when your father comes home." It came out sounding like a threat. With a loud, squeaky scrape of the chair legs, Sophie got up from the table and thudded upstairs.

Still feeling at a loss, Ellen reached for her mobile and called Alex. He didn't pick up, which she'd expected, but she left a message on his voicemail so he'd hopefully be prepared for a talk with Sophie tonight. Then she tidied up the kitchen and thought about doing some work, but she found she couldn't summon the energy. Worry was exhausting.

She looked through the stuff Ian Fletcher had sent on email: a photo of Sarah Mills's grave and a scan of her marriage in the parish register. Ian seemed to have become as interested in the mysterious Sarah Mills as she was, although perhaps he simply liked playing detective. He'd also written her a note on Sarah's cause of death:

*General Debility usually meant senility or death from old age, but since she was only twenty-two I doubt either of those apply. It's more likely that she had some sort of wasting disease, maybe tuberculosis, or consumption as they called it, which could have gone on for several years.*

*Regards,*

*Ian.*

Tuberculosis and a sister in the workhouse? Ellen shook her head, saddened by the tragic details of this woman's life. She clearly had nothing to complain about.

Annabelle came in from school a little while later, and trying to keep her voice light and friendly, Ellen asked her about Sophie.

"Have you noticed anything going on with Sophie?" She raised her eyebrows, her smile quizzical. "I know you've been spending a lot of time with her lately."

"What?" Annabelle looked guarded as she stood in the doorway of the kitchen, half-poised for flight. She'd stopped hiking up her skirt, Ellen noticed, and undoing the top two buttons of her blouse. She looked... normal. "No."

"It's just she got in trouble at school today." Ellen's smile slipped and her voice wobbled. "For bullying. And it doesn't seem at all like her."

"Bullying?" Annabelle's eyebrows snapped together, and for a second Ellen thought she'd say something. Then her expression closed down and she turned towards the door. "I don't know anything about it," she said, completely dismissive. She was up the stairs before Ellen could ask anything else.

She made tea, her mind still seething with unanswered questions, and checked on Sophie, only to find her closeted with Annabelle yet again, music pounding. Gritting her teeth, Ellen knocked on the door of Annabelle's bedroom.

"Annabelle? Sophie? Tea in ten minutes."

A muffled "fine" was the only response, and Ellen couldn't tell which girl it came from.

Back downstairs she found Alex in the kitchen, his bicycle helmet dangling from one hand as he riffled through the day's post with the other.

"Alex." Relief pulsed through her at the thought that she finally had an ally, someone who could help her navigate this new minefield. "Did you get my voicemail?"

Alex looked up from his perusal of an alumnae magazine. "What voicemail?"

"About Sophie." Ellen pushed away the disappointment she felt at Alex not having picked up the message. She could hardly point the finger for not checking voicemails. "She's been suspended from school."

"What?" Alex's expression of incredulity was almost comical. "What on earth for?"

"For... for bullying. I can't believe it, but apparently she's been bullying a girl in her class, Chloe Dawson. But I think Chloe must have been doing something first..." She hoped.

"Bullying?" Alex shook his head slowly. "What kind of bullying?"

"I'm not exactly sure. Name-calling and... and pushing." Ellen bit her lip, the awfulness of it all hitting her afresh and bringing her near tears. "We need to talk to her about it. She's refusing to say anything to me."

"OK." Alex glanced at his watch. "I'm taking Annabelle to her parent/teacher conference in ten minutes."

"What?" Ellen stared at him blankly.

"I mentioned it last week."

"Right." Vaguely she remembered him saying something about it, and her suppressing a vague feeling of hurt that she was not included in the conference. She didn't even know how Annabelle was doing in her subjects, but presumably Alex did. "That won't take too long, surely?" she said, trying to rally. "An hour or so? We could still talk with Sophie when you get back."

Something flickered across Alex's face; Ellen couldn't tell if it was annoyance or guilt. "We're going to dinner after, to discuss her university applications," he said. "There's an open day at Manchester next week that I wanted her to attend."

Ellen swallowed, caught between tears and fury. "This is important, Alex."

"I know, Ellen, but this is important too. This is Annabelle's future."

"Haven't you talked about her university applications during your date nights?" Ellen demanded, her voice veering towards a snarl. "You've spent plenty of time with her in the last month. Can't you spare Sophie a single evening, when it's clearly so important?"

Alex stared at her for a long moment, his eyes dark and hard, his jaw tense. "I've missed out on Annabelle's entire childhood," he said. "I missed out on all the things I did with Sophie – teaching her to ride a bike, telling her stories, the lot. I'm not bailing on her now, Ellen." Ellen opened her mouth to protest but Alex cut across her before she could frame so much as a syllable. "I get that Sophie needs us both right now, and something is clearly going on. I'm not ignoring that, or her. But Annabelle is counting on this dinner—"

"And what if it's Annabelle that's making Sophie this way?" Ellen burst out. Alex stared at her, his expression turning even more grim.

"What do you mean by that?"

"Maybe... maybe she's been a bad influence on Sophie."

As soon as she said it, Ellen knew she shouldn't have. She'd just shut down any hope of a reasonable conversation, and she wasn't even sure she really thought that. Did she?

"I'll try to get back before Sophie goes to bed," Alex said, and walked out of the room.

# CHAPTER 22

## SARAH

Kendal, 1870

A week before they were to move to number four, Belmont, Clara came to the doorway of the kitchen, looking mutinous.

Sarah, having just set the week's bread to rising, eyed her askance. "Do you need something, Clara?"

"Yes. No. I don't know." Clara wrapped her arms around her middle and jutted out her chin. Sarah's wariness increased, a dread seeping into her stomach the same way the river water flooded the garden, dark and slimy.

"What do you mean? Is something wrong?"

"Yes." Clara's head was lowered so Sarah couldn't see her face. "Yes, I think something is. But I'm not sure."

"You must tell me what you mean, then," Sarah said, holding on to her patience with effort, but Clara remained silent. Sarah eyed her for another long moment as Lucy slid closer to her, half-hiding in her skirt, although she was getting too big to hide behind Sarah in that old way; in the last year she'd grown several inches, and her body was starting to be that of a woman, with slight, girlish curves.

"It's nothing," Clara said after a moment. Her face was pale and pasty-looking and she shook her head. "It's nothing," she repeated, less convincingly, and Sarah, exasperated and out of patience, let it lie.

Still the conversation, or lack of it, niggled at her for the next few days as they prepared for their move. The future loomed so close and bright and yet with every step nearer to the shining, perfect life Sarah envisaged in number four, Belmont, she had a growing terror that it would be snatched away. Hadn't everything else been?

She pictured Ruth Teddington's smiling face as she poured her another cup of tea from the big brown pot, back in the Goswell days when her mother hadn't been so terribly ill and Ruth had felt like a second mother, a friend.

"Don't borrow trouble," she would have said. "There's enough to go round as it is."

And so there was. Another two days passed with Clara seeming more and more out of sorts, skulking around the house or lying on the sofa, lazier than ever. Sarah tried to rouse her once or twice, but Clara simply turned her face away from her.

Then, one morning after James had left whistling for work, Clara rose from the breakfast table and dashed outside to the privy. From the kitchen, Sarah heard the sound of retching and she froze.

Ten endless minutes later Clara returned, looking pasty-faced and wiping her mouth.

Sarah turned to face her, taking a deep breath, her hands on her hips. "You'd better tell me what's going on."

Clara stared at her sulkily for a moment, the back of her hand against her lips, before she muttered, "You've most likely guessed, considering your own *blessed state.*" The two words were said on a sneer.

Sarah's stomach churned and for a moment she felt light-headed. "You can't mean... surely you can't mean what I think you mean," she whispered.

Clara glared at her. "What do you think I mean?"

"But how...?" She was at a complete loss, spinning in a void of shocked disbelief. "You never even go anywhere! How on earth could you have possibly..." She couldn't finish the thought. She couldn't grasp the possibility that Clara might have destroyed her prospects so utterly and appallingly. And what of her? When James discovered this atrocity, he would blame her. Completely. She knew that already, full well.

Clara's arms were wrapped around her middle, protectively, her shoulders hunched. Sarah sank onto a stool, Lucy leaning into her side.

"Who?" she asked faintly. "What man took these liberties with you?" Because she would have to marry him, if they could somehow contrive a way to make it happen. "What unscrupulous bounder took such liberties with you?" she demanded, and Clara didn't answer. Sarah glared at her, her voice ringing out. "Well? Answer me, Clara!"

"The curate," she said after an endless moment, her voice low. "Mr Fairley."

"Mr Fairley..." Sarah's breath came out in a defeated rush. She had no real affection for the man, cheerful as he was, but it still felt like an even worse betrayal. "A man of the cloth... a man who has accepted our hospitality..." She shook her head, her mind still spinning. "I can hardly countenance it. I did not know you had met with him. When...?"

"It doesn't matter."

"It does," Sarah returned fiercely. "Don't you realise your father shall blame me for your indiscretion? I'm responsible for you, and your wellbeing lies at my door. For this to happen..." She closed her eyes, not wanting to think of what James might do to her, or to Lucy. "We must speak to Mr Fairley right away," she said. "He will have to marry you. Reverend Cooper will have to give him permission, but perhaps we can contrive for him not to know the circumstances. How far along are you?"

Clara shrugged. "I started feeling sick a month ago."

"A month..." She had to be three months' gone, then, too late to pretend it was a wedding night baby. "Why did you not tell me then?" Sarah asked. "We could have arranged something sooner..."

"I didn't know," Clara cried, her voice thick with tears. "I didn't know that was how babies came about. I only realised when I saw how I was like you, getting sick in the mornings, and my dresses going tight."

"Oh, Clara." Sarah gazed at the girl with a rush of sympathy. She was nearly seventeen but she was still such a child. And Andrew Fairley had taken terrible advantage of her. "Still, we can manage," she said resolutely. "Mr Fairley will have to marry you." She shuddered to think of James's reaction to this turn of events, but there was nothing she could do about that now.

"I don't want to marry Mr Fairley," Clara said, her lower lip starting to tremble. "I can't. I won't."

Sarah stared at her, flummoxed. "No one else will have you now. You have no choice, Clara, and neither does he."

"I don't want to marry him," Clara insisted. Her tone was that of a child who didn't want to eat her supper or go to bed. Sarah half-expected her to stamp her foot. "I *won't*. There must be some other way."

"What other way could there possibly be?"

"Mr Fairley won't marry me anyway," Clara continued sulkily. "He doesn't even like me. He likes you better."

"He liked you well enough to get you into this state!"

"He'll deny it. Why wouldn't he? He could lose his position if it became known." Clara looked almost triumphant at presenting this bit of logic, confounding Sarah further.

"Then what do you suppose will happen to you, Clara?"

she asked quietly. "You'll have this baby and it will be given away and no one will so much as speak to you, or to any of us, in the street again. We shall all be completely shamed, and you will live out your days with even less comfort and companionship than you have now."

Clara didn't look at her as she answered in a low voice, "There must be another way."

It took Sarah a stunned few seconds to realise what she meant. "You mean... get rid of it? Of a child? That's a terrible sin, Clara, and very dangerous." She shuddered to think of it. "We could both go to prison." She pressed one hand against her own burgeoning middle, and felt the faint flutters of her own much-wanted baby. "I could not do that. I would not."

Clara looked up, her eyes swimming with tears. As miserable as she was, she looked strangely lovely in that moment, her face pale, her eyes shining, the very picture of helpless femininity. "Please, Sarah. Surely there is some way...? I can't let Father know. It would destroy him. He might blame you, but he'd blame me as well. He'd never look at me the same again, or love me. He's all I have. I can't lose his respect. *Please.*" Tears trickled down her face and Sarah sighed, wretched and defeated.

"I don't know what else to do. But I will think on it for a day or two. We can't wait much longer than that."

For the next two days, Sarah's mind went round in circles, finding no alternatives or ways out of Clara's terrible predicament. She lay awake at night, James snoring softly next to her, and stared gritty-eyed into the darkness, wondering how she could rescue Clara – and herself.

Then, on the way back from the fish market on Finkle Street, she saw Andrew Fairley walking towards the church, his step as light as ever, his smile welcoming when he caught sight of Sarah.

"Mrs Mills! How lovely to see you."

Something in Sarah snapped. She bustled towards the curate, Lucy by her side, a basket looped over her arm. "You have some audacity, sir, to address me thus," she said, keeping her voice low so as not to cause a scene. Andrew Fairley's fair eyebrows drew together in a comically puzzled frown.

"I beg your pardon?" He studied Sarah's narrowed and pursed lips for a moment before adding, "I fear something has happened of which I am not aware."

Against all caution, Sarah ploughed on. "Then you should be aware! Clara has suffered at your hands, sir, suffered dreadfully under your shameful treatment."

"My shameful..." Andrew Fairley shook his head slowly. "My dear Mrs Mills, I really do not have any idea as to what you refer. The last time I spoke with Miss Mills was at your house, when you kindly invited me to supper."

Sarah opened her mouth to refute such a bold-faced lie, only to close it again. Andrew Fairley's gaze was as clear and innocent as any she'd ever seen. She couldn't discern so much as the merest flicker of uncertainty or shame in his open, honest face. And now that she was standing here with the man in front of her, she realised how unlikely it was that he'd had some dalliance with Clara. He'd barely looked at her during the meal several months ago.

Sarah took a step back, scrambling to reassemble the shreds of her dignity. "I apologise," she said stiffly. "I believe I have spoken in error. Good day to you, sir." She turned and began to walk quickly away, pulling Lucy along with her.

"Mrs Mills, wait." Andrew caught up with her easily, and was brash enough to touch her sleeve. "Please, if something is distressing you, I would like to know about it. Is Miss Mills... is she in trouble?"

"It has naught to do with you," Sarah said. She could feel a flush of mortification scorching her cheeks. To think she'd almost blurted Clara's secret to this man. Why had the girl lied to her? "Good day," she said again, and pulling her arm away from him, she hurried down the street.

Back in the house Sarah slowly took off her bonnet, trying to think how to get the truth from Clara. All around her their possessions were packed into boxes and crates; they were moving in just five days. Five days until life was meant to start afresh for all of them, and yet that dream felt more distant than ever. How would they hold their heads up at number four, Belmont, with an unwed mother in their midst?

Slowly Sarah went to the kitchen, where she seemed to spend most of every day. She put her basket of fish for dinner on the table, her body aching with tiredness. Her baby fluttered within her and she pressed her palm against her middle, cradling that little life.

"It's all right, little one," she whispered. "You shall be safe." Although Clara had ruined her child's chances along with her own. How long in a small town such as this before their shame was forgotten, or at least forgiven?

Clara appeared in the doorway of the kitchen, wearing the same dress as the day before, her hair in a tangle about her blotchy face. She had spent most of the last two days in her room sleeping, waiting for Sarah to sort everything out.

Sarah took a deep breath and turned from the table. "Why did you lie to me?" she asked evenly.

Clara's eyes widened. "Lie..."

"Don't prevaricate now, Clara. I confronted Mr Fairley, and it was clear he had no idea what I was talking about."

Clara's blotchy face paled. "You didn't..."

"Of course I did. What else was I to do?" Sarah shook her head, exasperated beyond all measure and underneath that, afraid. "Why lie to me about this? It serves no purpose, and will only lead to more gossip." She pointed one shaking finger at Clara. "Who is responsible for your condition?"

Clara stared at her for a long moment, her eyes wide, her

lips trembling. "Eddie," she finally mumbled, and Sarah stared at her blankly.

"*Eddie?*" She'd never heard the name before.

"The butcher's boy."

"The butcher's..." For a second Sarah pictured the gormless lad who skulked by the kitchen door with his goggly eyes and pimply face. She thought of his dirty neck and the way he scratched himself, and a wave of fury crashed over her so she could barely see. "You stupid, stupid girl," she hissed, and then she drew her arm back and slapped Clara hard across the face.

Clara let out a cry, throwing one arm across her face as she reeled back. She steadied herself, lowering her arm, and glared at Sarah with both hate and hurt. "How dare you strike me—"

"How dare you bring such shame upon my household!" Sarah returned, her voice low and savage. She felt incandescent with rage, with the futility of everything she'd worked for and tried to build. Clara, in her selfish stupidity, was going to take it all away. "You have no sense, so shame, no dignity!" she continued, choking on the words. "You have ruined us all, and for what... some ill-begotten fumble with that idiot of a boy in the garden..." She shook her head, tears of anger and grief welling in her eyes. "You are even stupider than I thought."

"Don't," Clara said, her voice as low and savage as Sarah's. "You can't treat me this way—"

"Why not? Will you tell your father? Tell him everything, by all means. He will be as angry with you as he is with me, and well you know it!"

"I hate you," Clara choked. She raised her hand and Sarah stood still, bracing herself for Clara to strike her. But Clara, ever knowing what would hurt Sarah the most, didn't hit her. She hit Lucy, her fist ploughing into the side of Lucy's head so hard that Lucy went flying, letting out a scream, the only sound Sarah had ever heard her make.

"*Lucy...*" Sarah reached for her sister as Lucy scrambled to her feet, staring at Clara in wide-eyed terror before she turned and ran straight into Sarah, burying her head in Sarah's stomach so she stumbled back, her temple striking the corner of the range before she crumpled to the floor with Lucy on top of her.

For a few minutes Sarah was too dazed to speak. She could feel blood trickling down her face and Clara loomed above her, face as pale and round as a moon.

"Sarah..." she whispered. She looked terrified.

"I'm all right," Sarah whispered. All of her anger had drained out of her, leaving her stunned and empty. It had all happened so fast... her slapping Clara, Clara hitting Lucy... She closed her eyes, overcome. They'd been screaming and slapping like two coarse fishwives.

"Sarah," Clara whispered, her voice shaking. "You're bleeding."

Sarah touched her cheek. "I know..."

"Not there," Clara said, and it was only then that Sarah felt the terrible wetness between her thighs and she registered the bands of pain that started in her back and tightened around her middle, a painful squeeze as her hope bled out of her.

# CHAPTER 23

## ELLEN

Alex did not return before Sophie went to bed. Ellen sat on the edge of her daughter's bed while Sophie lay so her back was to her, her knees tucked up to her chest. She'd refused a bedtime story.

"Sophie," Ellen said, and then stopped, because she felt at such a loss. She'd taken Sophie's sunny disposition for granted, she realised. In actuality she'd been a bit smug about it, as if Sophie's cheerful childhood had been down to her excellent mothering skills rather than simple genetics. Now, faced with this sulky Sophie whose eyes blazed defiance, Ellen had no idea what to say.

So she said nothing, stroking Sophie's narrow back, her thumbs finding the knobs of her spine as she remembered doing when Sophie was a newborn, cradled in her arms, red, wizened, and perfect. "We'll talk tomorrow," she finally said, wanting the words to be to a comfort rather than a threat. Sophie did not reply. Ellen squeezed her shoulder once and then rose from the bed. She turned out the light and went downstairs to the emptiness of the kitchen, too distracted and on edge to work or even tidy up.

She ended up sitting in the conservatory in the semi-dark, slowly sipping a glass of wine and planning what she'd say to Alex when he returned. An apology seemed like the best option, the choice most likely to bring harmony back to her life and marriage. But she didn't *feel* like apologising. She *did* believe Annabelle was a bad influence, whether Alex thought that was unfair or not. If Annabelle hadn't come to live with them, then Ellen didn't think they'd be in this position, with Sophie sulky and defiant, suspended from school for pushing a girl.

By eleven o'clock, Ellen was feeling tired and played out and she went upstairs, turning off all the lights and putting Pepper to bed, silent but pointed reminders to Alex that he'd stayed out too late.

She didn't think she'd be able to sleep but she ended up falling abruptly into one of those deep, dreamless slumbers that had her starting awake when Alex came in the room at past midnight. She lay still, her eyes closed, as he moved around the room, dropping change onto the bureau with an irritating clatter and leaving his clothes on the floor.

Ellen pretended to be asleep as he got into bed, the mattress dipping beneath his weight. For a second she thought he'd touch her, give some kind of silent message of his understanding, but then he rolled onto his side away from her and a few minutes later he was snoring. Now it took her a long time to fall asleep.

Alex was up by five for his bike ride to work and Ellen couldn't summon the energy for a conversation, much less an argument. She stayed in bed, feigning sleep until she heard the front door close, wondering how it had got to this. They'd never been like this before. They'd never even argued, not really. Alex was too rational for that; he always came at her with logical arguments, reasonable suppositions, and Ellen didn't mind because she'd had enough of the screaming and slanging matches with Jack. Yet right now this cold and stony silence seemed worse than any set-to she'd had with her ex-husband.

At seven she got up and made coffee, putting out bread and jam and cereal for when Annabelle came down at a quarter to eight.

"Good morning," she said in a voice that was far too chirpy. Annabelle narrowed her eyes. "You had a late night last night."

"Yeah." Annabelle pulled her shiny hair into a tight pony-tail, effectively dismissing Ellen.

"How was the parent/teacher conference?" Ellen asked, determined to persevere. "I know you haven't been there that long yet, but did they have some..." She struggled to find the most positive spin on the question. "Insightful comments?"

Annabelle's lip curled. "Insightful comments? Yeah, I guess. They didn't seem to think I was a *bad influence*, so that's something."

Oh, not again. Why did everything she wanted to keep quiet get overheard? "Annabelle..." Ellen began, her hands clenched around her coffee cup, the blood draining from her head. "I'm sorry..."

"Yeah, right." Annabelle turned, her long ponytail swishing, to get her bag. "It's not like I haven't known what you think of me, so you can just drop the mumsy act, OK?"

Ellen took a deep breath. She could feel her temper starting to fray because, for heaven's sake, she was tired of everyone blaming her. "You know," she said, an edge to her voice, "it's not as if you've made any of this easy for me."

"Easy for *you*?" Annabelle's perfectly shaped eyebrows rose and her mouth twisted in a snarl. "How do you think it feels for me? I'm the one who got dumped here like some return-to-sender parcel. I'm the one who has to fit myself into your perfect little family when it's so frigging obvious that there's no place for me. You don't want me here, you never have, and no amount of stupid throw pillows or home-made cakes is going to change that so just drop the act, OK? Save us both some time."

Hoisting her bag onto her shoulder, Annabelle stormed from the room, leaving Ellen feeling shaky and sick. She heard the door slam and sank onto a kitchen chair, wondering if the day could get any worse.

Fifteen minutes later Sophie slumped into the kitchen, and Ellen decided she would redeem this day, no matter what. "How about we make a cake?" she suggested to Sophie, as her daughter sat at the table, shovelling in her breakfast with a list-less air.

Sophie glanced up at her dolefully. "A cake?" she repeated around a mouthful of cereal. "What kind?"

"What kind would you like to make?"

Sophie's eyes brightened a little. "Can we make a chocolate volcano cake?"

Of course. The one cake that required a huge amount of faff, a special pan, and a lot of mess. Ellen smiled. "Of course."

An hour later they'd assembled all the ingredients on the kitchen counter, and Sophie was happily measuring flour while Ellen creamed the butter. Standing there in a pool of sunshine, the house peaceful and quiet, Ellen could almost forget all the vitriol and tension she'd experienced recently. She could almost pretend it wasn't a Wednesday morning, and Sophie wasn't suspended from school. She'd turned her phone off around the time of the school run to avoid the well-meaning but gossipy questions of other mums as they learned about Sophie's suspension. Explanations were beyond her at this point.

Friday, when Sophie went back to school, would be hard enough. And tonight, when Alex came back, would be hard too.

"Sophie," Ellen began hesitantly when they'd mixed the cake and were pouring the thick chocolatey batter into the Bundt pan, "what did Chloe Dawson say that made you push her?"

Sophie's face closed up and she looked away. "I don't want to talk about it."

Ellen couldn't help but feel her daughter had learned that line straight from Annabelle. "I want to talk about it," she said firmly. She would not be managed by a ten-year-old. "I want to know exactly what happened."

Ellen waited while Sophie maintained a sullen silence for a few seconds and then gave a long, drawn-out sigh as she scuffed her foot along the floor. Finally she said, "It was all really stupid." And then stopped, as if that would satisfy her mother.

"I need more than that, Soph."

"Chloe's always going on about how cool she is and how everybody else's stuff is really naff." Naff? When had her ten-year-old learned that word? "And you know she's got this posh handbag, and Emily Hawes had a knock-off one and she, like, completely rubbished it..."

"Wait." Ellen held up a hand, feeling almost dizzy. This was *Sophie*. She did not talk about posh handbags and naff knock-offs. She didn't even know what those things were. She skipped down the street with Merrie and read books about ponies or fairies.

"What?" Sophie jutted her lip out, looking mutinous. "You *asked* me to tell you."

"I know, but..." Ellen shook her head slowly. "I didn't even think you talked to Chloe Dawson."

"I didn't," Sophie said, with an emphasis on the past tense.

"So you have been talking to her recently?"

Sophie shrugged. Ellen couldn't help but feel Annabelle was involved in this somehow. "Did you talk to Annabelle about Chloe?" she asked.

"What?" Sophie's eyes rounded. "What does that have to do with anything?"

"Just answer the question, Sophie."

"Maybe. I don't know. I don't remember."

"Don't you?"

Sophie glared at her. "Why would I?"

"Because I can't help but feel you're not telling me something here. You never even mentioned Chloe Dawson and now it's all handbags and arguments? What's been going on?"

Another shrug. "What did Annabelle tell you?" Ellen demanded.

"Why are you so obsessed with Annabelle?"

"Because you are sounding a lot like her and I want my own daughter back!" Too late Ellen realised how shrill she sounded. "Please, Sophie..." Her voice broke a little, and her heart broke even more when Sophie's expression hardened and she flounced from the room.

Ellen got through the rest of the day on autopilot – bills to pay, an article to proof, tea to make. She dragged Sophie out to walk Pepper with her, avoiding the high street and taking the shortcut through the back of the garden to the golf course, not wanting to see anyone and invite questions or worse, sympathy.

When had her life become such a *mess*? She was Ellen Tyson, bubbly and on top of it all – laughingly, just – cheerfully disorganised but still managing to bake gorgeous meringues for the bake sale, shrugging at life's idiosyncrasies and enjoying – only a bit smugly – its benefits.

Goodness, but she wanted to give her former self a slap upside the head, tell her to clamber off that high, high pedestal she'd scrambled onto without even realising it. She wanted to shake her own shoulders and tell her that nothing was that safe, that the family life she'd thought she'd cultivated and earned might only be a mirage. Too bad her former self wouldn't listen.

Now she strode through the tussocky grass between the golf course and the coastal path, a surprisingly brisk wind biting at her, Pepper frisking at her heels. Sophie had lagged behind and was atypically dragging her feet – although what was typical of this new Sophie, this Annabelle-in-waiting? Ellen didn't know any more.

She breathed in the salty sea air and let the damp wind sting her cheeks, telling herself when she got back she'd be different, she'd make it up to Annabelle and Alex, she'd be honest and even-tempered and loving. She glanced at Sophie, who was shivering slightly in the brisk wind.

"I suppose we ought to go back."

Back at home the post-baking mess of chocolatey bowls and spills of flour and sugar greeted her, along with a volcano cake that had one large, sticky slice taken out of it. Ellen stared at the cake, silently fuming, amazed that even Annabelle would have the gall to help herself to a piece of cake that she had to have known was meant for dessert – and taken it upstairs, judging by the slamming door Ellen had heard as she'd come in the house. Ellen had lost the opportunity to offer a cheerful welcome as well as safeguard her cake. Just as well, perhaps, she decided as she made herself a cup of tea. She wasn't sure she could face Annabelle right now.

As soon as they'd got home, Sophie had disappeared upstairs, and Ellen winced as she heard Annabelle's door slam for a second time.

By the time Alex came home, supper was on the table, admittedly only sausages from the freezer, and mash, and the post-cake mess had been tidied up. Sophie and Annabelle had not come downstairs.

"Hey," Ellen said, pitching her voice light as she tried for smile. "How was work?"

"Fine." She couldn't tell anything from Alex's tone or his expression as his head was bent as he looked through the day's post, all bills and brochures.

Ellen called Sophie and Annabelle downstairs while Alex went to change, and a few minutes later they sat down for tea, all happy families, at least on the surface.

When Ellen brought the cake out, with the sunniest smile she could manage, Sophie clapped her hands and seemed almost her old, excited self.

"You'll have to tell us if it's any good, Annabelle," Ellen said lightly, "seeing as you're the only one who has tasted it." As soon as she said the words, and saw the way they landed in the centre of the table like a grenade casually thrown, she wished them back.

"Nice one, Ellen," Alex muttered.

She hadn't meant it like that. At least, she didn't *think* she had. Yes, she was annoyed Annabelle took a slice of cake, up to her room no less, without asking. But she'd been... well, she didn't know what she'd been thinking. Maybe she'd simply felt the need to address the cake's missing slice. Maybe she had been acting out of petty spite, but not *consciously*. Was that worse?

"It was OK, I guess," Annabelle answered in a tone that suggested it was the worst cake she'd ever eaten, eyes snapping angry defiance, and Ellen did not reply.

They ate the cake in silence, all of the goodwill Ellen had put into making it leaching out, unnoticed, ignored. After supper Alex disappeared into the conservatory with his laptop, and Annabelle and Sophie headed upstairs. Again. Ellen tidied up alone.

She tried to use the time to calm her temper, but it didn't work. She was, she realised, quite furious. She was bloody tired of everyone blaming her for everything that went wrong. And she needed Alex to realise how his own actions were affecting their family life, as much as hers were.

Taking a deep breath, she steeled herself for what was ahead and went into the conservatory.

"May I talk to you for a minute? A few minutes?"

"What is it?" Alex did not even look up from his laptop.

"Alex. Can you give me your attention, please?" Already

her voice possessed an edge, and Alex noticed. He lifted his gaze from the screen with exaggerated, weary patience, making Ellen grit her teeth. "You know, Sophie was home from school on suspension and you haven't even asked about it."

"What is there to ask? She was home all day, right?"

"Don't you *care*?" Ellen burst out. "It's as if... it's almost as if... you don't care about us any more."

Alex sighed. "Ellen, you're being melodramatic."

"Melodramatic? Our daughter was suspended from school for two days at only ten years old and you don't even ask why or what we should do about it."

"Did Sophie tell you why she was suspended?"

"Miss West told me. She pushed a girl in the class."

"OK."

"*OK?*" Ellen repeated in disbelief. "Aren't you curious? Concerned? It's not like Sophie. Don't you think it's a bit... strange?"

Alex shrugged. "She's ten. Ten-year-olds do strange things sometimes."

"You sound completely unconcerned."

"Not completely, Ellen," Alex answered, an edge in his voice to match hers, "but I'm pragmatic. She's ten. She pushed a girl. I think the school is most likely overreacting because they have to be seen to crack down on bullies. I don't think Sophie is going to turn into a mini-thug. I also don't," he added, his steely gaze focused on her, "think Annabelle is a bad influence."

"So that's what this is about? You're refusing to take an interest in Sophie because I said that?"

"I'm not refusing to take an interest in Sophie. For heaven's sake!" Alex slammed the lid of his laptop down and then rubbed his temples. Maybe she was giving him a headache. "Why do you keep insisting on turning this into a battle?" He looked up at her, resentful and despairing. "Why do I have to take sides?"

Ellen blinked, stung. "I don't want you to take sides," she said quietly. "But with the way Annabelle is—"

"Don't—"

"I can't help it, Alex! Nothing I do works with her!" Ellen's voice came out high and shrill, a near-shriek of total exasperation. "Why can't you see that? Why can't you accept that I'm trying?"

"I've never said you weren't."

"But it's not enough for you, or Annabelle."

Alex just sighed and shook his head. They always came to this impasse, and there seemed to be no way to get across it. Slowly Ellen walked over to a sofa and dropped herself onto it. "Did you ever think," she asked slowly, hesitantly, "what a mess this would all be?"

Alex frowned. "What do you mean?"

"The fact that we're both on our second marriages." Ellen's throat felt tight. They *never* talked this way. "The fact that we've both got all this emotional baggage."

"Do we?" His voice sounded ominously neutral. "I didn't realise."

"I've never even asked about your marriage to Sandra. You've never told me anything."

"That's because it was in the past."

"That's what I thought, but it doesn't feel that way now."

"Ellen..." Alex leaned back against the sofa cushions and closed his eyes. Now she'd exhausted him. "Why are you bringing all this up?"

"Because having Annabelle here has made me realise how little I know of her. Of Sandra. I don't even know what she looks like."

"Why should you want to know that?"

"I don't know. It's just..." Ellen shrugged, unsure if she could explain or if she even wanted to. "Suddenly it seems important."

"It isn't," Alex said firmly. "The last thing we need is to drag Sandra into all this."

"All this? What exactly is 'all this'?"

"You know what I mean. Things haven't been easy lately."

"Annabelle mentioned something," Ellen blurted. She knew now was not the time to bring up this particular nugget of information, and yet she couldn't help herself. She needed to know. "She said something about your crap."

Alex stilled. "What are you talking about?"

Ellen was really wishing she hadn't said anything. "Annabelle said something about Sandra putting up with your crap."

Alex's eyebrows rose. "Seriously? You're hitting me with that now?"

"There's just so much I don't know—"

"I don't ask about you and Jack—"

"Because I told you everything!" The first few months they'd dated Ellen had poured it all out, the regrets and hurts, the arguments and infidelities on Jack's side. Alex had listened and hugged her and she'd been so sure he was different. So grateful. And he *was* different. "Alex, it's reasonable for me to want to know—"

"What? How I failed as a husband? Is that what you're looking for? You want some catalogue of crimes I committed against Sandra so you can compare?"

"No..." Ellen's voice came out in a whisper. She'd never seen Alex look so coldly furious.

Alex shook his head in disgust and shoved his laptop away. "I'm going to bed," he said, and stalked out of the room.

# CHAPTER 24

## SARAH

Kendal, 1871

Sarah stayed in bed for a week after the bleeding started. She slept for most of it, too bone-weary to so much as open her eyes, and then when she finally wakened she simply stared out the window, feeling as if the very will to live had left her along with her hoped-for baby, slipped from her body so quickly and quietly, and whisked away by a midwife before Sarah had so much as glimpsed her face.

Clara tended to her, creeping in to change her bedclothes or feed her broth. They never spoke; what could they possibly say to one another? Sarah had no more words.

They did not move to number four, Belmont. James, pale-faced but resolute, said they had no need of it any more. Sarah did not argue. In truth she was not even surprised. It had always felt too good to be true, a shining promise just out of her grasp. Of course it would have slipped away.

After a week, she knew James's husbandly concern had started to ebb; Clara was neither cook nor housekeeper and he wanted his hot meals and his ironed shirts. Sarah rose from her bed.

She felt shaky and weak as she came into the kitchen, surveying its dark dankness and realising with a numb and leaden certainty that she would never leave this place. She would never see anything but the four damp walls of this awful kitchen, bending low over the open range, endlessly turning the mangle's handle, Lucy anxious, pressed to her side. She took a shuddering breath and began to make their midday meal.

She dragged herself through several days, her mind a blur, her body aching, as she cooked and washed and scrubbed and starched, the surprisingly balmy summer days passing her by completely. Then Clara cornered her in the kitchen while James was at work, her hands clenched in her apron, her expression a mixture of fear and resentment.

"Sarah, it's been weeks. What am I going to do?"

Sarah looked up from the basin of soapy water where she'd been soaking James's collars, half-surprised to realise how indifferent she felt now to Clara's predicament. Clara had a baby she did not want and Sarah had nothing but an empty, sagging belly and a weighed down heart.

"You'll have to tell your father."

"I *can't...*"

"Well, what am I do?" She felt a spark of ire that roused her briefly from her numb complacency. "Why should I clean up your despicable mess?"

Clara's face crumpled and Sarah watched as two fat tears slid down her pasty cheeks. "Please, Sarah," she whispered. "I... I know I haven't been kind to you." She glanced guiltily at Lucy who was crouched by the table, drawing patterns on the linoleum. "Or Lucy."

"*Kind?*" Sarah's voice rang out scornfully. "You haven't been *kind?*"

Clara bowed her head. "Please."

Sarah turned back to the soaking collars and closed her eyes. She was so very, very tired, and nothing seemed to matter much any more. But why should Clara's life be destroyed along with her own? The disappointment and shame James would surely feel would not help any of them, and she wasn't even angry with Clara. She didn't have the strength to be.

"There is one possibility," she said quietly, the words drawn from her with slow reluctance.

"Oh, what is it? Please, what? I'll do anything."

"I'll do it," Sarah answered. "I'll write my mother's friend, Ruth Teddington."

That night while James was in the front room reading the paper and Clara had hidden away in her room, Sarah took out pen and paper and a bottle of ink and sat at the kitchen table, the dishes dried and stacked, the floor cleanly swept, and wondered what to write.

She rested her chin in her hand, her body aching with tiredness, and looked around the kitchen that she both loathed and accepted. She couldn't think of the bright, cheerful kitchen of number four, Belmont – it was far too painful to think of that. She couldn't think of the bedroom Lucy could have had, the change in all of their circumstances that would have been so welcome, had felt so needed. She especially couldn't think of the baby she would have cherished and loved, the child that would have been her own, beloved and blessed.

Sighing, she looked back down at the blank paper and began to write.

*Dear Ruth,*

*It has been quite a while since I have last written you, I know, but circumstances compel me to pen a few lines. Life has held many trials and burdens these last few months, not least the loss of my own hoped-for child. My stepdaughter, Clara, however, finds herself in delicate circumstances...*

Gritting her teeth, Sarah continued writing, throwing herself on Ruth's mercy for Clara's sake.

*If you could take her in, and see that everything is satisfactorily arranged... I know you have wanted to help us in the past, and in your great kindness you will surely not shirk your Christian duty towards my family, considering the desperate straits we find ourselves in.*

In fact, Sarah suspected Ruth would very much wish to shirk said duty. She would not welcome an unwed girl and her unwanted child, but she would do it, Sarah hoped, out of long-held guilt for the way she'd once failed both Sarah and Lucy. Clara could, with some help from the hand of Providence, a hand Sarah still regarded with deep suspicion, live quietly in Goswell, give birth, and leave the child in the home for orphans in Whitehaven. It pained Sarah to think of Clara's child being left like a parcel, while hers...

But she couldn't think about hers.

She sent the letter the next day, and Ruth's response came a few days after that, filled with lamentations for "dear Sarah and poor Lucy", and a deep reluctance to take "such a daughter as which you find yourself", and yet, at the end of the missive that was filled with misgivings, Ruth agreed to the thing.

Now, Sarah acknowledged with yet more weariness, she simply had to get her husband to agree. She sat across from him at supper the next night, watching him methodically chewing the saddle of lamb she'd made and Sarah felt absolutely nothing. She was completely numb inside, and she'd decided, after some reflection, that it was no bad thing. Far better to feel nothing than to feel pain and grief and sorrow, all of which seethed beneath the surface of her mind like black, churning water beneath the cold, frozen ice.

"Clara has seemed a bit worn out as of late," she said after supper, when the dishes had been cleared away and James was in the little parlour, his booted feet stretched out towards the empty grate. The brief blazing days of summer had given way to grey and rain, but he had not wanted to spare the coal for a fire. "A bit out of sorts."

"Well, it's been a difficult few weeks," James replied, and snapped his paper, his gaze scanning the headlines.

Sarah watched him, wondering what he thought about his daughter. He spoiled her, yes, but he could also be remarkably indifferent to her. Would he have been the same to their child? And perhaps, one day, although she could not truly think of it yet, she would know. Perhaps she would have another chance at a child. And yet she both feared and felt in her very bones that there would not be a chance – her mother hadn't had many chances. Briefly she closed her eyes.

"I wonder," she said as she opened them again, "if she might like a change."

James did not look up from his paper. "A change?"

"For a few weeks." Or months, most likely, since Clara was not yet five months gone by Sarah's reckoning. Fortunately she was not showing yet, besides a plumpness that could have been attributed to the chocolates James brought her. "Somewhere fresh, where she could meet new people, respectable acquaintances."

James finally looked up from his paper, his eyebrows drawn together in a frown. "What on earth can you mean?"

"It's only that my Aunt Ruth—" the lie slipped easily from her lips "—is in want of a companion for a short time. Goswell is on the sea, and I think the air could be good for Clara. It would be an opportunity for her."

"An aunt? I thought you had no relations."

The easy lie had become a snare. "Aunt Ruth is my only one."

"And she did not see fit to help you in your time of need?"

"She would have done, of course, but her husband was poorly at the time." The lies tumbled thick and fast, entrapping her. "He's passed to his reward recently, God rest him, and that is why she would enjoy some company." She held her breath, wishing she had not said Ruth was her aunt. She'd simply thought it would sound more respectable and convincing if Ruth was related to her.

"I don't know." James managed to look both thoughtful and impatient. "Why should she go anywhere?"

"Why should she not? She is a young girl on the brink of life. A change could be good for her." Sarah paused, weighing her words. "And perhaps," she said, softening her voice, "for us."

James stared at her for a moment, nonplussed. Sarah was not surprised. Sometimes it did not feel that there was an "us", not in the way she could still remember had been with her parents.

"Perhaps," he said at last. "I shall think on it."

Sarah knew better than to push him. She waited two days, endless days where Clara paced and wrung her hands and Sarah noted the growing soft swell of her belly with alarm. They could not wait much longer.

Then, after dinner when he was sated and mostly content, she asked again. "Have you thought on Clara's situation?"

James frowned and Sarah waited, a faint smile of docile acceptance on her face, her hands clenched in the folds of her apron.

"Does she wish to go?" he asked irritably, and Sarah drew a careful breath.

"Ask her yourself by all means," she said. "But I believe she does."

She arranged the train fare the next day.

Sarah had not thought much beyond James's agreement. She helped pack Clara's things, and wrote again to Ruth, and then saw her to the train station where she'd stepped off herself over three years before. Clara gave her a tremulous smile, biting her lip, her eyes full of tears.

"Sarah..." Her voice trembled, and she said nothing else.

"Godspeed," Sarah said briskly. She was surprised to find her chest was tight with emotion. She had not expected to miss Clara, who had made her and Lucy's life such a misery for so long, and yet she thought she would, at least a little.

The house was quiet upon their return; James had returned to work and Sarah moved slowly about their rooms, relishing and despising their silence at turns. Then her thoughts went to Clara's bedroom and a smile bloomed across her face.

"Lucy," she called, holding her arms out to her sister. "How would you like your own bed?"

James resisted the idea at first, claiming Lucy would get too used to it and resist her inevitable return to the kitchen, but Sarah would not be swayed. "You cannot countenance keeping her in the kitchen like the lowliest servant when there is a spare bed!" she said, her voice rising despite her best efforts to remain calm and reasonable. "James, please. This is but a small boon to my sister, and therefore to me."

He relented, grudgingly, and Sarah stood on her tiptoes to kiss his cheek. "Thank you," she whispered, and James looked at her in surprise.

"Does it mean as much to you as all that?"

She simply nodded, wondering how, after so many years, he could possibly ask such a question.

The next few weeks passed in a cautiously pleasant blur. Lucy revelled in her room and bed, and Sarah found that although it had been unsettling at first, she soon relished the peace and quiet of River Cottage without Clara lounging in her room or skulking around corners. Lucy began to blossom, offering more genuine, wide smiles as she took delight in simple things without bracing herself for a pinch or slap. In the guilty quiet of her own mind, Sarah wished Clara would stay away forever.

She wrote weekly, dutiful letters to James that detailed a life Sarah questioned the reality of – walks along the beach taking the sea air, and gentle pursuits with "Aunt Ruth". She enclosed a bit of inexpert needlework as proof, and James seemed satisfied. She did not write to Sarah.

Two months after Clara had left, James began to ask, in an indifferent sort of way, when she would return. Sarah put him off and wrote to Clara, asking her to request to stay longer. Clara did so, an effusive letter detailing the charms of Goswell, the people she'd met. Sarah read it and wondered if any of it was true.

And then, a month later, Clara wrote to Sarah alone. She sat in the sitting room, Lucy playing with a handful of spillikins, and read the missive with its round, childishly formed letters, in growing disbelief.

*Dear Sarah,*

*So much has happened since I have come to Goswell. You were right in that I did need a change, and being here has helped me so wonderfully. Oh Sarah, I have met someone – a good man, a kind man. He is a carpenter and he has been so tender with me; he does not even mind the child and will allow me to raise it as our own. I know you and Father had aspirations for me beyond a simple carpenter, a man who cannot even read, but he loves me and I love him and I have no wish to go back to the stuffy confines of the house in Kendal. I am to be married shortly, and I will make my life in Goswell. Please tell Father for me. I cannot bear his disappointment or disap-*

*proval. By the time you receive this letter, I will be Mrs Frampton!*

*Yours sincerely,*

*Clara*

Sarah put down the letter with shaking hands, caught between a sudden, rising fury – that Clara should presume so much! And act as if her trip to Goswell had truly been for the sea air and a rest rather than to hide her pregnancy! – and also a thankfulness that poor, wretched Clara, unkind as she had been, should find some happiness, and in such an unlikely situation. Yet she had left Sarah to tell James? Her stomach clenched at the thought. James, she feared, would not take such news well – but perhaps she was being fearful. Maybe he would be pleased to see Clara well-placed.

She told him that night, after Lucy had gone to bed. "Clara wrote to me today," she began, her voice quavering a little. She had no idea what to expect from him.

"She wrote to you?" James sounded faintly surprised but mostly uninterested. "We should book her tickets to come back. She has been gone too long."

"She seems happy there." James shrugged, and Sarah continued, her voice tentative, too tentative, "James... she wrote to me that she has met a man. A man she intends to marry."

James stared at her blankly for a moment before he drew back, his face already starting to turn red with masculine affront. "What? That is not possible!"

Sarah tried not to gulp. She'd been hoping, nonsensical as such a wish might have been, that James might be pleased at Clara's good fortune. "It is, James," she said, trying to placate him. "She wrote to me herself—"

"Let me see the letter."

Sarah stared at him, shocked and dismayed. "I... I'm not sure where I put it..." She could feel her heart starting to hammer, her palms to sweat. He couldn't see that letter, not with its mention of the baby. Why had Clara been so imprudent? Why had she?

"You must know," James answered flatly. "It was obviously important." His eyes narrowed. "What are you hiding from me, Sarah? What are you keeping from me about my own daughter?"

Sarah did not answer. She could not form a lie, not now, when James was glaring at her, when he looked as if he knew. "I..." Her mind spun and swam. She did not know what to say.

"Fetch me the letter," James said in a cold, hard voice she'd never heard before, a voice that made her quake inside. "Right now."

Wordlessly, her stomach starting to heave, Sarah retrieved the letter from the top drawer of the bureau where she'd hidden it beneath her underthings. She didn't know what else to do; she couldn't think of a way to keep it from him.

James took the letter silently and scanned the lines. Sarah knew the exact moment when he read about Clara's child. He jerked as if he'd been hit, and then his features ironed out, his fingers clenched on the single sheet. A long moment passed after he'd finished reading; Sarah waited, bracing herself, and yet for what? She did not even know. She was afraid to think.

Finally James looked up. "You deceived me."

Sarah licked dry lips. "For Clara's sake..."

"You led my daughter astray."

"No—"

"You permitted her to... to *fornicate!*" He snarled the word, and then hurled the letter towards the empty grate. It missed, fluttering to the floor in a slow, lazy way that seemed like a mockery. James let out another snarl of pure fury and reached for the paper, tearing it into bits that fluttered around them in terrible confetti.

Sarah blinked, holding herself steady even though her heart felt set to beat its way up her throat. "I am sorry, James," she whispered. "I did not know what to do. Clara begged me..."

"Who is the father of her ill-begotten child?"

"I..." Sarah faltered, looking away, and then she gasped when James grabbed her chin and forced her to look at him.

"Sarah! Who is the father of my daughter's bastard child?"

"The... the butcher's boy," Sarah whispered. Tears formed in her eyes and spilled down her cheeks. James, his face now white with tight-lipped fury, did not soften in the least. "He came round the house with a barrow twice a week."

"The butcher's boy," James repeated tonelessly. His fingers were squeezing her chin hard enough to hurt, and he dropped his hand. "The butcher's boy."

"Yes..."

James shook his head slowly, now looking winded, and Sarah wondered what hurt the most. The fact that Clara had so lowered herself, or that he had been deceived? All of it an affront to him as a man, a husband, a father. She swallowed hard.

"I really am so very sorry, James. I had no idea—"

"I do not care for your apologies." His tone was flat and cold. "We will talk about this in the morning," he said, and he got into bed.

Slowly Sarah followed suit, blowing out the candle and lying there in the dark, her body as stiff as James's. She could hear him breathing, and knew when he dropped off to sleep. She remained relentlessly awake, her heart beating with dull, resigned thuds, long into the night.

The next morning James shook her awake, one hand rough on her shoulder. Sarah blinked muzzily; she was usually up by dawn, but bright light poured through the windows.

"I'm sorry…"

"Get dressed," James ordered. "I'm taking you out."

"Out…?" She didn't trust the cool, resolute look in his eyes, the firm set of his shoulders. There was no smile.

"Yes. Out."

Sarah washed and dressed as quickly as she could; she could hear James pacing downstairs, and with a quaking heart she wondered where on earth he was taking her. Were they going to travel to Goswell to fetch Clara? It would be hours on the train.

She plaited Lucy's hair and put a fresh pinafore on her, trying to smile for her sister's sake, although she could tell Lucy knew she was nervous. Her sister placed one hand on her cheek and gazed up at her solemnly, a question in her eyes.

"It's all right, Lucy. James is taking us out on a trip." Sarah tried to inject a jolly note in her voice. "Won't that be fun? It's a lovely day, nice and crisp. The leaves are starting to turn."

As they stepped outside of River Cottage she saw that James had hired a carriage, and for some reason her unease grew.

"Where are we going?" she asked as he helped her inside.

"You'll see."

The horses began to jaunt across the uneven cobbles and Lucy clutched on to Sarah as they jostled down the road. They did not travel very far. The carriage stopped at Windermere Road, and when Sarah peered out the window she went cold all over. They were in front of the Kendal Union workhouse.

"No…" The word came out of her in a groan from deep within. "No, please…"

In the dim interior of the carriage she saw the resolute iron in James's eyes, his pursed mouth. "You took away the person I most loved," he stated. "Now I will do the same to you."

Sarah grabbed onto his arm. "No, James, please. Please don't this." Her voice came out choked, tears spilling down her

cheeks. She swiped them away impatiently; this was too important to give way to such useless emotion. "Please, I'll do
anything. Just please keep Lucy with me..."

James shook her arm off and climbed out of the carriage. He
turned to Lucy with a bright, hard smile. "Come on, poppet."

Lucy glanced at Sarah and then at James, and then at Sarah
again. She shook her head. Sarah pressed one fist to her lips,
helpless, wanting only to snatch Lucy and hold her forever.
"Please," she whispered, but James was already reaching into
the carriage and hoisting Lucy into his arms.

Lucy, sensing Sarah's grief and fear, began to kick and strug-
gle. Two attendants from the workhouse stepped forward to
take her, bundling her away towards the grim stone building
that signified all that was hopeless, and Sarah heard an
unearthly keening sound, a sound of terrible sorrow and fear.
She thought it was coming from Lucy, and it wasn't until James
had got back into the carriage and closed the doors that she
realised she was making it herself.

# CHAPTER 25

## ELLEN

On Friday Ellen walked a silent Sophie to school, keeping her head high and trying not to meet anyone's compassionate or curious gaze. She'd kept a very low profile since Sophie's suspension, turning off her phone and staying off the high street. She'd even let Jane's call to their home phone go to voice-mail, which felt both mean and cowardly, but she couldn't face the prying questions or even the genuine concern.

The mood in the house over the last two days had been one of frozen hostility. Alex left for work before Ellen rose, and last night he'd immersed himself in his laptop – except when he'd taken Pepper for a walk with Annabelle. Ellen had watched them head off towards the gate at the bottom of the garden and wondering why such a simple, pleasant scene – her husband and his daughter walking together – had the power to hurt.

She'd gone over her own feelings and motives endlessly, questioning whether she was truly petty and spiteful to feel hurt and angry about Alex's choices. Had she been unfair to Annabelle? Was there any way to make it up to her, as well as protect Sophie from her teenaged influence? Or maybe she was completely off base, and Annabelle wasn't influencing Sophie at all. Maybe Sophie's sudden sullenness was more about being almost eleven than anything else.

Jane made a beeline for her as soon as she reached the playground. *"Ellen..."* Her voice was full of confusion and sympathy, and it forced Ellen into the kind of brave smile she didn't feel remotely like giving.

"Hi." She nodded towards Sophie. "I'm going to take her in today."

"Of course." Jane gave Sophie a brief, sympathetic smile that Sophie ignored. Another chip broke off Ellen's fragmenting heart.

She kept her gaze straight ahead and so did Sophie as they entered the classroom. She'd tried to give Sophie a pep talk that morning, telling her that everyone made mistakes and this was a fresh start, blah, blah, blah as far as Sophie was concerned. She eyed Ellen with ill-concealed disbelief before turning away.

Now Ellen gave her teacher, Miss Forrester, a tense smile as Sophie headed to her desk. Thankfully Miss Forrester gave Sophie a quick hug, nothing too over the top, said good morning, and then moved on. Ellen felt a little of the tension knotting between her shoulder blades loosen. She saw Merrie bounce up to Sophie and she decided she could leave.

Out in the playground, Jane was still waiting. "Fancy a coffee?" she asked, forehead furrowed, and although Ellen didn't really feel like it, she knew that first awkward conversation had to be got through. And Jane was a good friend, maybe even a best friend. If she couldn't be honest with Jane, who could she be?

"Mine or yours?" Jane asked and Ellen shrugged. They fell into step together and started down the high street towards the old vicarage. "Do you want to talk about it?" Jane ventured, and Ellen gave a weary laugh.

"Not really, but I suppose I should."

"You don't have to..." Jane sounded half-hearted.

"It's just all a mess," Ellen said flatly. "Everything. And I feel as if I can't do anything right. Worse, I feel like..." Ellen stopped on a half-gulp, realising with alarm how close she was to tears – and not just tears, but full-on noisy, messy sobs. She took a deep, steadying breath. "I feel as if I'm losing Sophie."

"It was just a suspension," Jane protested. "And *I've* been tempted to give Chloe Dawson a bit of a push—"

"So I guess everyone knows what happened," Ellen said, managing another sort-of laugh.

Jane made a face. "Sorry..."

"Is everyone talking about it?" Ellen knew how small Goswell really was. Nothing happened in the primary school without it flying around the playground.

"Not really," Jane said after a telling pause. "Yes, there was a bit of chat. But it was well-meaning. People are concerned. Sophie is such a sweetheart..."

"She *was*," Ellen agreed. They'd reached the old vicarage and she stood aside while Jane scooped up the two pints of milk that had been left on the steps by the milkman and ushered her inside.

"What do you mean, was?" she called over her shoulder as she headed towards the kitchen in the back of the house. "She hasn't had a personality change."

"Sometimes I think she has."

"Oh, Ellen." Jane had, Ellen thought, the sympathetic but slightly exasperated tone of someone who feels they've already experienced what you were bemoaning. "Look, she's going through a rough patch. It happens, especially as they transition to the teenage years—"

"She's ten." Ellen felt a flare of annoyance and suppressed it. "I don't see Merrie acting the same way, Jane." She felt restless, unable to sit down even though Jane had switched on the kettle. She couldn't talk about this over cups of tea and a couple of digestives as they usually would. She just couldn't. "I appreciate you're trying to help," she said in as even a tone as she could manage. "I really do. But making light of it or acting as if it's no big deal... that doesn't help."

Jane blinked, looking surprised and a bit hurt by Ellen's plain speaking. Even so, Ellen couldn't regret it. "I'm sorry," she said, only semi-meaning it. "But you haven't gone through this."

"I've had some issues with Natalie..."

Ellen sighed, deflated. Yes, Jane had had some bolshy behaviour from Natalie when they'd first moved to Goswell. But Natalie was doing fine now, happy and bouncy and settled, the way Sophie used to be. It didn't feel the same.

"I'm sorry," she said again. The kettle switched off.

"Tea?" Jane asked, and Ellen shook her head.

"Sorry, I'm just not in the mood for a chat." Ellen grimaced. "Sorry," she said for the fourth time. "I think I might take a walk to clear my head."

"OK." Jane put the mugs back in the cupboard. "Well, I'm here if you change your mind."

"Thanks." Ellen offered her a lopsided smile before heading for the front door. She shook off her guilt over leaving Jane so abruptly and headed for the beach road.

It was a brisk, breezy day, grey clouds scudding across the sky, and even though it was almost July, it didn't feel summery at all. Ellen didn't mind. The cool and grey suited her mood.

The tide was rolling out when she got to the beach, leaving only a narrow strip of damp sand for Ellen to walk on. She walked the length of the beach and back, and didn't feel much better for it. She still had no answers about anything – Alex, Annabelle, Sophie. And even Alyssa – she'd sent an email reminding Ellen that she was off to Lanzarote with her father tomorrow.

Back down the beach road, Ellen's steps slowed and on a whim she turned into the church. She breathed in the strangely comforting scents of dust and wax, wondering where the vicar,

Simon Truesdell, was. Obviously he didn't hang about the dim, empty church, waiting for someone to pop in. Then she saw a handwritten sign on a table by the door: "For inquiries to the vicar, please see him at the vicarage, 42 Vale Road."

Of course. He had an office at the vicarage – her childhood home.

She hadn't been up Vale Road in years, and now she climbed the steep road that afforded tremendous views over the sea. The vicarage was at the very top; Ellen could remember as a child feeling as if she could be blown down the hill with one strong gust. In fact, she felt that way now – as if everything was just as precarious, her whole life perched on a precipice, about to topple.

Simon Truesdell answered the door with a ready smile even though Ellen didn't think she'd had a conversation with the man outside of school fetes and Christmas Eve services.

"Ellen! Lovely to see you. Tea?"

"Oh. Uh. No thanks." She stepped into the small hallway, smiling awkwardly in response to his gently enquiring look. "Actually, I wanted to ask about the old parish registers."

"Ah." Simon rocked back on his heels. "Doing a bit of genealogy?"

"Sort of. I'm interested in the people who once lived in my house."

"Of course."

"Samuel and Clara Frampton. I thought you might have a record of their wedding? Or births...?" Ellen trailed off, feeling faintly ridiculous. Who cared about the people who lived in her house nearly a hundred and fifty years ago? Yet it was better than thinking about the people who lived there now.

"Of course. I'll have a look through and let you know."

"Thank you."

Simon cocked his head. "Was there anything else you wished to talk about?"

To her embarrassment Ellen could feel herself flush. What did he know? She decided to be blunt. "Well, not really. My stepdaughter has come to live with us, as you might have heard. It's a bit difficult." A bit? She wasn't going to be that blunt.

"Yes..." Simon nodded encouragingly, and Ellen felt compelled to continue.

"These blended families. Not what God or at least the church intended, I suppose, eh?" She tried for a laugh.

"We live in a broken world," Simon agreed. "But much good can come out of difficult or sorrowful situations."

"Hmm." She wasn't sure about that. "Well, I should be getting on. Thank you for looking into the parish registers."

Back at home both laptop and laundry awaited her. The house felt almost eerily silent, the only sound the hopeful wagging of Pepper's tail against the table leg. As she folded Sophie's vests she tried to think logically. Somehow she needed to get her family back on track. She needed to make up with Annabelle, and figure out what was going on with Sophie. As for Alex... Ellen tried to suppress the hurt that needled her at the memory of how cold he'd been. She needed to be honest with Alex, and he needed to be honest with her. Talking to him had started to feel like battering her head against a brick wall.

By the time she went to pick up Sophie at three, she was feeling slightly more optimistic. Less brittle, anyway, and able to meet other mums' eyes as she walked to school.

Jane gave her an uncertain smile as she reached the playground, and with a firmer smile back, Ellen approached her.

"Hey. Sorry about this morning."

"It's OK. I was just worried about you." Jane glanced at her, assessing her. "You seem a bit more cheerful."

"I feel a bit more cheerful," Ellen said, although that wasn't strictly true. She felt more determined, at least, not to let her family be destroyed. "I'm going to talk to Annabelle and Alex tonight. Get things straight."

"Annabelle and Alex?" Jane looked confused. "What about Sophie?"

"Oh, well..." She hadn't told Jane about the tension between her and Annabelle and Alex. "Everybody, really. We all need straightening out." Fortunately she was saved from having to say anything more because the doors had opened and children started running out. Sophie, usually one of the first to come out, plaits flying and with a wide smile, was nearly last.

Ellen watched her daughter trudge through the school doors and felt that fierce determination start to waver.

"Do you want to come round?" Jane asked. "With Sophie...?"

"No, I think we'll just go home and see how things are. But I'd like to have that coffee sometime." Jane nodded and Ellen turned to Sophie. "So. How was it?" she asked, managing to keep her voice from sounding maniacally bright. Just.

"Can we go home?" Sophie asked, and kept walking.

Back at home, Sophie started to slope upstairs and Ellen called her back. "Sophie. Tell me how your day went." Shrug. "Were... were people friendly?"

"Yeah. I guess."

Ellen peered at her daughter, studying the sulky mouth, the downcast eyes. What was going on?

"Are you angry at me?" she asked after a moment.

Sophie lifted her gaze for one brief second before offering another shrug. "No."

"Why are you acting this way, then?"

"What way?"

"*Sophie.* Are you really going to pretend you're not giving me some major attitude?" Exasperation crept into Ellen's voice despite her best efforts to keep it friendly and light.

"Major attitude?" Sophie bristled. "What is that supposed to mean?"

"I just want you back to normal," Ellen said, knowing the

words were wrong as soon as she said them. But what words were right any more?

"Thanks a lot," Sophie huffed. "So now I'm not normal?"

"I didn't mean that—"

"Whatever." Before Ellen could say anything else – not that she even knew what she'd say – Sophie disappeared upstairs, the requisite door slam audible afterwards.

Ellen sank onto a chair at the kitchen table, her head in her hands. First healing conversation of the afternoon was officially a failure. The second one was, as well. Annabelle strode in, gave Ellen one dark look and bolted upstairs before Ellen could say more than, "Hell—" Which said it all, really. Ellen started making tea. Alex came in an hour later, when the kitchen was clean, a lasagne in the oven, and Ellen had rediscovered her determination, despite the muffled thump of techno music from the second floor.

"Hey." She blew a strand of hair out of her face and gave Alex a bright smile. "How was work?"

"Fine." He put down his briefcase and picked up the post.

"Alex, we need to talk." Alex glanced up from the post but didn't say anything. "We can't go on like this," Ellen continued, wincing slightly at the melodramatic sound of the words. "At least, I don't want to go on like this. All this tension and these fraught silences – it isn't good for anybody. I know I've made some mistakes, but I am trying to make this work."

For a second she thought Alex would come back with one of his usual retorts, a mixture of disappointment and accusation. But then he sighed and dropped the post and said, "I know."

"So we'll talk? Tonight?" He nodded. Ellen let her breath out in a rush of relief. "All right. Let's have tea, then."

By eight o'clock Sophie was in bed and Annabelle was barricaded in her room, giving the downstairs at least a semblance of peace. To pave the way for their discussion, Ellen took the liberty of opening a bottle of wine and bringing two brimming glasses into the conservatory where Alex was sitting with his trusty laptop. As she handed him a glass, he closed it with a slightly resigned air.

"So." Ellen took a sip of wine for fortification.

"We talk."

"We talk."

Cue silence. Ellen took another sip. Where to start? How to navigate this emotional minefield that had sprung up so suddenly? "Are you angry with me?" she asked.

"No."

"Disappointed?"

"Ellen." Alex looked exasperated. "We can't just... *fix* this."

"What?" She blinked, surprised and more than a little afraid. "Why not? What else are we supposed to do?"

"I don't know." Alex raked a hand through his hair. "I just mean your attitude sometimes is so... simplistic."

"OK." She wasn't going to feel hurt. She *wasn't*. "So what do you suggest I do? Say? I'm open here, Alex. I'm looking for a little guidance, because lately it feels like everything I do or say is wrong."

"Maybe that's because you're analyzing everything to death. I take Annabelle out for a meal and it means I don't love Sophie as much. It's not tit for tat, you know."

"I'm sorry." She swallowed, trying to ignore the burning in her chest. "I suppose I feel... threatened."

"Why? Why should Annabelle threaten you?" Alex shook his head. "I suppose that's what I don't understand. She's seventeen. My relationship with her for ten years has been absolutely nil. Why on earth would you feel threatened by a couple of dinners, a few films?"

When he put it like that Ellen felt unbearably petty. "I don't know," she whispered. "It's just... she disdains me so much. And takes offence at everything, even when I'm really trying to be nice. And since she's come you *have* ignored Sophie, you can't deny it—"

"Ignored Sophie?" Alex's eyebrows rose. "How?"

"Ignore might be too harsh a word," Ellen allowed. "Neglected, maybe—"

"*Neglected?* Seriously? It's not a competition, Ellen. This is exactly what I mean."

She was losing this argument, Ellen knew, because her husband was so bloody logical. How could she explain how she felt day after day, as if Alex and Annabelle were one unit and she and Sophie were another? Except Sophie wasn't even part of her unit anymore. Ellen was spinning away from everyone, alone.

"What about Sophie's suspension?" she asked. "That was a time when I really needed you. And Sophie did, as well."

Alex sighed. "I am sorry about that. I probably could have handled that better. I know I could have. But I couldn't just walk out on Annabelle's teacher conference. How would that have looked—"

"You didn't have to have dinner together until eleven o'clock. Can't we have some compromise here?"

"Yes. Of course. I suppose I feel like things with Annabelle are... fragile. I don't want to jeopardise them."

"At the moment things are pretty fragile with Sophie, as well," Ellen returned more sharply than she'd meant to.

"OK, I get it. I'll take her out this weekend."

Ellen should have been pleased, but it didn't feel like a compromise. It felt more like a sop. "OK." They were both silent, sipping their wine as darkness settled over the garden. "I was thinking," Ellen ventured after a moment. "What about a holiday this summer? I know we haven't booked anything..." They hadn't because of the cost of the room renovation and then Annabelle's arrival. "There might be some last-minute deals," Ellen persisted. "To France, even. We could rent a *gîte*...

have some family time, all of us..." She trailed away because Alex was already shaking his head, looking, at least, genuinely regretful.

"I've booked a trip with Annabelle to look at universities. I can't really take more holiday than that."

"What...?" Ellen stared at him, numb inside. So after all the talk of compromise, this was what she got? "Your entire summer holiday is with Annabelle?"

"It's not like that, Ellen. We talked about this, anyway."

"We talked about her visiting universities, yes, but—"

"And I'm not saying I can't take any summer holiday. Just not a long trip to France. I can take days out. We could go to that theme park near York..."

So instead of a proper holiday, he was offering a day out at a second-rate theme park. Ellen swallowed down her resentment, knowing there was no point. "Fine," she said. Alex looked relieved.

"We'll get through this," he said, smiling, and Ellen just stared. Yet another sop to his conscience. And they hadn't even talked about Sandra yet. Now didn't feel like the right time, but she didn't know if there would ever be a right time.

"OK," she said, and Alex opened his laptop.

The next morning Sophie came downstairs in her usual sulk and Ellen was too tired to force the bright smile, the chirpy voice. What was the point, anyway? It didn't work. Nothing she did worked.

After her talk with Alex she'd checked her email and seen that Simon Truesdell had got back to her. Clara Frampton's marriage was recorded in the parish register; she was listed as coming from Kendal. It would have intrigued her a few weeks ago, but now Ellen couldn't summon the energy for any interest. She'd emailed Simon back thanking him for the information and left it at that. She didn't need the distraction of Sarah Mills and the people in her life. Her story seemed to be one of sorrow and tragedy, and Ellen had enough of that in her life already.

Now she dumped some cereal into a bowl and pushed it across the table to Sophie, who took it silently. A flash of livid pink on Sophie's arm made her still.

"Sophie, did you hurt yourself?"

"What?" Sophie looked up warily. "No." Quickly she pushed down the sleeves of her cardigan so they covered her hands.

"Wait a second." Ellen's heart was beating hard and there was a metallic taste in her mouth. She reached across the table to grab hold of Sophie's wrist.

"Get off—" Sophie tried to jerk her arm away but Ellen held on.

She rolled the sleeve of Sophie's cardigan up so she could see the three pink lines on her inner arm – livid and puckered, newly made. Naïve as Ellen knew she could be, she recognised these marks. Her daughter, her golden girl, was cutting herself.

# CHAPTER 26

## SARAH

Kendal, 1872

It had been six months since Lucy had entered the Kendal Union workhouse. At first Sarah visited her every day, although the Master of the lunatic ward didn't like her coming so often. "It agitates her when you leave," he told her flatly. "The only way to subdue her afterwards is to beat her with a stick."

After that Sarah came less often, though it hurt her unbearably to do so. The visits hurt too, because Lucy was a shadow of her former self. Sometimes when Sarah would sit with her, Lucy rocked and moaned softly without seeming to recognise her at all. Other times Lucy would cling to her, arms and legs wrapped around Sarah's waist, head burrowed into her breast, until one of the attendants would pry her off, declaring such conduct was not seemly.

There was, Sarah had thought with unmitigated bitterness, nothing seemly about anything in the workhouse, from the rag-like uniforms to the monotonous meals of thin gruel or suet pudding, to the frigid air and the walls that ran with damp.

Newly built after the Poor Act had been passed in 1834, it was not, in Sarah's opinion, fit for human habitation.

The Master in charge wasn't an evil man, not like some she'd heard of, but he was tired with little money and many demands, and he'd seen the harder side of human nature for too long. He had little time for anyone, and especially not for a declared imbecile who was, he'd told Sarah, a "harmless idiot". Neither did he have time for that imbecile's sister, who was clearly subject to "all manner of a female's weak humours".

Going to the workhouse for her weekly visits became the lifeline to which Sarah clung, even as she dreaded the place. It was full of unfortunates, scabby-faced children and work-worn single mothers, despairing men who hadn't been able to find paying jobs, the crippled and lame, the blind and the old and the infirm – the dregs of a society that would rather shut them away so they could pretend they did not exist.

Sarah had heard that the workhouses had been built to be unappealing to their inmates – the food and clothing were poor on purpose, to keep them from wanting to stay. As she walked down the narrow halls, peering into gloomy rooms with small, high windows, and listening to the hacking coughs and sickly moans of those too ill to break stones or pick oakum, she'd believed it.

The day James had pried Lucy away from Sarah and hustled her into the workhouse was the day Sarah's life had changed forever. The frail, faint happiness she'd managed to find amidst the hard circumstances of life at River Cottage had been leached from her life, leaving a colourless palette of duty and work without so much as a shred of kindness or pleasure to liven it.

When they'd returned from the workhouse, Sarah had done everything she could to convince James to change his mind. She'd cried and screamed, begged and pleaded. She'd moaned and wept and torn at her hair, until James had insisted she stop making such a spectacle of herself and get his dinner.

Sarah had looked up into the once-placid face, the eyes she'd thought had been kind, and saw only impatience and ill temper, with perhaps the faintest flicker of regret – but not enough, she realised dully, for James to change his mind.

Over the next few months they fell into a joyless pattern of living; James went to Gawith Hoggarth & Co. and more often to the Cartmel races, and Sarah continued her long days of hard work at River Cottage; with only the two of them there was less laundry and cooking, but the lack of water and the old-fashioned range still presented their usual difficulties.

She missed Lucy with a fierceness that could steal her breath. Although her sister had never spoken, she'd communicated, and Sarah missed the sudden, shy smiles, the way Lucy would lean against her or hide in her skirts, the delight her sister had taken in a tabby kitten or the pattern of sunbeams on the floor.

It was all gone, leaving an emptiness inside Sarah that could never be filled. A month after Lucy "went into college", Clara wrote to say she'd married Samuel Frampton and been delivered of a healthy baby boy. She'd enclosed a precious photograph from her wedding day, asking Sarah to show it to James.

Sarah had stared at the man with the sticking-out ears and unruly hair and marvelled that Clara had found such happiness. She'd tried to show the picture to James, but he'd refused to look. And so Sarah had put it in her drawer, where she'd once kept Clara's letter. Occasionally she'd noticed her things were rumpled, and she'd wondered if James had secretly gone to look at the photograph. The possibility made her sad, even as she felt as if her heart had become encased in iron when it came to her husband. She'd once thought she could love the man, if he'd only be kind to her and Lucy. She'd been wrong on both counts.

One icy afternoon in March, Sarah left the workhouse for

the walk home, drawing her shawl around the shoulders as she ducked her head against the unforgiving wind that funnelled down Windermere Road.

Lucy had been inconsolable today, screaming silently as she clung to Sarah, until an attendant had pulled her off. The Master had met her at the door, shaking his head as he said severely, "These visits are not helping anyone, Mrs Mills. You really must ask yourself if you are pleasing yourself or your sister when you persist on seeing her."

Sarah had not replied. She could not think of ending the visits to Lucy, both for her sister's sake and her own. What would happen to Lucy if she never saw her again? Her sister's last frail thread linking her to reality, to hope, would snap, never to be mended. She could not do it.

She was just turning onto Stricklandgate, shivering in the cold, when someone fell in step beside her. Sarah turned to see Andrew Fairley giving her a friendly but uncertain smile. She stiffened, because she had not spoken to Andrew Fairley since she'd made those unjust accusations some months ago. She and James had, by mutual silent agreement, stopped going to church, and Sarah was glad to see the back of the place, with its new roof and benevolent vicar. She had no use for any of it.

"Good afternoon, Mrs Mills," Andrew Fairley said now. "You are well, I hope?"

"I am as well as to be expected," Sarah answered shortly.

"I have not seen you at church services," he replied gently. "I was worried you might have been ill."

"No, I have not been ill." Sarah left it at that and quickened her pace. Andrew Fairley matched it.

"And Miss Mills is well?"

"She is Mrs Frampton now. She married a man up in Goswell."

"Then I wish her much joy."

Sarah shot him a cold look. "I will make sure to tell her in our next correspondence."

"And your sister?" the curate pressed, infuriating Sarah. "How is she?"

Sarah stopped and turned to face him, shaking now with both cold and outrage. "My sister," she informed him, "is not well. She has been relegated to the workhouse these six months last."

Andrew Fairley's eyes widened and then he shook his head sorrowfully. "I am grieved to hear that."

"*Grieved?*" Sarah repeated. It offended her deeply that this man, this *stranger*, could say he was grieved by her sister's predicament. What did he know of grief, of endless disappointment, of the emptiness inside you that hollowed your heart right out until you felt like nothing more than a shell, a husk? "What use is your grief to me, sir?" she demanded. "You have many fine sentiments and fancy ways of telling me of them, but they do me no good at all."

Andrew looked almost comically astonished by her outburst and Sarah did not wait to hear what he said in reply. Pulling her shawl more tightly now, her toes numb inside her worn boots, she hurried towards the market square.

"Sarah—" The use of her Christian name, called out in such an unthinking fashion, almost made her stumble. Sarah slowed instinctively and Andrew caught up with her.

"Please forgive me. I meant to sympathise with your trials, not add to them."

"More pretty words."

"Shall I use words that are not pretty?" He touched her arm, turning her around to face him. "What has happened? Why is Lucy in the workhouse?"

"Because my dear husband put her there," Sarah spat. The bitterness she felt was like a poison inside her, a canker that festered and grew, choking every other emotion. "He was angry with me and he sought to punish me in the way he knew would hurt me most."

"But why would he do such a thing? I thought he was fond of Lucy..."

Sarah thought of how James had chucked Lucy under the chin, offered her smiles and baubles. Cheap, easy ways to win affection. He'd called her poppet when the carriage had been at the workhouse door. "No."

"I am truly sorry. If there is anything I can do..."

The pointlessness of the question, and its accompanying gall, infuriated Sarah all over again. "And what do you think you could do? What have you ever done, besides flap your hands and say how sorry you are? You stood by and watched while Reverend Cooper lined his own pockets with my aunt's inheritance—"

"That is not true," Andrew said quietly. "That money belonged to the church. Reverend Cooper did not line his pockets at all."

"No, he lined the roof. And he had only twenty-five pounds to throw my way." Sarah shook her head wearily; bitterness was so exhausting, yet she did not know if she was capable any more of feeling anything else.

"Reverend Cooper was in a true quandary," Andrew protested. "He could not simply hand the money over to you—"

"I know." Sarah held up a hand. "I have no wish to stand in the street and argue the point. Perhaps we should say farewell, Mr Fairley, and seek each other out no more."

"Will you return to church?"

She laughed, a hollow sound. "Why should I? When has God done anything for me?"

"God has done much for you, Sarah Mills," Andrew returned with feeling. "Whether you acknowledge it or not. You are alive and loved by Him, no matter how much you rail. It is people who have disappointed you so terribly, myself included, and not God."

She stared at him, his earnest face and anxious eyes, and for one terrible moment she wished things could have been different with a yearning that frightened her in its sudden strength. "Thank you, Mr Fairley," she said quietly. "I shall think on it."

"You would be welcome to come to Sunday services on any—"

"Thank you," she said again, and turned and began walking towards River Cottage.

Spring came, as damp and cold as winter. Rain caused the garden to flood and Sarah came downstairs one morning in May to find several inches of dark, brackish water covering the kitchen floor. She pushed it out the back door, shivering in her soaked boots, and stared at the leaden sky above, feeling nothing. *You are alive and loved.* One of those was true. Just.

An epidemic of cholera raged through the workhouse and Sarah couldn't visit Lucy for several weeks. When she finally returned, the numbers in the workhouse were much depleted and Lucy was even more withdrawn and listless, barely raising her eyes when Sarah came into the damp, dank room where her sister spent her days, with no amusements or company save for other unfortunates like herself.

"Lucy." Sarah reached for her sister but Lucy flinched away, tearing at her heart. Usually her sister would burrow into her, arms snaking around her waist as she accepted that first necessary embrace, such a paltry effort to right the multitude of wrongs. "I'm sorry I didn't come," Sarah said quietly. "There was so much illness, they told me to stay away." Her absence felt selfish now. What did she care for her own life? "But you're all right?" Sarah pressed, her gaze roving over Lucy, noting the pale, expressionless face, the slack jaw, the shuttered eyes. Every time she came to the workhouse her sister retreated further and further into a place Sarah could not reach, a world she did not understand. "I've brought you sweets, Lucy." Sarah placed the bag of mint humbugs on the plain deal table. "Your favourite." Lucy did not so much as look at the sweets. Sarah pushed the bag towards her and Lucy flinched again. "Lucy." Sarah's voice wavered, broken. "It's me, Sarah. Don't you want your sweets? Won't you look at me?" Her sister wrapped her arms around her knees and began to rock.

Looking at her sister, knowing she could not reach her, despair was like a wave that lapped at her, eroding the last of her fragile resources. Everything in Sarah ached, yet she was too weary to rage against all the disparate elements that had brought her to this moment – her father's death, and then her mother's, Ruth Teddington's reluctance and Aunt Edith's accident. Reverend Cooper's bland determination and Clara's foolishness, borne from a childish heart that longed for love. James's intractable cruelty, even though his revenge had not satisfied him in the least. Sarah bowed her head.

An hour of interminable silence later she headed back towards River Cottage. Every breath felt laboured, her legs heavy as she trudged down the street. The sky was low and grey with clouds that promised rain and yet more flooding. There was no end in sight to any of it, Sarah thought. Not one thing.

Back at home she took off her bonnet and shawl, smoothing her damp hair back. Her breath came in ragged gasps. She stared at the fussy ornaments in the china cabinet that had belonged to James's wife, Amanda. A rosy-cheeked shepherdess and a glass-eyed kitten, both appallingly insipid. She had a sudden urge to hurl them to the floor, watch them shatter into porcelain fragments. She wanted, perversely, to see something destroyed, to witness someone else's pain. Taking a shuddering breath, Sarah set about making tea.

She chased out the beetles and puddles of river water from the kitchen with a broom. There was nothing but vegetable soup for their supper, a few potatoes and carrots and half a cabbage. James hadn't done as well at the Cartmel races as he used to.

*You are alive and loved.* Even now Andrew Fairley's words echoed in her mind, both a taunt and a promise. If it were true, if she could hold onto that idea that there really was something greater than herself... if she could believe that a force was at work, that all would come well eventually, no matter how she suffered now...

Sarah had a sudden memory of her father, his head bent, his dark hair falling over his forehead as he studied his fusty books by the light of a smoking tallow candle. She could picture the scene in its heartbreaking entirety: her mother with her feet stretched towards the coal fire, Lucy in her basket, a baby whose placid quietness had not yet held any alarm. *All shall be well and all manner of things shall be well.* She could almost hear his voice, the kindly, patient tone. She could almost see the weary yet certain smile. Even when the fever had raged through his wasted body, he had not doubted.

Perhaps she would not doubt if so many things hadn't gone wrong, one after another, the humble aspirations of her life falling like dominoes. Perhaps she could hold onto whatever frail faith she'd once had if she wasn't so tired. The soup bubbled on the range and rain fell from the sky. Sarah swayed on her feet. Her head felt light, her chest painfully constricted. She could hear her father's soft voice even now, comforting and sure, although the words were not audible. She could almost feel his hand touching her hair.

An hour later, James came home to a quiet house, the bottom of the soup pot blackened, and Sarah collapsed on the kitchen floor, rainwater lapping at her boots.

# CHAPTER 27

## ELLEN

Sophie tried to yank her arm away but Ellen held fast. Her heart was beating so hard she could feel it through her whole body.

"Sophie," she said, her voice unnaturally calm, "what are these?"

Sophie yanked her arm again. "Get off."

"Sophie!"

"I ran into some brambles," Sophie said sulkily, and pulled her arm once more. This time she succeeded, and she pulled the sleeve of her cardigan down with a defiant look.

Ellen wanted to believe her. She wanted, quite desperately, to believe that those three neat incisions, equidistant from each other, barely starting to heal, were mere bramble scratches. She wanted to believe it with every fibre of her being, because the alternative was unthinkable. Sophie was *ten*. She was her golden girl, her cheerful soul, the bubbly, excitable, *lovable* darling of the family, the whole village! She could not be intentionally harming herself. She could not.

"I'm going to be late for school," Sophie said, and slid from her chair. She hadn't touched her cereal.

"Sophie, wait. We need to talk about this."

"I told you, it was brambles!" But instead of sounding exasperated or impatient, her daughter sounded scared. Her voice rose shrilly and she wouldn't look Ellen in the eye. Every maternal instinct Ellen possessed rose to the fore, alarm bells clanging so loudly she could not ignore them.

"It was *not* brambles." She held Sophie's gaze, challenging her daughter, daring her, risking what felt like everything on this moment. This instinct. "You've been cutting yourself on purpose."

Sophie's lips trembled. Her gaze darted away. "Why would I do that?" she tried to scoff, but her voice wobbled.

"I don't know. But I know I'm concerned, Sophie. Very concerned. The last thing I'd ever want is for you to hurt yourself." *Why* did girls cut themselves? Ellen scrambled to recall the articles she'd read online and in doctor's offices, the school safety notices she'd never, ever thought would apply to her and her smugly perfect family. She wanted to slap her old self silly. She wanted to tell the old Ellen to watch out, to stay alert, that no one was ever safe or immune.

"It's not like that," Sophie said in a low voice. She scuffed a shoe along the floor, lowering her head so her blonde curls bounced against her shoulders. Tears pricked Ellen's eyes.

"Why, Sophie?" Sophie just shook her head. "I didn't even know you knew about that. I mean..." Ellen took a deep breath. She was stumbling through the dark now, hands thrust out in front of her as she walked blindly forward, feeling for the words. "I know some girls... harm themselves... because they're stressed or anxious about things. Boys or friends or schoolwork. But I didn't think... I didn't realise you felt that way." Sophie hunched a shoulder. "How... how did you make those cuts?"

A long, telling silence. "A razor," Sophie mumbled.

Ellen closed her eyes. "What razor?" Sophie didn't even shave. Not yet, she was too young. Too *young*.

"Annabelle's razor."

Annabelle. It always came back to Annabelle. "She... she gave you this idea?"

Wordlessly Sophie nodded. She looked up, her eyes huge and glassy. "Don't blame her," she implored. "It's not her fault. She just told me..."

"Told you." Told a ten-year-old to cut herself with her own razor. A rage that felt like a black, boiling cloud billowed up over Ellen so thick and fast she was choking on it, unable to speak or think.

"Don't blame her," Sophie insisted, angry now. "It's not her fault."

"Sophie, I understand your concern, but—"

"I knew you'd blame her!" Sophie shouted. "I *knew* you would. You blame her for everything. You hate her!"

"I don't—" Ellen began, but Sophie had already grabbed her school bag and was running out of the house.

Ellen stood in the kitchen for a moment, the sound of the door slamming echoing through her, before she grabbed her keys and headed out after Sophie. By the time she'd almost caught up with her, Sophie was at the school doors. Ellen stopped and watched in frustration and fear as Sophie disappeared into the school. At least she was safe there. At least Ellen hoped she was.

She walked slowly back home, avoiding the sympathetic smiles and curious looks, her mind spinning. When she came into the house she could tell Annabelle had left for school, from the spill of sugary cereal on the kitchen table to the wet teabag flung near, not in, the sink. Ellen threw her keys onto the table. *Now what?*

She called Alex, but of course he didn't pick up. He wouldn't have his mobile in the high-security area. Ellen slammed the receiver several times in the cradle simply because it felt good. Then she felt childish and out of control and she let her head fall into her hands. What on earth was she going to do?

The ringing of the phone had her leaping towards it, grabbing it from the abused cradle, a desperate hope firing her words.

"Yes?"

"Ellen?"

The sound of surprise in the stranger's voice had Ellen closing her eyes. She must have sounded alarmingly fierce. "Yes, this is Ellen."

"It's Ian Fletcher from the Kendal Historical Society."

"Oh." Realising how ungrateful she sounded, Ellen tried and failed to inject some cheer into her voice. "Sorry, I've had a hectic morning and I was expecting another call."

"Oh, sorry. Is this a bad time...?"

Ellen gazed around at the messy kitchen. Pepper nudged her knees. "No, it's fine."

"I've done a bit more digging on your Sarah Mills."

"Oh?" Belatedly Ellen realised how unenthusiastic she sounded.

"Well, more about her sister, Lucy. She was in the workhouse, and she was admitted by Sarah's husband, James. His signature is on the records."

"Right." It all seemed irrelevant now, as well as terribly sad.

"Furthermore, I've managed to dig up the workhouse records of visitors. Bit of a surprise, that. I wouldn't have expected it to be kept, but someone in the historical society has a special interest in the workhouse."

"Right," Ellen said again.

"Anyway, Sarah visited her sister quite regularly for some time. But then the visits stopped about a month before her death."

"Understandable, since she would have been ill, I suppose."

"Yes." Ian Fletcher's voice held a jarring note of enthusiasm, even excitement. "But the really interesting thing I've found out is—"

Ellen's phone buzzed from the table where she'd flung it along with her keys. Alex's picture flashed on the screen. "I'm sorry, Ian," Ellen interjected, cutting off the long-winded explanation he'd started on about headstones and inscriptions that Ellen hadn't really been listening to. "I've got an urgent call on my mobile. I'll have to call you back."

"Of course."

Ellen hung up the phone and grabbed her mobile. "Alex?"

"You rang me four times." Alex's voice was touched with impatience. "I assume it's urgent? I tried calling the house line but you were engaged."

"Yes, but never mind about that. Alex..." A sob clutched at Ellen's chest and she dashed at her eyes. "Alex, I caught a glimpse of Sophie's arm this morning and she's... she's cutting herself."

Silence. Ellen waited, her breathing harsh and ragged. "Cutting herself?" Alex repeated neutrally. "You mean, on purpose?"

"*Yes*."

Ellen didn't know what she'd been expecting. Alex to fly home from his lab like Superman? To rush into Goswell Primary like an avenging superhero? She wanted rescuing. She needed a saviour. And instead she got: "We'll talk about it when I get home."

"That's *it*?"

"What do you want me to say?"

The sob that had been threatening to erupt dissolved. "Nothing," Ellen said dully. "Absolutely, bloody nothing."

She took Pepper for a long walk because she needed to move, to feel as if she was doing something. When she got back home she steeled herself to do the prerequisite online searches, going on the medical and psychology sites about self-harm, appalled and still disbelieving that she was actually needing to do this for her own daughter.

A throbbing headache had started around lunchtime; she hadn't eaten anything all day. Ellen walked back up to school to collect Sophie, no nearer any answers or even a game plan than she'd been that morning, when she'd stared at Sophie's deep scratches in horrified shock.

Sophie came out of school head down, refusing to talk. Ellen put a hand on her shoulder. "Sophie..."

"Let's just go home, OK?" Her daughter shrugged off her hand and started walking, leaving Ellen no choice but to follow.

Annabelle was in the kitchen when they arrived home, raiding the fridge and looking infuriatingly insouciant. Sophie slouched inside, glancing warily between Ellen and Annabelle. Ellen placed her keys on the table with a deliberate *thunk*.

"Annabelle."

Annabelle looked around, surprised and then on guard.

"Mum..." Sophie began, but Ellen held up a hand. She hadn't planned on saying anything to Annabelle. The saner, self-controlled part of her brain told her to wait. Wait until Alex had got home and they'd discussed everything, agreed on an approach. Wait until she wasn't lashing out of anger and terror and pain. *Wait.*

But another, larger part of herself rose up in a howl of indignation and rage. Remembered every sneering slight and insult this girl had thrown her way, every thankless task and kindness she'd performed for her. The bedroom, the vegetarian meals, the smiles and humour and the determination to bond. All of it wasted. All of it costing her Sophie.

"What is it?" Annabelle said in a bored voice. She reached for a cola from the fridge and popped the lid with her thumb, giving Ellen that dreaded death stare of indifference – except she didn't dread it any more. She despised it. In that moment she despised everything about this young woman, from her expertly shaped eyebrows now raised in affected boredom to the painted toenails she knew Annabelle had given Sophie. Matching black, with silver skull decals. Not exactly appropriate for a ten-year-old in Ellen's opinion, but she'd said nothing. She'd said nothing about anything. She'd been so *good*, and she'd been blamed for so much.

"Annabelle," she said again, her voice cold and clear. "I want you to stay the hell away from my daughter."

Annabelle flinched and Sophie let out a whimper. Ellen took a step closer to Annabelle, hands balled into fists. "You have abused my hospitality, my welcome, more than I can stand. You have corrupted my daughter. Yes!" She snarled as she took in Annabelle's look of confusion. "Corrupted. Do you know what that word means, with your English A-Level? Do you know what I saw on her wrist this morning? *Do you?*"

Sophie let out a strangled sob and raced upstairs. Annabelle held her ground, although she'd lost her veneer of bored disdain. "What did you see?" she asked. Ellen couldn't tell anything from her tone.

"Cuts on her arms. She cut herself with your razor, at your instruction." Suddenly all the rage Ellen had felt deflated, leaving her in one huge whoosh. She sagged against the table, near tears. "She's cutting herself, Annabelle, and she's only ten. I didn't even think she *knew* about that kind of thing. She didn't, until you came along." There was no accusation in the words, just weary fact. Suddenly Ellen felt so tired, too tired to cope with all of this alone. "What do you have to say about that?"

"Nothing," Annabelle whispered. Ellen stared at her helplessly, hopelessly, and Annabelle stared back, her expression fixed and blank. Then, after a long, tense, silent moment, she walked quickly out of the room, leaving the fridge door open. After a moment, feeling almost too tired to move, Ellen shut it.

She sank onto a chair and rested her head in her hands, wondering what on earth she should do now.

She didn't do much of anything. She sat there for a while, and then paced the kitchen while Pepper got in the way, claws clicking on the floor as she weaved between the table and Ellen's legs, as anxious as her owner. Ellen went upstairs, knocked on Sophie's closed bedroom door and listened. No reply.

"Sophie...?"

"Go away." Her daughter's voice was muffled, as if she was speaking into her pillow. Ellen could picture her lying on her bed with its pink ruffled bedspread, clutching her pillow as she cried. She leaned her forehead against the door.

"Sophie..."

"Go *away*."

Not knowing what else to do, Ellen went. She paced the garden and then sank into one of their old, weathered deckchairs, tracing a splinter in the wood with her fingers. When had they all started to break apart, pieces chipping off? When had her family started to splinter? Had there always been cracks in it, like in this weathered wood, cracks and weaknesses from age, from experience, from the fact that this was the second time around for both of them?

Her ignorance about Sandra, which she'd so blissfully agreed to, now felt like a weakness. Annabelle's absence in their lives for so long, which had felt convenient, now felt like a mistake. Was there any way to right the wrongs? Could they find a way forward through this emotional mire?

Heaving a sigh, Ellen rose from the chair. She needed to say something to Annabelle before Alex came home, although she had no idea what it was. But when she came to the top floor and peered into the room that had once been meant to be hers, it was empty. Annabelle was gone.

Alex came home a short while later, looking tired and

drawn, the lines from his nose to mouth more pronounced than usual.

"Sophie...?" he asked quietly.

"She's in her room."

"I'm sorry, Ellen." Alex's apology took her by surprise. What exactly was he sorry for? The awfulness of the last few weeks, or simply what had happened to Sophie?

Ellen took a deep breath. "Alex, I went upstairs to talk to Annabelle and she wasn't there." Alex frowned, waiting, and she continued, knowing it needed to be confessed, "I... I spoke harshly to her before, in the kitchen. About Sophie."

"You spoke harshly to Annabelle?" Alex looked incredulous. "What does she have to do with this?"

*Everything.*

"Sophie told me Annabelle showed her how. She cut herself with Annabelle's razor."

Alex looked like she'd sucker punched him. He shook his head slowly, sinking into one of the kitchen chairs. "Anyway," Ellen continued in a low voice, a pressure building behind her lids, "She isn't anywhere in the house. She might have just gone for a walk to cool down, but..." Ellen shrugged, spreading her hands. "I'm sorry."

Alex stared into space, still looking dazed. "I thought everything was going so well."

Ellen almost laughed at that. Well? When had anything been going well? "I mean," he clarified, "with me and Annabelle. I know we've had our difficulties, but I was making up for lost time, Ellen. I thought we were really getting somewhere. I thought she was happy here."

It took Ellen a few seconds to realise his concern was entirely for Annabelle. "And what about Sophie? What about the cuts on her arm?"

He refocused his gaze on her. "Why does it always have to be—"

"Because it *is*. Since Annabelle has come into our lives you've only been thinking about her, Alex. It's like she's replaced us! I'm sorry if that makes me sound petty and childish, but it's how it feels. Can't you see that, when you swan off to dinners and the cinema and plan our bloody summer holiday with her, leaving us out of all of it? Don't you think Sophie has felt that, too?"

His mouth tightened. "So you're blaming what happened to Sophie on me. Me and Annabelle."

Was she?

"No, I blame myself too," Ellen said more quietly. "Of course I do. I seem to have botched everything up again and again, and I don't know how to stop. But I want to be a team, Alex, fighting for our family. And instead for the past few months I've felt like we've been fighting each other."

Alex raked a hand through his hair. "First we need to find Annabelle."

Had she got through to him at all? Wearily, Ellen sighed. "I suppose I could call Jane. Annabelle has been friendly with Natalie."

An hour later they were no closer to locating Annabelle. Ellen wasn't truly worried, not yet, when it was still light out and barely past dinnertime. She put a frozen pizza in the oven and the three of them ate it in silence, Sophie having slouched down from her room without a word.

"Sophie," Alex asked when their picked-at meal was finished, "do you know where Annabelle could be?"

Sophie shook her head. Her eyes were huge and full of tears and she bit her bottom lip. Ellen wanted to hug her, but Sophie shied away from so much as a brush of her hand.

At eight o'clock Alex had had enough waiting. "I'm going to drive around and look for her. Call me if she comes back or you hear anything."

"OK." Ellen watched him stride out of the house, car keys clenched in one hand.

Fifteen minutes later the phone rang and Ellen practically flew to it. "Yes?" she said breathlessly.

"Ellen? It's Ian Fletcher of the Kendal Historical Society—"

Not again.

"I'm sorry, Ian, but it's really not a good time—"

"I'm not calling about Sarah Mills this time," Ian cut her off with a dry chuckle. "Someone a bit more current. I've got a young woman with me whom I think you've been looking for."

"What...?" Ellen blinked, too stunned to take it in for a few seconds. "You mean Annabelle? She's in *Kendal*?"

"I found her in the graveyard of the parish church. Funny place to be, but I gather she got on the first train out of Goswell, and then took a bus."

"But..."

"I think she wants to go home."

"We'll come and get her right away."

"We'll be waiting."

Ellen called Alex, but his mobile switched over to voice-mail; he had to be out of signal. She paced the kitchen, chewing her lip, before she decided she'd go herself. Maybe it was better that way. She had no idea why Annabelle had gone to Kendal, but she felt it had something to do with her rather than Alex.

"Sophie," she called upstairs. "Come on down. We're going to get Annabelle."

# CHAPTER 28

## SARAH

Kendal, 1872

The first time Sarah spat blood into her handkerchief, a month after James had come home to find her collapsed in the kitchen, she almost laughed. Laughed with the cynical weariness that here was her fitting end, to wither away as her mother once had, dying an invalid of a weak chest and poorly lungs.

Who knew how she'd got the contagion. Through the damp humours that pervaded River Cottage, or the cold, wet walks each week to the workhouse, where infection bred in every corner? Perhaps it had been inside her all along, festering, growing, waiting to spread and kill. It didn't matter, not really. She had precious little to live for now. The end, when it came, would only bring relief.

In July, the same month she'd married James four years earlier, she took to her bed. He'd had a neighbour nurse her while he'd gone to work when he'd thought she had a chest cold, but when Sarah told him she had consumption he looked shocked, dazed, as if she'd hit him, hurt him with the news.

"But I haven't had a doctor in," he protested. "How can you know?"

"It was the same with my mother." Sarah's voice came out in a rasp, and every breath hurt her weakened chest. She lay her head against the pillows, already drained. "I know the signs. I nursed her through it."

"But people with consumption can live for a long time." He sounded truculent, like a child. "They get better when it's warm and dry."

Sarah let out a sound that was meant to be a laugh but sounded more like a wheeze. "It is neither warm nor dry here."

James stared at her, his lower lip thrust out, his eyes clouded. "You *will* get better, Sarah. I'll send for the doctor. I'll get the best medicine. We can move house…"

Sarah simply shrugged, the coverlet sliding over her thin shoulders. She didn't suppose it mattered much to her either way.

The doctor duly came, and prescribed several syrups and powders while offering no real hope. "The case has progressed for some time," he told James, his voice low although Sarah could still hear him. "It is difficult to stay its progression now, but I can at least alleviate some of the worst symptoms."

Give her a little time, Sarah surmised. Yet what for? After the doctor had left, James sat by her bed, hands pleated, brow furrowed.

"I'll get another doctor."

"Doctors cost money, James." Money they didn't have. "And another one won't say any differently."

"You're young and strong. There's no reason…"

Sarah shook her head. She'd been young and strong once, maybe, but years of hard work in comfortless conditions had taken their toll. Losing Lucy had sapped her of the strength to fight, to live. "Perhaps it's better this way," she said, wearily disconcerted by her need to comfort him now. "You could marry again."

"I don't want to marry again." James struggled to find words. "Did you think I wouldn't care?" he finally asked, and Sarah looked at him in surprise.

"Not terribly much," she admitted.

"Sarah. I... I love you." She said nothing and a flush touched his cheeks. "I know I haven't... I haven't been the best of husbands. And Clara was spoilt, I know she was, but..."

"James." Sarah stayed him with one fluttering hand. "There is no need for this now. I could have borne it all, and gladly, save for Lucy."

"Lucy..." James looked away, a flush staining his cheeks.

Sarah closed her eyes, too tired to speak any longer.

The days drifted by, a haze that was strangely not unpleasant. Nothing seemed to matter as much as it once had, as if the tethers that had bound her to this earth were being loosed, one by one. Small things had the power to please her – the pattern of sunbeams on the floor, a patch of blue sky. James came in and out of the room, and the doctor came twice more, with more powders. Distantly Sarah heard him say it wouldn't be long.

How long? She wondered. How long had she been lying in this bed? Time ceased to have any meaning. Day and night blurred together. Then one afternoon she woke to see Andrew Fairley sitting by her bed, a prayer book in his hand.

"What are you..." she began in a papery voice, only to lose the strength to say anything else.

"I heard you were ill," Andrew said quietly. "And I came to visit you, and pray."

"Pray for what?" Sarah managed to choke out. "My soul?"

"I wish you well, Sarah. I wish you, even now, to know the joy of being a precious child of God."

*Precious.* She'd never felt precious, not since her father had died. And yet he had believed. He had told her what Andrew

Fairley was telling her now when she'd been a child at his knee, when he'd taken her to the beach and they'd watched the surging sea. Everything in creation had pointed, he'd believed, to a great and loving God.

When had she lost her faith? Had it been chipped away at by life's sorrows, until there was nothing left? Or perhaps only a fragment remained, weathered by time and broken by trials. She closed her eyes.

"May I pray for you?" Andrew asked, and with her eyes still closed, Sarah nodded. The words washed over her in a strangely soothing tide. She felt comforted, at least a little, but at the same time she felt quite suddenly unbearably sad, the emotion surprising her with its strength. She'd thought she was past that.

She opened her eyes. "Will you visit Lucy?" she asked. "In the workhouse?"

Andrew did not hesitate. "Of course."

"She won't know you, but at least you'd be someone. Someone to try to reach her..." A coughing fit overtook her and her body shook with the force of it. She subsided, breathless, blood speckling her lips. Silently Andrew dabbed at them with a handkerchief and she submitted to his ministrations, unable to do it herself. "I would have liked to have seen her again," she whispered, "even though the last time I saw her she barely looked at me. But she wouldn't want to see me like this. It would upset her, I know."

"I'm sorry, Sarah, so sorry for all of it."

"Life hasn't been kind to me, Mr Fairley. I know that. I know it hasn't been kind to many people, and I suppose you think that doesn't reflect badly on God." The effort to say all of that exhausted her and she closed her eyes, dozing off for a few minutes before she was able to rouse herself again.

"I think it reflects badly on a broken world," Andrew answered quietly. "A world that will be made new one day."

"I would like to see that. I would like to see my father and mother and Lucy all made new and whole again." She smiled faintly at the thought. "I'd like that very much." But it sounded like a fairy story to her, something too good to be true, too wonderful to hold onto.

There was a sound at the door and then James was there, on her other side. His eyes were bright, his cheeks wet.

"Sarah," he whispered, and held her hand. Something about his tone made Sarah realise the gravity of her situation. Was this it, then? Was this what dying looked like, felt like? She gazed around the room; through the window she could see it was raining, the drops spattering against the glass. An afternoon in July, not much of a summer, and she would slip away from this world, perhaps in a few minutes, even? She felt a tremor of fear at such an unknown. She turned suddenly to Andrew, desperate now. "I want to believe."

"Then believe," he said simply.

Was it that easy? A matter of mere words? Sarah formed them soundlessly. *I believe.* Then other words came.

"Why did you take her from me, James?" She rasped out the question, her gaze burning into his, needing to know this last thing before she slipped from this world, to understand how he could have been so cruel. "Why would you do something so terrible, so unkind? She'd never done anything to you. You said you'd take care of her. It was why I married you. I was prepared to love you, you know. On account of your eyes..." She dozed again, sleep like a tide that lapped at her senses, dark and light, pulling her under, bringing her closer.

When she opened her eyes she could see James was weeping. "I'm sorry," he said, again and again. "I'm so sorry. I was angry, I let it control me. I'm so sorry, Sarah..."

Sarah stared at him. She'd never seen him look so emotional, so penitent, the tears dashing his cheeks. She tried to reach for his hand, amazed at how claw-like her own looked as she raised it, yellowed and thin. She must have wasted away completely, and she hadn't realised. "Then take care of her for me," she whispered. "Bring her back here and take care of her for me, James. It's not too late." She glanced at Andrew, seeking confirmation. "It isn't, is it? For Lucy, at least?"

"And it's not too late for you," Andrew assured her, his hand finding and patting her own.

"I will," James whispered, his voice choked. "I promise, Sarah. I give you my solemn vow. I haven't been a good husband to you, I know it, but I promise this on my very life."

*On his life.* The words floated through her mind like wisps of vapour. And her life was already floating away, the last tether snapped. Sarah closed her eyes, her hands, one held by James and the other by Andrew, already starting to relax. The tide lapped over her, like the warmest, gentlest sea. She could hear her father's laughter, the smile in his voice, and her mouth curved into the smallest of answering smiles, a welcome ready, at last, at last. *I believe.*

# CHAPTER 29

## ELLEN

It poured rain the entire way to Kendal. Alex called when they were halfway there, distraught, and Ellen assured him she would bring Annabelle back safely.

"Why on earth as she gone to Kendal?" he asked.

"I don't know. Ian Fletcher found her in the churchyard—"

"Who on earth is Ian Fletcher?"

"The head of Kendal's historical society. We came down here once, the girls and I, to research Sarah Mills." Alex was silent and Ellen clarified, "You know, the death certificate that was found?"

"Oh. Right. So you think she was going to look for something...?"

"I don't know. But it's the only link I can think of."

Alex was silent for so long Ellen thought she'd lost the connection. Then he spoke. "Ellen, I'm sorry. I've been a stupid fool about all of this. I've been so worried about Annabelle, and so guilty because I know I failed her before, when she was little. I worked all the time and I disengaged, and I know I'm doing the same thing again, but I feel like I can't do a damn thing to stop it. I hate that, I really do, and yet I keep doing it."

"Oh, Alex." Ellen blinked rapidly, her eyes on the road.

"I know now isn't the time for a heart to heart, but I just wanted you to realise... I get it. At least some of it. I really do. And when you get back, when you all get back, we'll talk. Properly."

"OK," Ellen whispered, and blinked back more tears.

After Alex had hung up, Ellen took a deep breath and then glanced at Sophie who had been silent and pensive for the whole trip, gazing out the rain-smeared windows.

"I'm sorry I lost my temper before, Sophie," she said quietly. "I shouldn't have. I was angry and afraid, but I shouldn't have lost control like that."

Sophie gave a tiny nod but still didn't speak. Ellen turned to gaze back at the rainy road. "Will you tell me why you cut yourself?" she asked gently. "I looked it up online and it seems a lot of people do it to relieve pressure, when they're feeling stressed about things. Was that how you felt?"

An entire minute ticked by before Sophie gave another small nod. Ellen's heart felt as if it was being wrung right out. "What are you stressed about, Sophie?"

"Everything." The word was a near-soundless whisper. "You and Dad fighting all the time—"

"We're not fighting—"

"Just because you're not shouting doesn't mean you're not fighting," Sophie answered with a shrewdness Ellen hadn't expected. And it was true. She and Alex *had* been fighting. She just hadn't liked to think of it like that. "And Annabelle..."

"What about Annabelle?"

"She knows you don't like her."

"I don't dislike her," Ellen protested. "But she hasn't exactly been easy to like, you know."

"But that's not supposed to matter, is it?" Sophie said quietly. "To a mum."

Ellen felt skewered by that comment. So it really was her

fault. Maybe not all of it, but definitely some. She needed to accept that. "I'm sorry," she said after a moment.

To her surprise, Sophie reached out and touched her arm. "I know it's been hard for you too, Mum."

"Oh, Sophie." Ellen sniffed. "You shouldn't have to worry about whether it's hard for me. I just want you to feel happy and safe."

"And what about Annabelle?"

"I want her to feel happy and safe as well," Ellen answered. But she couldn't feel about Annabelle the way she felt about Sophie. If that was unfair or cruel or just plain wrong, then so be it. She couldn't manufacture feelings, but she could have acted differently. She knew that.

They arrived in Kendal and Ellen parked in the market square before walking to the address on Lowther Street where Ian said he lived. It was a tall, narrow house in a row of Victorian terraces, with flowerboxes out the front and a ginger cat peering from the front window.

"Hello." Ian gave her a wide, friendly smile as she stepped into the small, crowded porch. "It's filthy out, isn't it? Annabelle's just in the kitchen, having a cup of hot chocolate." He glanced at Sophie, eyebrows lifted. "You fancy one?"

Sophie nodded shyly. "Yes, please."

Ian led the way down the narrow hall to the kitchen in the back, giving Ellen a sympathetic look as they walked. "She's all right," he said in a low voice. "Don't you worry."

Ellen nodded, not sure what response to make or how she even felt. Her emotions had been stretched perilously thin over the last few days. The kitchen was a pleasant room with a dark blue Aga, another cat perched on top of one its lids, tail swishing. Annabelle sat at the pine table in the centre of the room, hands cupped around a mug of hot chocolate. Her hair was damp and curling about her face, and looking at her then, Ellen realised with a pang how very young she was. Somehow, between Annabelle's glossy looks and endless attitude, she'd forgotten that. "Annabelle." She tried for a smile and then realised that wasn't enough. It wasn't what she felt. Instead, she dropped down on her knees and put her arms around Annabelle. "I'm so glad you're safe."

To her shock Annabelle began to cry, thin shoulders shaking with the force of her sobs. It took Ellen a few seconds of murmuring soothing nonsense as she patted Annabelle's back before she realised what she was saying.

"I'm sorry. I'm so sorry..."

"You don't need to be sorry," Ellen said, and meant it. Where had this grace come from? She certainly hadn't possessed it before, and yet she felt it now, truly.

Ian gave Sophie a cup of hot chocolate and then quietly absented himself. Ellen sat back on her heels, looking up at Annabelle's tear-stained face. "I think we need to start again," she said. "Properly."

"Can we?" Annabelle asked, a touch of disbelief in her voice, but Ellen just smiled.

"We can." She knew it wouldn't be easy. Not much had really changed, despite the sweetness of this moment. But for the first time she actually believed in the possibility.

Annabelle broke away from her loose embrace and took a slurping sip of hot chocolate. The sleeve fell back on her jumper and Ellen saw the cuts, so similar to Sophie's. Had Sophie got the idea from seeing Annabelle, or hearing about it? Did it even matter? There were two very distressed, hurting girls Ellen knew she needed to take care of.

"Why did you come to Kendal, Annabelle?" she asked as she sat at the kitchen table. The cat, seeing an opportunity, jumped into her lap and began to purr in plaintive demand.

"At first I just wanted to get away. I got on the train and took it to Millom, and then I saw that there was a bus outside the station that went to Kendal. I remembered going there, and how you'd been trying to learn about Sarah Mills... so I went. I don't really know why I did."

"I'm glad you did, in a way, so Ian Fletcher was able to find you." She tried for a small smile. "Good thing there wasn't a bus to Aberdeen."

"Yeah." Ellen was rewarded with a tiny smile back. "Ian told me what he's learned about Sarah. He said he didn't get a chance to tell you on the phone—"

"No, I was distracted, I'm afraid. Something about a headstone?"

"Yes." Annabelle looked genuinely animated. "He found James Mills's headstone. He was Sarah's husband, and he died in 1902. You know what was on his headstone?" Ellen shook her head, mystified and intrigued. "Beloved father to Lucy and Clara!"

"Father to Lucy... but she was in the workhouse..."

"Ian checked the workhouse records and she wasn't in the next year's register. He thinks James Mills took her out and brought her home."

"After Sarah's death," Ellen said slowly, marvelling.

Annabelle nodded. "It's a happy ending of sorts, isn't it?"

"Yes, I suppose it is." Ellen sat back, her mind reeling with this new information. "And Clara... that must be Clara Frampton, who lived in our house. She was from Kendal. I didn't even ask Simon what her maiden name was, but I'll bet it was Mills."

"So why did she hide the death certificate?"

Ellen shook her head. "That we'll probably never know." She touched Annabelle's shoulder, surprised by the sudden emotion that rolled over her. "You're all right?" she asked softly. "It must have been scary, coming all this way on your own, not knowing where you were going..."

Annabelle's eyes filled with tears. "I never meant for Sophie to hurt herself. I never wanted that. I didn't realise..." She gulped, sniffing back tears. "I didn't think she'd seen me do it."

"I know," Ellen said, because in that moment she did. "Your dad is really worried about you," she continued. "We should get back before he tears out what's left of his hair."

Annabelle smiled at that, and Sophie pretended to pout. "Daddy's not that bald," she said, and for a second, in the gleam of laughter in Sophie's eyes, Ellen thought she saw a glimpse of her golden girl.

"Not too bald," she agreed. "Not yet, anyway."

Ian Fletcher chose that moment to make a self-deprecating entrance, offering refills of hot chocolate, but after giving him her heartfelt thanks, Ellen said they had to go. They'd come a long way, but they still had a lot of distance to cover, in a lot of different ways.

"It's so interesting, about James Mills," she said as they stood in his doorway, preparing to leave. The rain had stopped and it was looking to be a spectacular sunset, all oranges and reds. "You really think he came back for Lucy?"

"I'd like to think he did," Ian answered. "Considering his headstone, and the fact that she wasn't in the workhouse the following year. But we'll never really know, will we?"

"No," Ellen answered. "I don't suppose we will."

She put her arms around both Sophie and Annabelle and began to shepherd them towards the car. Perhaps she'd never feel towards Annabelle what she felt for Sophie, that deep-seated, gut-level, maternal love. But she cared for this girl. She saw that she was hurting and she wanted to help. She wanted to move past her mistakes and find a new way, a better way, forward. Not just for Sophie and Annabelle, but for her and Alex. And now she knew they would find it.

"Come on, girls," she said, and squeezed their shoulders. "Let's go home."

# EPILOGUE

## Kendal, 1875

She holds the little boy by the hand, her heart pounding as she stares at the tumbledown cottage she once disdained to call home. She'd been such a child, then. Such a petty, selfish little girl, and she'd hurt so many. But perhaps now things can be different.

"Mama?" The boy looks up at her, his gaze a question. She smiles down at him and squeezes his hand.

"This is where your grandfather lives, Peter. Where your mama grew up." It has been nearly four years since she left Kendal, pregnant and miserable, her future a looming unknown. Four years since Sarah, kind, kind Sarah, made her future and her happiness possible. And now Sarah is long gone, lost to illness and suffering and grief. But happier, she hopes. At peace, at last.

After four years she has finally worked up the courage to come home. To see if her father will forgive her many, many mistakes.

River Cottage doesn't look as tumbledown as it once did.

The stone wall in the front is mended, the door freshly painted black, and there are flowers in the garden. A cat winds its way through a tangle of sweet peas before jumping elegantly onto the top of the wall and staring at them unblinkingly.

She takes a deep breath and opens the gate. Peter lags behind, shy and apprehensive, and she gently pulls him along. "It will be all right. Your grandfather wants to see you." She hopes. She prays.

She knocks once on the door, blinking in surprise when it is opened by a young woman with blonde hair kept back in a neat bun, her expression placid. She doesn't speak but she smiles at her before stepping aside. It is Lucy, she realises with a ripple of shock. Lucy, now a grown woman. She looks far more composed and content than she ever expected, neatly dressed and tended, and it makes her glad. She steps into the front room, Peter hiding in her skirts. Lucy smiles at him.

Inside, the house is tidy and welcoming, a vase of fresh flowers on the mantel. Lucy closes the door behind her and she hears the sound of footsteps coming from the kitchen. Peter presses closer. Then James rounds the corner, stopping in shock when he catches sight of her, his gaze moving to the boy, his mouth opening soundlessly.

Her lips tremble as she tries to form a smile. "Hello, Papa."

"Clara," James says, his voice catching a little, and he opens his arms.

# A LETTER FROM KATE

Dear reader,

I want to say a huge thank you for choosing to read *The Bride's Sister*. If you found it thought provoking and powerful, and would like to keep up to date with all my latest releases, just sign up at the following link. Your email address will never be shared and you can unsubscribe at any time.

*www.bookouture.com/kate-hewitt*

*The Bride's Sister* was inspired by a real-life event—after a small house fire, a builder discovered a death certificate underneath the floorboards of our attic. The details of that death certificate were the same as the ones in this story—Sarah Mills, aged 22, died of general debility, address River Cottage, Kendal. Of course my writer's brain went into overdrive trying to figure out how a death certificate got into such a place! As I began to try to find out who Sarah Mills was, I discovered a Lucy Mills at the Kendal workhouse in 1872, listed, as was the terminology of the time, an imbecile. I do not know anything more about the real Sarah and Lucy Mills, but these details were enough to have my own characters spring to life.

Life in Victorian times was unbearably hard for so many people, and I tried to convey this in my novel, along with the prospect of hope that can be found in the direst of circumstances. I hope you loved *The Bride's Sister* and if you did, I would be very grateful if you could write a review. I'd love to hear what you think, and it makes such a difference helping new readers to discover one of my books for the first time.

I love hearing from my readers—you can get in touch on my Facebook page, through Twitter, Goodreads or my website.

Thanks again for reading!

Kate

www.kate-hewitt.com

 facebook.com/KateHewittAuthor
twitter.com/author_kate

# ACKNOWLEDGEMENTS

There are many people to thank in helping this novel come about – my lovely editor, Jessica Tinker, my copy-editor, Sheila Jacobs, and the rest of the lovely team at Lion Hudson, who first published this book. I'd also like to thank all the team at Book-outure for giving the Goswell series a second outing, as well as my family for being patient with me when I'm deep in the writing cave, and also for brainstorming with me about reasons why a death certificate would be hidden under the floorboards. And last but certainly not least, I'd like to thank the builder whose name I don't know who found the real death certificate of Sarah Mills under the floorboards of our attic. Without you this story would not have been written!